CHRISTOPHER C DOYLE graduated from St. Stephens College, Delhi, with a degree in Economics and studied Business Management at IIM Calcutta. Since childhood, his literary mentors have been Jules Verne, HG Wells, Isaac Asimov, Robert Heinlein, JRR Tolkein, Robert Jordan and Terry Brooks.

Christopher has written articles on management and business for several publications, and is regularly invited to speak at conferences. He worked with leading multinationals before setting up a strategic consultancy in India in partnership with a US-based firm. He is also a certified Executive Coach and works with senior executives to help them achieve better results in the workplace.

Work aside, Christopher is a musician and lives his passion for music through his band called Mid Life Crisis which plays classic rock.

He lives in Gurgaon with his wife, daughter and two dogs.

The Mahabharata Secret is his debut novel.

Please visit:

www.facebook.com/authorchristophercdoyle

www.christophercdoyle.com

THE MAHABHARATA SECRET

CHRISTOPHER C DOYLE

Om Books International

Reprinted in 2015 by

OM
Om Books International

Corporate & Editorial Office
A-12, Sector 64, Noida 201 301
Uttar Pradesh, India
Phone: +91 120 477 4100
Email: editorial@ombooks.com
Website: www.ombooksinternational.com

Sales Office
107, Darya Ganj, New Delhi 110 002, India
Phone: +91 11 4000 9000, 2326 3363, 2326 5303
Fax: +91 11 2327 8091
Email: sales@ombooks.com
Website: www.ombooks.com

ISBN: 978-93-83202-31-7

10 9 8 7 6

Printed in India by Gopsons Papers Ltd.

O, Duryodhana! O great Kuru!
The gods smile upon us once more!
We will carry a silent death to the Pandavas
Unseen, unheard,
they will not know Death when it approaches
We will lay waste to their cities
Decimate their armies
And emerge victorious on the fields of Kurukshetra!
Rejoice O Kuru, for victory is at hand!

—Anonymous

For

My parents,
who introduced me to the joys of reading and
encouraged me to write through my growing years;
My wife Sharmila and daughter Shaynaya
who were my audience as *The Mahabharata Secret* took
shape; who also put up with my absences
while I wrote the book and researched for it.
Their support and encouragement was instrumental
in this book being published.
And Shaynaya's amazing knowledge of Indian history
and mythology helped me ensure I got my facts right.

Acknowledgements

This book owes its final form to many people, without whom it would have never seen the light of day. Every person mentioned below has contributed to the making of this book.

Artika Bakshi and Gurvisha Ahuja, who read the final draft of the book and gave me valuable inputs that kept the book on track.

Harmeet S. Ahuja, for his invaluable inputs on the physics of optics and for reviewing and validating my research and the section on optics that is so critical to the plot.

Sudhir Rajpal, for educating me on the process of evacuating a town in India.

Anand Prakash for his invaluable help in getting the website up and running and Denzil O'Connell who came up with amazing and innovative ideas to market the book.

To Ritu Rathour and Anand Prakash, who designed the brilliant cover of this book, thank you for creating a cover that brings the story to life.

My thanks go out to Gerald Nordley, Pat MacEwen, Kevin Andrew Murphy, Jaye Stoen, Ginger Kaderabek, Francesca Flynn, Mike Moscoe, Bert Ricci, Elizabeth Gilligan, Phyllis Radford, Karen Miller, Cindy Mitchell and Bob Brown, my fellow scribes in my writers' research group, who answered all my questions and provided me with the technical information that helped me ensure that scenes in the book that depended on research, especially the climax, were accurate and realistic.

A big thank you to all the people at Om Books International: to Ajay Mago and Dipa Chaudhuri for having faith in my writing and the book, and for taking the big leap of faith in publishing it. To Ipshita Sengupta Nag, my editor, who has done such a wonderful job of polishing my writing and keeping the narrative true to the plot.

While I acknowledge the contribution of people who have supported me in writing this book, I take full responsibility for all errors and omissions of fact or detail in this book.

Prologue

244 BC

Emperor Asoka and his courtier Surasen stood before the dark opening in the hillside, deep within the forest. The handful of soldiers accompanying them had been left behind before they approached the hill. The group had left Pataliputra ten days ago, after Surasen's return from his secret mission of inspecting the discovery.

On hearing Surasen's report, Asoka had insisted on seeing the cavern and its contents for himself and had decided to leave Pataliputra immediately. Surasen, realising the import of his discovery, had agreed to lead the Emperor to the cavern.

Asoka and Surasen now entered the passage that was the conduit to the cavern.

The emperor marvelled at the soft, dim light that played around them as they entered the passage. But nothing could match the wonder and awe with which he gazed upon the cavern when they entered it.

For a few moments, emperor Asoka stood still, transfixed by the sight that greeted him; despite having been prepared by Surasen on what to expect.

After overcoming his initial amazement, Asoka walked around the cavern in silence, inspecting every inch of it.

It was then that they made the second discovery. A secret so terrible that Asoka found himself wishing that it had remained buried forever – A secret that could destroy the world.

~

242 BC

Surasen stood before the heap of bark texts in the centre of the palace courtyard. He had chosen this place because it was in an older, secluded part of the palace, dating back to the time of Chandragupta, Asoka's grandfather. Few people ventured here, preferring the environs of the newer parts of the palace, built by Asoka.

He turned to the scribe who stood next to him, mournfully surveying the texts. They were all copies of The Mahabharata, collected from all over the empire, over the course of two years. After Asoka had determined his course of action, to hide the cavern's secret, he had turned his attention to its source.

The Mahabharata.

For, within the pages of the great epic lay the true story behind Asoka's discovery; a story which Asoka had decided to bury, with the secret, forever; erasing it from the memories of his subjects.

Royal messengers had been sent to the farthest corners of the kingdom to return with every existing text of the epic.

'Is this it?' Surasen enquired of the scribe. 'Every single text?'

The scribe nodded, his heart heavy. He knew what was to come.

Surasen ordered. 'Torch them.'

The scribe plucked a torch off the walls of the palace and lit the bonfire. The dry bark texts quickly caught fire and within moments the entire heap was engulfed in flames.

A choked sob escaped the scribe. He had obeyed the royal decree, but he hadn't understood it. No one had.

Only Surasen knew; as did eight of his fellow courtiers. All sworn to secrecy by Asoka.

As he stood watching the flames devour the texts, the Emperor's words on that fateful night echoed in his head.

'The myth must disappear from the knowledge of men, just like the secret it mentions. The world will know the Mahabharata but it will never know the dark secret it carries deep within.'

~

AD 500

Rajvirgarh

Pala handed the boy a coin. 'Now, begone before someone learns what you have been upto.'

The boy scampered away, thrilled with the reward.

Pala turned away thoughtfully. So, the stone book had been found and the connection between its story and the brotherhood had been made.

Someone knew about the brotherhood.

Someone knew about him.

And they would be coming for him.

He quickly put together his possessions. They were meagre. But these were not what he was worried about. He was the guardian of more treasures that belonged to the brotherhood; treasures that were no longer safe in Rajvirgarh. He had to hide them. And he knew exactly where to go.

In Bamiyan, many miles to the northwest, in a small monastery, lived one of the two members of the brotherhood whom he knew; Santhal, a monk.

He had to get the texts and the metal disk to Santhal. This was what had been agreed upon, when he had joined the brotherhood. Santhal was one of the two members who had revealed his true identity to Pala. If anything were to threaten the secrets either of them was responsible for, they were bound by oath to pass on the secrets to the other.

Pala stole out of the palace, and disappeared into the forest behind the palace. Deep in the forest, in a natural cave, were hidden the texts and the metal disk that he had sworn to protect with his life.

He placed the treasured possessions in a worn leather satchel and slung its strap around his neck.

Taking a deep breath, he left the cave, embarking on the long journey that would take him to Bamiyan.

And to his death.

~

March 2001

Breaking news on world television

'The Taliban have destroyed the Bamiyan Buddhas!'

The news anchor's face was replaced by a grainy video as she continued speaking. 'This video, released by the Taliban just hours ago shows the two statues being blown up. Archaeologists, historians and people all over the world have expressed their horror at the destruction of these 1500 year old statues.

'There is no doubt that the destruction of these ancient statues is very disturbing. But the academic world is excited about what the destruction of these statues has revealed. The tape released by the Taliban clearly shows caves hollowed into the cliffs behind the Buddhas. Concealed by the two figures for 1500 years, what do these caves conceal? This is the question that is on the mind of archaeologists and historians today.

'We also have unconfirmed reports from our correspondent in Bamiyan, of the discovery of a skeleton in one of the caves. The skeleton appears to be around 1500 years old. No further information is forthcoming at this moment.'

Present Day

Day 1
Jaungarh Fort, 130 km from New Delhi, India

Vikram Singh sat in the study of his ancestral fort and sipped his tea thoughtfully. He had just spoken to his nephew, Vijay, who lived halfway across the world in San Jose, California.

Tall and well-built, with a youthful face, Vikram was fit for his 65 years and looked 20 years younger. The only sign that betrayed his age was his unruly mop of white hair. His weekly call to Vijay was something he looked forward to, right from the time he had sent him to the US to study, as a 15-year-old, after the unfortunate death of his parents in a car accident.

Even today, Vikram often wondered if the car crash had really been accidental. It had been a head-on collision but they had never been able to trace the driver of the truck. Vijay had escaped only because he hadn't been in the car at the time.

Vikram shook his head. Perhaps he was being paranoid. But then, only he knew the threat that hung over his head today. Who knew if that threat had existed 15 years ago? It was this fear which had driven him to leave his comfortable apartment in New Delhi and live in the fort as a recluse.

His eyes strayed involuntarily to the soft board next to his desk, to the news clippings that he had tacked there. Eight people murdered in mysterious circumstances in the last two years; scientists, doctors, architects, engineers, located all over the world. Like him, they had all been men of knowledge and renown in their fields.

Vikram had been a nuclear scientist with a significant contribution to India's first nuclear explosion at Pokhran in 1974. Ten years ago, when he moved to Jaungarh, he had spent a small fortune fortifying the fort using cutting edge technology, and upgraded it over the years to make the fort as impregnable as it had been 500 years ago, when his ancestors had ruled from the fort.

He pulled his laptop towards him. Quickly keying in his password, he opened his mailbox and ran through the emails there, searching for a particular one. He found it and read it for the hundredth time. It had arrived six months ago, just after the last murder, and his blood ran cold even now as he read its chilling contents.

Since the mail arrived, he had often thought of talking to Vijay, of sharing the secret. But he could never bring himself to do that; it would only endanger Vijay's life as well. He would tell him but only when the time came.

Vikram swivelled around on his chair to gaze out of the large arched windows at the hillside, with the little village nestled at its foot, and sipped his tea. It was cold.

Something far below caught his eye. He stood up to get a better look. There was a sheer drop from the windows to the rocky hillside below. It was a moonless night.

He studied the area intently. Nothing moved. Then, he saw it. Two points of light moving up the road to the fort. Vikram frowned. Who could it be? He had few friends, and none of them would call on him without prior intimation. He screwed up his eyes and focused on the rocky slope below him, but there was no further movement.

For a while, he stood gazing out at the darkness, lost in his thoughts. Then, something struck him and he left the study, making for the entrance of the fort. The light on the hillside had disturbed him. If it was a car, it shouldn't have been there. And why had it disappeared after that brief glimpse? He opened the main door and gazed out at the night. Nothing seemed to be amiss. The garden beyond lay in darkness; silent and undisturbed.

As he turned to go back, he froze.

Beyond the manicured lawns stood the outer wall of the fort, a massive stone structure that rose 20 feet in height and snaked across the hillside, circling around the fort, a protection, in ancient days, against invaders. Set in this wall was an immense wooden door, studded with spikes; the only means of getting past the outer wall.

This gate had been locked, secured by the fort's security system, but it was now opening silently on well-oiled hinges. As it swung open, five shadows stole up the cobbled path. One of them stopped and pointed at Vikram as he stood silhouetted in the entrance.

A cold fear gripped Vikram as he realised that, somehow, the intruders had hacked into his sophisticated security system. There was no time to wonder how; he hastened back and secured the front door, arming the alarm as a single thought flashed through his mind.

They had come for him.

His instincts had been right about the car on the hill. Belying his age, he raced through the hallway and up the stone staircase, till he was at the door of his study. His breath now came in gasps.

His mind was a whirl of thoughts. An undefinable sensation washed over him, a peculiar mix of heady anticipation and dread.

He knew what the intruders were after. And he knew that the front door of the fort wouldn't pose a challenge to them if they had been able to open the main gate so easily. His butler had been given the day off. There was no one he could call upon immediately for help. But he wasn't worried about himself.

He could not allow the intruders to get their hands on the secret.

Neither could he allow it to die with him. He had no doubt about his own fate. It had been sealed 10 years ago.

Vikram gained the study and double-locked the door. He was aware that he couldn't stop the intruders, but the security system would buy him precious time; something which he had to put to good use.

He had to pass the secret on.

There was only one person he could trust with it. He sat down at his desk, breathing heavily from his exertions, and mentally rehearsed the words he had carefully chosen six months ago. There could be no mistakes if the message was to serve its purpose.

The minutes ticked away as he furiously typed away at his laptop and he heard footsteps ascending the stairs. The intruders were making no effort to conceal their presence. Perspiration beaded Vikram's forehead as he read and reread the words he had typed.

Abruptly, the door to the study swung open and a man with a pleasant, clean-shaven face and sharp eyes walked in, followed by three burly, bearded men and a shorter, slender, sallow-faced man bearing a black duffel bag.

'Good to see you again, Vikram,' the leader of the group greeted him affably. 'Though I don't suppose you will reciprocate.'

Without waiting for a response, the stranger settled into a chair across the desk. 'I was expecting you, Farooq.' Vikram forced his voice to stay calm.

'Where is it then? Perhaps you have it ready to hand over to me?'

Vikram said nothing but gazed defiantly at the stranger. His right hand quietly slipped over the mouse and he clicked on it.

The movement didn't go unnoticed by Farooq, whose eyes flicked to the mouse and back to the scientist's face.

'Where have you hidden the key?' Farooq persisted. 'Surely the secret isn't worth dying for!'

Vikram took a deep breath and exhaled, as if to steel himself. 'The key doesn't belong to you, Farooq. And you won't find it by killing me anyway. Your options are limited. You need me alive.'

A soft ping sounded from the laptop. Farooq pulled it towards himself and Vikram made as if to stop him, but the three henchmen immediately pinned Vikram to his chair. Farooq studied the laptop screen for a moment then reached for the mouse.

For a few minutes, silence hung heavy in the room, unbroken except by the click of the mouse.

'No options?' Farooq finally looked up from the laptop. 'I think you've just delivered the key to us.' He smiled. 'And this makes you dispensable, after all.'

A hollow feeling took hold of Vikram.

They had discovered his ruse! Would they succeed in finding the key as well?

But he put on a brave front. 'You're never going to find it. You need all the parts of the puzzle. It is why the secret has remained undisturbed for over 2,000 years.'

A flicker of doubt crossed Farooq's face, but was almost immediately replaced by a smug look.

'You'll be surprised at what we've managed to achieve with less than that.' He gestured and the sallow-faced man reached into his duffel bag and pulled out something metallic and black, which he handed to Farooq.

Vikram gasped when he saw what was in Farooq's hand. 'That is not possible!' There was panic in his voice as he gripped the side of the desk for support.

Farooq smiled unpleasantly and glanced from the metallic object to Vikram, 'I see you know what this is. I hope you are a religious man. It isn't everyone who gets to die with an ancient weapon used by a God.'

Vikram fervently hoped that he had planned well enough to thwart them. It was too late for him now to do anything more.

2

Day 1

San Jose, California, USA

Vijay frowned at his laptop as it pinged five times in quick succession, announcing the arrival of fresh mails. He had spoken to his uncle just 15 minutes ago. What could he be emailing him for at this late hour?

Curiosity got the better of him. Setting aside the report he was reading, he opened the mails in the order in which they arrived. He gaped as he read the first mail. It bore just two characters.

9!

He stared blankly at the mail, unable to comprehend it. Then he opened the second one, hoping that it would help him understand the first one. But this was even more baffling.

Everything isn't always the way it looks. Sometimes you need to look deeper within. Study, the Bhagavad Gita, it is the source of much knowledge. The subject of the Gita, though mixed up, is a mark upon us for our future lives and will lead you through the door to knowledge, which you must unlock. In an ocean of maya, there is always an island of satya.

Slowly, he clicked on the third mail and sat back puzzled. It was as obscure as the first two.

I have always followed the edicts of Asoka the Great. I urge you to follow them as well. They have served me well in my life and, believe me, they will lead you on a voyage of discovery.

Vijay shook his head, as if it would help him work out why his uncle was sending him gibberish about the Bhagavad Gita and a legendary Indian king who had ruled in the third century BC.

He hesitated at the fourth mail, then willed himself to click it open. As he read it, his bewilderment turned into utter confusion.

If something happens to me, you must seek out the Nine. If you look for a deeper meaning, you will find it. Two thousand years of history, which I have safely guarded for the last 25 years, is yours to unlock. Follow the path of truth and you will find your way through any illusion.

Now, he was concerned. His uncle had been fine when they spoke minutes ago. There had been nothing in his tone to indicate that he was anticipating trouble. And what had he been safeguarding for 25 years? He knew that, in addition to being a nuclear physicist, his uncle was a noted scholar of the languages of ancient India. Was the reference to 2,000 years of history related to an ancient language? He frowned, unable to work it out.

The old man was definitely not senile. They had spent time discussing the progress of his company's project to create a solar-thermoelectric device and his uncle's faculties had been as sharp as ever.

Vijay's hand hovered over the mouse, uncertain. There was one mail left. He hesitated for a few moments and then opened it. It was a cryptic message, again, consisting of four words.

Talk to Greg White.

It made no sense to him. He wondered why his uncle was sending him such ambiguous messages, when it was well past 11 pm in India. The phone buzzed. It was Joan, his assistant, reminding him about the project review meeting, which was due to start in the next five minutes.

Vijay looked at his watch. His uncle would have turned in for the night and his butler would have retired to his apartment as well. He decided that he would call him later that evening, when it was morning in India. The mystery behind the emails would have to wait.

Day 2

New York, USA

Terence Murphy awoke to the strident sound of the telephone ringing. He swore as he stretched out a hand for the receiver. He'd just got back on a red-eye flight from an assignment in Central Asia and had hoped to catch up on some sleep. At the sound of the voice on the other end of the line, however, he was instantly awake and alert.

'Murphy,' the voice was sharp and crisp, with a hint of a European accent. 'I have a job for you. It's urgent.'

'India!' Murphy exclaimed, as he took in the details.

'Yes. I need you to fly to Delhi immediately. You leave on tonight's flight to Delhi from Chicago; American Airlines.'

'The objective?'

He listened intently as the caller spoke, giving him instructions.

'And I report back to you?' Murphy asked finally. He wasn't surprised when he heard the response.

Murphy sat in quiet reverie for a while after his call ended. He had worked for his current employers for the last 10 years. His missions had taken him all over the world and had entailed surveillance, assassinations, kidnappings and coercion. But he had never been assigned a mission like this one.

3

Day 4

Jaungarh Fort

Vijay sat in a daze. He was still trying to come to terms with his uncle's death—his uncle's murder, he corrected himself, and his face flushed with anger.

He had got the news on the same day that he had received the bizarre emails. Homi Mehta, his uncle's lawyer, had called to inform him that they had found his uncle in his study. His head was severed from his body.

The study had been ransacked but none of the other rooms had been touched. Vijay had taken the first available flight to Chicago and flown direct to Delhi from there, arriving just the previous evening. Colin, his business partner, was scheduled to arrive tonight after taking care of a few things at the office.

There had been little time to recover from the jetlag. Vijay had performed the funeral rites this morning. The funeral was sparsely attended; his uncle had few friends and his reclusive life over the last few years had only served to distance him from his former colleagues and acquaintances in scientific circles. His death, however, had made news headlines and kept the news channels busy.

The last of the mourners had just left, leaving a handful of people behind. Apart from Homi Mehta, the lawyer, there was

Dr. Shukla, a close friend of Vikram Singh, and his daughter, Radha. Shukla was 65 and had sharp and alert eyes. His daughter was in her late 20s, slim, with long black hair and large almond-shaped eyes that gazed with commiseration at Vijay from under thick eyelashes. She had a finely chiselled face.

'I don't understand why...' Vijay finally voiced his confusion but his voice faltered and choked as he wrestled with a storm of emotions. He had been close to his uncle since he was a child, listening to stories of ancient India, and the death of his parents had served to draw them even closer.

The lawyer, Homi, had spent most of the previous day at the fort liaising with the local police, who were woefully ill-equipped to investigate this case.

The Jaungarh police post was manned by just three policemen and led by a sub inspector who had immediately thrown up his hands, saying he needed help from the state capital, Jaipur. A special investigation team from Jaipur had descended on Jaungarh. By the time Vijay returned from the funeral, they had completed their inspection of the murder site and collected all the evidence they could find, which they admitted was precious little.

'There are many unanswered questions,' said Homi, 'Nothing that could provide clues to the motive of the murderers. It was a perfectly planned break-in. They knew that the butler had his day off and chose a time when all the servants had left for the day. The strange thing is, nothing seems to have been stolen except for Vikram's laptop, which is missing. The study was a mess; books and files had been left scattered all over the floor but none of the other rooms seem to have been disturbed. It seems they were searching for something specific. Something that they thought was in the study.

'Each level of security has been breached without any obvious signs of a break-in. The police believe that the intruders knew their technology.' Homi shrugged. 'It beats me, though, why your uncle installed such an advanced security system. He must have spent lakhs on it.'

'Do you think uncle knew them?' Vijay frowned as he tried to sort out the possibilities through his jetlag. 'Perhaps he let them in?'

Homi shook his head. 'The police team from Jaipur brought a tech expert with them when they heard about the security system at the fort. I think they suspected foul play before they even got here. The records from the security log clearly indicate that each level was manually overridden from the *outside*, indicating a break-in.'

'And then, there is the manner of his death!' Homi seemed to be having trouble hiding the horror in his voice.

'I know,' Vijay muttered, 'They decapitated him.' His voice choked again.

'There's more to it,' Homi persisted, struggling with words. 'I'm really sorry to bring this up, but I didn't—I couldn't—tell you this before.' He paused again.

'They decapitated him, *but there was no blood on the floor*'!

There was silence as the others digested this information.

Finally, Shukla spoke up. 'Perhaps they mopped up the blood before they left,' he suggested, though he sounded as if he didn't really believe that the murderers would go to the trouble of cleaning up after a murder.

'No. There was no blood to mop up.' Again, Homi hesitated.

'Then what...?' Vijay frowned.

Homi replied slowly, choosing his words carefully, almost as if he thought they wouldn't believe him. '*The blood vessels in the neck were sealed.*'

'What do you mean?' Vijay demanded, not comprehending the meaning of the lawyer's words.

'It was as if they'd been cauterised at the same time that they had been cut, without a single drop of blood being spilt. A physical impossibility; yet, there's no denying it.'

Vijay didn't react to this news. A thought had begun to form in his mind. His uncle had secured the fort against intrusion. But the security system had been breached. And then there was the puzzle of his uncle's emails. When he considered the details Homi had provided, it seemed that his uncle had shot off the emails around the time of his death; probably just minutes before his murder.

Had his uncle been trying to tell him something? Was there a hidden message in his emails? And how was he to find out?

The Diary of Bruno Beger

Greg White sat down on the soft, white oversized sofa. He adjusted his tall and lanky frame on the comfortable sofa and glanced around the room. It was simple but elegantly furnished. He reflected on the flurry of events that had brought him here; to this farmhouse on the Delhi border. Three days ago, he had received a call in his office at Boston University, where he was a professor of archaeology and history. An invitation to visit India had been extended to him, with the condition that he had to leave

Boston the very next morning. Under normal circumstances, he would have politely declined such an outrageous offer, but two things had made him agree. First was the prospect of a funded visit to India. His special interest was ancient Indian history, with a focus on the Magadha empire. He couldn't possibly turn down an opportunity like this. The second reason had been provided by his host, in whose farmhouse he now sat. It was a reason that no archaeologist could ignore—an opportunity to research one of the greatest myths of ancient India, dating back to the time of Emperor Asoka the Great. This, more than anything else, had been the trigger for his acquiescence.

A large man entered the room. He was tall, well over six feet in height. Though his hair was grey, he was fit, with just a hint of the softening of muscles with age. White noted the fine cut of his suit and the silk tie and was suddenly aware of his own casual attire.

'Welcome to India!' His host boomed in a deep baritone with a strong British accent. He extended a large hand and shook White's hand with a vice-like grip.

'Er...thank you,' White replied, hesitantly, not sure how to address Indian royalty. For his host was none other than the former Maharaja of Rajvirgarh; a prominent businessman who had taken to politics two decades ago and now commanded significant respect and influence in the government.

The Maharaja noticed White's dilemma. 'I am Bheem Singh,' he offered, 'Please call me Bheem. I don't believe in all the formalities. Though if we meet in public, I'll request you to address me as "Your highness." It won't do for my subjects to know that I am so accessible to anyone.'

White nodded, noting that Bheem Singh had not said his 'former subjects'.

'Thank you for flying down to India at such short notice,' Bheem Singh said, as he picked up a silver bell from the table and shook it, gently.

As if waiting for the cue, a liveried waiter entered bearing a silver teapot and two cups on a silver tray.

Bheem Singh dismissed the waiter with a wave of his hand when he had served the tea, and continued,

'I truly appreciate your acceptance of my offer. We desperately need your expertise on this project.'

White decided to come straight to the point. 'What is the "significant evidence" that your secretary mentioned when we spoke? He said you'd stumbled upon something that conclusively proved that the myth is grounded in reality.'

The Maharaja didn't reply, but reached for the bell again. The waiter reappeared.

'Get me that book,' Bheem Singh pointed to a leather-bound notebook, old and worn, that was lying on a side table, not two feet from him. Its pages were frayed at the edges and the leather was creased and dirty.

White was amused. It seemed to be beneath the Maharaja's dignity to pick up a book from a table. He didn't understand. But then, he had never met a Maharaja before.

'Go ahead, take a look,' Bheem Singh invited him after the waiter left, placing the book on the table before them.

White did as instructed.

'This notebook was acquired by an acquaintance of mine from the family of a former US army officer. He had been a part of the US Counsel for the Prosecution of Axis

Criminality at Nuremberg, during the proceedings of the war crimes trials. It was part of a trunk full of Nazi documents that the officer had brought back with him when he returned home from Germany.'

'It's not in English,' White observed. 'It is a diary, written in German. Though there are a few notes in English in a different hand.'

Bheem Singh nodded. 'Yes. We got the entries translated into English.'

'And whose diary is this?'

'Have you heard of Bruno Beger?'

'The German anthropologist who was interested in racial research? The one who conducted his research in Tibet, believing that there were clues to the origins of the Aryans in Tibet?'

'The same Beger. This is the diary in which he kept records of that expedition to Tibet. What drew our attention were the entries that described their stay at the Temple of the Tooth, located around 200 miles from Lhasa.'

'Read it out loud,' Bheem Singh said pointing at an entry in the diary.

White cleared his throat and complied. *Found a 400-year-old temple called the Temple of the Tooth, 200 miles from Lhasa. Discovered ancient documents from India, in a secret vault one of the monks showed us. Don't think he was allowed to, since the head monk was furious with him. The documents are in Sanskrit, approximately from 500 AD, according to the monk. He says the vault belonged to an ancient, ruined temple upon which the present temple was built. Apparently, the texts are copies of much older documents that were brought to the original temple by a member of some brotherhood in India.*

White looked up from the diary. Bheem Singh was studying him closely, searching for a reaction.

'Intriguing, but not really conclusive.' White wasn't yet convinced.

The Maharaja instructed him to continue. He pointed to some writing in a strange script 'That's the reproduction of the verses in Sanskrit.'

White had studied Sanskrit to help him with his archaeological research. As he read, his jaw dropped open with amazement.

'That's right.' This was the reaction his host had been looking for. 'Here, look at this.' He pointed out another entry to White. There were more inscriptions in Sanskrit, longer than the earlier one.

Found a way into the secret vault. Our friendly monk tells us that the texts speak of a secret brotherhood called the Nine Unknown Men, founded around the same time the original documents were written. They also speak of flying vehicles and arrows that wreak great destruction. I have copied the texts. Need to get them translated by Professor Wüst. White's eyes were now shining with anticipation and excitement, mixed with wonder.

'So it *is* true,' White could hardly believe it. 'The legend of the Nine isn't just another myth.' A thought struck him. 'But what is this reference to flying machines and arrows of destruction? That sounds a bit far-fetched.'

'Not at all,' Bheem Singh responded. 'Have you read the Mahabharata? The epic is full of descriptions of flying machines and arrows that could kill thousands of warriors at one stroke and lay waste to entire cities. Have you heard of the *Vimana Parva?* The lost book of the Mahabharata that was never recorded when the oral tradition gave way to documentation? Few people know of it. It was discovered by an ancestor of mine, quite by accident, 1,500 years ago.'

White shook his head.

'Well, then, I must enlighten you.' Bheem Singh looked at his watch. 'Why don't you join me for dinner, and I can tell you all about it? Just one more thing, Greg. This is a top secret project. We know the legend of the Nine is a true story. But the government doesn't want to go public with the project. I'm trusting you to keep this to yourself. There are people out there, dangerous folks, who would kill to get their hands on the secret of the Nine. Do you know what happened at the Temple of the Tooth?'

White's face showed that he was unaware.

'13 years ago, there was a massacre of the monks at the temple. 21 monks were killed. And the documents, the texts that Beger has written about in this diary, disappeared. Somebody else knows the truth about the Nine. And they've been searching as well.'

White's face showed that he was beginning to realise the dangers associated with the project.

'There's one other person who knows the story is true,' White said slowly. 'I have a friend, Vikram Singh. He lives in a place called Jaungarh, not far from here.'

'Vikram Singh?' The Maharaja frowned. 'The nuclear scientist? How would he have known about the Nine?'

White shrugged. 'He told me about the Nine a few years ago, that he knew the truth about them.'

Bheem Singh wore an expression of concern on his face. 'I had no idea.' He looked at White. 'You don't know, I suppose, that Vikram Singh was murdered just three days ago? They found his body in the fort.'

'Good Lord!' White was aghast. No, I didn't know...I wasn't told...oh my god! Do you think his knowledge of the Nine was the reason he was killed?' He took a deep breath. 'I've got to go to Jaungarh then. He was a good friend.'

'We'll go together,' his host offered.' I had met Vikram a few times though I didn't know him well. We'll drive down tomorrow morning; it's not too far from here.'

White was still recovering from the shock. 'I think I'll go back to my hotel, if you don't mind. I...I need to be alone for a while. Thank you for your offer of dinner, but I hope you understand.'

'Of course,' Bheem Singh sounded sympathetic. 'I'm sorry; I should have been gentler in breaking the news. I just wasn't thinking.'

Through the 15-minute drive to his hotel, White's thoughts revolved around Vikram Singh. He recalled how, a few years ago, he had scoffed at Vikram when he had shared his idea about the Nine and their true purpose, over the centuries. And now, he was dead, murdered.

He reached the hotel and made his way up to his room, as if in a daze. As he approached the room, he gave a start. The door was ajar. Was one of the housekeeping staff inside?

White cautiously pushed the door open and peered inside. The room seemed to be in order. He reprimanded himself; Bheem Singh's words of caution and the news of Vikram's death had psyched him so much that he was imagining things.

The housekeeping staff had probably been negligent in locking the door after them. He made a mental note to complain in the morning. For now, he planned on having a large Scotch and a light dinner before turning in early. The jetlag, too, was beginning to take its toll.

He entered the room and shut the door, double-locking it behind him. Flinging his jacket on the bed, he bent down to open the mini bar. A shadow fell across the small refrigerator, but before he could react, something hard hit him at the base of his neck and everything went black.

4

Day 4

Jaungarh Fort

'Thank you for everything, Homi,' Vijay said gratefully, as he escorted the lawyer to the front door.

Homi nodded to Vijay. 'Let me know if you plan to visit Delhi in the next few days. We can schedule a meeting to complete the paperwork related to your uncle's will. Or, I can always get the papers to the fort. Whatever works better for you.'

Vijay returned to the living room and joined Shukla and Radha. They had offered to stay the night and keep him company.

'Thanks for being here,' he said. 'It would have been difficult to stay alone in the fort tonight.' He looked at his watch. 'I'd better be going. Colin's flight arrives at 5.45 pm. You can ask the butler for dinner. I'll eat when I'm back.'

Exactly two hours later, he was pulling into the parking lot of the T3 terminal at Indira Gandhi International Airport. He found a vacant slot for his uncle's BMW, and made a dash for the arrival hall.

There weren't too many international flights arriving at this time so there was a sparse collection of people who had come to greet the arrivals on the American Airlines flight from Chicago.

Vijay swiftly made his way to the arrival area. He quickly spotted the tall, blonde, young man, carrying a laptop and wheeling a large yellow suitcase, scrutinising the faces of those waiting for the passengers. Vijay shook his head and smiled. Even if he couldn't spot Colin, it would be difficult to miss that bright yellow suitcase!

He had met Colin Baker at MIT and, despite being from two different worlds, they had become close friends. Vijay and Colin had played together in the MIT rugby and football teams and shared a sense of humour which had cemented their friendship. After graduating, they had shunned employment and teamed up to start a technology firm in San Jose, which was now working on developing a technology to convert sunlight into electricity using the thermoelectric effect.

They were similar in many ways; both were tall and broad- shouldered and keen athletes, and spent at least one month in the year together, trekking, cycling and camping out. They shared a sense of adventure that seemed to be at odds with their aptitude for technology and enjoyed any activity that had any kind of risk associated with it. But that was where the similarities ended. Colin had blonde hair, blue eyes and filmstar looks, while Vijay was dark-haired and unconventionally good-looking. Colin was the life of every party while Vijay was more reserved.

'Colin!' Vijay whooped, and the tall, young man turned to look in his direction. A smile immediately spread over his face, the warmth reflected in his eyes.

The two friends embraced warmly.

Colin waved a hand at the people around them. 'I thought India had a large population and expected more people to turn up to welcome me. Is this all you could muster?'

Vijay shook his head in mock exasperation. 'Come on, let's get out of here.'

They made their way to the car park where the BMW was parked.

'Mmm, nice car,' Colin looked it over admiringly. 'The latest 7 series model. Your uncle's?'

Vijay nodded. 'Uncle bought this a few months back.' He paused, before adding, 'He liked cars and could afford a fleet, but never owned more than one at a time. I guess that's because there's space for only one car at the fort.'

'Are we going there straightaway?' Colin enquired 'I'm looking forward to staying in a real Indian fort.'

'You'll like it. Its 500 years old and more peaceful than the city.'

He turned onto the highway that connected Delhi with Jaipur and accelerated.

'Looks like New York,' Colin remarked. 'I mean the tight squeeze out there.'

Vijay grinned. The blaring horns of the tightly packed traffic could be heard even inside the BMW.

After a while, the highway suddenly broadened and traffic slowed.

'Gosh, will you look at *that* traffic.' Colin gazed out at the sea of cars, buses and trucks that stretched out before them.

'It's the toll plaza,' Vijay grumbled, manoeuvring his way through the densely packed traffic until he could proceed no further. 'There's a second one ahead that's as bad.'

'I have something to tell you,' he said once he managed to work out which queue they were in. Somehow, remarkably, the tsunami of vehicles sorted themselves out into lanes that led to the individual toll gates ahead.

Colin listened intently as Vijay brought him up to date on the events of the last three days. 'Wow!' he breathed, 'It's really sad about your uncle. I hope they find out who did it and why. But I don't understand why your uncle sent you those mails. They don't make sense.'

Vijay frowned. 'I just can't shake off the feeling that uncle was trying to tell me something. Suppose he knew the intruders? Let's say his alarm system warned him that it was being hacked and he realised his life was in danger. What would he do? Perhaps he felt he should leave behind something for me; a message hidden in emails that didn't make sense, so that whoever murdered him and stripped the study wouldn't find what they were looking for. But I don't know where to start figuring this out.'

Suddenly, Colin let out a yell. 'Look out!'

A black Mercedes with tinted black windows rushed out from an adjacent toll gate and overtook them, almost hitting the BMW in the process.

'Bloody idiot!' Vijay, shaken, slowed down the car and watched the Mercedes race away over the flyover.Once on the flyover, Vijay began moving back and forth between lanes to Colin's consternation. 'Slow-moving and fast-moving traffic mingle in India,' he explained to his friend. 'There isn't a concept of a fast lane. Well, in theory there is,' he corrected himself. Grinning, he looked in the rear-view mirror and prepared to change lanes again. His grin changed to a frown as he swung the BMW into the lane on the left. Almost immediately, he overtook the car on his right and swung back into the right lane, accelerating as he executed the manoeuvre.

'What's up?' Colin noticed his expression.

'It's funny, but there's a black Ford Endeavour that seems to be sticking to our tail.' Vijay glanced in the mirror again, and moved two lanes to the left.

Colin glanced back and sat upright. 'You're right. The Endeavour just changed two lanes. It's right behind us now.'

'Okay, I'm going to test him.' Vijay swerved to the furthest lane on the right, eliciting angry honks from the cars whose paths he cut across. The Ford followed suit, equally unconcerned about the indignation of the other drivers.

Vijay couldn't figure out why the Ford was sticking to them, but he was worried. He had heard stories of cars being stopped by goons in Gurgaon and the occupants robbed of their belongings and vehicles. He cut across to the left, heading for the nearby exit.

'He's right behind us,' Colin remarked, looking back.

Vijay swerved the BMW to enter one of the villages that dotted either side of the highway and immediately got swamped by cows, dogs, bicycles, tractors, cars and vans that slowly made their way between shops on either side.

The Ford was faring no better, its bulk slowing it down.

Colin asked, 'D'you know where you are going?'

Vijay shook his head. 'No idea. I just want to get that guy off our tail. Whoever he is, he's bad news.'

He spotted a gap in the traffic and an alley leading off the road they were on. It was narrow but it seemed to be free of vehicles. It was a concrete alley just able to fit two cars abreast.

Vijay hoped that they wouldn't come across another car coming from the opposite direction.

'He's turned in behind us,' Colin updated Vijay, who swore under his breath and accelerated.

The BMW came to the end of the alley. Ahead was the main road.

'Left or right?' Vijay wondered aloud.

'He's coming at us,' Colin warned. 'Just go left.'

Vijay stepped on the accelerator and the car lurched forward as he swerved sharply into the main road.

'Shit!'

A black Mercedes was bearing down upon them, from the right, while another black Ford Endeavour raced towards them from the opposite direction.

'This isn't good.' Colin shook his head. 'These guys are coordinating this chase. They've been with us for a while. That Merc was at the toll plaza.'

Vijay nodded, his eyes glued to the road as he weaved through the meagre traffic on the road. A quick glance in the rear-view mirror showed the two Fords, close behind, weaving through the traffic at high speed. The second Ford had made a U-turn and joined the one that had been chasing them so far.

Where was the Mercedes?

Suddenly, the traffic thinned out to almost nothing and Vijay pressed the accelerator pedal to the floor. The sudden rush of power to the engine propelled the car forward, but the near absence of traffic had given the Fords the opportunity to speed up as well.

A roundabout came into view up ahead.

Colin quizzed, 'You aren't going to slow down?'

Vijay nodded grimly. 'I think this car can take that turn at high speed. At least it will do a better job than the Fords. They are top heavy and I don't think they'll dare try.'

Colin grinned. 'This is more like it. I prefer this welcome to the one you gave me at the airport. This is *dangerous*.'

Vijay smiled despite himself. The adrenalin rush felt good, he had to admit. He forced himself to focus on their objective. They had to get rid of their pursuers. Whoever they were!

They gained on the roundabout, the Fords still at the same distance behind them. It looked like Vijay's plan was going to work. The roundabout was now just metres ahead of them and Vijay braced himself to handle the car as it rounded the bend.

Suddenly, he caught a flash of black out of the corner of his eye.

The black Mercedes!

The driver obviously had swung into the service road on the right, and had moved in parallel with the BMW, matching their speed. Vijay had been so intent on losing the Fords that he hadn't noticed the Mercedes racing in the same direction.

It reached the roundabout before them and slowed down as it swung around the roundabout and directly into the path of the BMW.

'Merc!' Colin noticed the car now.

Vijay didn't have an option. He slammed the brakes and swerved to the left in one action, to avoid crashing into the other car. The BMW's tyres screeched and the car wobbled on its suspension as they narrowly missed the Mercedes and screeched to a halt.

Barely had the car stopped than there was a loud crash, with the BMW being pitched forward violently; one of the Fords had smashed into the car.

The airbags ballooned, as Vijay and Colin were thrown forward with the force of the impact.

'Are you okay?' Colin enquired tremulously of Vijay.

'I think so,' Vijay grunted. 'Just badly shaken.'

Footsteps approached and they perceived five men standing outside the car. A thrill coursed through Colin as he realised that each one carried a 9mm mini UZI sub machine gun, capable of firing 1,700 rounds per minute in closed bolt position.

A few curious bystanders had gathered around, attracted by the accident, but scattered immediately when they saw the weapons. Two cars passed, slowing to observe the scene, but they, too, speeded up when they saw the guns.

Now, there were just the two friends and the armed men.

One of the men, apparently the leader of the group, barked orders in a strange language, his voice harsh and grating. The door of the BMW was wrenched open and Vijay and Colin dragged out. They didn't offer any resistance. It would have been foolish under the circumstances.

Vijay glanced at the Ford that had smashed into his car. The SUV was a wreck but the driver was climbing out, unhurt, with just a limp.

The two friends were rounded up and taken to the second Ford and dumped in the back, their hands bound behind their backs.

Outside, they saw one of the men get behind the wheel of the BMW. It started smoothly and after some instructions from the leader, the man drove the car away. The leader and another man got into the Mercedes and the other two settled into the remaining Ford, after blindfolding their captives.

In a few minutes, the convoy was driving towards the highway again, leaving the wrecked Ford behind.

Vijay and Colin sat helplessly in the SUV. They were prisoners but who were their captors? And why had they been taken captive?

5

244 BC

The Mauryan Empire, Ancient India

Surasen wiped the sweat from his brow. For the past three hours, they had cut a path through the jungle. It was the monsoon season and the humidity was stifling. Flies and mosquitoes buzzed around his ears. Surasen was breathing hard as the path sloped gently upwards.

The forest was still. To Surasen it seemed that the jungle and its inhabitants were holding their breath, waiting to discover what would happen when he reached the end of his journey.

He was aware that the forest had grown increasingly dense in the last few hours.

'There,' the jungle-dweller, who was leading them, said suddenly, as he pointed to the fronds and the closely packed trees.

Surasen held up his hand to halt the progress of the soldiers who accompanied him and they crowded around him in a tight knot.

'Stay here. Wait for me.'

'My lord.' The commander of the troops was hesitant. 'Is it safe to go on by yourself?'

Surasen shook his head firmly. 'I will be quite safe by myself. But, if I don't return in one *nadi* you may come after me.'

With these words he stepped forward and moved aside the curtain of leaves and creepers, revealing a hidden gully that sloped gently downwards, disappearing into the thick foliage and undergrowth. He took a deep breath and started down the gully, the thickly clustered creepers closing in behind him, concealing him from the others.

He drew his sword and slowly moved forward, squeezing through the trees and treading on a thick carpet of dead and fallen leaves that covered the floor of the forest. It was darker here than the rest of the forest. Looking up he discerned the reason for the gloom. Through the trees loomed the outline of a rocky outcrop, perhaps a small hill, which cast its shadow over this part of the jungle.

The path continued till it reached the base of the hill and disappeared behind a rock face that stretched for sixty feet around the foot of the hill.

Surasen approached the hill and hesitated; he stood before the crevice between the rock face and the hill. It was just wide enough for a man to squeeze through sideways, and led into a yawning black opening.

Stooping, he peered into the opening but nothing was visible in the inky blackness that stretched before him.

Clutching his sword tight, he stepped into the darkness, using the sword and his free hand to guide his path. As far as he could perceive, he was in a narrow passage, barely wider than the breadth of his shoulders. Slowly, he made his way through the passage, trying to ignore the claustrophobic feeling that was washing over him; and fending off the thought that he was walking through the base of the hill, with tons of rock sitting above him.

After a while, the walls of the passage abruptly vanished and he realised that it had widened. Almost simultaneously, a dim light pierced the darkness around him, as if the rays of the sun had somehow filtered through the layers of rock above and reached these depths.

Surasen could now make out that he was in a tunnel carved through the rock. Whether it had been created by natural forces or the hand of man he couldn't discern, but men had certainly been at work here, for the walls and floor of the tunnel were smooth and even.

He walked cautiously through the passage, testing each step before moving forward. There was no apprehension of supernatural beings anymore; he worried more about any possible traps that men may have laid to protect this place. Perspiration dripped down his face and body, drenching his clothes. Abruptly, the tunnel ended, opening into an immense cavern which was also dimly lit by the unseen source of light. Surasen gasped in disbelief. The roof of the cavern soared above him into the darkness, untouched by the light, and he couldn't see the far walls from where he stood.

But it wasn't the size of the rocky chamber that took his breath away. It was what lay before him that rendered him speechless.

A chill ran down his spine and a strange sensation, a mix of elation and horror, swept over him. He couldn't believe his eyes.

He now understood Emperor Asoka's words of caution and his cryptic instructions.

The legends of old were true.

What lay before him in the cavern could put the world in terrible danger.

6

Present Day

Day 4
Gurgaon

Vijay and Colin sat upright as the Ford drew to a halt. It had been
a long drive and they had spent much of that time speculating
about who their captors were and what they wanted with them.

'One thing I know,' Vijay said in a low voice, hoping the
men in front couldn't hear them, 'is that they aren't Indians.
I don't know what language they speak, but it definitely isn't
one of ours.'

'They were following us for a while, probably from the
airport itself,' added Colin.

'It was well-orchestrated,' Vijay agreed. 'They probably
planned to jump us on the highway, once we'd left habitation
behind. When I got off the highway, they decided to pool their
resources to stop us. But this was crazy. We could have died out
there, either by smashing into the Merc or when the Ford hit us.'

'I wonder what they want from us,' Colin said soberly. 'I
can't think of anything I have that could be of interest to anyone
else. And the same goes for you.'

A thought struck Vijay. It made him shiver. 'D'you think
they have some connection with Uncle's killers?' He voiced the

thought. Despite his blindfold, he knew immediately that this resonated with Colin.

They heard the rear door of the Ford being opened and were roughly dragged out of the car and into a building, down a staircase.

Their blindfolds were removed to reveal that they were in a windowless room, dimly lit by a single fluorescent tubelight. A stale smell hung in the air suggesting that the room had been locked or unused for some time. Three chairs stood in the room and they were swiftly bound to two of the chairs.

What now? Vijay wondered as the men left the room.

After a while, four men entered the room. Two of them were armed with Uzis.

One of the new faces, a medium-sized man with a pleasant, clean-shaven face and sharp eyes pulled up the third chair and sat facing the two captives. His demeanour indicated that he was the leader of this group. He stared intently at the two prisoners for a few moments. Vijay stared back defiantly. Though he was terrified inside, he didn't want to show his fear to his captors. But he said nothing. If his hunch was right, he didn't want to get Colin and himself into any more trouble than they were in already.

'You know what I want.' The man leaned forward and looked hard at Vijay. 'Where is the key?'

'The key?' Vijay echoed blankly, unable to comprehend.

The man's face grew hard and a menacing look appeared in his eyes. 'Don't play games with me,' he warned.

'I really don't know what you are talking about,' Vijay shook his head helplessly. How was he to convince this man?

Without taking his eyes off Vijay, his interrogator gestured to one of the burly men who stepped forward and lashed out with the butt of his Uzi, catching Vijay on his left cheek. Blood now trickled down his face.

'Did that help you understand?'

Vijay hung his head and shook it again, trying to hold back his tears, born more of terror than of pain.

Their captor pulled his chair closer to Vijay, until their knees almost touched.

'Now, listen to me, Vijay Singh,' he hissed. 'I know your uncle had the key.'

At these words, Vijay's head snapped back up and he found the other man's eyes boring into him. So these men *had* known his uncle!

The questioner misunderstood his sudden alertness as comprehension. 'Ah, so you do know. Your uncle told you about the disk with the verse, didn't he? And he left you clues to find the key in his emails. I know he did.' A sudden urgency crept into his tone. 'Where is it? Where is the key?'

Vijay struggled to control his emotions. The terror he had felt initially had been replaced by a raw fury, as he realised that these were the men who had murdered his uncle. But he had to be careful. These men wouldn't hesitate to kill Colin and him if they sensed that something was amiss. A plan began to form in his mind.

'Fine,' he finally said, keeping his voice low so the tremor wouldn't be noticed, desperately hoping that his deception would work. 'You're right.' He could sense Colin staring at him, bewildered, but he kept his gaze on the man before him.

'Uncle did send me the emails,' he admitted. 'But I haven't been able to decipher them yet. I haven't had the time.' The fact that he was being quite truthful helped him add conviction to his tone.

'Imtiaz,' the interrogator drew his chair away and addressed the sallow-faced man standing to the side. 'You have a printout. Give it to him.' He leaned back and studied Vijay for a while. 'I believe you,' he said, finally. 'For now. You have all night to study the emails and decipher them. You better have some answers by morning. Maroosh will not be so kind to you the next time.'

The burly man who had struck Vijay grinned cruelly as the leader rose and stalked out of the room, followed by Imtiaz. The two guards remained, stony-faced and hard-eyed. After a few minutes, Imtiaz returned with a sheet of paper which he placed in Vijay's right hand.

Vijay glanced at the paper in his hand. The familiar emails stared back at him.

'Where did you get these from?' he asked Imtiaz.

'Vikram Singh's laptop. And Farooq means what he says. Better get to work and figure them out. You saw what he did to your uncle.'

With that, Imtiaz turned and walked away, followed by the guards. The door closed and bolts were drawn, sealing them in.

Colin looked at Vijay. 'I sure hope you know what you're doing. These guys are no ordinary street thugs.

Vijay didn't hear him. He was lost in his thoughts as he stared at the printout Imtiaz had given him.

'So uncle did leave clues in the emails,' he mused. 'And now we know what they were looking for in the study. A key, he said. What does that mean?' He looked up suddenly at Colin. 'But that can wait. We've got a few hours before dawn. This Farooq guy is the one who killed uncle. Right now, I don't give a damn who he is or what he wants. We need to escape.'

'How?'

Vijay shrugged. 'Let's think. We have to work something out. If we can't, we're dead men.'

They sat there for a while, thinking hard. Their eyes explored every corner of the room. Vijay stood up, still strapped to the chair. Their legs were free and the chair was light, so he was able to shuffle his way around the room as he explored the walls and the door. But there didn't seem to be a way out.

As Colin watched, a thought came to him. He looked closely at the ropes, which bound his wrists but not his hands and fingers.

'I've got it.'

Vijay turned and looked at his friend. 'You have an idea?' He shuffled back to Colin and sat down next to him. Colin rose and slowly moved closer to Vijay, positioning himself in such a way that their hands were touching and he could tug at the nylon rope tying Vijay's hands.

The minutes passed slowly, agonisingly. But the knot refused to oblige. Perspiration beaded Colin's brow as he concentrated on the job.

His hand began to ache and the rope binding him cut into his wrist as he stretched his hand, adding to the pain. But he persevered.

They had no means to track the passage of time. There was no way of knowing when Farooq would come back, and desperation slowly began to get the better of them.

Colin sighed with frustration. He knew that time was passing them by. It was beginning to look hopeless. He gritted his teeth and tugged at the knot, willing it to loosen.

Suddenly, footsteps sounded outside the door. The sound of the bolts being drawn came to their ears. Vijay froze as he realised that time was up. A cold terror gripped him, paralysing him with fear. Maroosh appeared in the doorway and Farooq was visible behind him. What would Farooq do when he discovered that, far from deciphering the emails, they had been trying to escape?

Colin gave a cry. The knot had finally come undone because of his persistent efforts. Vijay's right hand was free. Vijay quickly pulled at the rope binding his left hand. His right hand throbbed with pain and his fingers were numb, but a rush of adrenalin gave him the strength to free himself completely, just as Maroosh walked into the room followed by Farooq.

Maroosh's eyes widened as he realised that Vijay was free, but before he could react, Vijay launched himself at the large man in a classic rugby smother tackle, wrapping his arms around the big man's arms, so that he was unable to use his gun. Maroosh went down heavily. His head hit the floor with a sickening thud and he went limp.

At the same moment that Vijay tackled the guard, Colin, still bound to his chair, launched himself at a surprised Farooq, who had also just realised that his prisoners were free. Farooq crumpled to the floor as Colin landed heavily on him, knocking the wind out of him.

'Can't let you take all the credit.' Colin grinned up at Vijay, who wrested Maroosh's gun out of his hand and rushed to

Farooq. He hesitated for a split second, then swung the butt of the Uzi against Farooq's head, knocking him out.

Vijay grinned back at his friend as he untied his ropes. But there was no time to linger. They had been lucky to overpower both men without an alarm being raised. There was no way of knowing if Imtiaz or any of the other guards were on their way here.

Colin sprang out of the chair, massaging his wrists, and the two friends crept to the door, peering out cautiously. The room was at the end of a corridor lit by a row of incandescent bulbs that hung from the ceiling. They moved stealthily down the corridor until they reached a staircase.

It seemed that the room where they had been kept captive was on the lowest level of the building. They waited for a few moments at the foot of the staircase, but there was no rush of feet coming downstairs; no sound.

Vijay hoped their luck would hold out. He glanced at Colin and with one accord they ascended the stairs, Vijay still clutching the Uzi he had taken off Maroosh.

Two flights of staircase. Still not a soul in sight. There was silence in the building. The stairway opened up into a large room, which was obviously the living room, as was apparent from the furniture.

There was still no sign of life. The first rays of the rising sun seeped through the windows lining the walls of the room.

Through one of the windows, Colin spotted the battered BMW parked outside and signalled to Vijay. The latter nodded; if the car had been driven here, it could be driven away.

Silently, they stole through the room and opened the front door. The hinges creaked loudly and immediately there was a shout from inside the house.

They froze.

The shout came again.

Then, all hell broke loose. The sound of running feet came to them from a level above.

Vijay and Colin didn't wait to discover who was now clattering down the staircase. They sprinted for the car. To their delight, the key had been left in the ignition.

Vijay risked a look around. Behind them was the building where they had been held through the night, a three-storey brick structure in the middle of nowhere. There was barren land all around and in the distance he could see the silhouette of the Aravali hills. He had no idea where they were.

Hurling the Uzi away, Vijay swiftly ducked inside the car. Colin was already in the passenger seat in front, strapping himself in. The engine roared to life as Vijay turned the ignition key. He stepped on the accelerator, raising a cloud of dust, as the wheels spun on the soft dirt path that led away from the house.

Colin turned in his seat and glanced behind, at the house. Two men had appeared in the open doorway, one brandishing an Uzi, which he now lowered and aimed at the BMW.

'Watch out!' Colin yelled. 'They're shooting at us!'

Bullets whizzed past them as Vijay swung the wheel wildly, zigzagging to avoid being hit. Despite his manoeuvres, bullets shattered the rear windshield and tore into the mangled rear fenders. Both men hunched down in their seats, hoping the bullets wouldn't find a target.

Vijay accelerated again in a final attempt to evade the shots and the car lurched forward. It was a blessing that the bullets had missed the fuel tank.

After a while, houses appeared on both sides of the road and Vijay realised they were in Gurgaon. He heaved a sigh of relief. They were safe.

For now.

7

Day 5

Jaungarh Fort

Bheem Singh stared thoughtfully at the battered BMW, the rear windshield glass shattered and the boot and rear fenders smashed in and pock-marked with bullet holes. His companion joined him in his inspection of the car.

Vijay had left the car on the road, in front of the massive entrance of the fort, when they had finally arrived at Jaungarh. Both Colin and he were exhausted from their ordeal. They had staggered into the fort where an anxious Shukla and his daughter were overjoyed to see them.

Radha had already called the local police station in the morning and filed a missing persons report when she couldn't get through to Vijay's cellphone.

The butler ushered the new arrivals into the sitting room, where Vijay and Colin were seated. Both men still looked a bit dazed, as if they couldn't quite believe they were back home safely. The cut on Vijay's cheek would require stitches. Radha had tried to convince him to let her drive them in the BMW to Gurgaon for proper medical attention, but he had brushed her away. While they had somehow made it back to Jaungarh, the car was in no shape for the long drive all the way to Gurgaon and back.

Moreover, Vijay's mind was still occupied with the mysterious emails from his uncle and what he had been trying to tell him in the last moments of his life.

'Please don't bother getting up,' Bheem Singh said, as Vijay began rising from the sofa with a visible effort. He walked over to Vijay and introduced himself and his companion. 'Bheem Singh from Rajvirgarh and this is Greg White, professor of archaeology and history at Boston Unversity.'

Vijay's jaw dropped as he introduced his companion and White walked over to shake his hand. In his last email, his uncle had instructed him to speak to Greg White! He had spent a long time trying to find out who, among his uncle's acquaintances, bore that name, but had drawn a blank. He had never imagined that the answer to the riddle would walk through his front door, in person.

Recovering his composure, he extended his hand. 'Pleased to meet you, Professor.'

'Greg, please,' White responded. 'Good to meet you, too, Vijay. Your uncle was a good friend. I was shattered to hear the news.'

'Yes,' Bheem Singh joined in, as White sat down next to him. 'Very unfortunate, indeed. I can't claim to have known Vikram so well, but we were...well, we moved in the same circles, you see, and I had met him several times. He was a good man.'

Vijay stared hard at Greg White. There was something familiar about him. But they had never met before. Then it struck him.

'You were on my flight from O'Hare to Delhi, three days ago. I was in 2B. American Airlines.'

White frowned, trying to remember. 'Three days back. Yes, I was on that flight. 3H. Courtesy Bheem's generosity. He's funded my trip here. But I'm sorry I really don't recall seeing you.'

Bheem Singh cleared his throat, visibly uninterested in whether Vijay and White had noticed each other during the flight to India. 'I saw the car outside. What happened'? He glanced from Vijay to Colin, and back, taking in the tense, harrowed look on their faces, the cut on Vijay's cheek and the gouges on the wrists of both the men.

Vijay shook his head. 'Somebody rammed our car when I was bringing Colin home from the airport and then kidnapped us.'

The Maharaja's face registered shock. He glanced at White, who looked horrified as well.

Vijay launched into a narrative of the events of the previous night, culminating in their escape, but left out the part about the key.

'You were very, very lucky,' the Maharaja mused. 'These people sound like dangerous criminals. But, why kidnap you? What did they want from you?'

Before Vijay could answer his question, the butler appeared at the door of the sitting room, followed by a policeman.

'Myself inspector Raunaq Singh,' the policeman announced as he entered the room. He was a middle-aged man, with a thick moustache and teeth blackened by years of chewing tobacco and betel leaves. 'I've come about the missing persons report. Who's missing?'

Radha rose. 'I had called the police station. They were missing all night.' She indicated Vijay and Colin.

'But they are back now. You should have informed us instead of wasting my time.' The inspector frowned and made to leave.

'Wait a minute.' Bheem Singh rose and drew himself up to his full height. 'I am Maharaja Bheem Singh of Rajvirgarh. These two men were kidnapped last night. Are you not going to do anything about that? They escaped with great difficulty and a lot of luck.'

Raunaq Singh stopped in his tracks. He had heard of Bheem Singh. He knew the Maharaja was a prominent politician and rumours of his power and influence had reached even the little police station in Jaungarh. He decided it was better not to rub the Maharaja the wrong way.

'You were kidnapped?' He addressed Vijay as he sat down on a vacant chair. 'Give me some more details.'

Vijay repeated the account of their kidnapping. 'Farooq and Imtiaz,' Raunaq Singh said, rubbing his chin thoughtfully, repeating the names that Vijay had given him. 'And you were imprisoned in a house in Gurgaon?'

Vijay nodded.

'Well, then, it is beyond my jurisdiction. This case belongs to the Gurgaon police.' He rose to leave.

'Aren't you going to register an FIR?' Bheem Singh enquired.

Raunaq Singh paused to choose his words carefully. 'They were kidnapped and held captive in Gurgaon. It is a matter for the Gurgaon police to investigate and check out the building they have described. And even if I was to register an FIR, how are we going to look for two men with only their first names as a basis for a search? Do you know how many Farooqs and Imtiazs there are in India?'

Bheem Singh considered this. 'I think you should still help out. Register an FIR so that the Gurgaon police take this case seriously. For God's sake, they could have been killed. I will make sure that the Gurgaon police follow up.' He nodded at Vijay. 'Leave that bit to me.'

The inspector finally nodded. 'Very well, sir. I will do as you say. But please don't expect anything more from me.'

Bheem Singh waited until the policeman had left and then turned to Vijay. 'You know, he's right. I don't think they have any chance of finding the two men purely on the basis of their first names. But it wouldn't have done to agree with him. They'd never take the matter seriously then.'

'That's why I didn't tell him what Farooq wanted,' Vijay said sourly. Ever since White had walked in, he had been torn between disclosing what Farooq had said about the key, and keeping that information to himself. He had concluded that, if his uncle had wanted him to speak to White, he should tell the archaeologist about the key. Perhaps White might be able to give him some insight that would help him understand his uncle's emails.

Bheem Singh raised an enquiring eyebrow.

'Yes. He was going on about a key and a disk with a verse. He said that uncle had given the key to me.'

Bheem Singh gave a visible start and exchanged a glance with White. 'I think we should tell them,' he said to the archaeologist.

White nodded. 'I was thinking the same thing, but I wasn't sure if you'd agree.'

Vijay looked at them quizzically, and was totally unprepared for White's question.

'Have you heard of the Nine Unknown Men?'

An Ambiguous Agenda of Terror

Imran Kidwai, Additional Director, Intelligence Bureau, strode down the corridor that led to the office of the Director. He had been urgently summoned by his boss. Imran was in his early 40s with a thick black moustache and piercing black eyes. He had kept himself fit despite the sedentary nature of his job at the Bureau.

He wondered what the urgency was about as he knocked on the door to the Director's office and then peered inside. Arjun Vaid, the Director, impatiently gestured to him to enter. Seated opposite Vaid was a foreigner with a mop of red hair, a laptop in front of him.

Imran took the chair next to the stranger and studied him curiously. 'This is Michael Blake,' Vaid said, introducing the foreigner. 'CIA. I think it's best he briefs you.'

Blake fixed Imran with a serious gaze. 'We've been alerted to a possible terror threat. We had a tap on the phone of a man who's a prime suspect in a recent high-level assassination in the Middle East. His name is Terence Murphy. We don't know who he works for and we hoped he'd lead us to them if we kept him under electronic surveillance. And this is what we got.'

He clicked on an audio file on his laptop. The playback of a recording began.

'Murphy,' a sharp voice instructed. 'I have a job for you. It's urgent.' The voice paused.

'We have a situation in India. Our partners operating there need help.'

'India'! Murphy exclaimed.

'Yes. I need you to fly to Delhi immediately. . You leave on tonight's flight from O'Hare to New Delhi. American Airlines. And the usual terms.'

'The objective?'

The recording ended with:

'All details will be given to you before you board your flight. Our partners operate under the leadership of a man named Farooq Siddiqui. That's all you need to know for now. '

'And I report back to you?'

'Negative. You'll report directly to a member of the Order. He is in India, personally supervising operations. You'll work with him and follow his directions.'

And one last thing. Read up on archaeology and ancient Indian history. You'll need it.'

The phone clicked as the caller hung up. Imran looked at Blake questioningly. 'There's more, isn't there? This is pretty inconclusive; hardly what I would call a lead.'

Blake grinned. 'I agree. We didn't think much of it either when we first reviewed it. But you must have heard of Farooq Siddiqui?'

Imran shrugged. 'Plenty of men with that name in India.'

Blake turned the laptop screen towards Imran. 'Watch this. We came across this video clip on a CD recovered from Bin Laden's hideout in Pakistan.' He clicked on an mp4 file and the video clip began.

The image was grainy, an amateur recording, but there was no mistaking the face of Al Zawahiri, the new leader of Al Qaeda. He was speaking in Arabic but there was a voiceover translating his words into English.

'The West will pay for the destruction of Islamic lives in Iraq and Afghanistan,' Al Zawahiri shrieked, brandishing an AK47 assault rifle. 'The infidels will die. They think they are superior, but now the Islamic world will have powerful weapons of a kind that mankind has never seen before; weapons that will help us achieve a victory for Islam!'

He turned and looked at another man, who stood by with a look of aloofness on his face, as if he had been compelled to be a part of the show.

'Brothers,' Al Zawahiri continued, 'this is Farooq Siddiqui. He is one of the nuclear scientists who helped Pakistan develop its nuclear bomb. He will vouch for what I have just said.'

Farooq coughed awkwardly and looked into the camera. 'We have a plan and funding from powerful sources. We have access to designs of weapons that people have never dreamt of. Our factories are being built to manufacture these weapons. We have the prototypes ready. And once the factories are ready, no one can stop Islam from asserting its rightful place in the world!'

The clip ended abruptly just as a group of hooded and armed men raised their automatic weapons to the sky and let loose a barrage of rounds.

Imran sat back, contemplating the last frame of the video which had zeroed onto Siddiqui's face. He would never have connected the name Farooq Siddiqui with the Pakistani scientist who had worked on the Pakistani nuclear bomb and then disappeared suddenly in 2003. It had been widely presumed that Farooq had been kidnapped or murdered by Islamic terrorists during an attempt to steal Pakistan's nuclear secrets. His body had never been found. Yet, here he was in an Al Qaeda video, with Al Zawahiri, no less.

'I don't get it,' Imran came straight to the point. 'What weapons is he talking about? And where are their factories?

Our intelligence has not picked up any such build-up anywhere. Have you guys heard anything?'

Blake shook his head. 'No idea. Farooq was careful not to describe the weapons and sounded deliberately ambiguous. This could be a recruitment video for attracting *jihadis* to Al Qaeda by promising them a technological superiority they haven't experienced yet. With Qaeda in tatters, this may just be an attempt to revive the group.'

'Farooq is the common factor between the phone tap and the video,' Imran summarised. 'And you think it is the same person?'

Blake shrugged. 'Could be. It is difficult to be conclusive. We only realised that we might be on to something when someone in the agency made the connection between the Murphy tap, the video clip and some documents recovered from Pakistan in a raid on a Lashkar-e-Taiba hideout. According to those documents, there is an LeT leader based in Pakistan by the name of Farooq Siddiqui. And we all know that LeT has links with Al Qaeda, possibly even ambitions of supplanting Al Qaeda as the foremost Islamic terrorist organisation in the world.' He paused to let his words sink in.

'As you say, there could be any number of Farooq Siddiquis in India,' Blake resumed after a few moments. He leaned forward to emphasise his words. 'The documents that named Farooq also mentioned a grand LeT terror plan, though there were no details. What if it is the same guy? Farooq Siddiqui, the scientist, swapping his lab coat for an AK47 and becoming an LeT leader? What if the reference in the Murphy tap wasn't to an Indian with this name, but to a Pakistani? And suppose the partner referred to in the call is LeT? Perhaps Murphy has been assigned to work with them on the project in India? It is plausible, since Murphy has connections in the Middle East as well.'

'Worth considering.' Imran looked at Vaid thoughtfully.

'If there is a link, we need to find it.' Vaid concurred. 'Kidwai, this one's your baby. Check on it and see if there is any substance to it. When you find Murphy, put a tap on his phone. We need to know who he speaks to. If our speculation is correct, there may be something really big underway and we need to stop it. I'll brief the Home Minister personally.'

Imran nodded. He had already begun planning his course of action. But two questions nagged at him.

Why was a renegade Pakistani nuclear scientist part of LeT? And what was he doing in India?

8

Day 5

Jaungarh Fort

Vijay shook his head and frowned. The Nine Unknown Men...
now, why did that sound familiar?

'Who are they'? He asked.

'The Brotherhood of the Nine Unknown Men is an ancient
secret society, perhaps the oldest in the world, going back
2,300 years.' White stopped, as Vijay sat bolt upright, his eyes
widening with surprise.

'You *have* heard of them, then'. White remarked.

'No, I haven't,' Vijay replied slowly. 'But that number—9—
was in an email my uncle sent to me on the day he was
murdered. I didn't understand what it meant, but when you
just spoke about the *Nine*, it suddenly struck me. I wonder if
uncle was referring to this secret society.'

'Your uncle certainly believed in the existence of the Nine,'
White said. 'He told me so on several occasions. You say he sent
you an email about the Nine?'

'Go on,' Vijay said impatiently, 'please tell me more about
this secret society.'

For a moment, White looked as if he wanted to find
out more about the email Vijay had mentioned. Then, he

glanced around the room. 'You have all heard of Emperor Asoka the Great.'

It was a statement more than a question, but Radha nodded. 'He was the legendary Indian king who lived in the third century BC. A fierce warrior who is said to have killed his brothers to ascend the throne, he fought bloody wars to expand his kingdom to cover almost the whole of present day India—except a bit of the south—and present-day Pakistan and Afghanistan. His last conquest was Kalinga, present-day Orissa. Thousands of soldiers on both sides were killed in the battle for Kalinga. Asoka is believed to have been overcome by remorse at the death and destruction he had caused, which led him to renounce violence and convert to Buddhism. History records that he was a great king, devoted to the welfare of his subjects. He spread Buddhism beyond India. His son Mahindra went to Sri Lanka. He put up edicts in stone all over the kingdom, propagating the law of *Dhamma*.'

White smiled. 'Very good. You certainly know your ancient Indian history. Asoka ruled from 260 BC to 223 BC. And you are right to call him legendary. The story of Asoka would have remained a legend if his edicts hadn't been first discovered and translated by James Prinsep in 1837. The discovery of another edict in 1915, mentioning Asoka by name, confirmed the historical authenticity of a king who, until the 19th century, had been considered a myth.'

'But there is another legend about Asoka, one less known and not established by historians.' Bheem Singh took up the narrative. 'It is said that he founded a secret society—The Brotherhood of the Nine Unknown Men. During Asoka's reign, it is a historical fact that while religion and peace flourished, science was cloaked in a veil of secrecy. It is believed that Asoka, having renounced violence, wanted to ensure that the scientific advances made by mankind were not put to military use or to cause destruction and death.

'According to the legend, the Nine were given the task of documenting all the scientific advancements made in history, by studying ancient texts and documents, to preclude the possibility of any known means of destruction falling into the wrong hands.

'Apparently, as members of the Nine died, new members were recruited, over the centuries, from the leading scientific minds of India, in order to preserve the continuity of knowledge. People even say that great Indian scientists like Jagdish Chandra Bose knew of and believed in the existence of the Nine; and perhaps even received help from them in their experiments. Why, it has even been speculated that Bose himself was one of the Nine.'

'But that isn't true,' White interjected. 'The Nine died out centuries ago. Legend has it that there hasn't been a member of the brotherhood alive for 1,500 years.'

'True,' Bheem Singh admitted. 'We know that for a fact because my ancestor, the first Maharaja of Rajvirgarh, has recorded the disappearance of the last member of the Nine in 500 AD. His court astronomer told him that he was the last one alive and asked him for protection because his life was in danger. But before my ancestor could do anything to help him, the astronomer disappeared.'

'I've heard the legend of the Nine,' Shukla murmured. 'They wrote books on different subjects.'

Bheem Singh nodded. 'Nine books, according to legend.' He ticked them off on his fingers. 'Psychology or propaganda and psychological warfare, physiology, microbiology, alchemy or chemistry, communication, gravity, cosmology, light and sociology.'

White nodded in agreement. The others simply stared at the Maharaja. This sounded unbelievable, yet it was coming from Bheem Singh whose persona seemed to lend this tale some sort of credibility.

'I'm sorry if I sound rude,' Colin found his voice, 'but I find it hard to believe that someone of your stature, a member of Indian royalty, would place his faith in a tale like this.' Colin didn't share the inhibitions of the other Indians in the room, who had a natural deference to a figure of authority like Bheem Singh. 'Books on chemistry, microbiology and gravity written over 2,000 years ago…I know India has a great history and science was pretty advanced in ancient times in India, but this is a bit far-fetched isn't it? We all know that Newton discovered the law of gravity. And microbiology…why, microscopes weren't even around at that time.'

'Oh, I'm not saying that I believe in this,' Bheem Singh smiled at their confusion. 'I'm simply telling you what the legend says. That doesn't mean the legend is true.'

'Yet uncle believed in this.'

White shook his head. 'I never said that. Vikram believed in the *existence* of the Nine, but not in the legend of the nine books written by them or any of the other fantastic stories about them. Somehow, he had stumbled upon the truth about the Nine.' He looked at Bheem Singh.

'You see,' Bheem Singh took the cue, 'Asoka the Great created the brotherhood to guard a great secret; one that had its roots in antiquity. The Nine were tasked to protect that secret which Asoka decided was too dangerous to be revealed to the world. All the other myths and stories about the Nine were fabricated to conceal this great secret from inquisitive minds and prying eyes.'

'And what was that secret?' Radha asked.

White shrugged. 'We don't know.'

'So how do you know that the purpose of the brotherhood was guarding this secret when you don't even know what that secret is?' Radha persisted.

White pulled out the leather notebook Bheem Singh had given him and placed it on the glass-topped centre table . They all stared at it but no one touched it; as if it was cursed in some way.

'Have you heard of Ernst Schafer?' Bheem Singh asked of no one in particular.

Everyone, except White, shook their heads.

'Okay, what about the *Ahnenerbe?*'

'Hang on, wasn't that the organisation set up by Hitler to research the origins of the Aryan race?' Vijay screwed up his face as he spoke, trying to recall his school history lessons.

'Correct.' Bheem Singh acknowledged. 'In 1935, Hitler authorised Frederick Hielscher to establish the *Ahnenerbe*, or the Bureau for the Study of Ancestral Heritage. One of its objectives was researching the origins of the Aryan race. They focused on Tibet.

'In 1937, *Ahnenerbe* was made an official organisation attached to the *Schutzstaffel*, the dreaded SS—the Protection Squad.

'Ernst Schafer, a hunter and biologist led two expeditions to Tibet in 1931and 1935, primarily to fulfil his hunting and biology research interests. However, in 1938, the *Ahnenerbe* sponsored a third expedition at the invitation of the Tibetan government. One member of Schafer's third expedition was the anthropologist Bruno Beger, whose interests included racial research. In 1937, Beger had actually proposed a research project in Tibet and, as a part of the Schafer expedition, intended measuring the skulls of Tibetans for his research on the racial characteristics of Tibetans.'

He indicated the notebook. 'This is Bruno Beger's diary in which he kept notes of everything he saw and researched.' He briefly explained Beger's stay at the Temple of the Tooth and his discovery of the texts there.

Shukla picked up the notebook and began leafing through it, stopping in parts to read some of the entries. As his eyes fell on one of the Sanskrit inscriptions that Beger had copied, his face lit up.

'You can read Sanskrit?' Bheem Singh noticed Shukla's attention to the verses.

Shukla nodded, not taking his eyes off the page. 'I studied ancient Indian languages when I was in college. Vikram and I both did; we were keenly interested in the past. Pali, Prakrit, Magadhi and Sanskrit. Even Kharosthi. That was before he decided to become a nuclear physicist. This is fascinating.' The last remark referred to the page he was reading.

'Well, then, perhaps you can translate for the benefit of the others.'

Shukla looked around and nodded. He cleared his throat and began reading aloud.

'I, Surasen, do hereby put down a record of my discovery as part of the secret library of the Nine Unknown Men, the glorious brotherhood created by our beloved Emperor Asoka the Great, Devanampiya Piyadasi. I will not say what this discovery is, for the Emperor forbids any record describing what I have found in case it falls into the hands of the enemy; for this is the reason the brotherhood of the Nine was founded. But I must record how I made the discovery.

'On the instruction of my Emperor, I accompanied the jungle-dweller to his forest habitat, a 10-day journey from the palace. Leaving him and my escort of troops behind, I proceeded cautiously to the foot of the hill that lay in the midst of the forest. 'Before me, I beheld a small entrance, a dark hole in the side of the hill, hidden by a larger wall of rock. I stepped through the opening into the darkness beyond. I was not afraid of demons, for I am not superstitious, but I was afraid of the unknown; and I knew not what lay before me, beyond the opening.

'As I passed through, a curious thing happened. A strange light, soft and dim, lit up my steps leading me through a passage to the mouth of the cavern. As I entered the cavern, I could not believe my eyes at what I beheld.

'But, as the wise Emperor has said, such a discovery can put the world in great peril. So I must hold my tongue and say no more.'

Shukla looked up. 'This is amazing.' His hands trembling with excitement as he resumed his study of the notebook.

Vijay's eyes narrowed. 'How is it that you guys are so well-informed about a secret society that has managed to stay hidden for over 2,000 years?'

Bheem Singh smiled. 'This is confidential, Vijay. But I'll share something with you. I'm leading a government project that is trying to secure the secret of the Nine. The brotherhood died out centuries ago. Now, someone else is after the secret. And the government wants to ensure that it remains concealed the way Asoka intended. If Asoka believed it could destroy the world, we can't allow it to fall into the wrong hands.'

'There's a reason you're telling me all this.' Vijay looked enquiringly at the Maharaja.

'A couple of reasons, actually. First, the original Nine Unknown Men went to great lengths to secure the location of the secret. They devised an elaborate system of riddles and clues and divided up the pieces of the puzzle among a few members of the Nine so that no one member could find the location on his own. The first part of the puzzle is a metal disk with a verse inscribed on it which can only be deciphered with the help of a key.'

'It's all here in the diary,' Shukla agreed. 'A metal disk, a key, a ball of rock and a riddle—four parts to the puzzle.' He then corrected himself. 'Sorry, two metal disks. They made a duplicate; probably just in case one got misplaced.'

Vijay's eyes widened. 'So you're saying that uncle was murdered because Farooq and his cronies are searching for the secret of the Nine'?

'That's the second reason why I've shared this with you because you told us what Farooq was looking for. Apparently he has somehow come into possession of one of the two metal disks, though how he came by it I can't imagine. It seems reasonable to conclude that your uncle was murdered and you were kidnapped because of your uncle's knowledge of the Nine. You need to know that you may be in grave danger. Especially if Farooq, whoever he is, believes that your uncle knew the location of the key and handed this knowledge to you. Did Vikram do that?'

'No, uncle never told me about any key.' Vijay toyed with the idea of telling them about the emails. But he wasn't sure he wanted to share the emails with anyone yet. If his uncle had intended the message behind the emails to be common knowledge he wouldn't have gone to such great lengths to disguise it.

Bheem Singh nodded. 'Anything you discover that might help in protecting the secret will be useful for us.'

'Sure, though I can't imagine how we can help.' Vijay couldn't help but feel that the Maharaja knew he was holding something back.

'In any case, please be careful,' Bheem Singh cautioned. He shared with them the details about the massacre at the Temple of the Tooth and the disappearance of the ancient texts that Beger had so painstakingly copied into his diary. 'And that's not all,' he added. 'Greg here was attacked last night.'

White nodded ruefully and his hand went to the back of his neck. 'I've got a bump here,' he said, 'from being mugged last night in my hotel room. I woke up to realise that the room had been searched.'

'There's nothing that Greg could have had with him that could help anyone on the trail of the secret. He had only just arrived in India and didn't even know the details. But his association with the project was, by itself, enough to draw attention to him.' Bheem Singh added and then addressed Vijay, 'We haven't lodged a police report because we don't want undue attention. I have asked Greg to move into my farmhouse. He will be safer there, as the farmhouse is well-guarded. I think you should also be very careful and watch your back. If this

Farooq guy is really after the secret of the Nine, then he will stop at nothing.'

The butler entered the room to announce the arrival of the lawyer, Homi Mehta.

'Vijay, my boy, are you alright?' Homi's usually genial face was creased with worry as he rushed to Vijay and clasped his hand, looking at his injuries from his earlier escapade.

'I'm fine, just a bit shaken,' Vijay assured Homi and then introduced him to Bheem Singh, Greg White and Colin.

Vijay once again narrated the details of their kidnapping and escape. He had intended telling Homi about the key since he considered Homi to be a part of the family, and had begun explaining what Farooq wanted, when he noticed Bheem Singh frowning at him. Realising that the Maharaja was averse to telling anyone else about the Nine, he quickly skipped over that part of the story.

'Radha called me this morning when you didn't return during the night,' Homi said, 'She called me again when you did turn up, so I decided to rush here as soon as I could.'

Bheem Singh and White exchanged looks and the former cleared his throat. 'Well, Vijay, I think we'll be going,' he said. 'I'd have been happy to take you to Delhi in my car and have you dropped back but, since Mr. Mehta is here, I guess that's taken care of. Let me know if there is anything else I can do for you.' He handed over his business card to Vijay.

'And me too,' White joined in, scribbling his phone number on the reverse of Bheem Singh's business card.

Vijay rose and shook hands with the two men and they moved towards the door.

'I've brought all the papers relating to Vikram Singh's will and estates,' Homi handed over a plastic folder to Vijay as he sat down. 'Apart from all his assets, there is…' He hesitated and glanced at Radha, Shukla and the two men walking out of the room.

Vijay understood. Homi was not comfortable discussing the details of Vikram Singh's will in the presence of others. He smiled reassuringly at the lawyer. 'It's okay, Homi. Everyone here is a friend.'

Homi nodded, still looking uncomfortable, but resumed. 'Your uncle had leased a locker, two years ago, in Delhi. Here's the key. I don't know what's in there, since Vikram was very secretive about it. There's nothing in the will about its contents either.'

White and Bheem Singh stopped at the door to the sitting room as they heard this, and turned. Their eyes met Vijay's. All three men were thinking the same thing.

Was the mysterious key that Farooq sought hidden in this locker?

However, without putting this thought into words, Bheem Singh and Greg White left.

'Why don't we check out the locker while we are in Delhi?' Vijay suggested.

He was excited about the revelation that his uncle had, indeed, hidden something away and he wanted to find out what it was; especially if it had something to do with a 2,000-year-old secret brotherhood.

Homi looked at his watch. 'I have a lunch appointment at one-thirty,' he said, 'so I'm sorry but I won't be able to drive you to the locker today.'

'Why don't you pick up my car on the way?' Radha suggested, as Vijay's face fell. She realised what he was thinking and understood his need for immediate action. 'We should anyway have a car at the fort, just in case, now that the BMW is out of action.'

'Good idea,' Vijay looked at her gratefully. 'We'll pick up your car once we finish at the hospital.'

Homi scribbled the address of the locker on a slip of paper, 'You'll need to carry an identification proof which has your photograph on it. The other papers that will give you access to the locker are in the folder I just gave you.'

Trapped!

Vijay and Colin accompanied the clerk down the stairs to the basement of the vault.

The lockers were in an underground vault accessed by a narrow staircase that was barred at the top by a solid steel door with two levels of security: an electronic password to open the first lock and a manual key to open the second.

The clerk stopped at a row of lockers, unlocked one of them and left. Vijay could now use his keys to open it completely. Vijay's hands trembled with excitement as he opened the steel box kept within the locker. Inside was a package wrapped in brown paper. He ripped off the paper to reveal a layer of bubble wrap. Carefully placing the package on the felt-topped table the clerk had left for them, he removed the bubble wrap, wondering what lay within that had to be preserved so carefully.

As the last layer of wrapping came off, Vijay and Colin stared at the object that lay on the table.

It was a solid slab, circular in shape, made from a strange dark metal, ancient in appearance but with no traces of rust. One side was smooth and polished. The other side had a circular hollow at the centre, circumscribed by what looked like a gear wheel with inscriptions around it. Forming a circular boundary to the hollow and the gear wheel was a final circle, also surrounded by inscriptions. It didn't seem like a key of any kind. As they stared at the disk a thought dawned on Vijay.

His eyes sparkled with excitement as he looked at Colin, who immediately understood what Vijay was thinking.

Just then, Vijay's mobile phone rang. He looked at the number. It was Homi. He put the phone to his ear, but could only hear someone breathing heavily.

'Homi...Homi...' he barked into the phone anxiously. 'Vijay,' a scratchy voice gasped, as if choking; Vijay could barely recognise the voice as Homi's. The words seemed to be coming between gasps. Or was it just a bad signal in this underground area? 'Vijay...please...they...address...locker...please...leave...' The voice faltered and fell silent, and Vijay heard a clattering sound as if something had fallen on the ground.

A cold fear gripped Vijay. He looked at Colin, who had replaced the metal slab in its bubble wrap packing and slipped it into a duffel bag.

'That was Homi. I think he was trying to warn us to get out of here. Now.'

He quickly dialled the ambulance number that was saved on his phone for emergencies, and asked them to report to Homi's office.

'Farooq?' Colin had caught onto Vijay's thought.

Vijay nodded grimly. 'Let's go!' He slung the strap of the bag across his shoulder and bounded up the stairs.

Suddenly, cries and screams filtered through the heavy steel door at the top of the staircase, which was open just a crack. Abruptly, the door slammed shut and the two friends, who had by now been joined by a few more people accessing their lockers, heard the sound of the bolts slamming home. Someone had locked the steel door!

The small knot of people looked at each other in surprise. There was, however, no cause for concern. If the steel door was locked, anyone wanting to leave the locker had simply to use the intercom and the door would be opened for them from the outside.

Vijay picked up the receiver of the intercom. There was silence; no tone. He waited for a while, hoping someone would come on the line, but nothing happened.

What was happening outside?

Abruptly, there were two sharp bangs and sudden silence. The screaming and shouting had stopped.

Vijay and Colin exchanged glances. Now they looked worried. They didn't know how many of the others had realised it, but the bangs had sounded a lot like gunshots.

'Let's step away from the door,' Vijay said as he and Colin tried to herd the others down the stairway. If those had been shots from a weapon, it was likely that there would be an attempt to break into the locker. There were only two ways the locker could now be opened: either someone from the vault would help unlock the steel door or it would be blown open. And if the latter happened, it would be best if there was no one near it.

A worried group crowded into the space between the rows of lockers.

Colin frowned. 'Do you think we've been tailed all the way here?'

Vijay shrugged. 'Perhaps. But I think we are safe here. I don't think their Uzis can penetrate that door of steel. It must be two feet thick.'

Just then, as if to prove him wrong, there was a loud explosion accompanied by an ear-shattering crunching of metal and the ground beneath their feet shook as if an earthquake had struck. Vijay and Colin looked at each other in dismay as the steel door bulged inwards from the centre, as if it had been struck by a powerful projectile. The thick hinges were bent and the door itself was twisted in places along the frame. Wispy trails of smoke drifted in through the cracks that had appeared between the steel door and its frame.

Voices could now be heard through these cracks. Men shouting at each other in harsh, guttural tones; sounds identical to what they had heard the previous evening.

Vijay and Colin exchanged glances.

Then, without a word, they split up and began searching along the walls for an opening, any orifice that might lead out of the vault. But there was nothing. The vault had been built to keep things in.

9

244 BC

Surasen stood silently and watched his Emperor pace the length of the chamber. Rarely, in his long association with him, had Surasen seen Asoka this distressed; this restlessness was uncharacteristic.

'Where are they?' Asoka stopped in mid-stride and turned to Surasen. 'Did you not command them to come here immediately?'

'My liege, I did,' Surasen bowed his head. 'It is midnight and they would have had to be roused from their sleep.'

Asoka turned away and resumed his restless pacing of the chamber. Silence descended on the two men, leaving Surasen to his thoughts.

He remembered the change in the Emperor's demeanour at the discovery in the forest. His mood had persisted since. So deeply had Asoka been affected that he had not spoken a word since then, except for a brief command, instructing him to immediately summon a few courtiers.

Surasen noticed that his emperor did not hesitate while naming the men who were to be summoned; clearly the emperor had, during the journey home, been dwelling on what he intended to do about their discovery.

There was a sound at the door, and a guard entered to announce the arrival of the courtiers.

244 BC / 69

Surasen noticed that the furrows had disappeared from Asoka's face. The mask of serenity was back. The Emperor was in control of himself once more.

The courtiers filed in, eight of them, and stood before Asoka in a semi-circle, each wondering what was so important for their Emperor to wake them up in the middle of the night. But they said nothing, waiting for his orders.

'Surasen, tell them what we found.' Asoka folded his arms across his chest as Surasen narrated the story of the forest dweller, his journey to the cavern and the discovery he had made, his subsequent journey back with Asoka and the second discovery they had made—the one that was deeply troubling the Emperor.

As he spoke, the faces of the other courtiers registered surprise, amazement, shock and wonder, in turn. When he finished, he knew they understood as well as he did the reason for them being here at this hour.

'So, you see,' Asoka took up the narrative, 'the myths of the ancients were not just stories. And I know that you, my wise courtiers, are aware of the danger posed to the world by what lies in this cavern. If it were to fall into the hands of the enemy, they could use it for untold gain. We cannot allow this to happen. This cavern and its contents have been buried for centuries. We will seal up the opening on the hillside. They must remain a secret. Forever.'

He drew a short dagger from the scabbard at his waist and beckoned the men.

'Hold out your left hand,' he said. Each courtier extended his left hand, palm upwards. Asoka made a small cut on the palm of each courtier, letting out blood that spilled across their palms. 'You are today joined in brotherhood,' he said as the men placed their hands together, their blood mixing and dripping to the floor. 'The Brotherhood of the Nine Unknown Men. And you will protect this secret forever, never letting the rest of mankind know that it ever existed.'

He looked at them gravely. 'Swear upon your blood that you will protect this secret with your life; that you will never betray your brotherhood or your cause, that no one will ever know about the true nature of your purpose in life.'

The nine men swore their allegiance to the newly-formed brotherhood and its mission.

'One more thing.' Asoka was not done. 'The *Vimana Parva*—the book of the Mahabharata that mentions the legend,—erase it from every record of the epic that exists. By royal decree, the memorisation of this book of the Mahabharata must also be discontinued. The myth must disappear from the knowledge and memories of men, just like the secret it mentions. The only place where it will continue to exist will be within the brotherhood. Create a book of stone that will record the *Vimana Parva* and hide it within the folds of the brotherhood, concealed from the eyes and ears of men forever. The world will still know the Mahabharata, but it will never know the dark secret it carries deep within.'

10

Present Day

Day 5
New Delhi

'I have an idea,' Colin suddenly whispered in Vijay's ear. 'Hang on.' He turned to the little group that clustered not far from them. 'Does anyone here smoke? Do you have a lighter or a box of matches?'

Vijay instantly understood. He glanced up at the ceiling. A network of pipes ran along the roof, with sprinklers protruding at regular intervals. There were smoke detectors fixed on the walls, which would set the sprinklers off.

One of the women in the group had a lighter and she handed it over to Colin, her hand trembling, her face betraying her anxiety. There was no time to lose. The shouts upstairs had subsided into a strange calm. Was it a lull before the storm? Both friends doubted that the door, thick as it was, could withstand another assault.

Vijay sprinted towards a ladder that was used to access the higher levels of the lockers and wheeled it over to one of the smoke detectors. Colin kept pace with him and jumped onto the ladder even before it came to a stop, shinning up the rungs at top speed. He reached the smoke detector and produced a flame from the lighter.

The seconds ticked by, seeming like hours.

Nothing happened.

There was another loud blast, followed by the sound of metal buckling under metal. The steel door was wrenched off its hinges, the bolts of the double lock snapping with a shattering sound as the door flew down the stairs. It skidded along the floor and came to a stop as it smashed with a resounding crash into a row of lockers against the far wall. The little group shrank back, sheltering behind a wall of lockers in an attempt to shield themselves.

Shouts rent the air and men came clattering down the stairs, following the path of the destroyed door.

Colin was grim-faced as he held the lighter to the smoke detector, willing it to work. *Why was it taking so long?*

Suddenly, the sprinklers came to life, dousing the group in the vault, soaking them thoroughly. The men charging into the vault were caught unawares and for a few seconds their downward progress into the vault slowed down.

'Quick, the ladder!' Vijay shouted to Colin.

With one accord, both friends lifted the heavy ladder and, holding it horizontal before them like a battering ram, charged towards the group of men racing down the stairs.

The men, though armed, hadn't expected to meet with resistance. The sight of a 10-foot ladder ploughing its way towards them brought them up short. The stairway was slippery with the water from the sprinklers, and the lower stairs had been damaged by the impact of the steel door earlier. The men leading the charge lost their footing and slipped on the stairs.

Vijay and Colin dodged them and ignored the water cascading down as they charged up the stairs with the ladder, hoping they wouldn't slip, mowing down men and carving a path for themselves to the room above.

There was only one thought in their minds. They had to get away.

As they emerged from the vault, two things greeted their eyes. The first was the prone body of the clerk who had led them into the vault, lying in a pool of blood, his head blown open at the back. The second was Farooq, Maroosh and three men standing around a peculiar machine that looked like an enormous metallic archer's bow, seven feet high, fitted on a solid metal pedestal. The entire contraption was made of a dark metal, not unlike the metal slab Vijay was carrying ensconced in the duffel bag.

Farooq's eyes widened with surprise as he saw the two men emerge with the ladder. Vijay and Colin had the advantage of surprise. Even as realisation dawned on Farooq, they summoned their last reserves of strength and heaved the ladder towards him and the contraption, causing the men to scatter to get out of the way.

The few moments this bought them were enough. The two friends dashed outside the building to where Radha's car was standing and leapt in. Vijay started the car and honked his way through a gathering crowd of curious onlookers, alerted by the sound from the vault.

As Vijay pressed his foot to the accelerator, he could hear furious shouts behind him as Farooq rallied his men. The sound of gunshots shattered the air. Vijay risked a glance in the rear-view mirror and saw Farooq's men piling into a mid-size truck that stood outside the vault. To his amazement, he saw three of them carrying a metal pedestal with a heap of metal piled on top of it into the truck. Was it the contraption they had seen? But that had been seven feet tall! It was almost as if they had been able to fold it into something that was not more than two feet tall. And they carried it as though it was not too heavy.

It seemed that Farooq and his men were going to give pursuit, when police sirens split the air and the truck suddenly veered in a different direction, giving up the chase.

Vijay and Colin grinned at each other. They had beaten Farooq once again. And this time, they had something to show for it.

Together They Guard The Secret

The little group sat in Vikram Singh's study, their eyes glued to the LCD television fixed on the wall.

One of the news channels was reporting the incident at the vault. At the bottom of the screen, the words 'Breaking News: Terrorist Attack on Vault in New Delhi' scrolled across repeatedly...'None of the terrorist groups have claimed responsibility.' A reporter was speaking into the camera.

Vijay sighed and switched off the television.

The incident was on all the channels. Speculation was rife about the purpose of the attack; with the most popular interpretation being that it was an attempt to accumulate funds for a terrorist group.

After leaving the vault, Vijay and Colin had rushed to Homi's office to find that an ambulance had reported and taken the lawyer to the nearest hospital. At the hospital, they had been assured by the doctors that he would live, though his condition was serious.

Vijay couldn't help but feel responsible in some way. After all, Homi had nothing to do with either Farooq or the secret of the Nine.

After leaving the hospital, Vijay had tried calling Bheem Singh, but his phone had been busy continuously, so he had called White and told him about the disk they had unearthed in the locker.

White had arrived at Jaungarh almost immediately, and was now seated with the others in Vikram Singh's study.

The study was a square room with large bay windows that overlooked the hillside below. In a corner by the windows, was a large polished desk. On the opposite wall, flanking the doorway, hung two large paintings. One depicted the scene from the Mahabharata, where the grandsire of the dynasty in the epic, Bheeshma Pitamah, lay dying on a bed of arrows. The other was a sketch of the Buddha with the word *Karma* in bold black letters above the sketch. There were also various Buddhist symbols like the Wheel of Law, the Bodhi tree, the lion and the footprints of the Buddha in bold relief below the sketch.

The other walls of the study were lined with bookshelves. Diagonally opposite the desk was a small glass-topped table surrounded by a comfortable seating arrangement, with a television on the wall; the place where the group now sat.

Vijay slowly walked to the desk to pick up his duffel bag. The shocking events of the day had driven away all thoughts of what they had actually found in the locker.

He sat down and pulled out the metal slab in its bubble wrap packaging.

'The key?' White enquired, leaning forward with interest.

'No. But I think this is one of the disks that were part of the puzzle.' He looked at Shukla. 'You'd mentioned that there were two metal disks.'

'Yes. That's what Beger wrote in his diary; it was a transcript of one of the texts that belonged to the Nine.'

Vijay unwrapped the metal disk and placed it on the table for everyone to see. 'The disk with the verse that Farooq had alluded to.' He indicated the inscriptions on the metal slab.

Shukla peered at the disk curiously. He reached out and picked it up, studying it intently.

'The script is Magadhi,' he said after a few moments. He looked up at Vijay, his eyes bright with excitement. 'You could be right. This disk could actually date back to the time of Asoka the Great, or even before him. This may just be the only other surviving artefact of those times.' He stared at the disk as if he couldn't believe he was holding it. 'Two thousand years of history in my hands.'

Colin looked sharply at him. 'That's exactly what Vijay's uncle said in one of his emails. *Two thousand years of history which I have safely guarded for the last 25 years, is yours to unlock.* Do you think he was referring to this disk?'

It was Shukla's turn to look enquiringly at Vijay. 'Vikram sent you an email referring to this disk?'

'You'd mentioned that Vikram had sent you an email talking about the Nine,' White interjected.

'I'm sorry,' Vijay confessed. 'I've been holding back something. I wasn't sure I wanted to share this with everyone yet. Only Colin knew. But I think the time is right to let you all into the secret.' He quickly told them about the emails, reading out the exact words of each one from a printout he had kept in the study.

'I believe uncle somehow knew that he was in danger. That is why he installed such an advanced security system in the fort. And hid the metal disk away in a locker without telling any one. How he obtained the disk, I can't guess. But he knew about the Nine and their secret.' He nodded to White. 'He told you about it. He may have told someone else and somehow the information filtered through to Farooq or whoever he is working for. I think that, on the night he was murdered, his security system alerted him about the intruders. Rather than protecting himself, his first thought was to ensure that the secret was safe. He sent me the emails, hoping that I would decipher them. That is why, I guess, he wanted me to speak to Greg, as instructed in his final email. He knew that Greg would tell me about uncle's belief in the existence of the Nine. I am not yet certain what he wanted me to do with this information. But I am sure he knew that someone ruthless, someone unscrupulous, was after it; someone who would stop at nothing.'

There was silence when he had finished. It was Colin who broke it.

'If I know you,' he raised one eyebrow at Vijay, 'You now want to try and decipher the hidden message in the emails and try and find the secret of the Nine?'

'Why not?' Vijay grinned at him. 'Are you afraid of a little secret that could destroy the world?'

'Who, me? Of course not. I'm game.' Colin grinned back. 'Maybe it will make us all rich! These ancient secrets have a way of attracting money. All I'm worried about is the *someone ruthless, someone unscrupulous*, who will stop at nothing. These ancient secrets have a way of attracting those kinds of folk as well.'

Vijay smiled to himself. He knew that Colin would be the first in line to jump into any activity that involved danger.

He looked at Shukla, who was still holding the disk. 'You said you could read Magadhi. Can you tell us what the inscriptions say?'

'I studied Magadhi,' Shukla agreed, 'but it has been a while since I last translated anything written in Magadhi. Let's see.' He bent his head over the disk.

After a few moments of studying the symbols around the grooves, he looked up, his face radiating excitement. 'This is a device that will provide directions to find something. Look at this.'

All eyes were on the disk in his hands as they bent over it. Shukla pointed to the concentric grooves. 'There are two sets of inscriptions,' he explained. 'One surrounding the gear wheel, and the other around the outer circle.'

He placed his index finger on the cogwheel and slowly moved it in a clockwise direction. To their surprise, it moved. The disk wasn't really one solid slab; the gearwheel was a separate disk, fixed to the slab, that moved independently of the outer circle.

As they watched, Shukla moved the toothed wheel until the inscriptions on its perimeter aligned perfectly with the characters on the outer disk to form nine distinct lines of symbols.

'Each row of inscriptions is a complete sentence now,' he explained, 'and together, the nine lines form a verse.'

He pointed to two lines of inscriptions, at two opposite ends of the disk. 'Those lines are the beginning and end of the verse. I will read it out to you.'

He adjusted his spectacles for a better view of the inscriptions and began reading aloud.

The Nine have gone forth to the edges of the empire
The first speaks in two tongues
The second, in appearance, is different from the rest
The third gazes over the sea, waiting for the ships to come in
The fourth speaks the name of the Emperor
The fifth is seventeen
The sixth doesn't have all that the others do; but is special for
he also has that which the others do not
The seventh pays homage to the Wheel of Truth
The eighth is greater by one than the other upright ones
The ninth writes with a hand that is different from the rest.
Together, they guard the way to the truth that is protected by
the Nine.

'And this is why we need the key,' Vijay mused. 'The key will lock the inner disk in place so that the resulting sequence of words in each line can be read in the correct order. Without the key, the correct alignment of words in each line of the verse will be impossible to find. Only the key can give us the correct verse.'

Shukla agreed. 'Without it, the disk is useless. There is no other way to say which combination of inner and outer inscriptions gives us the correct verse.'

Colin had been studying the printout with the emails. 'What's the Bhagavad Gita?' he enquired.

'Have you heard of the Mahabharata?' Shukla responded.

'Yeah, the ancient Indian epic about some battle fought between two sets of brothers.'

'Somewhat accurate,' Shukla smiled. 'It is an ancient epic, composed in antiquity. There are conflicting opinions about exactly when this was done, since it was orally transmitted from generation to generation, for centuries, before it was finally committed to writing, sometime between 500 BC and 200 BC. No one knows exactly when it was first documented. Set in ancient India, it tells the story of a war between two sets of cousins—the Kauravas, one hundred in number, and the five Pandava brothers. The epic traces the lives of each of the key players in the war that finally took place between the two groups on the plains of Kurukshetra in northern India.

'The Bhagavad Gita is part of the Mahabharata. It is the sermon delivered by Lord Krishna to Arjuna, a Pandava, on the battlefield of Kurukshetra. Lord Krishna was Arjuna's charioteer. The Bhagavad Gita explains the philosophy of life and entails the comprehension of five basic truths; *Isvara* (the Science of God), *Jeevas* (the constitutional nature of living entities), *Prakriti* (material nature), *Samay* (time) or the duration of existence of the entire universe or the manifestation of material nature and *Karma* (activities in our lives).'

'I've heard of *Karma*.' Colin studied the printout again. 'It's what influences your next life after rebirth, isn't it?' He frowned at the emails. 'I'm convinced the clue to finding the key to the disk lies in the second email. "*The subject of the Gita, though mixed up, is a mark upon us for our future lives and will lead you through the door to knowledge, which you must unlock.*' He looked around at the group. 'The only thing that will unlock the door to knowledge is a key. But what is the subject of the Gita that is mixed up and is a mark upon us for our future lives?'

'*Isvara, Jeevas, Prakriti, Samay, Karma*,' Shukla muttered. 'The five basic truths that form the subject of the Gita – But none of these can be described as mixed up.'

Silence descended on the group as they pondered this riddle. Vijay buried his face in his hands and concentrated hard. What was his uncle trying to tell him? He thought back to his childhood, the years he had spent with his uncle to find clues to his uncle's thought process.

Suddenly, it struck him.

'Anagrams!' he cried out loud.

The others looked at him curiously.

'It's an anagram,' he explained. 'Uncle was very fond of two things; solving crosswords and solving anagrams. He's used an anagram in the email.'

Colin smacked his forehead. 'I should have seen it. It's there in plain view. And it's the only basic truth that I knew.'

'What are you both talking about?' Radha interjected.

'Vijay explained, his face flushed with the thrill of having solved the first riddle. 'It isn't the truth that's mixed up. It's the word that describes the truth, an anagram.'

'Oh, I see it now.' An understanding spread through Radha's expression and even Shukla and White nodded.

Now that it had been explained, it was obvious. 'The subject that leaves a mark upon us for our future lives." A Mark." Unscramble it and you get *Karma*—the subject of the Gita that affects our future lives according to Hindu philosophy.'

'Okay, so how does *Karma* lead us through the door of knowledge?' Colin looked puzzled again.

Vijay's elation at having found the first clue slowly dissipated. They still didn't know where the key was.

'*You have to look deeper within*,' Radha read the second line of the email.

'I think your uncle was telling you to look deeper within this email,' Colin guessed. 'There's more in here than just the anagram.'

'Wait a minute,' Radha stretched both her hands out in excitement. 'Look at the third line.'

'*Study, the Bhagavad Gita.*'

White frowned. 'But we've already used that clue to find the anagram.'

Radha shook her head. 'Look deeper within,' she urged, quoting the email. 'Read the line again. There's a comma after the word "study." The line isn't an instruction to study the Bhagavad Gita. I think the comma was put there to draw attention to the word "study." It isn't a verb.'

'It is a pointer.' Vijay realised that Radha was onto something. 'The key is in the study.'

'And it has something to do with *Karma*,' Colin joined in, excitedly.

Vijay looked around the room, at the windows, the bookcases lining the walls, the paintings that flanked the doorway. If the key was in the study, why hadn't Farooq found it when he had searched the room after murdering his uncle?

'Where...?' He started to ask, then broke off and his jaw dropped. It had been staring them in the face all this while.

The painting to the right of the doorway in the study; the one that had the word *Karma* boldly printed above the sketch of the Buddha.

He slowly rose and walked to the painting. Was this it? Where was the key?

'Papa,' Radha broke the silence as they clustered around the painting, scrutinising it intently. 'Didn't the Wheel of Law propagated by the Buddha have eight spokes'?

'Yes. Eight spokes for the eight principles of *Dhamma*, the faith.'

As Shukla replied, they all realised why Radha had asked the question. The Wheel of Law depicted in the painting didn't have eight spokes.

It had nine.

They stared at the nine-spoked wheel for a few moments. The key had been hidden away in plain sight. Who would have thought of counting the number of spokes in the wheel?

'Ingenious,' Shukla muttered admiringly.

Vijay reached out for the wheel. It was embedded in the painting, barely a few millimetres protruding from the canvas. His fingers touched the wheel. It was metal; the same dark metal that the disk was made from. He grasped the wheel and tugged at it gently.

It refused to budge. But Vijay persisted.

Finally, there was an audible *click* and the wheel came loose from the painting.

Holding it tenderly, like a newborn, Vijay carried it to the coffee table and inserted it into the hollow innermost circle of the metal disk. With a soft click, the key slid into place. Elated, he moved the wheel in a clockwise direction. It had locked onto the gear wheel and both the circles moved together. Then, there was another click and the wheels came to a stop. They had locked themselves into place.

The rows of inscriptions were perfectly aligned once more. And this time they knew it was the correct sequence of lines.

Shukla took the disk in his hands and began reading out the new arrangement of words in the inscriptions.

'"*The Nine have gone forth to the edges of the empire*
The first, in appearance, is different from the rest

The second gazes over the sea, waiting for the ships to come in

The third speaks the name of the Emperor

The fourth is seventeen

The fifth writes with a hand that is different from the rest

The sixth is greater by one than the other upright ones

The seventh pays homage to the Wheel of Truth

The eighth does not have all that the others do; but is special for he also has that which the others do not

The ninth speaks in two tongues.

Together, they guard the way to the truth that is protected by the Nine."'

There was silence when he finished. The verse still didn't make any sense.

Colin gave voice to their feelings. 'The key does nothing more than re-order the combination of words.'

'This sounds a bit like a description of people,' White ventured. 'Perhaps it describes the original Nine Unknown Men?'

'And how are we to figure out the identities of nine men, who have been dead for over 2,000 years?' Vijay demanded testily but then checked himself. 'I'm sorry. This is getting to me. I thought finding the key would send us on our way. But it hasn't helped a bit. We are no closer to finding the secret of the Nine than we were yesterday.'

'I don't think this refers to the original Nine,' Colin said slowly. 'The Nine were a secret brotherhood. These secret societies operate on the principle that no one member knows the identity of all the others. Each member knows the identities of one or two others. And they never use their actual names when addressing each other. This ensures that betrayal by any one member doesn't lead to annihilation of the group. If the group is targeted by a traitor, they may lose a few members, but the brotherhood lives on.'

'How do you know so much about secret societies?' Vijay looked at Colin quizzically.

'Hey, all the thrillers about secret societies work on this principle.' An impish smile played across Colin's face.

Vijay threw a pen at him. 'You and your thrillers, again.'

'Colin is right in a manner of speaking,' Shukla explained. 'As a secret society, it is highly improbable that any reference to their members would be included in a riddle. First, their identities were secret, so how could anyone decipher the riddle when their names weren't known? Second, this riddle was meant to last for centuries, to be used when all else failed, and then only to protect the secret. The names of the original members would be forgotten, as they are now, even if they were known. That eliminates this possibility.'

'What about the emails?' Radha peered at the printout. 'Any other clues there?'

'The third email talks about following the edicts of Asoka and a voyage of discovery. And the fourth one mentions seeking out the Nine if something were to happen to Vijay's uncle. It also refers to a path of truth to find a way out of any illusion.' Colin's face was glum.

'How are we to follow Asoka's edicts?' Shukla wondered. 'Follow them, as in, apply the principles they preached, or physically follow them by visiting the sites where they were found? They are all over India and some are in museums.'

'Well, we have sought out the Nine in a manner of speaking, haven't we?' White pointed out. 'Finding the verse on the disk which is about the Nine; wouldn't that classify as seeking out the Nine? Perhaps your uncle was trying to tell you to get the metal disk from the locker. Which you did.'

Vijay frowned. 'You could be right. But what if uncle meant that we need to follow the clues in the verse to seek out the Nine, using the descriptions provided?'

'I'm hungry,' Colin announced, his stomach diverting his attention from the subject of the emails.

Vijay grinned, his mood lightening momentarily. 'The way to your heart is through your stomach. That's the advice I've always given your girlfriends.'

'Is that why they've always stuffed me with food?' Colin rolled his eyes. 'I used to wonder.'

'Let's have dinner, then,' Vijay suggested. 'Perhaps if we give this a break, the answers will come to us.'

'You'll excuse me,' White rose and held out his hand. 'I've got to get back tonight. There's work to be done for the project and I should also update the Maharaja on what we've found.'

'Well, there's not much to tell him, is there?' Vijay was despondent. 'Thanks for being here, Greg.'

11

Day 5

Intelligence Bureau Headquarters, New Delhi

'I don't understand it.' Imran Kidwai looked nonplussed. He was sitting in the office of Arjun Vaid, the Director. 'The vault wasn't on our list of possible targets. There was absolutely no intelligence to indicate a possible attack.'

'Yet, you believe it was a terrorist attack.' Vaid looked thoughtful. 'The forensic report doesn't help.' He picked up a file that lay open on his desk. 'They couldn't identify the explosive residue. Samples of the residue have been sent to Israel and the US to see if the compound can be identified. But eyewitness accounts say it wasn't a bomb that went off there.' He raised an eyebrow. 'Several people described the attackers as possessing a large contraption that was used to fire a projectile at the vault door; a contraption in the shape of a bow. In fact, one eyewitness even called it Lord Shiva's bow.' He snorted.

Vaid fixed Imran with a piercing gaze. 'If the eyewitness accounts are to be believed, a low-grade explosive must have been used to fire something at the vault door. But why go to the trouble of hauling a machine that fires projectiles? Why not simply blow open the door using explosives?'

'Imran shrugged. 'I can only guess that they wanted something from that vault. Something that was too important to risk damage by using explosives on the door. But, I can't see what they had to gain by targeting that vault. And no one has claimed responsibility yet, either.'

There was silence for a few minutes.

'What about Murphy?' Vaid looked quizzically at Imran.

'Good news and bad news. Homeland Security in the US was able to determine that he boarded an American Airlines flight three days ago under an alias. We traced his arrival in Delhi. He checked into a five-star hotel in Gurgaon, but checked out yesterday. That's when his trail goes cold. We're still trying to locate him, but so far we've had no luck. I've got the Gurgaon police involved as well.'

Vaid looked at the report again. 'Fine. I know you're on it. But I want to close this one way or the other. And soon. The Home Minister's breathing down my neck after this report. He's got enough on his hands and doesn't want something that can give the media another scoop. We have to find out if this is a real threat and contain it. Or put it to rest.'

Imran understood. There were five state elections looming, all critical for the ruling political party. That gave this matter a totally different perspective, apart from the more obvious one of national security.

He returned to his office and dialled a number. 'Pramod, listen carefully. I have a hunch.' He proceeded to give detailed instructions to the person at the other end of the line and then replaced the receiver in its cradle. He had no idea if his hunch would work. He knew he was grasping at straws. But what else could he do?

INTELLIGENCE BUREAU HEADQUARTERS, NEW DELHI / 89

Tour Around Jaungarh Fort

'I really haven't come been to the fort too often, so I don't know my way around very well,' Vijay confessed as he guided the group along the maze of corridors and narrow staircases that led from one room to another, connecting, through narrow staircases, the different levels of the fort, as it climbed the hillside.

They had finished dinner and Vijay had offered to take them on a tour of the fort to take their minds off the puzzle.

The stairways between the levels were steep. Five hundred years ago, the architects of the fort had designed it with the intention of thwarting enemies who managed to infiltrate the outer defences. Pursuit by the enemy on these stairs would be difficult. Each stairway ended in an intersection of four corridors, a design aimed at confusing and delaying an enemy in pursuit. These intersections had doorways leading out of them that were less than five feet high, compelling passage through them by bending; another device to slow the enemy while the inhabitants made good their escape through numerous secret passages and tunnels.

'Are these secret tunnels still accessible?' Radha asked excitedly.

Vijay shook his head. 'Some of them would have deteriorated and become dangerous to enter with the passage of time. I think uncle blocked them all up when he renovated the fort.'

They were now passing through the inner rooms of the fort which had smoothed, plastered walls with large, colourful murals painted on them.

'Frescoes of scenes from the Mahabharata,' Shukla observed. 'Your uncle loved the epic.

Vijay nodded. He recalled his childhood, sitting at his uncle's knee, listening to stories from the epic embellished with a child's imagination.

'That is a portrayal of the Bhagavad Gita being delivered on the battlefield.' Shukla pointed to a painting that covered the wall from floor to ceiling, with horses hitched to a chariot, stamping and tossing their heads while a man with blue skin clad in armour seemed to be preaching to another man armed with an enormous bow and a quiver of arrows on his back. 'Lord Krishna, the avatar of Lord Vishnu, delivering the Gita to Arjuna, the archer.'

There were other scenes from the Mahabharata, in the other rooms; the death of Karna—the son of Kunti, mother of the Pandava brothers, and Surya, the Sun God—as he tried valiantly to free his chariot's wheel from the mire; the famous scene where Draupadi, wife of the five Pandava brothers, is humiliated after she is gambled away over a game of dice.

It was nine o'clock when they finished the tour. Everyone was tired now, especially Vijay and Colin, who hadn't slept the previous night, and they all retired to their rooms, glad to be able to rest.

For a few hours, the puzzle of the verse was forgotten.

12

Day 6

Jaungarh Fort

Vijay shifted uneasily in his sleep. He hadn't slept well since he'd first received word of his uncle's death. It was the same tonight. Nebulous dreams filled his sleep.

He now dreamt of a king carving inscriptions on rocks, going from boulder to boulder, chiselling away until each rock's surface was fully covered with unreadable squiggles. Finally, nine rocks stood in a circle, like an eye gazing at the sky. And then he found himself watching the scene from above; looking down on the ring of rocks, in the centre of which stood the king, his hands triumphantly raised to the sky. In one hand he clutched a metal disk...

Vijay awoke suddenly and sat up in bed, dazed.

Then it came back to him; his dream, the king, the rocks. The inscriptions and the metal disk.

His dream, he knew, had its genesis in the events of the day: the discussion on Asoka's edicts, the brotherhood of the Nine and the verse on the metal disk. But, something tugged at his mind, some thought hidden away in a deep recess. He searched hard. He didn't know why, but that thought seemed important.

Then, it came to him—a line from one of his uncle's emails. *Follow the edicts of Asoka.*

Abruptly, it dawned on him. He knew what had woken him. He had found the second clue! The one that would decode the verse on the disk.

Vijay smiled. They were back on track.

Old Memories

Vijay looked up from his laptop as Radha entered the study, looking concerned. There were papers scattered across the desk and the printer was churning out more paper.

'What happened? We were wondering where you were. The butler told us you weren't in your room and we couldn't see you in the garden. I finally thought of looking for you here.' She stood by his side, looking down at him. 'Have you eaten anything? Everyone's had breakfast already.'

Vijay ran a hand through his tousled hair and shook his head. He had been up since awakening from his dream and had spent the time working in the study. Until now he'd been too preoccupied to give a thought to food. At her words, however, he realised he was hungry. But first he had to tell her what he had discovered.

'I've got it,' his eyes gleamed with exhilaration as he looked up at her. 'I've got the second clue.'

Radha smiled at him. 'Come on downstairs. I'll fix you breakfast. Once you've eaten, you can tell us about it.'

Vijay smiled back at her as she left. His thoughts went back to the day he met her, two years ago, for the first time after leaving the country. Vikram Singh had wanted something delivered to his old friend, Dr. Shukla, and Vijay had volunteered to be the courier.

Radha had been a childhood friend but he hadn't seen her for 12 years. All he remembered of her was a gawky teenager with braces on her teeth, and an attitude. He had wondered what he would find now. He had gaped at the attractive young woman, framed by the open doorway at Dr. Shukla's house.

Radha had been around when he had chatted with Dr. Shukla. The meeting had ended with him inviting her for dinner the next evening. During dinner, the next evening, he had told her about the start-up he and Colin had founded and had been pleasantly surprised to learn that she was a nuclear physicist working with the Department of Atomic Energy.

Vijay smiled as he recalled that evening. He had enjoyed her company. Ever since his last girlfriend at MIT, he hadn't had time or the inclination for another relationship. But Radha had been different. Though their relationship hadn't progressed beyond friendship, they had kept in touch. Returning to the present, he realised that he was hungry and decided to go downstairs for breakfast.

13

AD 500

Bamiyan, Afghanistan

From the moment his secret had been discovered, Pala had known that his life was in danger.

Court astronomer by profession, custodian of an ancient secret by volition, he had succeeded in concealing his true vocation for over 40 years. Until that fateful day that the book, written in stone and lost to the world for almost 800 years, was discovered while digging the foundation for a new fort. The book was whisked away to the Grand Palace and disappeared once more. As if it had never existed.

Only then had Pala realised that someone had made the connection between the stone book and a myth that was thousands of years old. He knew that he had to get the texts and the metal disk to Santhal, a monk and a member of the brotherhood, who lived in a small monastery that lay at the feet of the two giant statues of the Buddha that were being carved into the sandstone cliffs overlooking the valley. This was what had been agreed upon, when he had joined the Nine. Santhal was one of the two members who had revealed his true identity to Pala. If anything were to threaten the secrets either of them was responsible for, they were bound by oath to pass on the secrets to the other.

After leaving the palace, he had made his way through the numerous kingdoms of Western India that had risen as the mighty Gupta Empire disintegrated.

Pala came across three men, who were travelling to the same destination.

By the time he had seen through their deception and understood their motive, it was too late.

The group of four had struck out for the highlands that lay between them and the monastery. They had all agreed to continue travelling through the night and Pala now realised why.

It was a perfect night for betrayal and murder.

The moon lay hidden behind a wispy veil of clouds and no stars shone in the sky. Winter was upon them and in the bitter cold of night there would be no other travellers on the trail.

No witnesses!

Pala had tried to get away. But he was old and they were young and physically stronger. Then, he remembered hearing, at the last town, about caves that had been tunnelled into the cliffs behind the Buddhas, to service their construction. He had tried to conserve his energy, lagging behind the others at times, until they arrived at a gravel strewn gully. While his three companions had sat down to rest and wait for him to catch up he had made his break, striking out among the rocks and boulders, trying to get to the edge of the cliff where he would search for the caves.

It had worked for a while. Desolation and silence, twin sisters in the darkness, had aided him as he left the gully, and in the frosty night air the sounds of pursuit had been carried to him, enabling him to evade the others. But he knew it was just a matter of time; he would tire and his younger companions would soon realise where he was headed.

In the pale light of the veiled moon the rocks and boulders sketched shadows on each other, standing silent and grim like mourners at a funeral, as Pala furiously hunted for refuge.

Panting from his exertions, he finally found the entrance to the caves and clambered down a roughly hewn tunnel. It soon opened into a cave, barely four feet high so he had to stoop and walk. There was no light and Pala hunted around desperately, blindly, looking for a place to hide the contents of his leather satchel. His arms and elbows bled from scraping against the walls but he ignored the pain, intent on his purpose.

They might kill him, but they would never discover the secret he carried!

At one end of the rocky chamber was a smooth wall of sandstone which, he guessed, was the back of one of the Buddha statues. There seemed to be no crevices or niches in which to hide the contents of his satchel.

He heard the sounds of men scrambling down the tunnel and saw the glimmer from their horn lantern light up the cave with an eerie glow.

As the three men emerged, Pala knew he was going to die in this cave. There was fury in their faces; they had thought he would be an easy target.

One of them grinned at him. 'You thought you could outrun us and escape?' The leader chuckled, but the sound was devoid of humour.

Pala never saw the blow coming.

As he turned to face the man, something sharp and hard struck him on the side of his head. In the cold air of the cavern he felt something sticky and hot flow down his cheek. It was his blood, he realised, as his head exploded with sudden pain.

Pala sagged to the ground.

His last thought, before the darkness enfolded him, was that he had failed in his mission.

One of the men knelt down and rummaged through the contents of the dead man's satchel. It contained books of bark, bound together in the manner that was prevalent in northern India. He handed the books to their leader who leafed through them helplessly. None of the three men could read much more than their own names.

He threw the texts down in the dirt in anger and stamped on them, unmindful of the destruction he was causing.

His voice was hoarse with rage. 'We went to all this trouble for these strips of bark? The way he kept the satchel close to him as if he was guarding it with his life, I thought there would be something more precious in there.'

'Here, what's this?' The man peering into Pala's bag pulled out a metallic object. It was in the shape of a circle, made of solid metal. He handed it to his leader. The metal was black but definitely not tarnished silver. It was unlike anything he had ever seen before. One side of the circular slab was blank and smooth with a matted black finish. The other side had circular grooves with markings and inscriptions that he couldn't read.

He did not see any value in it and flung the disk at Pala's corpse.

'Curse the son of a dog!' he spat. 'We have nothing to show for our efforts.'

'What do we do with the corpse?'

'Leave it here. This cave isn't in use any more. We'll go back up and roll a boulder over the opening. No one will ever know.'

The three men made their way back up the tunnel, to the surface, and searched for the largest boulder. They finally had a huge one plugging the entrance, burying Pala's body and the contents of his satchel with him.

Little did they know that they had just buried the truth about one of the greatest ancient secrets of the world; a truth that would lie buried with Pala for the next 1,500 years.

14

Present Day

Day 6
Jaungarh Fort

The little group was assembled in the study again. They were all eager to find out about Vijay's discovery. Warm sunlight flooded into the study through the huge bay windows.

Vijay narrated his dream to them. 'What struck me was the fact that the king in the dream carved nine rocks. I realised that I was dreaming about Asoka and his edicts. When we read the verse yesterday, we naturally assumed that it referred to the Nine Unknown Men, describing them. But uncle, in his third mail, urges me to follow the edicts of Asoka, saying they will lead me on a voyage of discovery. It occurred to me that perhaps the verse referred not to the Nine themselves but to the nine edicts of Asoka.'

'So what we should be looking for are nine locations where Asoka placed his edicts.' Colin took up his train of thought.

'You got it,' Vijay grinned. 'Finally the years of knowing me have rubbed off on you. You're getting smart, my friend.'

'So I guess you also know which nine edicts the verse refers to, O Wise One?' Colin retorted.

Vijay held up a sheaf of papers from the desk. 'That's what I've been working on, while you were sleeping.' He sorted the papers. 'There are several locations where the edicts were found; some on rocks, some on pillars. I've been researching the net and have downloaded some information on the edicts and analysed it.'

He put the papers on the table. 'I've summarised information about each site where the edicts were found. I wasn't sure how exactly we were to associate the locations with the lines in the verse, so I've tried to cover everything—location, script, variations. Not all locations had all the edicts. Some had only the major edicts and others only the minor ones. There were 14 major rock edicts and three minor ones. I've listed them all. There were also seven major pillar edicts and two minor ones. But there were also variations between different locations. For example, the one in Dhauli omits any reference to the Kalinga war. Scholars believe this was probably because Dhauli was in Kalinga and Asoka didn't want to offend his conquered subjects.'

Colin's forehead furrowed. 'So we have to go through this list and try and match the clues in the verse to the locations?'

'It's not that tough. I even managed to get us off to a start by deciphering the ninth line of the verse. *The ninth speaks in two tongues.*' Vijay quoted from the verse. 'I thought it must be the one at Kandahar, where there was a bilingual edict in Aramaic and Greek. Two tongues.'

The others nodded, seeing the logic in his deduction.

'Maybe it won't be that difficult to find the others,' Radha said slowly, 'We may not have to study all locations in detail in order to find the ones that match the verse. I think the first line of the verse—*the Nine have gone forth to the edges of the Empire*—provides us with a direction. If the verse had referred to the Nine themselves we could have interpreted this, quite literally, as the members of the brotherhood travelling to the borders of the Empire. But since we now think the verse refers to locations, we should be looking for nine sites on the borders of Asoka's empire.'

'Great thought.' Vijay walked back to the desk and started typing on the laptop. 'Let me find a good map that depicts the full extent of Asoka's empire.'

Colin was studying the list of locations while Vijay searched for the map. Suddenly he looked up.

'I think I've found another one. The third location is Maski. The verse says, *The third speaks the name of the Emperor*. Maski is the only edict to mention Asoka by name.'

Shukla nodded approvingly. 'Good work.'

Colin beamed and went back to the list of locations.

The printer hummed. Vijay plucked the sheet and carried it back to the group.

'Here's a good map. It shows the location of his edicts. Asoka's empire covered most of present-day India, Pakistan and Afghanistan. Kandahar is in Afghanistan, the western extremity of Asoka's empire. Maski, while not on the edge of the empire, is close to the southern border. It could be a likely candidate.'

Colin scowled at him with mock indignation. 'I find something and you try and dig a hole under it. Can't you just accept and get used to my intellectual superiority?'

'Okay, Mr. Wow,' Vijay retorted. 'Let's see your superior intellect come up with a few more locations.'

Despite their light-hearted banter, there was excitement in the air. The group pored over the papers, occasionally glancing at the map, trying to find the links between the sites marked on the map and the clues in the verse.

Radha found the next one. 'The first one is Girnar. The edict that looks different from the others, as the inscriptions are all separately engraved and separated by horizontal lines. *The first, in appearance, is different from the rest.*'

'I've got two,' Shukla announced after a while. 'The seventh one is Sarnath. And the fifth is Shahbazgarhi.'

'I don't get the connection,' Colin confessed. Vijay shrugged in agreement.

'*The seventh pays homage to the Wheel of Truth,*' Shukla quoted. 'The Buddha gave his first sermon at the Deer Park in Sarnath; he preached the concept of the Wheel of Dharma or the Wheel of Truth, also known as the Wheel of Law, to his five disciples. He glanced at the paper he held. 'According to this, the seventh edict stands at Sarnath, carved into a highly polished sandstone pillar.'

Colin and Vijay nodded, impressed by Shukla's knowledge.

'The edicts at Shahbazgarhi,' Shukla continued, 'are inscribed on two rocks, one on the slope of the hill and the other in the valley. Shahbazgarhi is in present-day Pakistan. The verse says... *The fifth writes with a hand that is different from the rest...*this particular edict is the only one that is written in the Kharosthi script which is read from right to left. Earlier, this script was known as Indo-Bactrian and Ariano-Pali and is derived from Aramaic. All the other edicts are written in the Brahmi script. So, the hand that is different from the rest is the script.'

He saw the expression on Colin's and Vijay's faces and smiled, shrugging self-deprecatingly. 'You shouldn't be surprised. I studied ancient Indian languages.'

'I've got another one, I think,' Colin spoke up after a while. 'The eighth line says... *The eighth does not have all that the others do but is special for he also has that which the others do not...'* He looked up, beaming, delighted. 'It's the one at...,' he peered at the sheet of paper, 'Dhauli, is that how you pronounce it?'

Vijay nodded, but looked like he didn't understand. Colin couldn't resist a barb. 'Okay, I'll explain. Make way for my grey cells, my friend.'

Radha smiled. The good-humoured exchange between the two friends and the insults that they traded frequently only revealed the depth of the friendship. 'The carving at Dhauli,' Colin resumed, 'doesn't contain edicts 11 to 13, so doesn't have all that the others do; but it also has two other edicts that the others do not have.'

'Lucky guess,' Vijay muttered. 'And now he'll go on about it for the next 10 years.'

'I think I know what the second one is,' Shukla offered. 'I should have got it much sooner, since I've read about it before. The second one is supposed to gaze over the sea, waiting for a ship to come in.'

'It's a port,' Colin interjected.

'Yes,' Shukla smiled at his excitement. 'In Ptolemy's time there was an ancient sea port called Soupara, which was a commercial centre. Its ancient name was Supparaka. Today, according to this map and your research, it is known as Sopara.'

Vijay beamed with delight. 'We've got seven now. Just two more to go.'

'I've got another one,' Colin grinned. 'The sixth one... *The sixth is greater by one than the other upright ones*...the upright ones are the pillar edicts. All the pillars have six edicts, except one. Topra has seven edicts. It is greater by one than the other pillar edicts.'

Vijay looked at him. 'Seems logical.'

'Grey cells again,' Colin beamed. 'I'm awesome. What would you do without me? What...'

'There's one left,' Vijay interrupted him, smiling. '*The fourth is seventeen*...what could that refer to?'

Radha frowned. Something in the printed notes had struck her but she couldn't quite put her finger on it. Silence descended on the group. What could this line of the verse mean? It certainly couldn't refer to the age of the edict.

Suddenly, Radha looked around, flushed with excitement. 'Yerragudi.'

Questioning looks were directed at her.

'Yerragudi is a small town in Andhra Pradesh,' she explained. 'There doesn't seem to be much significance attached to it since there isn't too much in the notes but it has both the major and minor rock edicts.'

Blank faces gazed at her.

'Don't you get it? There were 14 major rock edicts and three minor ones; 17 in all. Yerragudi had all 17.'

Vijay shook his head. 'Unbelievable. The locations of all the edicts were cleverly disguised.' He turned to his notes. 'So the locations, in the order they are mentioned in the verse, are: Girnar, Sopara, Maski, Yerragudi, Shahbazgarhi, Topra, Sarnath, Dhauli and Kandahar.'

'What are we supposed to do with them?' Radha wondered. 'This still doesn't lead us anywhere.'

'In all the books I've read,' Colin said thoughtfully, 'when people decipher clues like these, they normally visit each location and find additional clues. Perhaps if we visit all nine locations we will find nine more clues that will lead us to something else and so on, until we find the secret of the Nine?'

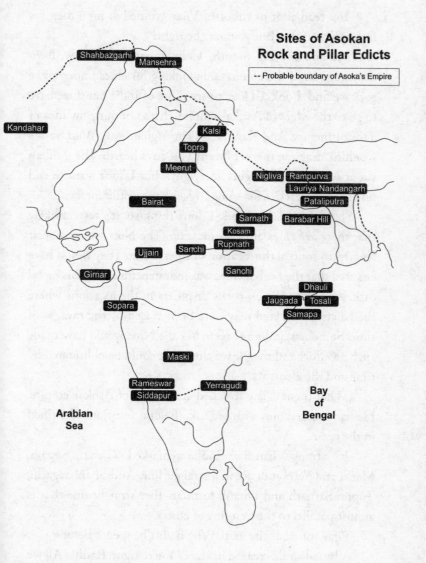

Sites of Asokan
Rock and Pillar Edicts

-- Probable boundary of Asoka's Empire

Shahbazgarhi

Mansehra

Kandahar

Kalsi

Topra

Meerut

Nigliva   Rampurva

Lauriya Nandangarh

Pataliputra

Bairat

Sarnath   Barabar Hill

Kosam

Rupnath

Ujjain   Sanchi

Sanchi

Girnar

Dhauli

Jaugada   Tosali

Sopara

Samapa

Maski

Rameswar   Yerragudi

Siddapur

Arabian
Sea

Bay
of
Bengal

'You read a lot of rubbish,' Vijay grinned at him, then his face grew serious. 'But you may be right.'

'Me and my big mouth,' Colin groaned. 'Now we'll go traipsing round the countryside looking for clues under every rock we find. Look, I'd love to see more of India but if we have to go to the edges of Asoka's empire, that's not quite my idea of a tour itinerary. And Kandahar is in Afghanistan. Wild horses wouldn't drag me there. Haven't you guys heard? The Taliban shoot Americans on sight. Sorry guys, but I don't want to end up as target practice for some trigger happy militants.'

Shukla shook his head. 'I don't think so. It's very unlikely that there are clues at every location. The Nine went to great lengths to conceal the location of their secret. They would have ensured that the trail of clues was indestructible, like this metal disk. Any clues left on rocks or pillars in the locations where the edicts are located may have been erased by the ravages of time. Somehow, it doesn't seem like the Nine would have made such an effort and then leave clues that could be obliterated by time and the elements.'

'What then?' Vijay frowned at the map of Asoka's empire. He had marked out, with red ink, the nine locations identified in the verse.

'It's strange, isn't it?' Radha remarked. 'Girnar, Sopara, Maski and Yerragudi are in a straight line. And Shahbazgarhi, Topra, Sarnath and Dhauli form another straight line that is almost parallel to the first line of edicts.'

Vijay stared at the map. Why hadn't he seen it before?

A broad smile creased his face. 'You're right, Radha. All we have to do is follow the edicts of Ashoka. That's what uncle said in his mail. Look at this.'

Vijay took a ruler and red pen and connected Girnar to Sopara, then extended the line to connect Maski and Yerragudi. As Radha had observed, all four locations were in a straight line. He then placed the ruler along the dots that represented Shahbazgarhi, Topra, Sarnath and Dhauli and drew a second line connecting these four locations. This line was parallel to the first.

'Let's follow the edicts of Asoka in the order they are mentioned in the verse on the disk,' he grinned at them, enjoying himself, now that the puzzle was clear to him. 'We go from Girnar to Sopara, then to Maski and Yerragudi. Next, the trail goes from Yerragudi to Shahbazgarhi in the north.' He connected Yerragudi and Shahbazgarhi with another straight line. 'From Shahbazgarhi, we follow the line through Topra, Sarnath and on to Dhauli. Now, look at this. The last stop is Kandahar.'

He took the ruler and once more drew a straight line, this time between Dhauli and Kandahar. Then, he sat back and watched as the others took in the pattern that had emerged on the map.

The line connecting Yerragudi to Shahbazgarhi and the second line from Dhauli to Kandahar intersected. At the point of their intersection lay another site with Asoka's edicts.

Bairat.

'Together they guard the way to the truth that is protected by the Nine!' Vijay declared with a flourish.

'This is incredible.' Colin shook his head. 'When you put it this way, it jumps out at you.'

Vijay grinned wickedly at him. 'I thought you were the brains between the two of us?'

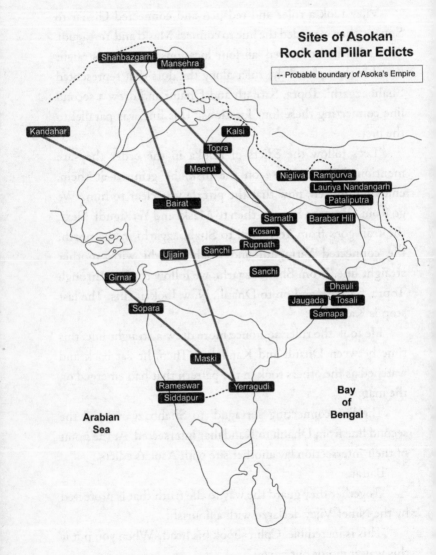

Sites of Asokan Rock and Pillar Edicts

-- Probable boundary of Asoka's Empire

Shahbazgarhi

Mansehra

Kandahar

Kalsi

Topra

Meerut

Nigliva

Rampurva

Lauriya Nandangarh

Pataliputra

Bairat

Sarnath

Barabar Hill

Kosam

Rupnath

Ujjain

Sanchi

Sanchi

Girnar

Dhauli

Jaugada

Tosali

Sopara

Samapa

Maski

Rameswar

Yerragudi

Siddapur

Arabian Sea

Bay of Bengal

'Yes, but you couldn't have done it without the help of your uncle's email,' Colin retorted immediately.

Vijay simply grinned back at him, delighted with what they had achieved.

'Colin is right,' Radha agreed. 'If someone was trying to decipher the verse and didn't know that they had to follow the edicts, they wouldn't get too far. And they'd also need to know a lot about Asoka and his edicts.'

'So, we go to Bairat?' Colin enquired, looking at Vijay.

'That's logical, isn't it?'

Radha pulled out a sheet, from the printouts, and read from it. 'Bairat is a small town in Rajasthan, forty two miles northeast of Jaipur. This little town has the distinction of having the oldest freestanding Buddhist structure in India – the ruins of a third century BC *chaitya*.'

'What's a *chaitya*?' Colin wanted to know.

'Broadly speaking, a Buddhist chapel,' Shukla informed him.

'There are also brick and timber shrines of the same period,' Radha continued. 'A fragment of the rock edict of Asoka is now housed in the building of the Asiatic Society in Kolkata.'

'It's gotta be Bairat,' Colin said. 'It can't be coincidence that there was a rock edict of Asoka *and* remains of structures from his time at this location, especially when it lies at the intersection of these two lines on this map.'

'It can't be too far from here,' Radha remarked. 'It's on the Alwar-Jaipur highway, so it shouldn't be more than an hour's drive.'

'Let's go then,' Colin's eyes shone with anticipation. The others nodded, sharing in his excitement at the thought of finding a 2,000-year old secret.

'What do we do if we find the secret?' Shukla asked quietly, bringing an element of sobriety into the atmosphere.

'We'll inform the Maharaja,' Vijay replied, promptly. 'He'll know what needs to be done to keep the secret safe.'

'So why don't we tell him now?' Shukla pressed.

Vijay frowned. 'I don't know. Suppose we are wrong and there's nothing there? What if we've read the clues all wrong and got the wrong location? I'm not sure we should tell anyone until we find out for ourselves. But I'll call Greg and ask him if he'd like to join us. I'm sure he'd love to be a part of the discovery of a 2,000-year old secret.' He looked at his watch. 'I'm going to pack a few things. See you down in the hall in half an hour.'

15

Day 6

Intelligence Bureau Headquarters, New Delhi

Michael Blake sat in Imran Kidwai's office. Imran had called him, with no explanation other than a statement that they had come across some information that Blake might find interesting.

'It was a stroke of luck,' Imran began. 'A hunch that paid off. Nothing more.'

'Regarding Farooq?'

Imran nodded. 'When I saw the report on Murphy, I got an idea. Murphy had checked into a hotel in Gurgaon. Why Gurgaon? Why not Delhi? It was quite possible that there was no particular reason and it was a random choice. But what if it wasn't?'

Blake frowned. 'I see what you mean. Murphy could have chosen Gurgaon simply because the LeT team was also based there.'

'Exactly. Which includes Farooq and, perhaps, the member of the "Order" who was mentioned in the call you guys tapped into. So I got this crazy idea. While the Gurgaon police was engaged in trying to locate Murphy, I also put out a call to locate anyone whose name began with Farooq or ended with Siddiqui.'

'And something came up.'

Imran nodded, beaming. 'Yes. You're not going to believe this. The Gurgaon police actually had a case registered with them against a person named Farooq; a kidnapping case. Apparently this Farooq and an accomplice, named Imtiaz, had been involved in the kidnapping of two men and holding them captive in Gurgaon. But here's the interesting part. The case was referred to the Gurgaon police by the SHO of Jaungarh, which is a small village en route to Jaipur from Delhi. It seems that the two men, who were kidnapped, live there.'

Blake looked thoughtful. 'And you think this might be Farooq? But why would he kidnap two men from an obscure village? It doesn't make sense.'

Imran picked up a folded newspaper from his desk and handed it over to Blake, who unfolded it and gazed at the headlines.

'Read the leading byline.'

'*Mysterious murder of nuclear scientist*,' Blake read aloud and scanned the contents of the news article. 'So, this prominent retired nuclear scientist was murdered under mysterious circumstances. No clues were left at the murder scene. A Pakistani hand is suspected.' He shrugged and grinned. 'That's normal isn't it? *Police are investigating but have little to go on*.' He folded the newspaper and placed it back on the desk and waited. He knew there was more to come.

'One of the kidnapped men from Jaungarh was the nephew of the murdered scientist.'

Light dawned on Blake. 'I get it. So you think that Farooq Siddiqui may have been involved in the murder of the scientist and the kidnapping of the nephew. But why would he murder this scientist?'

'I haven't been able to figure out what LeT is doing in India. We are making a lot of assumptions, but if our conclusions based on the video and the phone tap are correct, then LeT and Murphy's employers are working together on some project in India. Farooq is leading that project. He is also a nuclear scientist. Both he and Vikram Singh, the murdered Indian scientist, were involved in the production of their respective country's nuclear bomb. Too many coincidences! What if Farooq was after something that Vikram Singh had? Information, plans, designs...I don't know. And the nephew may know something too, which is why he was kidnapped. But he managed to escape and filed a police report giving the names of two of his captors.'

'What's the plan, then?'

Imran grinned at him. 'We go pay Vijay Singh, the nephew, a visit at Jaungarh. Let's find out if our deductions amount to anything.'

Bijak-ki-Pahari

Radha drove slowly along the highway connecting Delhi and Jaipur. Trucks, cars and jeeps whizzed past them at high speed. Vijay sat in the passenger seat next to Radha and Colin and Shukla were seated at the back. White had expressed his inability to make the trip as he was accompanying the Maharaja to a meeting. He had sounded quite miserable at being left out of what would definitely be a momentous discovery. But since Vijay was quite insistent that the Maharaja shouldn't know about Bairat until they had returned, there was no excuse White could think of that would be strong enough to excuse himself from the meeting with Bheem Singh.

According to the map of Rajasthan they carried with them, they realised, there should be a left turn that led to Bairat but they had seen no road leading off the highway, except for a few dirt paths that snaked though the fields. Nor were there signs along the highway marking the road to Bairat.

Vijay gazed at the map. 'We passed Pragpura just now. The turn on the map lies between Pragpura and Shahpura. Those are the only landmarks on the map.'

'It should be somewhere here, then.' Colin had been gazing out of the window, studying the milestones they passed. 'We're just fifteen kilometres from Shahpura.'

'Let's ask someone.' Radha spotted a cluster of trucks parked next to a row of rustic wood and thatch buildings.

Vijay and Colin alighted and walked towards the nearest hut. Inside, they saw truckers lounging about on rough *charpoys*.

'How do we get to Bairat?' Vijay asked the nearest trucker in Hindi.

'Keep going straight along the highway for around six kilometres and you'll come to a left turn which will take you to Bairat,' the man replied, studying them curiously. 'The left turn's just before the market.'

After getting the directions, they resumed the drive until they came across signs of habitation, probably the outskirts of Shahpura. As instructed, Radha turned into a road to the left.

A rickshaw driver confirmed they were on the right track and they sped down the road, which was smooth to begin with, but soon degenerated into a patchwork of potholes . On either side of the road was scrubland—expanses of sandy soil with thorny bushes.

Beyond the expanses of sand rose the Aravali hills; low, rocky hills upon which little vegetation grew. Boulders were stacked in clumps upon each hill and there was no sign of habitation around them.

Colin wondered aloud why Asoka had thought of choosing such a desolate region for one of his edicts.

'It was different in those days,' Shukla answered 'Two thousand years ago, Bairat was probably an important confluence of trade routes. Asoka had wanted his edicts to be read by as many people as possible. He had them set up at ports, important towns and places where travellers would have stopped to rest on their journey. Bairat must have been one such place.'

There was little traffic on the road. Twenty minutes later, fields on either side of the road replaced the sand and bushes. As the fields gave way to clusters of mud houses, they realised they had reached the village of Bairat. At this time of day, few people could be seen.

'Where do we find this hill?' Colin wondered.

'*Bijak-ki-pahari*,' Shukla murmured, recalling the name of the hill where the Asokan edict and the ruins of the *chaitya* and the monastery were located, according to the information they had downloaded from the internet.

'Hang on, there's a sign here.' Vijay craned his neck to read the minute inscription on a three-foot-high sandstone plaque planted alongside the road.

'Department of Tourism.' Vijay read out. 'According to this, the *Bijak-ki-pahari is four kilometres from here.*'

Radha grinned mischievously. 'I could have saved you the trouble.' She indicated another sign mounted on a wooden post and shaped like an arrow. Upon the sign, crudely written in white paint, were the words *Bijak-ki-pahari*. The sign pointed down a mud track that branched off to their right.

Vijay looked doubtful. 'Are you sure that sign is right? That doesn't look like a road leading to a historical site.'

But Radha was already pulling onto the track. It was a narrow path, just enough to accommodate a single car, and walled in on either side by thorny plants with sharp, spiked leaves, that rose to a height of around 20 feet.

Radha negotiated the track cautiously. It was potholed and rutted by years of use by camel-drawn carts. The track wound right and left, and they occasionally, saw a small child standing in a break in the foliage, looking curiously at the car as it bounced along the path.

After being jolted around for a while, they came to a small clearing to the right of the path in which stood a small mud hut with whitewashed walls. A man was standing next to the hut.

Radha poked her head out of the window and hailed him in Hindi. 'Where is the *Bijak-ki-pahari*?'

He approached them and pointed down the track. 'I'll show you the way if you want,' he offered.

He introduced himself as Chunnilal and asked them to drive on while he joined them on foot.

The path changed from a mud track to a concrete road which had seen a lot of wear over the years. Eventually, , the road opened up into a large clearing paved with smooth stones. A small pillared structure occupied one corner of the clearing. All around them, small, misshapen rocky hills rose to a height of two to three hundred feet.

Chunnilal came up as they got out of the car and stretched their legs.

Groups of small monkeys with little black faces frolicked on the roof of the pillared building as they followed Chunnilal up the nearest hill, along a path, paved with stones and thorny bushes. The stone paved track soon gave way to a mud path and then to a well-paved stone path, that led to broad stone stairs that ascended the hill.

'The government constructed this stairway recently,' the well-informed Chunnilal told them.

The stone stairway skirted boulders that towered ten feet above them and passed under rocky overhangs; turning at sharp angles as it wound up the hill. The hillsides were strewn with rocks and immense boulders inclined at almost impossible angles. Stunted trees with spiny leaves and dry, thorny plants were the only signs of vegetation, as far as the eye could see.

Vijay and Colin bounded along ahead of the others. Shukla was helped along by Radha.

The stairway finally ended, opening up into a natural terrace dotted with huge rocks. To the left of the stairway stood a stone wall around five feet in height; it was evidently a recent reconstruction. Clinging to this were the remains of an ancient brick structure, not more than a couple of feet in height. The bricks had blackened with age and appeared to form a stairway leading to the terrace which lay behind the stone wall and was not visible to them from where they now stood.

'That's probably where the *chaitya* is,' Vijay whispered to Colin, his eyes gleaming with excitement.

Chunnilal gestured to follow him as he walked away from the stone wall and, to their right, a long, oblong-shaped rock leaned at an angle of 25 degrees upon a smaller rock. Its raised tip had a large indentation in it, giving it the appearance of a rather angry looking giant slug that gazed out over the hills around.

As Radha, supporting her father, reached the terrace, she looked around but there was no one in sight. She yelled out for Vijay and he appeared from behind the slug-shaped rock.

'Come here,' he gestured to them. 'You've got to see this.'

They followed him and came upon a cemented platform constructed outside a natural cave beneath the slug-shaped rock. Colin was sitting crosslegged on the platform, looking distinctly uncomfortable, and before him sat Chunnilal and another man, dishevelled, his hair unkempt and his beard straggly. Both men were smoking *bidis*.

'The old man is the baba who looks after the temple within the cave,' Vijay explained quietly. 'He's completely blind and lives on donations from the villagers and tourists who come by.'

Colin grinned at Radha as they joined him. 'This is amazing,' he remarked. 'Apparently this cave has a 5,000-year-old history. It's connected with the characters from the Mahabharata, which you told me about. Awesome, isn't it, how we've been talking about the Gita and the clues and now we come across a site connected to the Nine and Asoka the Great, which also has a legend about the Mahabharata? Apparently the five brothers had come here; what was their name?'

'The Pandavas,' Shukla prompted and asked, 'There is a legend about the Pandavas?'

'Yes. The legend says they had come here with Lord Krishna during their exile. They were requested to stay overnight for a wedding. But Krishna was carrying a lot of gold and jewellery and there was no safe place to leave them. So, he placed them in this cave which was later converted into a temple. He never returned for the valuables, though, and, according to the locals, the treasure is still buried here. Some say that you can see the treasure within the cave but when you enter it the vision disappears.'

'An ancient story about a buried treasure.' Shukla looked thoughtful, 'Many ancient legends were born out of a need to protect something. What if the story referred to the secret that the Nine hid here? The legend and the temple would have been great ways of ensuring that no one would ever try and look for a treasure that was inaccessible.'

'Shouldn't we move on and look at what we came to see?' Vijay was growing impatient. He nodded to Chunnilal and bowed to the baba, handing him some money. Together with Chunnilal, they walked along a dirt path that led up a slope studded with small rocks and flanked by a stone wall. Where the incline ended, a short flight of stairs led to a second level, where another wall enclosed the remains of the *chaitya*. A mud path bordered by stones led to a brick platform. Where the bricks hadn't been cemented over during preservation work, their age was evident. Most of the bricks used here seemed to have been the original ones.

On the brick platform stood a circular wall, with an opening to the east. While the inside wall of this circle had a cement face, the exterior was exposed brick.

But what they didn't expect to see was the structure that lay within the circular wall. It was shaped like a gear wheel and had a gap between the teeth that perfectly aligned with the opening in the surrounding circular wall. The cog wheel was completely cemented all around, with not one brick visible.

Chunnilal, in the meanwhile, had wandered off to one side, gazing into the distance as they took in the sight.

Above them loomed a second terrace, over 50 feet higher, built on the summit of the hill and enclosed by a stone wall. A flight of stone stairs led to this.

'What's in there?' Colin wondered.

'Let's check.' Vijay started for the staircase.

He sprinted up the stairs, and reached a small landing that lay ten feet below the upper terrace. The stone wall that enclosed the ruins on the upper terrace rose from this level. To his right, adjoining the wall, was a stone platform built entirely of brick.Before him rose the stairway with the final stretch of nine stairs. Vijay quickly dashed to the top and surveyed the ruins that lay before him.There was nothing left of the structures that must have stood here centuries ago. All that remained now were the foundations; brick walls that stood six inches above the ground.

Colin and Radha joined Vijay and gazed at the ruins.

'Was this the monastery?' Colin asked, looking around.

Radha nodded. 'Probably.'

To their right, a series of square brick platforms, two feet high, lined the terrace, their purpose a mystery.

'There's nothing here.' Vijay turned back and began descending the staircase, followed by Colin and Radha.

As they reached the foot of the staircase and arrived at the lower level, Chunnilal shared another legend with them.

'This *chakra*,' he indicated the cog wheel, 'dates from the time of the Pandavas.'

'What do you mean?' Shukla asked, interested.

'The design of the *chakra*,' Chunnilal explained, 'is based on a game of dice that they played in ancient times. This structure was built for the Pandavas to play dice.'

'And why would they play dice on top of a hill?' Colin wanted to know.

'Because this hill has special powers,' Chunnilal replied. 'According to legend, this hill has the ability to imbue people with immense knowledge and learning; so they would be able to play well.'

Colin couldn't understand how knowledge and learning helped in a game of dice which was based on chance. He opened his mouth to remonstrate but Shukla interrupted him, his eyes gleaming with excitement. 'I'll explain later, Colin.' He turned to Vijay. 'This is the place. There is no doubt about it.'

'But where do we look?' Vijay gestured around him. 'Everything is cemented over. If there were any signs left by the Nine, they would have been obliterated aeons ago or covered up by the restoration.'

'I don't think so,' Radha said slowly. While they had been talking, she had been walking among the ruins, lost in thought. 'I think they left us a sign; a very obvious one. Let's go back to the hotel and I'll tell you.'

16

Day 6

Gurgaon

'They went to Bairat?' Farooq's face twisted into a frown as he contemplated this piece of news. 'And you tell me this now?' There was anger in his voice, but he controlled it. It wouldn't do to lose his temper now. Not, at least, with the man who was on the other end of the line.

'How does that matter?' The voice was curt and seemed to have sensed Farooq's mood. 'The point is why did they go to Bairat? They are on the trail of something.'

'What's there at Bairat?' Farooq looked at Imtiaz, who had been typing at his laptop ever since he had heard the word Bairat. He had googled the word and come across the same information that Vijay and his friends had.

'If there are ruins from the time of Asoka at Bairat then there must be a link to the Nine.'

Farooq shook his head. 'It doesn't make sense. The topography is all wrong.'

'What do you mean?'

'Remember the description of the cavern? It was in a hill surrounded by forest. Bairat is in Rajasthan. It's a desert out there. No evidence of a forest even 2,000 years ago. And the text spoke of a single hill with a cave at its foot that led to the cavern where they found the secret. Bairat is surrounded by hills.'

'They wouldn't waste their time going there if there wasn't something there.'

'I'm not saying there's nothing there. All I'm saying is that this isn't where we'll find it. It's not the hiding place.'

'In any case, you'd better go and see what there is to be found at Bairat.' There was a click and the caller hung up.

Farooq stared angrily at the telephone receiver in his hand. With a visible effort he recovered his composure and looked at Imtiaz. 'Get the men and equipment ready. We leave in 10 minutes.'

Devious Clues!

Radha stood facing the rest of the group. They were gathered in Vijay's room at their hotel in Jaipur.

'It occurred to me when I walked around the cog wheel,' she began, picking up the metal disk with the verse inscribed on it. 'Look at this disk. And then try and recall what you saw at Bairat.' She held up the disk with its inscribed face turned towards them, so they could see the inscriptions.

It struck them immediately.

'It's the structure at Bairat.' Colin slapped his forehead.

Vijay groaned. 'What idiots we are!'

Radha grinned. 'While you guys were going on about the Mahabharata, I counted the number of teeth on the cog wheel at Bairat. There were twenty-seven in number; exactly the number of teeth in the cog wheel on this disk.'

'So this cog wheel has a link to that gear like structure that Chunnilal claimed was used by the Pandavas to play dice.' Colin summarised and threw up his hands. 'Devious clues!'

'I think there's more,' Radha continued. 'Both the cog wheel and the outer circle on this disk have gaps corresponding to the gaps in the structure we saw at Bairat. However, when we align the inscriptions to get the verse the gaps in the outer circle and the cog wheel are not aligned. What happens if we align the two gaps?'

'But the key locks the disks in place,' Colin pointed out. 'The only way to get the circles to move is to take the key out.'

Radha removed the key and rotated the cog wheel, so the gap in the wheel aligned with the gap in the outer circle.

There was a soft click.

'What happened?' Colin squinted at the disk.

But nothing seemed to have changed. Radha frowned. She picked up the disk from the table to study it closely and gasped.

The metal slab had split into two parts; the slab that contained the outer circle and the first and last lines of the verse had separated from the slab that had been affixed below it and which contained the cogwheel and the hollow for the key.

'Amazing,' Shukla murmured in wonder. 'I did not see the joint between the two slabs. Whoever created this slab possessed amazing workmanship; or amazing technology.'

'More likely workmanship,' Vijay remarked. 'Technology over 2,000 years ago? Kind of like the story of the nine books written by the Nine.'

Radha carefully separated the upper portion of the slab from the lower one and placed the part with the gear wheel on the table.

Inscribed on the slab, enclosing the gearwheel, was a circle with a gap at its lower end, aligning perfectly with the gap in the teeth of the cog wheel. Around this outer circle were randomly scattered circles, squares and rectangles etched into the dark metal.

Colin saw it first. 'It's a map of Bairat.'

'And the squares and circles around the gearwheel are the locations of the ruins on that terrace,' Radha finished.

'What's that there?' Vijay pointed to a small hollow in the shape of a parallelogram that lay directly above the gear wheel. 'All the other shapes are etched as outlines. Why is this three dimensional?'

Almost before he had finished speaking, the answer came to him. 'It's a trapdoor.'

'But where is it located?' Colin scratched his head. 'We looked everywhere.'

'It's in a spot that is on the opposite side of the gaps,' Radha pointed out.

There was silence for a few moments as everyone thought hard. Then, Colin spoke up. 'I think I know where,' he beamed. 'Let's go back there and I'll show you.'

17

Day 6

Bairat

Vijay stood and gazed upon the hill that was now shrouded in darkness. There was a half moon in the sky that cast a pale glow upon the trees, rocks and shrubs around.

'Let's go.' Vijay strode purposefully towards the hill. He pulled out a portable lamp from his bag. A powerful beam of light swept up the hillside, cutting through the darkness and illuminating the cobbled path.

He beckoned to the others, 'Let's see what the Nine hid out here.'

They climbed up to where they had seen the cog wheel earlier in the day. 'Okay, so where's the trapdoor?' Vijay looked at Colin.

Colin produced the metal slab with the gearwheel. 'Okay, this is how I see it. This is the only shape that isn't a circle, square or rectangle. It is a parallelogram. Why? All the structures here with straight lines as edges have only right angles. No parallelograms. The only thing I can think of that would justify the parallelogram is that the trapdoor is located at a different elevation than the cog wheel.'

Understanding dawned on Vijay. He swung the beam of light to illuminate the raised platform on the small landing that lay between the two larger terraces.

They marched up the stairway to the mid-level terrace and studied the platform. It was built using the same bricks that were found in the ruins of the *chaitya* below them and the monastery above.

Vijay trained the light on the surface of the platform.

Nothing there.

'Now what?' Radha wondered.

Vijay reached into his bag and pulled out another lamp. 'Here.' He handed it to Colin. 'This will help you guys to look around as well.'

He returned to his scan of the platform and the others joined him.

Suddenly, he froze as a familiar symbol among the bricks jumped out at them in the light of the torch. It was the only decoration on the bricks.

A nine-spoked wheel.

They looked at each other in excitement. This had to mean something.

'This could be a marker for the trapdoor,' Shukla suggested, looking a little doubtful. 'But I don't know how reliable it is. Remember, this platform, along with much of the ruins, has been restored. Where is the guarantee that this brick with the wheel was put back in its original position during the reconstruction?'

Vijay now had his nose to the platform as he ran the lamp along the surface.

'You sniffing out the trapdoor?' Colin chuckled.

'Looking for anything in the brickwork that will indicate where the trapdoor lies.'

Slowly, they covered every inch of the surface but found neither crack nor joint in the brick masonry.

'You were right,' Vijay admitted to Shukla. 'It looks like the reconstruction obliterated any sign that may have existed, or maybe even the trapdoor itself. Otherwise wouldn't the trapdoor have been discovered during the reconstruction?'

They looked at each other glumly. What chance did they have of finding a 2,000-year-old clue in ruins that must have been restored less than 50 years ago?

Radha took the lamp from Colin and shone its light on the brick with the wheel, peering at it curiously. Something had struck her as odd about the sign.

Of course! All the bricks on the platform were rectangular. All, that is, except the brick on which the wheel was inscribed.

The brick with the sign was circular in shape.

What did that mean?

She voiced her observation.

Two lamps were trained on the circular brick now and the little group stared hard at it, trying to fathom what this meant.

'There is another possibility,' Shukla spoke up. He was sitting on the platform, off to one side.

All eyes turned to him.

'Perhaps this brick was put here to indicate a spot.' He traced the outline of the brick with his finger. 'It could be that there is something hidden underneath it.'

Vijay nodded. They had been looking for an entrance of some sort, a trapdoor among the bricks that made up the surface of the platform. But what if the brick marked a spot where something was hidden?

He produced a chisel and hammer from his bag. Handing the lamp to Colin, he gently chiselled away at the circumference of the brick, dislodging the mortar around it.

The mortar came off in chunks. Soon, there was a gap separating the circular brick from the others. Vijay now drew out a screwdriver from the bag and slowly using it as a lever, gradually prised the brick from the platform.

When it was protruding halfway he grasped hold of the circular brick, with both hands, and gently tugged at it.

But the brick held fast. Vijay clicked his tongue in exasperation. He didn't want to use the screwdriver to extricate the brick for fear of damaging whatever lay underneath it.

'Here,' Colin said. 'Let me help you.'

He grasped the brick with Vijay and they pulled together.

For a brief moment the brick refused to yield; then, without warning, it jerked loose and came away in their hands.

A receptacle within the platform gaped out at them. The lamps were immediately trained on it , and there was a collective gasp.

White stone gleamed back at them. Etched into the stone was another wheel.

A nine-spoked wheel.

'We should have brought a crowbar,' Colin grumbled.

Vijay reached within his black bag and pulled out a crowbar. He handed it to Colin and grinned.

'So that's what you had in your bag.'

'Believe it, sonny, I'm always better prepared than you. You've got this high opinion of yourself but it just isn't true.'

'It's justified,' Colin retorted. 'I'm the brains between the two of us. I'm also the good-looking one...'

'Guys,' Radha interjected. "We've got a trapdoor to find.

Colin wordlessly searched with the crowbar for a hold among the bricks. He finally found a gap. Vijay picked up a rock lying nearby and Colin used it to lever the brick out of place.

More white stone gleamed at them.

'There's something underneath this layer of bricks,' Radha said excitedly.

Vijay and Colin took turns to take apart the surface of the platform. Shukla peered at them as they worked. 'The workers who reconstructed this platform obviously didn't bother to see what lay below it,' he remarked. 'They simply placed the original bricks back on top and cemented them into place.'

After half an hour of labour, clearly visible in the lamplight was the faint outline of a square; there was a stone slab inserted here into the platform. On the surface of the square stone slab were the outlines of two rectangles.

There were two rectangular slabs of stone embedded in the square stone slab.

'This is the entrance we were looking for,' Vijay said finally.

He inserted his screwdriver into the outline of one of the rectangles and dug at the dirt settled in the crack. Once the joint was free of most of the dirt, he levered the screwdriver upwards. A rectangular piece of stone popped out revealing a handle underneath, made from a dark metal. He repeated the exercise with the other rectangle to disclose a second metal handle.

'Come on, man,' he said to Colin. 'Let's get this show on the road.'

He took hold of one handle while Colin grasped the other and, together, they heaved at the stone slab.

It was heavy and didn't budge, despite their efforts. The two men looked at each other, drenched in perspiration with their exertions. And then, with one accord, they bent down again and with combined effort wrenched it out of its resting place.

Finally, it stood at an angle of 45 degrees to the platform. Their hands ached with the struggle. 'Dr. Shukla,' Vijay gasped, 'there's a thick coil of nylon rope inside my bag. Please pass it through the handles while we hold the slab upright.'

Shukla did as he was directed.

'Okay,' Vijay said, 'Everybody grab hold of the rope. One final heave and we're done.'

As Radha and Shukla held the rope, Vijay and Colin let go of the handles and grasped the rope instead, stepping back to put some distance between them and the stone.

'Right,' Vijay said when all four had firmly gripped the rope. 'Heave!'

Together, the group yanked hard on the rope and the slab fell forward with a crash that split the stillness of the night.

For a few moments they stood there, wondering if the noise would have attracted attention, worried that the baba at the temple might have woken up. But the silence of the darkness descended upon them once more. They picked up the lamps and directed the beams into the opening in the platform.

A stone stairway came into view, descending into darkness.

'I'll go first,' Vijay said and clambered down the staircase, holding a lamp aloft, without waiting for agreement from the others.

'Be careful!' Radha shouted down the opening as he disappeared from view with only the light from his lamp visible.

Vijay slowly made his way down the stone staircase. He seemed to be in a large cavern carved into the belly of the hill. Finally, the staircase ended and he hit the floor. He shone the lamp around the cavern and gaped.

'Come on down here,' he shouted to the others. 'You have to see this!'

On The Trail

Arjun Vaid gazed thoughtfully at Imran who sat across his desk, next to Blake. 'Are you sure about this, Kidwai? You could be playing with fire.'

Imran shook his head. 'Sir, I can't be sure of anything right now. It's just a hunch. But it's the only thing we have to go on for now.'

Vaid tapped the desk with his pen. 'You haven't met this nephew of Vikram Singh yet, though. So you haven't yet been able to do a positive ID on Farooq. You could be wrong about this.'

Imran's gaze didn't waver. 'I could be wrong. We would have known for sure today if we had been able to meet Vijay Singh in Jaungarh. I've left instructions for them to call me as soon as they return. In a day or two, we'll get to know if the Farooq who kidnapped Vijay Singh is Farooq Siddiqui. But there's something that doesn't make sense. The station-in-charge at Jaungarh reported that Bheem Singh, the Maharaja of Rajvirgarh, had insisted on a report being filed with the Gurgaon police to investigate the kidnapping. Which is fine, but where does he fit in? What is his interest in the matter? I'd like to know; especially since it is going to be next to impossible to solve the case with only a first name—Farooq—to go on.

I, myself, know five Farooqs. And only three of them are Muslims. The other two are a Christian and a Parsi. Secondly, the Gurgaon police reported that there was pressure from the Haryana government to drop the kidnapping case. Why would anyone want to pressurise the police against pursuing an obscure case with few leads, which may never be resolved? I don't understand.'

'Fine. But be careful. Bheem Singh is powerful and has connections in the government. And the Haryana Chief Minister is close to the Prime Minister. Don't rub either of them the wrong way. I don't want the Home Minister calling me.'

Blake suppressed a grin. He figured that Imran had got into trouble before and Vaid had had to bail him out.

Imran smiled grimly. 'I will. I just want both my questions answered. Nothing more. And I'll only meet Bheem Singh and the Haryana Chief Secretary if we get a positive ID on Farooq.'

Vaid nodded. 'Let me know how it goes.'

18

April 2000

The Temple of the Tooth, 200 miles from Lhasa

Pema Ngodup shivered as he crouched in the little closet in the main hall of the monastery adjoining the Temple of the Tooth. The temple itself was 400 years old, having been built upon the ruins of a much older temple, which was rumoured to be over 2,000 years old.

Pema didn't know it, but the ancient temple whose ruins formed the foundations of this Temple of the Tooth had been built over 2,000 years ago by a courtier of Asoka the Great. A courtier who had travelled from Pataliputra to spread the word of Dharma, and had carried with him texts that spoke of the brotherhood he belonged to—the Nine Unknown Men. These texts had been hidden away in a vault below the ancient temple, safeguarded through the centuries by the monks who had lived in the monastery adjoining the temple.

Through the sliver of a crack in the ancient wooden door of the closet, Pema had a clear view of the main hall. Twenty-two monks inhabited the monastery; 10 of them were lined up in the hall, kneeling with their heads bowed.

The terror had begun 10 minutes ago when the staccato beat of helicopter rotors had broken the stillness of the morning. The monks, unaccustomed to visitors, had flocked to the courtyard, curious to see who was aboard the two large helicopters that slowly touched down.

Pema had been completing his morning chores—as the youngest member of the monastery, just 12 years of age, he had yet to be initiated into the routine the other monks followed. On hearing the choppers, he had rushed to the closest window, driven by the same curiosity as his brothers. He watched wide-eyed as the two large flying machines descended and landed on the thin carpet of snow; residual evidence of the light snowfall the previous day.

Then, the shooting started.

Men armed with automatic rifles poured out of the choppers. Five monks dropped where they stood, dead before they hit the ground, their lifeless bodies riddled with bullets.

The few remaining monks scattered, shouting warnings to their brothers inside the monastery.

As Pema watched, horrified, the armed men pursued the fleeing monks, lobbing grenades. The pristine white snow turned red in patches, greedily soaking up the blood of the fallen monks.

With great difficulty, Pema tore himself away from the terrifying and rushed to find a secure hiding place. He knew exactly where he would hide. Two months after he had been brought to the monastery to join the order, some six years ago, he had discovered a loose wooden panel in the wall of the main hall, which concealed a small closet. He had no idea what its original purpose had been, but unless you knew it was there, it looked like just another wall panel. He squeezed in there just before the attackers began herding the monks into the hall.

As he watched, the men rounded up the monks, ejecting them from the places where they had sought refuge.

When ten monks were lined up in the main hall, Pema saw a tall man enter. He was clearly the leader of the attackers and was the only one not wearing a ski mask. He walked slowly over to the monks and asked the man in the ski mask standing next to him.

'Are these all?'

The masked man nodded. 'Ten dead. Ten here. We've scoured the monastery and the temple. There's no place left to hide.'

The leader's voice was sharp. 'The intel was that there were 22 monks. Where are the other two? You sure you've looked everywhere?'

'We'll run another check to be sure.' The man barked orders and a group of armed men left the room on a run.

'So, who's your leader here?' The tall man asked the monks, looking each one in the eye. He turned to the man in the ski mask as he came to the end of the line. 'Make them kneel.'

Men stepped forward to force the monks to their knees.

The tall man took out a gun from a shoulder holster and aimed it at the head of the monk nearest to him.

'I'll ask again. And this time, if I don't get an answer, I'll shoot. Who is your leader?'

Again, silence greeted him.

Pema held his breath as the moments passed. Would he shoot?

An ear-splitting sound broke the silence and monk sagged to the ground; the bullet had shattered his head like a watermelon. 'Don't shoot!' An elderly monk spoke up. 'Our leader is dead— he was shot in the courtyard—but I am the eldest here.'

'Finally! An answer.' The man walked to the monk and stood before him. 'Where is the vault?'

'I don't know of any vault,' the old monk quavered. 'Shoot me if you want, but I'm telling you the truth.'

'Oh, I don't need to shoot you. Not yet.' The man pointed his gun at a young monk who knelt beside the elderly monk. 'So you don't know about the secret vault that was part of the older temple and which was preserved when this temple was built? That's funny, since someone saw the vault a few decades ago. Perhaps this will jog your memory.'

The man fired at the young monk who collapsed to the ground in a pool of blood.

Pema covered his mouth with his hands, stifling a scream; his blood ran cold.

The man knelt before the old monk and gazed into his eyes. 'See, I'm going to find that vault. And if you don't tell me, I will kill each one of your remaining monks before your eyes. One by one.'

A tense silence followed his words.

Then, the elderly monk bowed his head as if ashamed at what he was about to do. 'If you promise to spare the others, I will tell you where the vault is.'

'Great.' The man with the gun turned to the masked man. 'Take him and empty the vault. Ensure that you get all the documents. Leave nothing behind. And take care that none of them are damaged. These are ancient texts and have to be treated with great care. And let me know if you find a metal disk.'

The man nodded and left with the elderly monk and a handful of men, heading in the direction of the temple.

The group that had left the room earlier returned. 'Negative,' said one of the men. 'No one else.'

'So where are the other two?' Their leader gazed sharply at the remaining seven monks.

Another elderly monk looked up at him. 'They went to Lhasa yesterday. To get supplies for the monastery.'

The man with the gun looked at him suspiciously and was silent for a few moments, as if considering this possibility. Pema knew the elderly monk had lied. Only one monk had gone to Lhasa the previous day.

The moments passed in agonising silence, each minute seeming like an hour to the young monk. His leg had begun to develop cramps and he was not sure how much longer he could hold out in his tiny hiding place.

Just when he thought he couldn't bear it any longer, the men returned with the elderly monk.

'Got everything,' the man who had led them out reported to his leader. 'No metal disk, though.'

The leader frowned, then whipped out a satellite phone and dialled a number. 'Murphy here. Mission accomplished,' he spoke into the phone. 'But no disk. What do you want us to do?' He listened to the reply then disconnected the call and put the phone away.

'Now that you have what you wanted, let us go,' the elderly monk pleaded.

'Oh, I will,' Murphy smirked. He gestured to his men, who immediately opened fire on the kneeling monks.

The elderly monk looked on horrified. Then, a scream came from somewhere inside the wall. Pema could take it no longer; horror and panic had overcome him.

Murphy looked surprised. 'Find him,' he barked.

Four men went to work, ripping out the wooden panels until they found Pema, cowering and shivering in his little closet. They pulled him out roughly and flung him on the floor. Pema lay there, sobbing and trembling.

'He is only a child. Have mercy,' the elderly monk pleaded.

Murphy smirked. 'My orders are to leave no survivors. There's no age bar.' He aimed his gun at Pema and pulled the trigger.

Tears ran down the old monk's cheeks as Pema's body lay sprawled on the floor, his blood pooling with the blood of his brothers. He knew that the contents of the vault would not help these men achieve their objective. That was his only consolation as he watched Murphy point the gun at his head and pull the trigger.

19

Present Day

Day 6
Bairat

Radha led her father down the stairs with Colin bringing up the rear, holding the lamp to light their way. As they reached the foot of the staircase and stood beside Vijay, they stared at the sight that greeted them in the combined light of the two lamps.

They were in an immense circular cavern. But what was striking wasn't just the size of the cavern. It was the appearance of the walls. Rocky shelves had been carved into the walls, so that the entire cavern was lined with pigeonholes carved into the rock. Only the wall opposite the staircase was bare.

Vijay shone the light of his lamp on the floor and they gasped. Etched on the floor in bold relief was an exact two dimensional replica of the gear wheel that lay above. In the very centre of the wheel stood a square pedestal; about four feet high. On the smoothly polished surface of the pedestal was carved a familiar symbol: the nine-spoked wheel.

This cavern had obviously been made by the Nine or at least used by them for some purpose, now long forgotten.

Below the nine-spoked wheel on the pedestal was an inscription.

Shukla once more assumed his role as translator and read out the words etched on the slab.

Four Brothers
Offered by the Emperor
The eldest brother
The first of the four
Echoes the secret
Of the Nine.
A riddle.

'The metallic disk, a key, a ball of rock and a riddle,' Shukla mused, recalling the entry in Beger's diary. 'Is this the riddle?'

'What do you think this place is?' Colin asked, shining his lamp into the pigeonholes .

No one spoke for a while.

Then, Shukla offered: 'I suspected this when I heard Chunnilal's tale of the Pandavas and the dice this afternoon,' he said slowly. 'I'd say we're looking at what must have been a secret library of the Nine, perhaps the one described in the documents that Beger had transcribed. And the legend of the dice that Chunnilal narrated to us today would support this possibility. This hill was supposed to have powers that enhance knowledge and learning. Could that have been another way of saying that a library of ancient knowledge once resided here? The legend about the dice could have been a convenient way of hiding the true secret that was hidden here, just as the legend of the treasure was meant to keep people from looking for it.'

Shukla gestured to the pigeonholes. 'These must have been the receptacles where the texts belonging to the library were stored. In those days, they used bark to write on. The bark was dried in the sun and then these strips were used to write on and then bound together to form what we would call books.'

Vijay nodded. 'This does seem an extremely likely place for a secret library. The rock would have sheltered the documents and the dry, arid nature of the soil here would have ensured the texts didn't decay.'

'So what happened to the library? Where are the texts?' Colin wanted to know.

'Bark wouldn't survive two thousand years even in a place like this,' Shukla explained. 'There has been no record of any written texts from 2,000 years ago, apart from the inscriptions of Asoka's edicts, which were carved into rocks and stone.'

'Or,' Radha suggested, 'the library may have been removed by subsequent generations of the Nine, for safekeeping.'

Shukla looked around in wonder, tinged with visible disappointment. 'Imagine the knowledge that must have lain in this cavern; centuries of accumulated wisdom. Who knows what we might have found in those texts'?'

'Hey, what's this?' Colin had wandered off towards the far wall of the cavern. He was peering closely at something on the wall.

The others joined him to see what he had discovered.

'Look at this.' Colin trained the lamp on a section of the wall and they saw a hairline crack tracing the outline of a rectangle bounded on one side by the floor of the cavern.'It's a doorway, an entrance of some sort,' Colin concluded excitedly. 'There must be a hidden chamber behind this wall.'

'How do we open it?' Vijay frowned. The doorway itself was barely discernible and he had seen nothing in the cavern that looked like a mechanism to open a hidden door.

Something struck Radha. She abruptly grabbed Colin's lamp and hurried back to the pedestal with the inscription on it.

'What's the matter...,' Colin began to protest, but was cut short by Radha as she trained the lamp on the surface of the pedestal.

'I thought the nine-spoked wheel looked a bit different.' She beamed at the others, who hastened to join her.

In the light of the lamp they all noticed what had escaped their attention earlier. In their excitement at finding the riddle, they had failed to observe that there was a hollow at the centre of the wheel. Where the hub should have been, there was, instead, a depression scooped out of the rock and lined with black metal.

Vijay and Colin looked at each other. They were thinking exactly the same thing.

'Do you think...'

'Try it and see.'

Both men spoke together and smiled. Vijay reached into his bag and pulled out the key they had used to decipher the verse on the disk. He inserted it into the hollow and gently turned it clockwise. It fitted perfectly and locked into place with a click.

'Here we go,' Vijay grasped the key and twisted it. Nothing happened. He twisted it in the opposite direction. There was still no result. He frowned and tried pulling the key out but it wouldn't move. It was stuck.

'Why isn't it working?' Frustration crept into Vijay's voice.

'Perhaps we're being too optimistic,' Radha suggested. 'This cavern and the doorway are over 2,000 years old. And we are assuming that the doorway will open through a system of gears and levers activated by the turning of the key. In books and Hollywood movies you find trapdoors and hidden entrances that work even after thousands of years, but that doesn't happen in real life. It would be surprising if that doorway opened after all.'

'Hush!' Vijay hissed, suddenly. 'Quiet! I hear voices.'

For a few moments there was no sound to be heard. Then, the sound of voices came to them, faint at first and then growing louder. Someone was climbing the stairs from the lower terrace to the level on which the platform lay.

'The light from our lamps must be streaming through the open trapdoor,' Colin guessed.

'Who could it be?' Vijay whispered.

There was a loud exclamation and a hurried exchange of words. The newcomers were probably at the platform and had seen the open trapdoor. Their voices were loud now and they were making no effort to be stealthy. But the words were unintelligible.

A thought crossed Vijay's mind and he looked at the others in dismay. He didn't need to voice his thoughts. They understood immediately. As if to confirm their suspicions, Farooq's voice cut across the other voices, speaking in a strange language they didn't understand.

'What do we do?' Radha looked worried.

They were trapped. The group of four backed up against the wall as men appeared at the foot of the staircase and advanced into the cavern. They were carrying Uzis. Vijay and Colin recognised Maroosh. He had a nasty bruise on his right temple, swollen and purple.

Maroosh saw them, too, and grimaced; whether from pain or anger they couldn't tell. But a grim purpose entered his stride and he marched menacingly towards them. Farooq appeared behind the men, walking calmly and slowly down the staircase. As he stepped off the final stair onto the floor, he stopped and swivelled around, taking in the contents of the cavern. Then he nodded to himself and walked towards the group from Jaungarh.

'Well, well, well,' he smiled unpleasantly. 'If it isn't the innocent young men who didn't know anything about the clues in the emails or the key to the disk! I suppose you found your way to this chamber by sheer chance?'

He advanced until he stood before Vijay. 'So, you fools thought that you'd discovered the secret of the Nine? Look around you. What do you see? Empty pigeonholes.'

One of the men gave a shout. He had spotted the inscription on the pedestal. Farooq turned immediately and walked over to the pedestal. Without taking his gaze off the inscription, he barked an order. Maroosh grabbed Shukla by the arm and dragged him roughly to where Farooq stood.

'Don't hurt him,' Radha screamed, tears welling up in her eyes as her father winced in pain.

Farooq gestured to the inscription, his eyes glued to the pedestal. 'Dr. Shukla, I know you are a linguist and a specialist in ancient Indian languages. Please translate this verse for me.'

Shukla stood his ground, his face white but determined. 'And what if I refuse?'

'You won't.' He barked another order and two men advanced towards Radha. One grabbed her by the hair, the other gripped her arm and together they dragged her away from the rest of the group.

'Don't hurt her!' Vijay advanced two steps and three Uzis were immediately trained on him. He froze, knowing that Farooq wouldn't hesitate to give the command to cut him down. He would be of no help to Radha and the others if he was dead. 'For God's sake, Dr. Shukla, give him the translation!' He was beside himself with rage and fear now and he felt his hands trembling.

'I'm sure you value the safety of your daughter.' Farooq resumed his study of the pedestal.

Shukla's lip quivered as he watched Radha struggle against the iron grip of the men who held her. They sneered. Radha yelped in pain as one of them pulled her hair and jerked her head back.

Farooq looked inquiringly at Shukla, who blurted out the meaning of the verse.

'Four brothers.' Farooq looked puzzled as he turned the verse over in his head, trying to make sense of it. 'You're sure of this translation?' He looked at the old man and saw the terror in his eyes and nodded. 'No, I don't think you are dissembling.'

'Let her go now,' Vijay said fiercely. He glanced at Radha, still held by the two men, her head at an awkward angle as the man gripping her hair twisted her head back. 'You have the translation.'

Farooq glanced at the inscription again as if to reassure himself that the translation was, indeed, correct. He gestured to his men and issued some more instructions. They stepped back from the group, their Uzis still trained on them, and the two men holding Radha released her.

Colin didn't like the look on Farooq's face. 'I don't think he intends freeing us,' he whispered to Vijay.

His voice must have carried to Farooq, whose face twisted into a cruel grin. 'I don't mean to let you go so easily,' he addressed Vijay. 'Not after the hard time you've given me. And not once but twice. You are as bad as your uncle.'

Without bothering to explain, he turned on his heel and headed back up the staircase. His men backed away from the group, guns ready in case someone tried to make a break, and followed him up the stairs. Radha joined them as the last of the men disappeared.

'You okay?' Vijay asked her, concern in his voice. She nodded numbly, still dazed.

'He's going to drop the trapdoor on us.' Colin had a worried look on his face. 'There's no other way out of this cavern.'

As he spoke, the sound of the trapdoor crashing down into its resting place echoed down the stairway and into the cavern. They looked at each other grimly. The stone trapdoor had been difficult to lift from the outside. How would they raise it from below?

Suddenly, a blast shook the cavern and the ground underfoot trembled as the roof of the cavern above the stairway came crashing down. The stairs disappeared in a pile of rubble. Almost simultaneously, the walls of the cavern shook and groaned, and the wall behind them, with the secret doorway, began to disintegrate and rain down in shards of stone.

They fled from the collapsing wall, bending double, trying to shield their heads from the shower of rocks from the wall and the stone roof.

As the collapse of the wall subsided in a cloud of dust they straightened up, coughing and flapping their hands in an attempt to wave the dust away from their faces.

'He's blasted the trapdoor opening with explosives.' Vijay's voice was surprisingly calm, belying the horror that gripped him with the realisation of what had happened.

They were trapped underground, deep within a hill, with no way to escape.

20

March 2, 2001

Bamiyan, Afghanistan

The air was thick with the sound of explosions. Scores of Taliban soldiers stood around and cheered as the anti-aircraft rounds ripped through the giant statues of the Buddha that had been carved into the sandstone cliffs, 1,500 years ago. Now, they were doomed—fated to be reduced to a memory occupying a corner of history—on the orders of the Taliban, rulers of Afghanistan. These statues had seen successive rulers of Afghanistan come and go, but they wouldn't survive the rule of the Taliban.

The stone scultpures exploded in clouds of dust and a rain of rubble that cascaded down the sides of the cliff. Within moments, where the statues had stood, there remained only two hollows.

Some of the Taliban men picked up a rock or two, souvenirs to take home. They would tell their children and grandchildren about the day they destroyed the infidel statues.

Baran paused at the foot of the cliff, a rock in each hand, and looked up at the hollows left by the statues. The cliff was a jagged wall of stone where the statues had stood; solid, except for five black dots that marked the face of the cliff in the larger hollow.

He shouted to the others and pointed to the dots.

It seemed that these were caves which had been hidden behind the statue with no record of their existence. Within minutes, ropes and rough climbing equipment were organised and two nimble-footed Afghans began climbing up the rock face.

Baran was one of them.

They quickly scaled the cliff, using to their advantage the jagged surface left behind by the breaking of the statues. Baran's fellow climber, a younger man, reached the caves first and disappeared into one. He came out quickly and, with a shout of disappointment, climbed to the next one.

Baran reached an opening and pulled himself over the edge and into the cool darkness of the cave. He blinked as his eyes gradually adjusted to the gloom inside.

But there was nothing there. It was a small, shallow cave, barely four feet deep and not more than five feet from floor to roof. He quickly clambered his way to the next one.

His fellow climber had finished exploring the third cave and was on his way down.

'It's useless,' he cried to Baran. 'There's nothing in the caves.'

Undeterred, Baran kept going. There was no way he was going back without checking the second cave. He knew there would be jibes at his manliness and jokes about age catching up with him, with the younger man checking out three caves in the time he had taken to inspect one. But he also knew that the taunts would be worse if he turned back now.

He reached the last cave and pulled himself in. It was slightly larger than the earlier one and its interior was shrouded in darkness. It had to be quite deep.

He switched on a flashlight and shone it around the cave. The back wall was discernible now, at least 25 feet from the opening. There was nothing to be seen here, though.

Hoping to find something of value, Baran walked deeper into the cave, stepping warily and crouching to avoid hitting the ceiling. While the cave had been sealed for long enough to ensure there were no wild animals here, he wasn't so sure about snakes. The light from the torch lit up the rocky walls as he walked past them. They were bare.

Suddenly, he spotted something white on the floor.

He kneeled and focused the flashlight to get a better look.

What he saw chilled him to the bone.

It was a human skeleton; bones that appeared to be very old.

The skeleton was intact, not a bone out of place. The bones lay on the stone shards that made up the floor of the cave. Baran couldn't imagine how or why, but the man seemed to have died here, in this cave.

There was something else here, half-buried in the gravel.

Baran trained his flashlight on the object. It was metallic, but unlike any metal he had ever seen. He pulled it out and examined it; the circular metallic slab was smooth on one side and had grooves and inscriptions on the other. In the centre of the slab was a hollow scooped out of the metal.

Baran stared at the slab for a few moments, trying to fathom its nature and purpose. The metal was dark, appeared really old, but was not rusted. He hefted it in his hand to assess its value. It was light. He made a face; it was probably worthless.

Disappointed, Baran scoured the ground around the skeleton with the flashlight one last time before he reported his find. Then, he saw some tattered strips of bark, bound together, scattered as if they had been thrown there by someone.

He quickly tucked them along with the metallic slab into the folds of his robe.

Suppressing a triumphant grin, he made his way to the cave opening to announce his discovery, of the skeleton, to the crowd below.

Once Baran had come down, the men gathered in a huddle before the local commander of the Taliban, Hamid, who beckoned to Baran. 'Now, let us see what you have found.'

Baran's chest swelled with importance. He now sat before Hamid in the little semicircular space left by the crowd at the very front of the gathering.

Hamid examined the texts. Though a bit frayed at the edges, and torn in parts, they were still in surprisingly good condition considering their age. He leafed through the strips of bark and attempted to read the lines that were inscribed on them.

Finally, he looked up, his face betraying his frustration.

'I can't read these,' he announced. 'The script is unintelligible. Who knows what they could be? Perhaps his shopping list?' He chuckled at his own joke and the crowd laughed with him.

Hamid gathered up the texts and tossed them at Baran.

Next, he picked up the circular metallic slab and studied it, turning it over in his hands, frowning at the inscriptions and grooves that marked one face. Something struck him. He stuck one finger out and rubbed it across the inscribed face of the slab. To his surprise, the toothed wheel on the slab moved under his touch. He grinned and looked up at the men seated before him, then tossed the slab to Baran.

'Keep them,' he declared grandly. 'The texts are worthless if they are not readable. And the metal object is a toy. Definitely of no use to us.'

Whether Hamid considered them worthless or not, the texts and the disk were centuries old. Baran decided that he'd keep them as a souvenir of the destruction of the infidel statues. And who knew, they just might have a price on the black market in antiquities.

Little did Hamid or Baran know the true worth of the texts and the secret buried within them. For the second time in 1,500 years, the texts had been discarded by those who couldn't see beyond the words inscribed on them.

21

Present Day

Day 6
Bairat

Vijay and his companions stared in horror at the wall of rocks that now blocked the exit. Vijay grimaced. 'I should never have got all of you into this.'

Radha responded immediately, her eyes flashing, 'You didn't exactly coerce us into coming here. We came of our own volition. And now, we...we,' her voice faltered as she couldn't bring herself to articulate their situation.

'Guys, you gotta see this.' Colin was staring in the opposite direction.

The others turned to look.

All that remained of the wall with the hidden doorway was a heap of rubble on the cavern floor. What lay before them now was the secret chamber. The far wall of the hidden chamber was polished smooth and lined, from floor to ceiling, with inscriptions that they couldn't read. And in the centre of the wall was a hollow receptacle in which something glinted brightly at them in the light of their lamps.

The dust was beginning to settle and all thoughts of their predicament were momentarily forgotten in the excitement of this discovery. This, then, was the true secret of the cavern.

'What is it?' Vijay found himself whispering, though he didn't know why.

Shukla was beside himself with excitement. He had already begun to translate the inscriptions and was visibly delighted with what he read.

'It is a summary of one of the books of the Mahabharata.' He couldn't keep the excitement out of his voice and it trembled as he spoke. 'The *Vimana Parva*. This is amazing.'

Colin had advanced swiftly to the object that was shining in the niche and he gave a whoop as he studied it.

Vijay and Radha hurried to Colin's side while Shukla remained glued to the writing on the wall of the cavern, reading it with undisguised pleasure.

'What is it?' Vijay asked, as Colin reached into the recess and brought out the object.

They all stared at it.

It was a ball that, at first glance, appeared to be made of glass. Colin slowly held his hands out and they realised that it was actually a perfect sphere carved out of stone and polished to a degree that it shone and took on the appearance of glass.

Vijay placed the rock ball carefully in his bag. He didn't know what it was, but if it was concealed in a secret chamber in this cavern, it had to be important.

Radha walked to her father's side. 'What is it, Papa?' She knew her father had read the Mahabharata a 100 times over, if not more, and could quote verses from the epic. There must be something different about the inscriptions on the wall to get him so excited.

Shukla couldn't contain his excitement. His eyes shone as he looked at her. 'The book which is summarised here is the

Vimana Parva. The Mahabharata consists of books, each one narrating a section of the tale that is reflected in the title of the book; the *Karna Parva* is the story of Karna, the *Bheeshma Parva* is about Bheeshma Pitamah, and so on. But I've never come across the *Vimana Parva* in any version of the epic that I've read. As far as I know, it doesn't exist.'

'What is this book about?' Vijay had come up and heard Shukla's explanation. He gazed at the wall with interest.

'A *vimana* is a flying craft,' Shukla began. 'There are several references to *vimana*s in the epic.'

Vijay remembered hearing stories from the epic that involved flying machines narrated to him by his uncle years ago. 'What is the story in this book?'

Shukla opened his mouth to reply, but there was a shout from Colin, who had wandered off to explore the rest of the secret chamber.

'There's a stairway here!'

Vijay walked over to Colin, who was peering into a crack in the wall. They examined the crevice in the light of the lamp. It led to a niche from which a stairway rose, cut into the rock, spiralling upwards and disappearing into the darkness beyond the reach of the lamplight.

'I wonder where it leads to,' Colin mused.

'Probably a hidden exit.' Shukla and Radha had joined them. 'Most ancient structures, especially when carved into rock or built underground, had two access routes. For ventilation and as an escape route in case one got blocked up for some reason. Considering what was concealed in this chamber, they would definitely have ensured that there was more than one way to get in and out.'

They looked at each other, their hopes rising. Perhaps they could still make it out of this underground prison.

'I'll go first.' Vijay started up the stairway. Shukla and Radha followed him, with Colin bringing up the rear.

The staircase wound upwards. At regular intervals, holes were visible in the walls of the staircase.

'Ventilation shafts,' Shukla explained. 'They probably lead to openings in the hillside that allow fresh air to circulate in the cavern.'

Their progress began to slow down and they began to wonder when they would reach the top. Suddenly, the stairway ended and opened up into a small square rocky chamber.

They stood for a few moments, getting their breath back after the climb. Vijay looked at Shukla, concerned, but the linguist nodded back at him reassuringly to indicate that he was fine.

They shone their torches around the little chamber but there was no joint or crack in the wall to indicate a hidden doorway. The walls were solid rock. In one corner was a short staircase that ended abruptly halfway up the wall.

'What now?' Vijay wondered.

Radha saw it first.

In the roof of the chamber, just above the stairway in the corner, was the square outline of an opening. Vijay advanced up the stairway until he stood on the top stair, crouching, and studied the stone slab that seemed to be their passport to freedom. He extended his hands and positioned them against the slab and tried pushing it open. It was heavy and didn't move.

Vijay beckoned to Colin, who immediately bounded up the stairs and joined him.

The two friends looked at each other and nodded. With one accord, they pushed against the stone slab.

Nothing happened.

They stared at each other, helplessly.

There seemed to be no way out.

Where It All Began for Farooq

Farooq sat back in the black Mercedes and mulled over the verse he had discovered in the cavern at Bairat. He wasted no time on thinking about the group he had left trapped in the cavern. His thoughts flitted back 11 years in time to his first meeting with the European, shortly after he had joined Al Qaeda. Columbus, the man had called himself. Farooq smirked, amused even after all these years; if the man had to choose an alias without people knowing it wasn't his real name, he couldn't have chosen a worse name. But then, again, it didn't matter what the European was called. He was powerful and could deliver on his promises, using a vast network of politicians, businessmen and criminals across the globe, as Farooq had witnessed several times in the past 11 years.

Columbus was tall and distinguished looking. He oozed power and wealth from every pore. In his first meeting with Farooq, he had left a deep impression. Not the least because, as a parting shot, he had shared with the scientist a secret known to few people alive.

The secret of the Nine.

'Someday,' Columbus had asserted, 'we will find the means to unearth the nature and location of the secret they hid.' How the man had come to know about the secret and what gave him confidence in the truth the myth hid, Farooq hadn't known at the time, but Farooq hadn't revealed his own great secret— which was also connected with the Nine.

It was amazing, Farooq thought, that just one year later, when he was forced to go underground, he had met Mohammed Bin Jabal. Perhaps it was destiny.

Farooq was deeply religious, having been raised in an orthodox Islamic family, and his father had enrolled him in a *madrasa*, which had a deep impact on him. He had grown up believing that Allah had a plan for him and today he was firmly convinced that he knew what that plan was. And what a grand one it was!

It had to be more than coincidence that Bin Jabal had shown him ancient texts and a metal disk that bore inscriptions that no one could decipher. But Farooq had cannily got them translated, suspecting that there was something of importance in the texts and the disk. He had been right.

He had shared the discovery with Columbus and the journey had begun; a journey that was going to culminate in the next few days with the discovery of the secret of the Nine. They had come a long way since then. The texts had led them to a hidden location where they had found artefacts that further reinforced their beliefs. They had redoubled their efforts to find the missing links that would lead them to the secret.

But first, he had to figure out the meaning of the verse.

He frowned. What could it mean?

Caved In!

Vijay and Colin tried, once again, pushing with all their strength against the stone slab at the top of the unfinished stairway.

Still nothing.

They walked down the stairs despondently. Four disconsolate faces stared at each other. Were they doomed to remain trapped here in this cavern?

Vijay put his lamp on the floor and sat down. He was tired and the cut on his cheek was throbbing. He closed his eyes and buried his face in his hands.

Radha noticed his dejection and bent down to put her hand on his shoulder. And froze.

'What's it?' Colin noticed her stiffen suddenly.

'There's something on the floor.' Radha pointed to where Vijay sat. In the interplay of light and shadows, a vague design on the floor of the chamber was visible.

Vijay perked up immediately. They had studied the walls of the cavern but the thought of examining the floor hadn't crossed their minds. He sprang to his feet and directed the lamplight on the floor, along with Colin.

Etched in the floor was a representation of the gear wheel, with 27 teeth. At the centre of the toothed wheel was a hollow, sheathed in the dark metal that they were so familiar with, by now.

'The key!' Colin couldn't contain his excitement. 'Do you think there is a mechanism here to open that trapdoor?'

His enthusiasm was dampened somewhat as soon as he spoke these words and the same thought struck the others. The key was stuck in the pedestal that stood in the cavern below them! And even if they could retrieve it, there was no guarantee it would work. After all, the secret doorway in the cavern below had refused to open using the key.

'Let's give it a shot.' Vijay squared his shoulders.

'I'll go down and get the key,' Colin offered and disappeared down the stairway with his lamp.

The others waited. Silence descended on the chamber like a death shroud. They tried to keep their thoughts away from the fate that awaited them, if Colin failed in his attempt to retrieve the key. While there was sufficient ventilation in the cavern and this chamber, they would surely die for want of water and food. None of them wanted to contemplate that awful possibility.

After what seemed like an eternity, Colin's lamplight appeared again, bobbing up and down as he dashed up the stairs, and he entered the chamber, a broad beam on his face.

'It wasn't easy to take out, but it definitely wasn't stuck like before,' he explained jubilantly. 'Perhaps the collapse of the wall loosened the key in some way.'

Now that they had the key, their hopes revived.

Colin inserted the key into the hollow in the floor. The others watched with bated breath. Would it work? Or was the mechanism to open the trapdoor jammed like the one in the cavern below?

He gently turned the key clockwise. There was an audible click, followed by a series of staccato clicks accompanied by a sharp whining sound. Something was happening! The floor of the chamber shuddered gently for a few moments.

Then, everything went quiet.

Their eyes went to the trapdoor in the ceiling of the chamber. It hadn't moved. Something within Vijay snapped. The tension and frustration that had been building up broke through. With a roar of rage, he charged up the short stairway in the corner and hammered with all his strength at the stone trapdoor, venting his feelings.

To his great surprise, as he pounded at the trapdoor, he felt it give slightly. He stopped his pounding and applied pressure instead.

The stone slab moved upward by a few inches. It was heavy.

He let it drop and faced the group. The mechanism had worked after all.

'I think the key unlocked the trapdoor. There must have been some sort of mechanism locking it in place which has been released. We can do it.'

Colin joined him immediately and the two men squatted and then rose up together, hitting the stone slab simultaneously. The trapdoor lifted reluctantly and then toppled over with a crash that resounded through the small chamber.

With a whoop, Colin hoisted himself over the top of the opening and held his hand down. 'Quick, let's get out of here.'

Together, he and Vijay helped Shukla and then Radha out. Vijay retrieved the key from the floor of the chamber and clambered out after them. They looked around and found themselves in a small cave formed by three 20-foot high boulders leaning against each other.

'I know where we are,' Colin recognised the place. 'On the upper terrace.'

Vijay breathed in the sweet night air and savoured their freedom.

'Farooq didn't see the key in the pedestal,' Radha said thoughtfully.

'The key probably looked like part of the design on the surface of the pedestal,' Vijay speculated. 'It is a good thing he didn't notice it.' He motioned to his bag and grinned wickedly. 'He'll never know what he missed.' He turned to Colin. 'Let's replace this slab. The trapdoor is destroyed but if we leave this open, the secret cavern of the Nine is still accessible.'

'Yes, we can't allow that to be discovered,' Shukla agreed. 'Once we inform the Maharaja, the government can take over and restore the library of the Nine or do what they want with it. Until then it should remain a secret.'

Vijay and Colin lifted the stone slab and dropped it back into place, concealing the opening. They then hurried towards the staircase that led to the lower terrace. As they passed the platform they saw, in the dim light of the half moon, the destruction wrought by Farooq's men on the platform through which they had accessed the cavern.

They followed the path down the hill, silently, to their car. There was no sign of life on the hill. The baba in the temple hadn't been roused by the explosion.

Vijay got into the driver's seat.

'Now, all we have to do is solve the riddle and find the meaning of the verse.' With these words, he drove down the path that would take them to the road leading to the highway and back to the fort.

22

Day 7

Jaungarh Fort

Greg White stared at the smooth, polished ball of rock that rested on a cushion. Vijay had called him early in the morning and told him briefly about their excursion to Bairat, though he hadn't disclosed the events of the night or what they had found. White, eager to hear the details and see the discovery, had rushed to the fort as soon as he could leave Bheem Singh's farmhouse.

They were now assembled in the study and Vijay had shown him the rock ball. He fervently hoped that White might be able to tell them something about it that might help them decipher the cryptic verse they had found at Bairat.

White shook his head slowly. 'This is an amazing specimen,' he remarked. 'It has been polished to a degree that you can see your reflection in it.' He gazed at his own face reflected in the ball. 'But I've never seen anything like this before or heard of any artefact like this being discovered anywhere in the world.'

Vijay was disappointed. 'So there's nothing you can tell us that might help?'

'I'm afraid not. Sorry.' He looked at Vijay. 'So this is what you found at Bairat?'

'And also a verse.' Vijay told him about the verse and also narrated their experience of the previous night, their encounter with Farooq, and their ordeal after he had trapped them in the cavern.

White looked solemn when Vijay had finished. 'You really should have informed Bheem Singh. He could have provided an armed escort for you. This Farooq guy sounds dangerous. This is the third time he's attacked you violently, apart from playing a role in Vikram's murder.'

'Yes, but the violence at the vault wasn't aimed at us,' Vijay reminded him. 'He was after the contents of the locker. Not us. We just happened to be in the wrong place at the wrong time.'

'Still, there's no saying what he might do next. We should take Bheem Singh's help if we want to be safe. I know this personally. Remember, I got mugged, too.'

'I agree with Greg,' Shukla joined in. So far, you've been lucky; we've all been lucky. The next time we cross Farooq's path, our luck may not hold out. Bheem Singh offered to help and he has the resources and the backing of the government. We should take his help.'

Vijay pondered this for a few moments. Then, he shook his head, his face grim. 'I know that Farooq is dangerous. But he's probably nothing more than a treasure hunter who somehow chanced upon the story of the Nine and thinks that their secret is a hoard hidden away. And I know that doesn't make him less dangerous.' He looked at Shukla and White in turn. 'But my uncle wanted this search to remain a secret. That is why he went to such great lengths to devise clues in the emails he sent to me. And Bheem Singh also wants this search to be covert. Taking an armed escort and going around with an entourage will attract attention; including Farooq's.'

A thought suddenly struck him. *How had Farooq known that they were going to Bairat? Were they being shadowed by his men?*

But he didn't voice the thought. Their experience last night had shaken the others. Raising this question now would only set them on edge. Instead, he decided to voice another thought that had been taking shape in his mind for a while.

'I think, from here on, I'm not going to involve the rest of you, except Colin, in the search. It is too dangerous. I have no right to put your lives in danger. Uncle intended me to solve this puzzle on my own and that's what I am going to do.'

He hadn't reckoned on Radha's reaction. She glared at him, her face hardening, 'You can't be serious. You want us to drop out of this search after all we've been through? Vijay, don't forget, no one compelled us to join you. I know you are concerned about our safety. But, if you think you can do this on your own, think again. You'll need us.'

'You'll need me to decipher any other inscriptions that you might find,' Shukla looked at him with a smile.

'And I'm not going to miss being a part of the discovery of the century,' White added. 'I couldn't make it to Bairat but the next time, I'm going to be with you.'

Vijay looked at Colin, who shrugged. 'I didn't intend leaving all of you out of the thrill of the discovery,' he remonstrated. 'It's just that it might get really dangerous from here on. Farooq's going to be more desperate than ever. He knows the verse and may get the meaning behind it, but he doesn't have the ball. Not that he's ever going to know. And I don't want to put any of you in any more danger than you've been in so far.'

He was thinking to himself that if Farooq was keeping them under surveillance, though he couldn't fathom how, he would definitely get to know where they were going next.

'But if you are all determined to accompany me until the end, I'll welcome your company and help. God knows I'll need it,' he concluded. There were cheers from the others.

A soft cough sounded from the doorway to the study. It was the butler.

'The police are here, sir.'

Two men walked into the room. Vijay, who had been expecting Raunaq Singh, stood up in surprise and advanced to greet them.

'How can I help you?' Vijay asked Imran, after the IB officer had given his name and introduced his companion, Deepak, a police artist.

Imran had rehearsed this conversation several times. 'The Gurgaon police are investigating your kidnapping and we'd like to get a portrait done of the two men whose names have been mentioned as suspects in the FIR.' He had deliberately chosen his words to give the impression that he worked for the Gurgaon police without actually lying about it. 'Will you and your friend help us?'

'Of course.' Vijay beckoned to Colin, and led Imran and Deepak out of the study to the sitting room on the ground floor. There, they described Farooq and Imtiaz to Deepak, who busied himself sketching the faces of the two men.

When he had finished, Vijay and Colin gazed at the sketches. 'The portrait of Farooq's a pretty good likeness, don't you think?' Colin glanced at Vijay, who nodded his agreement.

'But the sketch of Imtiaz isn't too good.' Vijay looked at Deepak. 'I'm sorry, it is probably because we focused our attention more on Farooq than Imtiaz.'

'That's okay,' Imran responded, staring at Farooq's portrait. 'This is a great help. At least we can try and get a visual match for one of them. And you said he was the leader of the group, right?'

Both Vijay and Colin nodded.

'Thank you both. We'll keep you posted on the investigation.' Imran smiled, and they were shown out of the fort.

Vijay and Colin returned to the study where Shukla, Radha and White were still trying to work out the meaning of the riddle.

'What did they want?' Shukla enquired.

Vijay told them about the portraits, but was more interested in solving the riddle. 'Have you guys had any luck yet?'

'Well, we discussed the possibility that this is an allusion to four members of the Nine,' Radha said. 'But that doesn't seem likely; just as the verse on the metal disk didn't refer to the original Nine.'

'So you think that, using the same logic, this verse could refer to four edicts of Asoka?'

'Well, we were just speculating that this verse could refer to four structures. Built by Asoka or constructed during his reign, if the Emperor in the second line is assumed to refer to Asoka.'

'You mean like a stupa or a pillar or something?' Vijay responded.

'Perhaps they are temples of some sort?' Colin ventured. 'Temples would be offered to the gods in some sort of consecration ceremony, wouldn't they?'

White shook his head. 'Asoka was a Buddhist. I can understand Hindu temples being offered to a god or deity on completion but I haven't heard of a stupa or *chaitya* being offered to the gods. That's not the way of Buddhism.'

'But it doesn't say that the offering was made to the gods,' Colin persisted, taking another line of reasoning. 'What if they were offered to Buddha himself? Or to the people? Asoka had this thing about his people, didn't he?'

'Hang on,' Radha interjected. 'Suppose we ignore the second line for now and focus on trying to identify structures that Asoka built, which would fit the description of being four brothers?'

Vijay looked at White. 'Good idea. Come on Greg. You're the historian here.'

'Not many structures built during Asoka's reign have survived,' White frowned and continued, 'Asoka built lots of things—pillars, stupas, monasteries, palaces and, of course, his edicts. None of the palaces have survived. Some of the stupas are still in existence today. It could be any one of them.'

'The riddle was meant to be interpreted after Asoka's time,' Radha said thoughtfully. 'So if the reference is to four structures, they would have to stand out in some way; unique features or special associations which could be identified by someone who was familiar with Asoka.'

'And they would have to be structures that would be virtually indestructible. At the very least, they should be capable of withstanding the ravages of time and weather,' Shukla added. 'We've seen that the Nine have been fastidious in their selection of sites and landmarks. They left very little to chance, so it is highly unlikely they would choose to compose a verse like this around structures that might disappear with time.'

'Suppose,' Vijay suggested, 'We follow the edicts once more, as urged by my uncle. The edicts seem to be the only durable things that were created by Ashoka. Are there any edicts that are somehow related to each other? Linked in some way that could lead to them being perceived as "brothers"?'

Colin produced the sheaf of papers that Vijay had distributed earlier when they had deciphered the clues on the disk. He passed them around and the group bent over the papers, studying them, searching for a clue that would help find the meaning of the riddle.

The clock ticked by as the minutes passed in silence, broken only by the rustle of papers.

Suddenly Colin gave a whoop and looked up, beaming. 'I think I've found something. Listen to this.' He read from the sheet of paper in front of him. 'The Barabar hill caves were carved out of the Barabar hills in the 3rd century BC, during the reign of Asoka the Great. These caves have one or two chambers and their interior walls are highly polished.'

Vijay involuntarily glanced at the polished rock ball at these words. Coincidence? Or was this a possibility? He rose and walked to the desk and typed out something on his laptop.

Colin continued, grinning and enjoying the attention. 'These caves were donated by Asoka to the...the,' he faltered then slowly pronounced the phonetics of the next word. 'A-j-i-v-i-k-a. Did I get that right?' He looked around. The others nodded, eager for him to complete.

He returned to the sheet. 'Asoka donated these caves to the Ajivika sect and the caves were exact copies of the wooden beehive-shaped huts that were used by monks of that time. And here's the clincher. There were four caves carved out during the reign of Asoka. The oldest cave was carved out in the 12th year of Asoka's reign.' He looked around again. 'Well, what do you think?'

'Four caves,' Vijay mused. 'Four brothers...polished walls. And we have this ball of polished rock. It may make some kind of sense. What's wrong with you?' The question was addressed to Radha, who had a curious expression on her face.

'I am so stupid.' Radha shook her head. 'I can't believe I didn't get it.'

'What do you mean?' Colin asked.

'I'm certain now that you are right about the Barabar caves being the four brothers.'

'It certainly seems plausible, but how can you be certain?' White wondered.

'Have any of you read EM Forster's book, *A Passage to India*?' No one had.

'Well, in his book, Forster describes caves with polished interior walls in a group of hills, near an imaginary town called Chandrapore. He called them the "Marabar caves." Forster's description of the Marabar caves was inspired by the Barabar caves. The similiarity in their names was more than a mere coincidence. Forster had visited the caves on one of his two visits to India and one of the central events of that book occurs in the cave.'

She paused and shook her head once again, chagrined at not having thought of this earlier.

'Now, here's the clincher, as Colin put it. One of the outstanding features of these caves, which Forster describes in his book as well, is their extraordinary echo. The caves echo!'

'*Echoes the secret of the Nine*,' White murmured, quoting the verse. 'This is almost unreal. It's like pieces of a jigsaw puzzle falling into place. Now that you've explained this, the verse really does seem to make sense.'

'It certainly does,' Vijay agreed. 'The four caves are the four brothers. They were donated by Asoka—*offered by the Emperor*. And each cave has an echo. That last line has two meanings. It sums up the purpose of the caves, to lead us to the secret of the Nine. But it also describes the one unique feature that makes the caves stand out, differentiating them from all the other structures built by Asoka.'

He had been clicking away at his laptop and he now looked at the screen. 'I googled "Barabar." The caves are around 20 kilometres from Gaya. From all accounts, it's in the boondocks of Bihar. Here's another description which says that from Bela there is a dirt track leading to the caves..'

He looked up from the laptop. 'Well, what do you think? Could the secret of the Nine really be hidden away there?'

'A likely candidate,' Colin answered immediately. 'Miles from civilisation; the last place anyone would suspect a secret to be hidden.'

'I have to say I agree with Colin,' Shukla put in.

'My vote goes to Barabar.' White raised his hand.

'I'm with them,' Radha said excitedly. 'Vijay, this has to be it.'

'Okay,' Vijay beamed at them. 'We leave for Patna tomorrow morning. I'll organise our tickets immediately.' He glanced at Shukla. 'But first, there's one thing I have to clear up. I had forgotten about it in the excitement of interpreting the verse.'

Shukla looked enquiringly at Vijay, unsure of what he was alluding to.

'The inscription on the wall in the secret chamber at Bairat,' Vijay explained. 'You said it was a book from the Mahabharata about aircraft. I didn't get it.'

'Oh, yes, of course. I was going to tell you about it when we discovered the hidden stairway.'

'You mean when *I* discovered the hidden stairway,' Colin protested with mock indignation.

Vijay made an impatient clicking sound and Colin subsided, grinning.

'The inscription on the wall was a brief summary of the *Vimana Parva*,' Shukla explained. 'Literally translated, it means the book of flying machines. But here's the strange thing. In all versions of the epic that have been handed down through the centuries, there is no mention of this book. It doesn't exist. But here it was—at least a summary of it. On the wall of a secret chamber that belonged to the Nine. Or so we believe.'

'Hang on a minute,' Colin interjected. 'I'm confused here. The Mahabharata is an epic that is hundreds of years old. So how can a book go missing?'

'I'm guessing here, but there could be a logical explanation,' Shukla replied, thoughtfully. 'The Mahabharata was documented relatively recently. The exact date isn't certain, but probably somewhere between 500 BC and 200 BC. Until then, it was transmitted orally, across generations.'

Realisation dawned on Colin. 'You mean that it could be possible that this missing book was transmitted orally down the generations but when the epic was written down, it somehow got left out?'

'Exactly. Why and how is a matter of conjecture but it certainly seems to be the most probable explanation.'

'So what does the book say? Anything about the secret of the Nine?' Vijay was impatient to unravel the meaning behind the presence of the inscription on the cavern wall.

Shukla shook his head. 'I don't know. At least, I couldn't see anything in the summary suggesting a secret that could destroy the world. The book told a story, like all the other books of the Mahabharata. The *vimana* or flying machine has several references in both the Mahabharata and the Ramayana. These flying machines are usually the chariots of the gods, or *devas*, used in battle to defeat their enemies. The *Vimana Parva* tells the story of the King of Magadha, who was allied with the Kauravas. According to the inscriptions, he secretly set out to build a fleet of *vimanas* equipped with a secret celestial weapon that would decimate the Pandava army. But the summary doesn't reveal the name or nature of the weapon of the gods that was to be employed against the Pandavas. It concludes by saying that the plans of the King came to naught because the war ended before the fleet could be completed. The Pandavas won, the King of Magadha was killed and that was the end of the plan.'

'A secret weapon that could decimate an army?' Colin was incredulous. 'That sounds a bit far-fetched, doesn't it?'

Shukla smiled. 'You must remember,' he explained, 'the epics often talked in metaphors. Several weapons in the Mahabharata are described as "celestial weapons," weapons given by the gods to the warriors who wielded them.'

'Yes,' Vijay murmured, recalling the tales his uncle had narrated to him when he was a child. 'I remember. The *Brahmastra* was one such weapon. Arjuna used it in the war.'

Shukla nodded. 'That is correct. There are many such weapons in the epic. Arjuna also released a weapon called *Mahendra*, which was given to him by Indra, the king of gods. It showered hundreds of thousands of blazing arrows upon the Kaurava army. Then, Dhristadyumna used a weapon called *Pramohana*, which deprived the Kaurava army of their senses so they fell to the ground, helpless. To counter this, Dronacharya, the guru of the Pandavas and Kauravas, released a weapon called *Prajna*.'

He looked around. 'There are more examples. When the demon, Alambush, covered the battlefield with a dense darkness, Abhimanyu countered this illusion by releasing a solar weapon that lit up the battlefield and dispelled the darkness. Another celestial weapon used by Arjuna was the *Vayavya*, which created a hurricane. And, of course, one of the most famous weapons is the *Anjalika*, which Arjuna used to kill Karna. It is described as measuring three cubits and six feet long, with the brilliance of the sun. When Arjuna put it to his bowstring, the earth trembled and sounds filled the sky. The weapon was released with the sound of thunder and severed Karna's head from his body.'

'Wow,' Colin was overwhelmed.

'Of course, none of these descriptions can be taken literally,' Shukla continued. 'The storytellers of the epic often took dramatic licence to enhance the stories and make them more interesting for listeners, in ancient times. Over the centuries, these embellishments became part of the story and it was difficult to distinguish between the original story and the enhanced versions. So, the *Vimana Parva* isn't unique. Flying machines, for example, may well have referred to swift chariots that *flew* into battle, so to speak.'

'So, why was a summary of this book inscribed on the wall of a secret chamber hidden in what may have been the library of the Nine?' Vijay wondered aloud.

Shukla shrugged. 'Perhaps this book was part of the library?'

'That's interesting,' Radha remarked. 'They must have had some reason for doing that. They must have known that this inscription would last much longer than the other texts in the library. After all, Asoka, their Emperor, was inscribing his edicts on stone as well.'

'I can't help thinking that there is some significance around the inscriptions.' Vijay frowned. 'But what can it be?'

He hoped they would find the answer at Barabar.

23

Day 7

Intelligence Bureau Headquarters, New Delhi

Imran nodded with satisfaction as he surveyed the portrait before him. Blake, who was sitting across the desk from Imran guessed correctly at the reason for his obvious pleasure.

'It's a match.'

Imran nodded, smiling now. 'It was a long shot, but it paid off.' He shook his head in disbelief. 'Sometimes I wonder if there's a force behind stuff like this. Coincidences like this just don't happen. I mean, what are the chances that we'd find that the person who kidnapped the nephew of a murdered nuclear scientist was a Pakistani nuclear scientist who appears in an Al Qaeda video and whose name is mentioned in a telephone call with a suspected assassin?'

Blake smiled. Their suspicions that Farooq Siddiqui was involved in something big in India had been confirmed. What that was, however, was still a mystery.

'So what are you going to do now?' Blake was painfully conscious that the success of his mission depended on how Imran Kidwai moved from here on. But his experience with the IB officer so far gave him confidence. The man's intuitive ability and perspicacity was admirable.

Imran grinned back at him. 'Two things; first, I've given an order to tap Vijay Singh's mobile and landline phones. If Al Qaeda and LeT are interested in him, there's got to be a reason. Second, I'm going to interview a Maharaja, Bheem Singh.'

Blake raised an eyebrow. 'You managed to pull that off?'

'We had to pull strings in the Home Ministry to get an appointment. And I have a feeling it won't go well.'

Blake grinned mischievously. 'Why do I have this feeling that you'll come out on top?'

Focused Agenda

Farooq's face darkened as he listened to the speaker on the other end of the line. The call had come through a few minutes ago and the caller had immediately launched into a critique of the operation at Bairat.

'If you'd controlled your impulses, you would have discovered the hidden chamber as well.' The speaker had an acerbic edge to his voice. 'I don't understand why you are in such a hurry to get rid of Vijay Singh and his friends. Once we've achieved our goal, I don't give a damn what you do to them. What happened at Bairat could have cost us the search if we didn't have our backup plan in place.'

Farooq listened but said nothing, restraining an impulse to respond, as the caller continued. 'So far, we've been getting publicity that we can do without. But we don't seem to be any closer to our goal. We really can't afford to miss out on any information that might help us. And, don't forget, the deadline for the announcement is near. We don't have time for games.'

Farooq decided that it didn't make sense to try and justify his actions. And there was a modicum of truth in what was being told. He had missed out on getting his hands on vital information at Bairat. He admitted that some part of him was guided by a personal agenda. He was still smarting at having been outwitted, more than once, by Vijay. He wanted to strike back. But he couldn't allow his own emotions to get in the way. He wanted the mission to succeed as much as anyone else. There was too much at stake for things to go wrong. 'We'll get there,' he promised. 'No more diversions or distractions.'

'I'm glad to hear that. You know the consequences of failure.'

The caller hung up. Farooq stared at the telephone receiver in frustration.

There was a knock on the door and Murphy entered, unbidden.

Farooq glared at him. He didn't like Murphy. Somehow, the American had managed to upstage him in this project. And Farooq didn't like being upstaged.

'What do you want?'

'I've been asked to work directly with you. Support you from here on.'

Farooq scowled, his displeasure showing.

'It's better in a way,' Murphy said, reading Farooq's emotions. 'We communicate directly. It's more accurate. Saves time. And don't worry, I'm here to help. I won't get in your way.'

'And you think you can help?'

Murphy shrugged. 'I think you guys have it all wrong.'

'Now you're trying to teach us?'

'No. I think you guys are experts at what you do. No one can beat you at causing terror. But this one's not up your street.'

'And you think you know better?'

'This is what I do for a living.'

'So what's your solution then?' It was a challenge.

'I've been told we have very little time to go before the declaration. Once that happens, the countdown begins. We have to find what we seek. There is no room for failure.' Murphy paused, seeking the words to explain. 'Rethink your strategy. You've tried force. But what have you achieved?'

Farooq was silent.

'Exactly. Now, what if you abandon all efforts to try and force the secret out of them?'

'We can't afford to sit back and relax.'

'That's not what I meant. Look, let's face it. You couldn't decipher the mails. They did. You've now got a new riddle from Bairat. And they have found a ball of rock from the secret chamber. How are you going to unravel those clues?'

Farooq understood. 'You're right. They're good at this game. They have reached this far and will go further. All we need to do is follow them. And they will take us to our goal.'

Murphy smiled.

Farooq nodded. 'Fine. We'll leave them alone. Let them lead us to the secret. And I know exactly when we should step in and take control.'

Murphy leaned forward, interested. 'How would you know that?'

Farooq grinned maliciously. 'Let's just say that I learned from what happened at Bairat.'

A Royal Rebuff

Imran sat in the ornately furnished study and glanced around. He looked admiringly at the mahogany desk, at the quill pen in its crystal holder and the crystal inkpot at its side. The walls of the study were lined with bookcases from top to bottom. The Maharaja seemed to be an avid reader.

The door of the study opened and the Maharaja entered; imposing in his dark grey Nehru jacket with gleaming black brogues.

'Your Highness—,' Imran began, getting to his feet, but was cut off almost immediately by Bheem Singh.

'I know why you're here. The Home Minister briefed me.'

Yeah, like he reports to you.

Imran suppressed a snigger at the Maharaja's arrogance.

Bheem Singh rounded the mahogany desk and sat down in the luxurious leather chair behind it. No invitation was extended to Imran to sit down.

'That's great,' Imran responded, sitting down anyway. He was damned if he was going to stand and interview this man! He may be a former Maharaja and prominent politician, but Imran wasn't going to let him have the upper hand in this conversation. 'Then we can get straight to the point.'

Bheem Singh said nothing, but folded his arms across his chest, as if waiting for Imran to continue.

'We are investigating a man named Farooq Siddiqui and his activities in India,' Imran began cautiously, looking for a reaction. There was none. 'I believe that you insisted that a case be filed against this man for kidnapping one Vijay Singh from Jaungarh.'

'I insisted that a case be filed against a man named *Farooq*,' Bheem Singh corrected him. 'I know nothing of a man with the surname of Siddiqui.'

'Thank you. Can I ask what your interest in this matter is?'

'I don't think that's any of your business.'

Imran was taken aback.

'I'm sorry, your Highness, but we're investigating this case and we need to have answers to all our questions. How do you know Vijay Singh?'

'Vijay is the nephew of Vikram Singh, who was also from a royal family. Vikram and I moved in the same circles. I don't know Vijay, but I had gone to pay him my condolences on his uncle's death, when the SHO of Jaungarh police station paid us a visit. He was refusing to investigate the case and I simply insisted that he should do his job. Are you going to arrest me for that?'

Imran took a deep breath. This was going to be tougher than he had thought.

'No, your Highness, I didn't mean any offence.'

'Well, then, if that's all, I have to be going. The American Vice President is in town, as you probably know, and he's scheduled to visit me tomorrow.' Bheem Singh stood up.

Imran steeled himself for what was to come. 'Your Highness. I have just one more question.'

The Maharaja sat down grumpily and looked at his oversized Rolex watch.

'I'll be quick,' Imran assured him. 'We also received reports that the Gurgaon police were being pressurised by the office of the Haryana Chief Secretary to close the case as unsolved.'

He watched Bheem Singh carefully. Again, there was no reaction. Imran thought, either the Maharaja genuinely knew nothing about this case or he was a very good actor.

'Do you have any comment on that, sir?'

Bheem Singh placed his palms flat on his desk and leaned forward. 'I am a busy man,' he boomed. 'I didn't give you an appointment for you to waste my time with frivolous questions. If that is all you need to ask me, then I have nothing to say and you can leave now.'

It was meant as a dismissal, but Imran didn't move. He looked straight at Bheem Singh and continued talking.

'Your Highness, this is a matter of national security. We have, just a few hours ago, positively identified the man Farooq, who kidnapped Vijay Singh, as Farooq Siddiqui, a missing Pakistani nuclear scientist, who has conclusively been linked to Lashkar-e-Taiba.'

Bheem Singh's face registered surprise.

'So, your Highness,' Imran pressed home his advantage, 'I need you to answer my question.'

Bheem Singh sat back in his chair and studied Imran. 'I have no comment,' he said finally, his face passive again. 'How would I know what is happening in Haryana or Gurgaon? I have no constituency there.'

Imran took another deep breath. 'Perhaps, then, you will help me understand why the Haryana Chief Secretary's office claims that you are the one who has pressurised them to withdraw or close the case against Farooq Siddiqui?'

A succession of emotions flitted across Bheem Singh's face—shock, followed by confusion, which gave way to anger.

'What are you insinuating?' he thundered. 'Are you out of your mind? I hope you have evidence to substantiate your wild allegations! I will report you to the Home Minister. How dare you barge into my office, my home, and accuse me of something like this?'

He recovered his composure somewhat and stood up. 'You have no idea what you are dealing with. I am involved in a top secret government project. If you want details, go ask your boss. This interview is over.'

Without another word or glance at Imran, he stalked out of the room. After a few moments, two tall, well-built security guards entered the office.

Imran sighed. 'I was just leaving,' he told them, and they followed him out.

24

Day 7

Intelligence Bureau Headquarters, New Delhi

Imran sat in Vaid's office, across the desk from the Director, a sullen and defiant look on his face. Vaid looked both perplexed and angry.

'What were you thinking?' he demanded of Imran. 'Alleging that Bheem Singh was trying to suppress the investigation into the kidnapping case? You promised me that you wouldn't try and pull any stunts. Do you know the bollocking I got from the Home Minister?'

Imran stared back, unrepentant. 'Well, it's true. I got that from a reliable source in the office of the Chief Secretary of Haryana.'

Vaid leaned forward to emphasise his words. 'But you didn't get that as an official statement from the Chief Secretary, did you?'

'I know it is a hunch, sir, but I believe I am right,' Imran's gaze didn't waver. 'I think we need to tap Bheem Singh's phones. He claims to be involved in a top secret project, but how is it that the Home Ministry doesn't know about it? How come *we* don't know about it?'

Vaid shook his head firmly. 'The answer is no. After what happened today, there's no way I'm going to the Home Minister with a request to tap Bheem Singh's phones.'

Imran was prepared for this. He had spent some time planning this conversation..

'Well, then, sir, I'm going to ask you to get me included as part of the security detail for Steve Buckworth, when he visits Bheem Singh tomorrow.'

Vaid stared at Imran as if he had lost his mind. Curiosity kept him from rejecting this request outright. 'The US Vice President? And what will you gain by that?'

'Sir, we can't get an official search warrant on Bheem Singh. And I know I won't be allowed into that farmhouse after today. But, if I am officially assigned to Buckworth's security team, they can't stop me from getting in. While the VP meets Bheem Singh, I plan to slip away discreetly and conduct a search of the premises. I want to come back with evidence to back my hunch.'

Vaid sighed. He knew that Imran was perceptive and highly intuitive and had cracked several cases in the past, going purely by his instinct.

But that had been a different world. They had hunted down criminals. This was bigger. And potentially more explosive. They were not dealing with a petty criminal here. Imran had a former Maharaja in his sights, who was also a prominent politician with immense clout in the ruling political party. The fallout, if he was wrong, could destroy both men.

'I've done some homework before coming to you,' Imran was speaking again. He placed a dossier on the desk and flipped through the pages until he found what he was looking for. 'You know why Buckworth is meeting Bheem Singh.'

Vaid decided to play along. 'Bheem Singh put together a consortium through his business contacts across the world and the business they created in the US generated a 1,00,000 jobs in the last six months. The American VP, since he is in India on an official visit to push the aircraft carrier deal, is going to convey the American President's gratitude and appreciation for this job creation at a time when there is a recession and high unemployment in the US.'

'Correct.' Imran smiled. 'At least that is the official story.'

Vaid waited. He knew Imran was going to throw his punch now.

'Perhaps this is the true reason for their meeting,' Imran continued. 'But then, what reason would Buckworth have had for meeting Bheem Singh on earlier occasions?'

Vaid looked surprised. 'They've met earlier?'

'Several times.' Imran glanced at the sheet in the dossier. 'They've been meeting regularly since 2004, when the VP was a Senator. Different places each time. But they've met at least 15 times since then, including a meeting earlier this year; approximately twice a year, all low-profile meetings.'

'They could have been discussing Bheem Singh's business prospects in the US,' Vaid argued.

'Perhaps. But it wasn't a one-on-one meeting every time. On several occasions they were joined by others; Xen Haojing. Jacques Deaubois. Jeremy Martin. One or more of these others were also present at some of the meetings. Sometimes all of them were there.'

Vaid recognised the names. These were prominent politicians with very public aspirations to lead their respective countries; China, France and the UK. It was also no secret that Buckworth was going to run for President once the incumbent's term came to an end. It didn't make sense. What would prompt these men to meet so often over a period of nine years? And why hadn't any of these meetings caught the attention of the media?

'There's more.' Imran tapped the dossier. 'During many of these meetings, a European businessman was also present. Christian Van Klueck.' He paused to see if Vaid showed any recognition of the name.

He did. 'The Austrian businessman?'

Imran nodded. 'And Van Klueck is also part of the consortium that has invested in the US and created all these jobs that Buckworth is going to thank Bheem Singh for.'

Vaid looked puzzled. 'It certainly isn't possible that the consortium investment was planned nine years ago. All the publicity and hype around the job creation, talks about the investment being planned after the recession struck.'

'Exactly. So what were these guys meeting for, almost twice a year, for the last nine years? Five politicians and a businessman. If you don't count the fact that Bheem Singh is also a businessman. And look at the venues for the meetings; Estonia, Italy, Greece, Turkey, Poland, Slovakia, South Africa, Vietnam, Sri Lanka. All countries other than their own. No press releases to the media. No entourages. Almost as if they didn't want anyone to know they were meeting.'

'So you think that there is more to this meeting tomorrow, between Buckworth and Bheem Singh, than has been officially announced?' Vaid began to see where Imran was going with his logic.

'I think so. This is a one-on-one meeting between Bheem Singh and Buckworth. No delegation accompanying the VP or joining Bheem Singh A meeting to convey thanks from the US, would normally be accompanied by much more publicity, invitations to the press, a large delegation on both sides and all the frills. Why is none of that happening?'

'So what do you think they are meeting for?'

'I don't have a theory about that, yet,' Imran admitted to his boss. 'Like I said, it's just a hunch that something more is cooking.'

Vaid sighed. 'Fine. But you're going out on a limb on this one, Kidwai. I'll get you into the farmhouse. But I'm not getting the Home Minister involved in this. Not without a better reason than a hunch of yours. Once you're in the farmhouse, you're on your own. If you're wrong about this, just make sure that you don't mess up there. If something goes wrong, I won't cover you. Not this time. Is that understood?'

Imran nodded. 'Got it. But I'll find something. I can feel it in my bones.'

Right On Track

'So that's the plan,' Farooq said to Murphy. 'We won't move in until you give us the signal. And you'll lie low after that, until we reach the final phase of the plan.'

Murphy looked thoughtful. 'Seems like a good plan. The only problem I can see is if they find more clues at Barabar and the search goes on. We are now running against time.'

'I don't think this trail goes on for much longer,' Farooq sounded confident. 'We are going to where the Magadha Empire sprang from, where Asoka had his Capital. The location where the secret is hidden can't be too far. The description by Surasen, the man who first discovered the cavern 2,000 years ago, mentions a 10-day journey from the Capital of the empire.

We are close to finding it now. And I think our plan will ensure that they work to our deadlines.'

'Very well.' Murphy rose. 'You'd better not mess this one up. They aren't happy with you, I can tell you that.'

Farooq didn't reply. The secret of the Nine was within his grasp. And he would ensure that it did not elude him.

25

Day 8

The Patna-Gaya Highway, Bihar

Colin looked out of the window of the Nissan X Trail they had hired at Patna, the Capital city of the state of Bihar. They had decided to set up base at the Asoka Palace Hotel in Patna after arriving earlier in the morning. Two hours ago, they had left Patna and were now driving down to Gaya.

'One kilometre to Bela,' he announced as they passed a milestone. He glanced at the roadmap of Bihar that lay open on his lap. 'From Bela, we turn right, off the highway.'

'I'll be glad to reach the place.' Vijay shifted in his seat as he drove. Colin was in the passenger seat next to him, while Radha, Shukla and White were in the backseat of the X Trail. The drive had been tiring. The road was a two-lane highway and in poor shape. With alarming frequency, it would degenerate into a mass of potholes and cracks, making it difficult to maintain a good speed. Even when they did manage to speed up, Vijay often had to slow down as they passed through villages that would keep popping up on either side of the highway. Occasionally, they would have to stop for a tractor-trailer or bullock cart that emerged from the dirt paths that snaked away from the road and through fields on either side.

A signboard announced that they had reached the town of Bela and the car slowed down to a crawl as Vijay manoeuvred through the mass of bicycles, push carts, bullock carts, cycle rickshaws and motorcycles that thronged the road.

Cows and stray dogs mixed freely with the traffic and people and Vijay had to use the vehicle's horn liberally. He popped his head out of the window and hailed a hawker selling bangles.

'Where do we turn for Barabar?'

Though the question was aimed at the hawker, four men standing nearby gathered around the car, and began arguing about the best way to reach Barabar.

Vijay waited, patiently, as they discussed the merits of each route.

Finally, one of the men gave him directions, nodding his head all the time as if to reassure Vijay about the accuracy of his advice.

Vijay drove off only to stop a few metres ahead to validate the directions he had been given.

Relieved to find that they had been guided correctly, he followed the directions and they soon found themselves on the road to Barabar.

The road from here was rough and bumpy; mostly potholes and dirt. They had been warned, at Patna, about the state of the road beyond Bela, which had led them to rent the X Trail.

Forty-five minutes later, jolted and shaken by the ride, they arrived at the site of the caves. The landscape was bleak and barren; desolate scrubland with large rocks and boulders strewn around as if thrown there in anger by the hand of a giant. Clumps of straggling trees dotted the scene which was dominated by the hill.

Even as they approached, they realised that *Barabar Hill* was a misnomer.

The hill was more a huge black rock, not more than 30 feet in height. It rose from the ground like the back of a whale protruding from the ocean. The rock was bereft of any vegetation.

Vijay brought the vehicle to a halt at the foot of the rock.

They alighted and gazed at the desolation around them. Radha shivered. 'I can see why people are advised not to venture here alone,' she remarked, looking around.

White waved an arm at the rock-strewn landscape. 'Most people are probably unaware that this site has an association with Asoka the Great. Considering that it is one of the oldest surviving structures built during Asoka's reign, it shouldn't be so deserted.'

Vijay hauled out his black leather bag from the car and pulled out a sheaf of papers.

'According to this commentary,' he referred to the papers, 'The oldest cave is the *Sudama* cave. It lies on the south face of the rock. Going by the verse, *Sudama* will be the eldest of the four brothers. That's the one we need to check.'

Heaving the strap of the bag onto his shoulder, he started off for the southern rock face with Colin by his side. The others followed slowly with Shukla, who couldn't keep pace with the two friends.

They reached the southern face of the rock and began walking along the black rock wall.

'Just think,' Colin said, 'we are in some ways retracing the footsteps of a legendary Indian king who lived 2,300 years ago. I can't believe that I'm walking the same path that he'd have trodden. This is the great thing about India. Everywhere you go there's centuries of history, sometimes thousands of years of heritage. It's awesome!'

Vijay nodded. 'Yes,' he agreed, 'I had never thought of it that way.'

Suddenly, Colin grabbed his arm and pointed. Just ahead of them, cut into the black rock wall was a rectangular opening.

Vijay and Colin stood before the doorway, staring at the darkness beyond the entrance. Was this the culmination of their journey?

Vijay reached into the bag and pulled out two portable lamps. He handed one to Colin. The twin beams cut through the darkness that filled the interior of the cave, but revealed nothing.

Cautiously, Vijay stepped through the entrance, shining his lamplight all around him.

To his great surprise, he found the light reflecting off the walls. No matter where he trained the lamp, the beam of light shone back at him.

The cave was empty.

'Wow!' Colin whispered in awe, joining Vijay and experiencing the same effect. 'This is amazing!'

'It is remarkable,' Vijay agreed.

The artisans who worked in this cave had chiselled the inner walls to a high degree of polish, such that they were like mirrors. They had retained their glassy appearance even today, 2,300 years after they had been built.

The two friends gazed around the cave in awe. A shout made them jump; the echo rolled around the cave, the sound bouncing off from wall to wall, as effortlessly as the light reflected off them.

The others had joined them and Radha had chosen that moment to test the echo.

Vijay scowled at Radha, who was grinning from ear to ear.

'Why did you have to do that?' he complained. 'You scared me out of my skin.'

'You certainly did,' Colin agreed. 'That wasn't funny, sneaking up on us like that.'

'I've always wanted to do that.' Radha was still smiling broadly. 'After reading Forster's book and learning about these caves, I never believed that I'd be standing in one of them and experiencing the echo first-hand.'

'This is amazing.' White was looking around in wonder. 'Let's split up,' Vijay suggested. 'Radha and I will explore this side of the cave. Colin, you can team up with Greg and Dr. Shukla and check out the far side.'

With nods of agreement, the group split up.

'What exactly are we looking for?' Colin shouted across the cave at Vijay, momentarily forgetting to whisper. Immediately, they were surrounded by a volley of echoes, as each word repeatedly reverberated around the cave, the echoes overlapping with each other to produce an astounding effect.

Vijay walked over to the other group. 'Inscriptions,' he whispered.

'Well, then,' Colin whispered back, 'you've got your hands full. This wall's full of inscriptions.'

He shone the beam, at an angle, on the wall and immediately a mass of inscriptions jumped out at them. Line upon line of symbols etched into the stone, some etched over other symbols, sprang to life. Vijay gazed at the inscriptions in bewilderment.

'This can't be what we're looking for,' White said softly.

'Doesn't seem likely,' Shukla agreed. 'Some of these are in the Brahmi script, which is the one used for Asoka's edicts, and others are probably from a later era. Most likely, the inscriptions that have overwritten the earlier ones are from the Gupta dynasty, which flourished in this region in the fifth century AD.'

Vijay strode back to Radha and shone his lamp on the wall, at an angle. This wall, too, was covered with inscriptions. He quickly updated Radha on the conclusion the other group had reached.

Just then, there was a loud whoop from Colin and once again a medley of echoes filled the cave, melting into one another, a harmony of sounds as his whoop reverberated around the cave.

Shaking his head in mock frustration, Vijay grabbed Radha by her hand and they walked over to join Colin, who was now examining the rear of the cave.

'Sorry,' Colin grinned sheepishly as they regrouped around him. 'I keep forgetting about the echo. But look at this.'

He trained his lamp on the rock wall that formed the rear of the cave, revealing a doorway four feet high, in the form of an inverted U.

'Okay,' Vijay indicated the opening with a grin. 'You discovered it. You go first.'

'And get eaten by the protectors of the treasure or whatever monster guards the secret of the Nine? Have you watched "The Mummy"? No way!'

Sighing, Vijay bent and entered the doorway. It was the entrance to a small tunnel. In the light of the lamp, he could see that even the walls of the tunnel were as smooth as glass and reflected the light at him.

After a few feet of stooping and walking through the passage, he emerged into a chamber. While the outer cave was larger and had a barrel vaulted roof, the inner chamber in which he now stood had a roof that was hollow and semi-spherical.

The chamber was empty.

He shone the light back through the doorway and called out to the others. 'Come on in. It's alright.'

He noticed that this chamber didn't have an echo.

The rest of the group emerged from the tunnel. As they regrouped they found Vijay staring at the wall opposite the entrance.

'You've found something,' White observed as they came up to him.

'Yes,' Vijay answered. 'Do you notice anything about these walls that set them apart from the walls of the outer cave?'

White squinted at the wall. 'No inscriptions?'

'Exactly.' Vijay shone the light on the walls on either side of them and the wall behind them. 'None of these walls have inscriptions; except for this one.' He trained the lamp on the wall opposite the entrance and it jumped out at them.

A nine-spoked wheel. The symbol of the Nine.

They looked at each other. Whatever they were seeking, it was hidden in this inner chamber. All they had to do was locate it.

The Ominous Threat

'We've contained the media and they've agreed to cooperate... for now,' Imran reported.

Vaid stared back at him and rubbed his eyes as he stifled a yawn. The two men had been up since a little past midnight. He nodded. 'Good work. But we still need to monitor them. There's no saying when some journalist will decide that this is a career-boosting opportunity for him or her, and we can't afford any loose cannons right now.'

'We're on it. I've got men in the studios and offices of every major television channel and media network that received the email. A couple of television channels played hard to get initially, but fell in line when we told them a few things we knew about them.'

'I don't want to know what you threatened them with.' The shadow of a smile creased Vaid's face. He had seen Imran stretch the boundaries on previous occasions.

'Oh, I didn't threaten them,' Imran grinned. 'I gave them, you know, friendly advice. Just so I was sure they wouldn't put this on air the moment my back was turned.'

Vaid glanced at his watch. 'Time for my meeting with the Home Minister. I'll let him know that things are under control.' He looked pointedly at Imran. 'Are you sure you want to continue with your plan? This threat takes top priority. And your hunch about Bheem Singh has nothing to do with the threat. Remember, it's still a hunch.'

Imran nodded. 'I won't get another opportunity like this to get in there. Don't worry, it won't take long. I'll just take a look around and get out of there. It should not take me more than half an hour.'

'Keep me posted.' Vaid left the room and Imran followed him out.

As he walked down the corridor to his office, Imran's thoughts turned to the mysterious email they had received at midnight. It had been sent to 10 major news networks, both electronic and print media. But what perplexed him wasn't the source or the intention of the email. Both were very clear, surprisingly, for a terror threat.

He opened the door of his office and gave a start. Blake was sitting there waiting, his face haggard and worried. He, too, had been up since midnight, working with his colleagues in the CIA and with other government agencies in countries where similar threats had been received.

'We were wrong about all of this. We should have seen it coming. We saw the video clip,' said Blake as he settled down with some coffee.

Imran shrugged. 'There was no way we could have guessed. And don't forget, the video clip wasn't about LeT. It was about Al Zawahiri and Al Qaeda. What's the final word on the threat?'

'Twenty countries.' Blake looked at Imran significantly. 'All belonging to the G20. But we've managed to put the lid on the news in all 20. The media, for once, have behaved themselves.'

'And the message is the same?'

'Broadly the same with some variations. The common theme is the attack on the G20 economic summit in three months' time in Washington DC, which will be attended by all the G20 heads of state. And then, each mail goes on to list selected targets in each country that will be attacked on a specific date; like the targets identified in India in the mail sent to your media—nuclear installations, airforce bases, oil refineries, power plants. If you put them all together, there will be four attacks every day for a period of 10 days after the attack on the G20 summit. The intention is clear. Bring down the governments of the G20 member countries by killing their leaders at the summit, and then cripple their economies.'

Imran pursed his lips thoughtfully. 'That's quite evident. Look what they say in the email we received. And I presume this is common to all the twenty messages. If the G20 summit is called off as a result of this threat, *they will attack every single G20 member nation individually and destroy the seat of government in each country*. There's no mistaking their objective—they're targeting the governments. It's an ambitious plan. Plunge the world into chaos and precipitate a global political and military crisis.'

Blake nodded. 'This will make 9/11 look like child's play. And it will catapult LeT into the big league, right up there with Al Qaeda. So far, we've always viewed them as having a narrow focus on Kashmir. Only recently has the CIA begun to recognise that their ambitions are more global. But I don't see how they plan to pull it off.'

'That's exactly what I was wondering. Firstly, LeT doesn't have the kind of muscle that Al Qaeda has. Where would they get the kind of funding and resources required for an operation like this? Secondly, what's the point of publicising a terror attack so far ahead? They've literally given a time table for each target. Where's the element of surprise? Forget about the individual governments, how are they going to attack the G20 summit when security is obviously going to be beefed up after this?'

'Beats me,' Blake agreed. 'The US will be on high alert. The USAF and Navy will step up their patrols around the east coast, right away, and until the summit is over. And every government in the G20 is going to be on high alert as well.'

He frowned. 'Why issue this threat three months in advance? I don't get it either.'

'There's something else I don't understand.' Imran's face creased with thought. 'What does LeT achieve by destabilising these 20 countries? As a terrorist group, they achieve more by creating an atmosphere of uncertainty. But they aren't anarchists. So what exactly are they after?'

The same thought struck both men almost simultaneously. 'Good Lord,' Blake said quietly. 'The unknown partner of LeT. The ones who sent Murphy to India to work with Farooq Siddiqui.'

Imran nodded numbly. 'Yes. It ties in neatly with the Murphy tap and the video clip. But what is it that Farooq is doing in India that will help them execute this plan?'

The two men stared at each other, unable to unravel the riddle. One thing was clear to both. They had to find Farooq. And fast.

There was just one problem. They didn't know where he was.

26

Day 8

The Barabar Caves

'We found it.' Radha could hardly contain her excitement. She walked up to the sign and studied the wall in the light of the lamps. There was a hole in the wall, a perfect circle, approximately one foot below the nine-spoked wheel. She hesitated for a minute then shoved her arm into the opening.

'What are you doing?' Vijay was horrified. 'There may be a trap inside.'

Radha pursed her lips and shook her head as she withdrew her hand. 'Nothing there. It's empty.' She grinned sheepishly at Vijay and Colin, both of whom wore expressions of shock.

'That was silly,' Colin remarked. 'Hey, what's this?' He swung his lamp lower and trained it on another section of the wall below the hole.

There was a second, perfectly round, hole visible in the rock wall, one foot above the ground and slightly to the left of the hole above.

'Now don't go sticking your foot into that one,' Colin grinned at Radha.

White frowned. 'Why would they leave two holes in the wall? If something had been hidden away in either hole, it would have been taken out long ago.'

They stared at each other, puzzled, their hopes sinking. Had they come all this way to find a dead end? Was this the end of the trail?

'In the movies,' Colin said slowly, 'putting your hand into one of the holes would have triggered a lever that would have opened a section of the rock wall, revealing another hidden cave. Of course, in the movies, you also tend to lose the part of your hand that goes into the hole.' He grinned. 'But Radha's already tested that for us, hasn't she? And she's still got her hand.'

Radha slapped his shoulder lightly in mock exasperation. 'Your Hollywood fixation,' she muttered. 'This cave is from ancient India, not a Hollywood set.'

Colin grinned back at her, unfazed.

A thought suddenly struck Vijay. He passed his lamp to White and took something out of his bag. As he brought it into the light of the lamp, the highly polished spherical rock in his hand gleamed, reflecting the light and lighting up the chamber with an eerie glow. It was the rock ball they had found in the secret chamber at Bairat. He had been convinced that it had a purpose, though he wasn't clear what it was, and had carried it along, just in case. It was only now that he realised that the appearance of the rock ball matched the polished surface of the cave.

'Do you think that's from here?' White wondered.

'Looks like it, doesn't it?' Vijay held the ball, trying to work out what they should do with it.

'Here, let me try.' Radha took the ball from him and carried it to the wall, her forehead creased in thought. The others watched her, guessing what she was going to do. She slowly inserted the ball into the hole just below the wheel carved into the wall. It rested there, fitting perfectly.

Radha then gently pushed the ball into the hole.

With a rumbling sound, of stone grating against stone, the ball disappeared into the blackness of the hole. There was a loud click, as if the ball had hit the back of the hole, but instead of stopping, the rumbling grew in intensity and became louder.

As they looked on, wondering, the grating noise of the ball rolling within the wall rose to a crescendo. Suddenly, the ball shot out of the lower hole and landed on the floor of the cave, rolling to a stop a few feet away from the wall.

For a few moments they stared at the ball as it lay there, unmoving.

Colin shook his head. 'A chute for a ball of rock. Now I've seen everything!'

'This doesn't make sense,' Vijay agreed. 'There's obviously a tunnel within the wall connecting both the holes. But why?' He trained his lamp on the ball of rock. The light glanced off the rock, almost as if the rock was challenging them to unearth the secret it concealed.

'Wait a minute.' Shukla bent down and picked up the ball, turning it around in his hands to get a better look. 'There's an inscription on the ball. Where did that come from?' He looked at Vijay. 'It didn't have an inscription when we got it from Bairat, did it?'

'I'm sure it didn't,' Vijay asserted.

'Then it's not the same ball.'

For a few moments, they digested this.

Then Radha spoke. 'If it isn't the same ball, then there must have been another ball hidden in the tunnel, with this inscription on it. When I rolled the first ball into the tunnel through the upper hole, it dislodged the hidden ball, but got trapped itself within the tunnel somehow. And the hidden ball was ejected through the lower hole.'

'Ingenious,' White raised his eyebrows. 'You'd never discover the second ball if you didn't have the first one.'

'Like the rest of the puzzle the Nine created,' Shukla commented.

'What does the inscription say?' Colin wanted to know.

'It's the riddle,' Shukla answered. 'The fourth part of the puzzle. We've got the metal disk, the key, the ball of rock. All that was missing was the verse that is inscribed here.' He read out the verse.

> From the chambers that echo
> As we lift our eyes to the south
> To the harbinger of the Lord's birth
> In a dream
> Passing over the Mother
> Who lies amidst the forests green, reposing,
> Holding within her bosom,
> Hidden for Millennia
> The Secret of the Nine.

'That's just great.' Colin's voice betrayed his exasperation. 'What does it mean?'

Shukla shrugged. 'This is the final clue. We know that from Beger's diary, from the texts he copied that spoke of the Nine and their puzzle. And this is the first time the secret of the Nine has been explicitly mentioned. But I haven't the slightest idea what it means.'

'All I can figure out is that the secret lies in a forest,' Colin remarked. 'But who is the Mother? If we can work that out, we'll find it.'

'There's a lot of forest area in India,' Vijay scratched his head. 'Why don't we drive back to Patna and see if we can work this out?'

The others agreed.

Bright sunshine greeted them outside. The sun was still high in the sky and the brightness outside the cave hurt their eyes after the dark interiors they had left behind.

Wordlessly, they walked back to the X Trail. Vijay climbed into the driver's seat and started the long drive back to Patna.

Dangerous Discoveries

Imran shifted nervously in his seat, as the motorcade accompanying the Vice President of the United States of America made its way through the grand main gates of Bheem Singh's farmhouse. Yesterday's visit was fresh in his mind and he hoped that he wouldn't bump into the Maharaja. The commandant of the commandos, who formed the Indian section of the Vice President's security force, looked at Imran sourly. He hadn't been told why Imran was part of this team; only that one of his men had to be pulled out at the last minute to accommodate this special request from the Home Ministry. While he was unhappy about Imran's presence, he was curious about it. What was worse, he had been instructed to allow Imran to detach himself from the security team once they were in the farmhouse; to allow him to carry out his mission. What that mission was, of course, hadn't been disclosed.

The motorcade came to a halt. Three vehicles ahead, Imran saw Steve Buckworth alight from his limousine and greet the familiar figure of Bheem Singh. Both men disappeared inside the farmhouse, closely dogged by the US Secret Service agents.

'Ok, everyone out,' the commandant barked. They had orders to secure the farmhouse, but were not supposed to enter.

Imran took a deep breath and stepped out of the van. 'Thank you, sir,' he nodded to the commandant. 'This is where I leave your team.'

The commandant nodded back curtly and Imran headed off in the opposite direction. There was no way the US agents would allow him to follow Buckworth and Bheem Singh through the front door. He would have to scout around and find another way into the farmhouse.

This was easier said than done, he realised. The place was a virtual fortress, swarming with black clad guards, Bheem Singh's personal security force. Imran's blue camouflage uniform, the same as that of the commandos, identified him as part of the security team, so he wasn't stopped. But more than once, the security guards he passed flashed him questioning glances, though no one challenged him.

As he rounded the corner of the house, he noticed an open window with no grills. He looked around quickly. Unencumbered by an assault rifle, unlike the other commandos, he found it easy to vault over the low window sill and into an ornately furnished study. He adjusted the Glock in a holster at his waist, the only weapon he carried, and looked around.

It was the study; the same room where he had interviewed the Maharaja.

He glided to the door of the study and opened it a crack to look up and down the corridor. It was deserted. He stepped into the passage.

Which way should he go? He quickly made a choice and turned to his right. Where would Bheem Singh keep his secrets? Definitely not in the study or the rooms here; they were too accessible, too public. Large paintings by Indian and international artists hung on the walls of the passage and each doorway leading off the corridor was framed by antique-looking sculptures of stone and metal on ornate pedestals. The corridor ended in another passage perpendicular to it. Imran turned left and a short walk brought him to a stairway going downstairs.

A basement! Imran decided it was worth exploring.

Cautiously, he made his way down the stairs. As he descended, he realised that the stairway wasn't lit up. Neither was the basement. He cursed. The light from the corridor above barely reached this level, creating a murky gloom. He wished he had thought of bringing a torch with him.

As his eyes adjusted to the darkness, he realised that the basement extended in one direction, to his right, as the stairway ended. To his left was a wall. He made his way slowly down the corridor, discerning three doorways. He tried the doors to his left and right but both were locked. That left only the door that was directly before him.

He turned the handle. The door opened silently. He realised he had been holding his breath, and exhaled with relief. For a few moments, he stood still and let his eyes adjust to the deeper gloom within the room.

It seemed to be some sort of conference room. A semi-circular table occupied the space before him, with a few chairs around it. Beyond the table seemed to be a wall.

But he didn't have time to wonder. Voices floated down the stairway and he realised, with a shock that they were heading straight for this room.

A quick look around the room showed him that there were few places to hide. His best bet seemed to be under a small desk that stood in one corner of the room, next to the doorway.

Just as he squeezed himself into his hiding place, the lights came on and he heard Bheem Singh say, 'And this is where we'll speak to him from.'

Buckworth whistled. 'A telepresence room. Great idea! But what about the possibility of someone tapping into the lines?'

'You don't suppose I own a software company for nothing?' Bheem Singh's supercilious voice came to Imran. 'We've developed software that scrambles the signals both ways. Even if someone was to tap into it, they'd never be able to figure out what we were saying.'

'Impressive. So he's waiting for us to call him?'

'Yes. Everything's ready, I just need to dial in. Make yourself comfortable.'

Imran heard the notes of a touchtone phone as a number was dialled. He heard the telephone on the other end of the line ring. It was picked up immediately.

'Good evening, gentlemen.' A crisp voice said with a decidedly European accent.

Imran cautiously peered over the rim of the desk. What had seemed to be a wall beyond the semi-circular conference table was actually a bank of screens, arranged to form a composite screen on which a mirror image of the conference room was displayed. In one of the chairs, gazing out from the screen, was a tall, distinguished man with a high forehead, aquiline nose and silver grey hair, his grey eyes framed by rimless spectacles.

Imran sucked in his breath.

Christian Van Klueck.

The Austrian businessman, who had been present at earlier meetings between Buckworth and Bheem Singh.

Imran quickly ducked back under the table. If Van Klueck could see into this room, chances were he may notice Imran peeping out from behind the desk.

'Hey Christian.' Only Buckworth responded.

'I'm not happy getting into a conference like this.' Van Klueck got straight to the point. 'We are taking a big chance.'

'I don't like it either,' Buckworth replied, pugnaciously, 'but I managed to find a good reason to be here. If you had better control over your partners, we wouldn't need to meet like this.'

'Calm down, both of you,' Bheem Singh broke in, seemingly trying to defuse what sounded like a tense situation.

But Imran's ears had pricked up at Buckworth's words. 'It's true,' Buckworth persisted, though his tone was noticeably less aggressive now. 'They had no business issuing that threat when we are so close to accomplishing the mission. It can screw everything up. Do you know how much work we had to put in for damage control? And your government too. And all the governments that got their blasted message.'

Imran broke out in a cold sweat. Was he hearing right? Was this even possible?

'It doesn't matter.' Van Klueck still seemed miffed. 'Our plans are not affected by the announcement. We are on course. Bheem Singh has everything under control.'

'Of course,' Bheem Singh affirmed immediately. 'I got a confirmation today that the last clue has been found. They would have returned to Patna by now. Farooq is already in Patna. I've given them the word to take Vijay and the woman hostage. Once they solve this final clue, we'll know exactly where the secret is located. I think we should be through with this phase of the plan in a week from now.'

'That's great,' Buckworth's voice was calmer now. 'But can you rely on LeT to deliver? We've all got a lot riding on this. Haojing, Deaubois and Martin also feel the same way. They've been in touch with me since the announcement of the threat. None of them are comfortable anymore with your partners.'

'We can't do this on our own.' Van Klueck asserted. 'Not without the publicity that none of us wants.'

Bheem Singh agreed. 'We can't reveal ourselves. Not yet. They are the perfect camouflage…high credibility as terrorists. A perfect red herring. And don't forget that the reason they partnered with us was the prospect of being able to issue threats like this one. There's also a benefit for us, from what they've just done, even if it wasn't planned. While everyone is occupied with the terror threat, we'll complete our own preparations. There's a lot of work to be done, Steve, if you want to be the next President of the United States of America without being elected. And once LeT completes their mission, we'll be in control. Exactly like we planned it.'

'I see your point,' Buckworth grunted. 'But I don't have to like it.'

There was silence for a moment. Then, Buckworth spoke again. 'Assuming they find the location in a week's time, are we in a position to deliver on the timelines?'

'Perhaps you should show him the prototype,' Van Klueck suggested.

Bheem Singh seemed to hesitate before replying. 'It's not fully operational,' he said after a moment. 'I'll show it to you anyway. It will give you an idea of how ready we are. Once we have the secret in our grasp, it won't take long to make the prototype fully functional and test it. And then, it's just a matter of replicating the technology. We'll be ready to go well before the summit. Okay, Christian, we're signing off.'

'Let's connect in a week's time.' After Van Klueck's final words, there was silence and Imran guessed the conference was over.

'Come, I'll show you the prototype,' he heard Bheem Singh say, and the lights in the room went off.

For a few moments, Imran sat huddled, frozen. He couldn't believe what he had just heard. His hunch had paid off, big time, but in a most unexpected way. He extricated himself from his hiding place and stole to the door. He could hear voices coming from outside and peered into the corridor, which was now lit up.

There was no one there. The two men must have gone into one of the locked rooms. He knew he had to get close enough to hear what they were saying.

He ventured into the corridor. The door to his left, next to the staircase, was ajar. He sidled up to the door, and risked a glance inside the room. To his astonishment, there was no one there.

The voices had also fallen silent.

Imran slipped into the room and looked around. It was as if the men had vanished into thin air.

'Quite a collection you've got here.' Buckworth's voice suddenly broke the silence. It seemed to come from beneath the floor.

Imran realised that there must be a hidden level below the basement. Though, how the men had reached it, he couldn't fathom. There didn't seem to be any way out of the room, other than the door through which he had just entered. 'Yes,' Bheem Singh replied. 'The initial hoard that we found was very useful; helped us to make all this stuff.'

'What's this one? How does it work?' Buckworth had apparently found something interesting.

'Let me show you. I'll need to take my watch off for this. These are wrist bands which need to be worn together. They serve as armour and a weapon. I'll turn the intensity down and show you.'

Imran heard a crackle and a loud "pop" and guessed that Bheem Singh was demonstrating the weapon, whatever it was.

'That's cool. I haven't seen anything like this before, ever. Even DARPA doesn't have stuff like this.'

'They wouldn't. This technology doesn't exist. Outside the Order, that is.'

'So where's the prototype?' There was a trace of excitement in Buckworth's voice.

'Right here.'

'Where? I can't see it.'

'Step this way...that's right...a bit forward and to your left.' Bheem Singh seemed to be guiding Buckworth. 'Now wait while I...' There were a few moments of silence. Then, Bheem Singh spoke again. 'That's it.'

There was an exclamation from Buckworth. 'Well, I'll be damned!'

'Impressive isn't it? Even though it isn't complete yet. But once Farooq has found the secret, we'll be able to make it work perfectly. None of the G20 leaders have a chance.'

Buckworth's voice grew stern. 'Just make sure these guys don't screw up again. I haven't spent nine years waiting just to have a bunch of idiots flush my plans down the toilet.'

Imran heard footsteps, and realised they must be returning to this room. There was no place to hide here. He had to get out. The only place he could think of was the conference room. It wasn't likely they would go back there, and he could always hide under the desk again.

He hesitated, torn between the need to leave and the desire to know how the men had disappeared from the room. He also knew that he needed evidence if he was to nail Bheem Singh. No one was going to believe him if he returned to headquarters and related what he had just overheard. Bheem Singh had enough political influence to discredit his testimony. And the evidence he sought was in the hidden room.

As he backed up to the door, taking a last look around the room, the entire wall in front of him sank into the floor and disappeared. Beyond, where the wall had stood, was an opening in the floor and he could see the first few stairs of a stone stairway descending to a lower level which was dark, save for a dark blue, almost purplish glow emanating from it.

So that was the secret entrance to the lower level.

Tearing himself away from this discovery, he turned and slipped out of the door and back into the conference room, taking up his previous position under the desk. He heard

Bheem Singh and Buckworth talking as they left the other room and shut the door behind them.

Their voices faded away and he realised that they were going back upstairs. He waited a while longer to ensure that they had gone, then ventured into the corridor again. The lights had been switched off and the basement was once more in darkness.

He tried the door of the room with the disappearing wall. To his surprise and relief, it was unlocked. As he entered the room and shut the door behind him, darkness enveloped him. For the second time, he wished he had brought a torch. Remembering that he had seen a light switch to the right of the door, he brought out his mobile phone and used the dim light from the screen and keypad to search for the light switch.

He finally found it after a minute or so and hoped the light wouldn't be detected from the corridor outside. There was no way he would find the mechanism to move the wall without illumination.

Advancing to the opposite wall, he began studying it closely, looking for anything that might indicate a switch or a lever to activate the mechanism.

But the wall was bare.

How had Bheem Singh lowered the wall to enter the hidden chamber?

He examined the other walls of the room, but drew a blank again. Apart from the light switch there was nothing else on the walls. Sighing in frustration, he realised that there was nothing more he could do here. He dialled Vaid's number and waited as the call was diverted to his assistant, who informed him that

Vaid had been summoned by the Home Minister but was due back any time.

'Please ask him to call me back as soon as he returns. This is urgent.' He pulled out a small round Bluetooth earpiece and inserted it in his ear. Then, he fixed an even smaller Bluetooth microphone to his collar. The microphone was powerful enough to pick up the slightest whisper and had a noise reduction feature which would cut off external disturbances whenever he spoke. Setting his phone to auto answer to Vaid's number, he slipped it back into his pocket.

He stepped up once more to the disappearing wall and checked it in case he had missed something on his first inspection. Nothing. Shaking his head in disappointment and frustration, he turned to go.

And stopped short.

He wasn't alone in the room anymore. Bheem Singh had entered silently and stood before him now, regarding him with an expression in which curiosity mingled with anger.

27

Day 8

The Hotel Ashoka Palace, Patna

The X Trail drew up at the main porch of the hotel in downtown Patna.

'You guys carry on, I'll park and join you in a bit,' Vijay offered.

There were only two other cars in the parking lot. Vijay found a good spot where the X Trail would be seen from one of their rooms. As he emerged from the car, shouldering the bag, he realised that a man was staring directly at him. Vijay had noticed the man as he drove into the parking lot but hadn't paid him any attention.

Wondering why the man was staring at him, Vijay locked the car and turned to face the man.

Their eyes met.

It was Farooq.

After the initial shock, a cold fear gripped Vijay. How had Farooq known where to find him? He was no ordinary treasure hunter. If he had the resources to track him down in a location so far from Delhi, he was someone far more dangerous.

Vijay stroked the bag subconsciously. The rock ball was safely ensconced within.

Farooq began walking towards him. Two men emerged from a side doorway of the hotel and joined Farooq, who wore a sneer on his face now.

Vijay looked around and began walking quickly towards the entrance of the car park.

But that exit was blocked. Two men stood there. One of them drew a gun.

The two men with Farooq were also armed, their guns in their hands.

Vijay looked around wildly. The car park was enclosed by a four-foot-high brick wall, behind which ran a service lane. Thinking swiftly, Vijay ran towards the wall, hoping that Farooq's men would not resort to a shootout in a place as conspicuous as this.

He was wrong.

As he reached the wall, he heard a series of muffled claps, rather like the sound of a car door being shut, and bullets whizzed past his ears. With a shock, he realised that the guns were fitted with sound suppressors. He vaulted over the wall, just as bullets smacked into the brickwork of the wall.

As he lay on the ground, he could hear Farooq shouting orders to his men in Urdu.

'Fools!' Farooq roared. 'Get him!'

Vijay scrambled to his feet. He could hear the men running towards the wall. He had to get out of here.

The service lane opened up into a road that was perpendicular to the one on which the hotel stood. He dashed down the road, recalling that it led to one of the main roads of the city. There would be more people there and Farooq would not attempt anything with so many people around.

At least, Vijay hoped he wouldn't.

As he ran, he turned and looked over his shoulder. Farooq was nowhere to be seen, but three of his men rounded the corner, emerging from the service lane, in hot pursuit.

Vijay reached the main road and quickened his pace, glancing around. There was a hawkers' market to his right. He instinctively sprinted towards the market, hoping to lose himself in the crowd.

The bag was heavy and Vijay adjusted it as he dove headlong into the crowd, trying to lose himself in it.

He looked back. The three men had just reached the intersection where he had stood moments ago.

They looked around, searching. Across the crowd, one of the men looked straight at him and looked away.

Then, his head snapped back. He had recognised Vijay.

Quick words were exchanged between the men, and they broke up.

One of them made his way through the crowd towards him. The other two disappeared.

Where were they going? But there was no time to wonder. The man following him through the crowd was getting closer.

Vijay pushed through the crowd, trying to put as many people as possible between his pursuer and him.

He suddenly noticed a side alley. Looking back at his pursuer, who was busy jostling his way through the throng, Vijay quietly slipped down the alley. He had no idea where it led, but he had to get back to the hotel and warn the others.

Trees lined the alley, which had small brick and plaster houses on either side. This was a residential part of the city.

Suddenly, he saw a man move into sight directly ahead of him, raising his gun arm.

It was one of Farooq's men.

He must have circled around hoping to use this alley to access the hawkers' market. It was sheer chance that Vijay had chosen this very alley to escape.

Vijay cursed and ducked behind a tree. Bullets thudded into the tree and whined past him; the silencer muffling the sounds.

He thought fast. Slipping out from behind the tree, he wove his way down the alley, using each tree as a protective shield. The gunman kept firing whenever Vijay emerged from behind a tree, but Vijay kept him guessing.

How long would it be before his luck ran out and the gunman found his mark?

A plan began to form in his mind. The gunman had walked forward towards Vijay while shooting at him and was now just about 20 or 30 feet away.

It was now or never. Vijay unzipped the bag and took out the rock ball. He hoped he still had some of the athletic strength that had served him so well at MIT.

He emerged from behind the tree, hefting the ball in one hand. He would have only one chance to hit the gunman. If he missed...

Bullets thudded into the tree from behind him, zipping past his ears. Vijay whirled around and, to his horror, saw the man who had followed him through the market now entering the alley.

There was nowhere to hide. The two gunmen advanced towards him.

He was trapped.

Kidnapped!

Radha left the others waiting for Vijay in the hotel lobby and headed up to her room. The excursion to Barabar had been tiring and she wanted to relax for a while before they regrouped to discuss their latest discovery.

There was also something else that was troubling her. Of late, she had become conscious of a strong attraction towards Vijay. She couldn't explain it.

They had been childhood friends and when they met as adults two years ago, she had warmed up to him. Somewhere along the journey to find the secret, she had found herself thinking of Vijay more often. She could recall times when she wanted to share all his problems as well as his happiness.

Did Vijay feel the same way? She thought that she had sensed something in the way he had tried to protect her at Bairat when Farooq's men were manhandling her. But she couldn't be sure. And, she reminded herself, he lived in the US, he was an American citizen. Even if she was to believe, for a moment, that Vijay reciprocated her feelings, would this relationship even work? Radha sighed. An idea came into her head. Maybe she should speak to Colin. She got along well with him and she knew how close he was to Vijay. Perhaps he could help her?

There was a knock on the door. She jumped to her feet. Was it Vijay? She shook her head to dislodge the thought. It could be any one of the others, as well.

She opened the door.

To her shock, two men with guns stood there. Behind them was a pleasant-faced man with a smile on his face.

'Miss Radha Shukla?' he enquired amiably. 'I'm Farooq Siddiqui. Surely, you've heard of me. Please come with me. There's no point resisting or raising an alarm, unless you want to end up dead.'

Radha knew she had nowhere to run.

The Agenda Revealed

Imran didn't stop to wonder how long Bheem Singh had been standing there observing him or why he had returned. His training took over and he automatically reached for his Glock, holstered at his waist. Barely had his fingers touched the weapon, however, than he felt a jolt run through his hand, like a mild electric shock. Instinctively, he jerked his hand away.

Almost simultaneously, he felt his mobile phone vibrate and Vaid's voice spoke into his ear through the hidden earpiece.

'Kidwai? You called for me?'

Imran stiffened. 'Kidwai? Can you hear me?' Vaid repeated.

'I wouldn't try being a cowboy, if I were you,' Bheem Singh said calmly, as he toyed with the steel wristbands he wore. 'That was just a demonstration. I've now set these at a level that can stun you right as you stand there.'

Imran recalled the conversation he had overheard between Buckworth and the Maharaja. Bheem Singh had taken off his watch to demonstrate a weapon to the US Vice President. Wrist bands. He now understood the nature of the weapon. Somehow, these wristbands were capable of delivering an electric charge across a distance. What their range was he couldn't guess, but he was sure that they could pack a powerful punch when required.

What technology was this? And where had it been developed? He clasped his hands at his waist where Bheem Singh could see them. The Maharaja smiled. 'That's smart. My security has obviously failed, if you've made it this far. It's a good thing after all that I forgot my watch and came back for it. You made it in. That was the easy part.' He turned sideways and, grasping the handle of the door, turned it in an anticlockwise direction. The wall that Imran had been studying moments ago dropped away, revealing the entrance to the stairway that led to the subterranean chamber.

Vaid had fallen silent after his first words. Had he hung up or was he listening? Did he realise Imran's predicament? Imran could only hope that Vaid had recognised Bheem Singh's voice and stayed on the call.

'This is what you were looking for, isn't it?' Bheem Singh was saying, pointing to the door handle. 'You didn't think I'd make it easy for anyone to find this, did you? State of the art biometrics. Only I have access to this vault.' He motioned Imran down the staircase and followed him.

Imran found himself standing in a large rectangular room, flooded with the deep blue light, bordering on purple, which he had seen seeping out of the room earlier. It reminded him of a nightclub. The walls of the room glowed white and he saw two thick pillars that divided the room into unequal portions.

He realised that the room was illuminated by ultra violet light and the walls probably had fluorescent paint on them.

Even in the dim blue light, he could see that the walls were deeply gouged in places. To his right, along the length of the wall, ran a shelf that glowed white like the walls, on which were displayed a variety of metallic objects in different shapes and sizes. None of them were even vaguely familiar to him, but from what he remembered of Buckworth's reaction, he surmised they were all weapons of some kind, like the wristbands Bheem Singh wore.

On the other side of the room stood large mechanical devices, ranging in height from three feet to seven feet. A few of them looked like large metallic archer's bows mounted on platforms with wheels. Again, he couldn't guess what they were, though he could guess their purpose.

Where had Bheem Singh got these from?

'I've heard that you are one of the bright sparks at the IB.' Bheem Singh was regarding him with pity. 'Too bad you insisted on sticking your nose in matters that are none of your business. I tried to make it easy for you. I turned you away when you wanted to interrogate me. I put pressure through the Home Minister. But you have a nose for trouble. And what do you do? Break into my house. I don't know how long you've been here and what you've seen or heard, but I really can't allow you to leave now. And I don't think I can afford to keep you alive either. Too much bother.'

Imran's blood ran cold at these words. Hoping that Vaid was still on the call, listening in, he decided to try and get the Maharaja to talk.

'So you think these toys will help you in your plan to assassinate the US President and install Buckworth in his place?' He stared defiantly back at the Maharaja.

Bheem Singh looked at him for a moment then laughed, his teeth glowing in the UV light. Imran knew that he had struck the right chord.

'So you overheard my conversation with Buckworth.' The Maharaja chuckled. 'And you think this is all about making Buckworth the US President. Why would I want to do that?'

Imran decided to play dumb. 'Commercial reasons. You are a businessman and your consortium has global interests. What better way to increase your influence in global commercial activity than being a kingmaker for the economic engine of the world economy? Despite the recession, America is still important for global commerce and trade.' He was betting that the Maharaja had a king-size ego and would be goaded into boasting about his true intentions.

Bheem Singh appeared to consider Imran's words. 'I guess it won't hurt,' he said, finally, 'to tell you the truth. After all, you're not going anywhere.'

Imran smiled inwardly. He was right about the Maharaja's ego.

'This is much bigger than the US. By wiping out the leaders of the G20 countries and installing our own men in their place, we will control the most economically powerful countries in the world. This will give us unprecedented access to business opportunities across the globe and therefore global domination. Unhindered'. He beamed at Imran, visibly pleased with his own forecast.

'And just how do you intend carrying out your plan?' This was exactly what he and Blake had surmised earlier.

'Let me start with a discovery made by my ancestor, the first Maharaja of Rajvirgarh, 1,500 years ago.'

Bheem Singh explained the discovery of his ancestor and its link with the Mahabharata; informing Imran about a celestial secret weapon that had been lost in the mists of time and erased from public memory. While building a new fort, a book written in stone was discovered. It was remarkably well preserved and the inscriptions told a tale from the Mahabharata. A tale that was missing from all recorded versions of the epic.

When he had finished his story, Imran looked sceptical. 'How can you believe in a legend that goes back thousands of years? The Mahabharata is mythology. There may have been some truth about a fierce war fought thousands of years ago, but fanciful descriptions of weapons from the gods? Surely you can't be serious?'

'That's where you're wrong. Look around you. What you see are some of the so-called celestial weapons from the Mahabharata; ancient designs used to create modern weapons in modern factories. Whatever the truth behind the Mahabharata and its historical authenticity, those weapons existed; including this particular weapon that was described in the stone book. You see, my ancestor also made another startling discovery.

'Asoka the Great had unearthed the location where this weapon had been hidden away and cobbled together a secret brotherhood to conceal its location and ensure that no one ever found it. My ancestor's court astronomer was a member of this brotherhood. Unfortunately, however, before my ancestor had a chance to interrogate him and learn more, the astronomer disappeared and was never seen again. Until, eleven years ago, by an amazing turn of events, his bones were discovered in Afghanistan, along with texts that gave clues to the location where the weapon was hidden.'

'And you have found that location and plan to use this amazing weapon to further your plans.' Imran couldn't keep the disbelief out of his voice.

'Not really. We haven't found the location yet. But our partners are on the job. We already have a prototype of the weapon with us. The texts found in Afghanistan led us to another hidden location where we found more details on how to build the weapon. We've been assembling the prototype for the last three years. Unfortunately, those texts were incomplete. The prototype isn't perfect. We need a sample of the original weapon to complete it and make it fully operational.'

A sudden realisation dawned on Imran—Vijay Singh and his friends. Somehow, they were involved in this. So that was what Farooq wanted from them—the location of this weapon. But how had Vijay Singh come by this knowledge?

Another thought struck him. He had heard Bheem Singh tell Buckworth that he had instructed Farooq to take Vijay and another person hostage. The woman. He remembered her from his visit to the fort. She and Vijay were in danger!

'I still don't see how this ancient weapon will help you,' Imran persisted. 'After the announcement by LeT, you don't have a hope in hell of carrying out your plan.'

Bheem Singh smiled, and his teeth glowed again. 'Wrong again. The weapon will actually help us carry out LeT's threat. Let me show you the prototype and you'll see what I mean.' He gestured to a corner of the room.

Imran stared, unimpressed, at the device that stood there. 'This is it?'

Bheem Singh flicked a switch and suddenly the room was flooded with cool white light from compact fluorescent lamps.

Imran stared at the device he had seen in the ultraviolet light and sucked in his breath sharply. He couldn't believe his eyes now that the UV light had been switched off. This, then, was how they intended carrying out their plan.

The Maharaja was right. If they perfected this weapon, nothing could stop them from succeeding in their mission.

28

September 2001

Bamiyan, Afghanistan

Winter was upon them again and Baran opened up the trunk in which their winter clothes were stored.

He pulled out the simple robes, cloaks and shawls and dumped them in a pile by the side of the trunk.

As he pulled out a brown shawl something fell from within the folds of the cloth. It was a package which had been stored away for safekeeping.

He recognised the package as the one containing the metal disk and the texts he had discovered a few months ago, when the statues had been destroyed. He had forgotten about them.

A thought struck him. Mohammed Bin Jabal had arrived a few days ago. He had been introduced to him at one of the gatherings that had been held to facilitate the Al Qaeda leader. The destruction of the World Trade Centre in New York two weeks ago had created a buzz within the Taliban and respect for Al Qaeda and Bin Laden had risen by several notches.

Bin Jabal had come to review the operations of the Taliban in this part of Afghanistan, as rumours swirled fast and furious that America was planning to launch military operations in Afghanistan with the objective of flushing out Bin Laden.

But it wasn't the purpose of Bin Jabal's visit that Baran was now thinking about.

He had been told by one of his Taliban comrades that Bin Jabal was also an Al Qaeda expert on antiquities and a trader on the international black market. It was one of the means Al Qaeda employed to raise funds for its activities within Afghanistan and outside.

Baran looked at the package again. The novelty of the discovery had faded with time. Even as a souvenir, it had hardly matched up to the rocks—fragments of the fallen Buddhas—that Baran had brought home with him. Was there any further use of keeping them with him?

He made a decision. He'd speak to Bin Jabal and show him the texts. Perhaps he could read the script and determine if they were of any value. Surely Bin Jabal could help him get some money for them?

Money would be good. They needed new clothes for the winter. He strode out of the house purposefully, the package tucked under his arm, the pile of clothes at the side of the trunk totally forgotten.

29

Present Day

Day 8
Patna

For a moment, Vijay stood there, frozen, unsure if he should try something. Then, realising that the odds of succeeding were stacked against him; he sighed and slowly put the rock ball on the ground and straightened up, his hands in the air.

The two gunmen approached him cautiously. Farooq had instructed them to take him alive. They had been shooting at him only to deter him from trying any attacking manoeuvres and were taking no chances after his last escape from their clutches.

One of the men put the rock ball back into the bag, hefting it over his shoulder. The other man prodded Vijay in the ribs with the gun and together, the three walked away from the hawker market.

Vijay was surprised at how well the men seemed to know their way around the town. They were definitely not locals, by their accents or looks. The only other possibility was that they had done a thorough virtual recce of the area, which meant that they were well equipped with maps and GPS equipment. Whoever these men were, they were well-funded. And able to carry their guns with them wherever they travelled. He didn't know how they had managed to pull that off but the fact that they had was a scary thought.

Presently, they came to where two black Ford Endeavours were parked in a vacant parking lot. The place seemed deserted apart from the two SUVs and eight armed men waiting for them.

Vijay's hands were bound behind his back and he was roughly shoved into the Ford. He wanted to resist but he knew that it would be futile. As he sat there, wondering what was going to happen next, he realised they weren't moving on.

What were they waiting for?

Moments passed, and he could hear the men talking in guttural tones outside the SUV. He couldn't understand what they were saying so he tried to focus on keeping his thoughts optimistic. Maybe Farooq would let him off after taking the stone ball from him.

His hopes were rudely dashed to the ground as the SUV door opened once more and Radha, bound at the wrists, was forced into the seat next to him. His heart sank and something inside him seemed to cave in as he saw the terror on her face.

As he gaped at her, horrified at this turn of events, two men slid into the front seats of the vehicle and two clambered into the rear seats, and the SUV lurched forward and out of the parking lot.

Vijay wanted to comfort Radha, but words failed him. His own terror had given way to an inexplicable sense of despondency and all he could do was stare at her as if, by sheer willpower, he could secure her freedom.

Radha said nothing, but stared back, wide-eyed, at him. She knew there was little they could do to get out of this situation. And there was nothing that her father or Colin or White could do to help them either.

They were well and truly prisoners.

IB Headquarters On The Alert

Arjun Vaid listened intently, his entire attention on the speakerphone, ignoring the two IB officers sitting across his desk. He had recognised the voice of Bheem Singh, when he'd called Imran, and didn't have to listen too long to realise that Imran's hunch was correct. There had been a flurry of action after that, even as he stayed on the call, trying not to miss anything in the conversation.

The call was now being recorded and Vaid had even called up the Home Minister and patched the call through to him so he could hear the conversation for himself. The Home Minister was known for his integrity and Vaid knew that, whatever Bheem Singh was up to, the Home Minister wouldn't have known about it.

A team of commandos had been immediately despatched to Bheem Singh's farmhouse, with instructions to secure the building and ensure that none of the evidence was destroyed. With Bheem Singh's influence and political clout, Vaid wanted to ensure that they had enough to guarantee that he wouldn't get away after this. And he knew that he had a responsibility to get Imran out of this mess.

As the conversation progressed, the realisation dawned on Vaid that this entire situation was more complex and ran much deeper than any of them had imagined.

'So now you understand,' Bheem Singh was saying, a hint of triumph in his voice, 'that this plan is infallible. In a few months, we'll rule the world.' He chuckled. There was silence in response. It seemed that Imran had no answer to this boast.

'Enough about me,' Bheem Singh continued, as if Imran's response didn't matter. 'Let's talk about you. How do we end this? Let's see...' He broke off and there was silence again.

'You won't get away with this,' Imran said in a strained voice. 'Even if you kill me, they'll get you.'

'They?' Bheem Singh sounded puzzled. 'Who? Oh, I see, the IB. My dear fellow, how on earth do you think they'll ever know what happened to you or how I was connected with your disappearance? You don't think I'm naive enough not to cover my tracks?' He paused.

Vaid heard a buzzing sound over the speakerphone, but couldn't identify it.

'Now this is what Steve Buckworth would call "cool".' There was a trace of admiration in Bheem Singh's voice. 'An ancient weapon, as old as Indian civilisation itself. Kills cleanly.'

Vaid looked at his watch. Where were the commandos? Why hadn't they reached?

30

January 2003

Vikram Singh's apartment, New Delhi

Vikram Singh sat at his desk in his study, and gazed with mixed emotions at the strips of bark bound together. A sense of elation swept over him. But his delight was tempered with bewilderment at the mysterious emergence of these texts after their equally mystifying disappearance 1,500 years ago.

He looked up from the books to the man who sat on the other side of the desk.

Farooq Siddiqui beamed at Vikram. His guess had been correct. The texts were important.

'This is amazing!' Vikram's eyes shone with excitement.

'Can you read the script then?'

'Of course. It's in Kharosthi. An ancient language of India.'

Farooq leaned forward. 'And what do they say?'

Instead of reading the text, Vikram explained how the texts and disk had gone missing with an astronomer in the court of the first Maharaja of Rajvirgarh.

'The first Maharaja of Rajvirgarh? You mean the same Rajvirgarh that Bheem Singh's family ruled?' Inwardly, Farooq was smiling. So this is how Bheem Singh and Van Klueck had known about the Nine.

Vikram nodded. 'The same. The first Maharaja of Rajvirgarh was Bheem Singh's ancestor and started the dynasty. According to the legend, his court astronomer vanished one day. The Maharaja launched a search for him but it was like he had disappeared off the face of the earth. With him were lost some of the most secret texts of the Nine and one of the two metal disks that were part of the puzzle that the Nine had created to hide the location of their secret.'

'You mean a metal disk like this?' Farooq reached within his bag and drew out a circular slab of metal.

Vikram's hands trembled with excitement as he took the disk from Farooq. He placed it on the desk next to the texts and studied it. Suddenly, he looked up.

'Where did you get these from, Farooq? The texts, the metal disk, it's almost as if you met the missing astronomer and got these off him. These artefacts have been missing for 1,500 years. How did they suddenly re-surface?'

'They aren't fake, I assure you.'

'I know they aren't fakes. I'm just curious where you got them from.'

'Oh, I ran across a dealer in antiquities in Afghanistan,' Farooq replied, nonchalantly. 'He had these with him and didn't know their value. The moment I laid my eyes on them, I figured they were important. But I couldn't read the script, so I brought them to you.'

'These are in very good condition, for their age.' Vikram handled the strips of bark with a pair of forceps so as to not damage them. 'The only reason they have survived since the sixth century AD is because they've been written on the bark of the *bhoj* tree, which is resistant to decay and decomposition. And if they were found in Afghanistan, then the arid conditions and freezing winter temperatures would have helped preserve them.'

'And what do they say?' Farooq pressed.

'Lots of things. There's a list of the names of the original members of the Nine. There's a mission statement, the purpose for which the brotherhood was formed. There are also some instructions that look like directions to a hidden location.' A tremor entered his voice as he spoke the next words. 'And it has the lost book of the Mahabharata, the *Vimana Parva*, which was never documented officially. It describes the secret of the Nine.'

Farooq was astonished. 'You mean they documented all that? Why?'

Vikram shrugged. 'It's not like anyone could read this. Even if you knew Kharosthi, it would seem no more than the narration of an ancient myth and the story of the Nine. Even the *Vimana Parva* wouldn't be recognised by anyone not aware of its existence or familiar with its contents. The texts are in the form of verses. Few people would be able to interpret their true meaning.'

'You're well qualified for that, I know,' Farooq grinned. 'So, is the hidden location described in these texts the place where the Nine concealed their secret?'

Vikram shook his head. 'Can't be. That wouldn't make sense. Why would the Nine go to great lengths to devise a puzzle to protect the location of the secret and then document its location?'

'So, what's the secret of the Nine?'

Vikram smiled at him. 'Do you think you are ready and prepared for the answer? To know what it was that Emperor Asoka thought could pose such a great danger to the world?'

Farooq stared back, his face serious now. 'I believe I am.'

Vikram leaned forward and fixed him with his gaze. 'Then, I'll read you the *Vimana Parva*. Prepare to be amazed as I reveal to you the secret of the Nine!'

31

January 2004

The Dorchester Hotel, London

A tall, man made his way through the lobby of the hotel to the elevators. He had an aquiline nose and silver grey hair. The rimless spectacles he wore added to his stern visage. Anyone encountering him would speculate that he was a rich European businessman and immensely wealthy.

This speculation would not have been entirely wrong. Christian Van Klueck was Austrian by nationality and a businessman by profession; but his family had been wealthy for generations, having run a prosperous trading business that covered most of the globe. While the Van Kluecks traced their lineage back hundreds of years—some of Christian's ancestors had counted among the nobility in the Hapsburg court—some rumours went as far as to suggest that some of Christian's early ancestors were not the honourable men they were made out to be but had surreptitiously indulged in piracy on the high seas, looting and sinking ships, thus adding to their hoard of treasure and riches. Over the last three generations, however, the family had kept up with the times and diversified into businesses that were critical to global business and trade. Through this strategy, they had not only succeeded in multiplying their wealth several times, but they had also strengthened their influence in the political arenas of most of the countries in which they operated. Some said that the influence of the Van Kluecks was stronger than that of the United Nations, though they had never been known to wield this influence in any overt manner.

Van Klueck rode up in the elevator to the top floor, which housed the Harlequin Suite.

The door opened to reveal a man who was roughly the same age as Van Klueck and as tall, but broader in the shoulder and bulkier than the European. His mop of grey hair rested atop an aristocratic face.

Bheem Singh beamed at Van Klueck and motioned for him to enter.

So, what's the news? Bheem Singh asked him once he was seated on the couch.

'I met with Farooq. In Pakistan.' Van Klueck said, taking a gulp of the fine single malt whisky offered by his host. 'He wasn't bluffing. He's got what we want.'

Bheem Singh visibly perked up. 'The metal disk? Finally? You saw it?'

Van Klueck smiled at the Maharaja's perceptible excitement. 'Yes, I saw it. Held it in my hands. And not just the disk. Texts about the brotherhood and the lost book of the Mahabharata and a document with instructions to a secret location. He's got them all translated. They corroborate the documents you found in your fort. We were right about the secret. And now we have the means to locate it.'

Bheem Singh settled back in his chair. 'You mentioned instructions to a secret location. You mean there's a text that documents where the secret is hidden?'

Van Klueck shook his head. 'Farooq doesn't think it's that simple. The Nine wouldn't have created the puzzle if they had a text that gave away the answer to anyone who found it. He doesn't know what we'll find in this hidden location but he's quite sure it won't be the actual secret. For that, we have to follow the clues. But now that we have the disk, at least we have a starting point.'

'And there's a catch.'

'I don't know if you'd call it a catch. But yes, he had conditions.'

Bheem Singh looked at Van Klueck enquiringly. Van Klueck narrated his conversation with Farooq.

Farooq looked hard at Van Klueck. 'Those are my terms. I want the secret. And I know you can't find it without this disk.'

Van Klueck thought for a moment. 'You're right, we need you—or rather, we need this—to find the secret. But you need us too. Just getting the secret in your hands isn't enough. You need production facilities, R&D labs, engineers. Where do you think you're going to get those from? And even if you do manage to drum up the resources, you'll stick out like a sore thumb.'

Farooq pondered this. 'So what do you propose?'

'I'd like to first understand what you want to achieve once you get your hands on it.'

Farooq hesitated. Should he reveal his plan? But then, he knew he needed the European and his allies to carry out his scheme successfully.

'Fine,' he said finally. 'I think LeT's strategy has lagged behind its ambitions. It wants to be a global terrorist power but is still besotted with targets in India. I want to lead them onto the global stage; stage a disaster so big that the world will prostrate itself at our feet. I'm going to target governments of the world; the major countries, the enemies of Islam. An impossible task, normally. But, with the secret of the Nine in my grasp, it will be child's play. LeT's ability to strike terror anywhere, anytime, will finally be recognised. That is when Islam will rule the world.'

Van Klueck looked thoughtful. 'Brilliant idea! But there's a flaw in the execution.'

'What's that?'

'In order to sustain the fear and awe you wish to evoke as a global terrorist organisation, you need to have governments, law and order, peace in these countries. If you bring the governments down, your plan becomes anarchist and creates chaos. You are then competing with their internal chaos as a power to be feared and terrified of. Surely you don't want that?'

'And what is your solution?'

'That's where we come in. We help you find the secret. But, rather than hand it over to you, we use it productively. We develop the technology you need to execute the plan. And we have powerful allies in these countries. We can have standby governments ready to take over as soon as you wipe out the existing governments. Needless to say, the new governments will be more compliant, more supportive and more useful to you. It's a win-win for both of us.'

'What's in it for you?' Farooq was curious.

'Why, profit, of course. We get preferential terms for business, trade and commerce. We get government support for our investments and better conditions for business in all these countries.'

'That does sound like a good plan,' Farooq admitted.

'But I'm curious. How do you propose to take down all these governments? You are talking of 20 or 30 countries.'

'Simple. Bomb them. A plane carrying a payload that is targeted at the parliament or seat of government of each country,' Farooq responded confidently.

'I see. I can see where the secret fits in. So, do we agree on this?' Van Klueck extended his hand.

'Agreed.' Farooq shook hands with the Austrian.

'We have to begin preparations immediately. We're looking at early next decade as the target and there's a lot to do,' Bheem Singh noted after hearing the details.

'Why?'

'Because we've got four years to the 2008 US presidential election. Buckworth is just another Senator. He needs to start working on his image, his positioning as a future running mate for the President so he can become VP in 2008. We then have four more years to ensure that things go well and the President gets re-elected in 2012. It's the same for the others. They need a few years to establish themselves, build relationships that will help them when the time comes to place them. Also, we'll never be able to complete the search and build the factories in time. We need to find the secret, build the prototype and test it before beginning production. That'll take us to 2010.'

Van Klueck put his glass down. 'You're right. It will take time. We need to talk to our friends in these countries. It will take them a few years to build their profiles and position themselves appropriately.' He looked at Bheem Singh. 'Except in India, of course. That's all yours. Finally.'

Bheem Singh's eyes flashed. 'My dynasty has waited 1,500 years for this moment. Right from Rajvir Singh, the first Maharaja of Rajvirgarh, we've nursed the ambition of planting our dynastic flag on the map of India. Bringing back the glorious days when one king ruled over the entire country. God knows this country needs a king. Democracy doesn't work here. Grubby politicians, distasteful bureaucrats—you have no idea how I hate working with them—what they need is a king to rule over them and direct the affairs of the country as only a Maharaja can.

'You know, when I first found those texts in the secret chamber at the fort, I was disinclined to believe their contents. It all sounded too absurd. Then, you found Beger's diary.'

Van Klueck reminisced. 'If I hadn't bumped into that American whose father had been at Nuremberg during the war crimes trials, I'd never have come across that diary. The idiot thought I was German and proudly showed me the trunk of Nazi documents that his father had brought with him from Germany.'

'You killed him, didn't you?' Bheem Singh tried to recall the events of 14 years ago.

Van Klueck shook his head. 'Never. I don't get my hands dirty. I had Cooper take care of it.'

Bheem Singh murmured, 'It's taken 14 years. Destiny is finally with us.' He laughed and Van Klueck joined him.

32

Present Day

Day 8
Gurgaon

Imran stared at the device in Bheem Singh's hand. The Maharaja had first inserted his index finger into a hollow cylindrical metal tube which he held upright, and then inserted the tube through a hole in the centre of a circular disk with a serrated edge. As he withdrew his hand, the disk began spinning with the tube as its axis, somehow balancing without falling off or even touching it.

'Perhaps you recognise this?' Bheem Singh looked over the spinning disk at Imran. 'No? You've probably seen artists' impressions of this and computer generated imagery in television serials. This is the weapon said to have been used by Lord Krishna in his battles; the celestial weapon used by Lord Vishnu. If you were to put a gold plating on this, you'd recognise it as the *Sudarshana Chakra*. It's a wonder. Magnetic forces keep the wheel balanced and spinning around the metal axis unless the equilibrium is disturbed by an external force that can overcome the magnetic forces; like heaving it at someone.' He smiled. 'I've had a bit of practice with this, in this very room. I think my aim is reasonably good now. You won't feel a thing.'

Imran's eyes went to the gouges on the walls. He now understood how they had been created. He braced himself for the inevitable. So, this was it. He wished he knew whether Vaid had been listening in on the conversation or not.

'You wouldn't kill me here with this thing.' Imran was putting up a brave front. 'You're not going to risk having blood on your floor. Even in this secret room.'

Bheem Singh smiled smugly. 'That's where you're wrong. You, see, no one has ever seen the *Sudarshana Chakra* work. All that everyone's seen are artists' impressions, which invariably show the *Chakra* severing heads with blood flowing like a fountain. No one could ever guess that the great secret of the *Chakra* is that it kills cleanly without spilling a drop of blood. It has an inbuilt laser that cauterises blood vessels as it slices through them. Quite advanced for a weapon that is thousands of years old. And, unlike the artists who've never seen the *chakra* at work, we've had first hand experience.'

A horrible realisation dawned on Imran. He recalled reading newspaper reports about the dead scientist's corpse at Jaungarh. 'You had Vikram Singh killed with this thing.' His voice was low and strained.

'Correct.' Bheem Singh smirked at him. 'So it's been tried and tested. The people who designed this weapon knew what they were doing.'

Bheem Singh raised the spinning disk until it was over his head. He moved his hand back slowly as if preparing to hurl a javelin.

Suddenly, the staccato sound of automatic weapons, followed by two explosions, came to their ears, accompanied by loud shouts that resounded through the farmhouse.

Distracted and bewildered, Bheem Singh fleetingly took his eyes off Imran. That split second distraction was all that Imran needed. In one swift action, he dived towards the marble shelf, grabbed a round object off it and flung it at Bheem Singh as he hit the floor, hoping he would connect.

The object missed Bheem Singh but he had to jump aside in an effort to avoid it hitting him and lost his balance. As he stumbled and caught himself from falling, the spinning wheel jerked and detached itself from the metallic cylinder. With no magnetic force to control or stabilise it, the disk fell straight towards the Maharaja, still spinning at top speed.

Bheem Singh opened his mouth to scream, but the fast spinning disk slashed at his neck severing the arteries, before bouncing to the floor. Imran kicked and propelled himself out of the trajectory of the disk as it came to a rest on the floor.

He rose and cautiously made his way to Bheem Singh's prone body, his gun aimed at the corpse. The Maharaja must have died instantly. Despite himself, Imran couldn't help marvelling at the device. It had severed the arteries but no blood had been spilt. Making his way to where the disk lay, Imran picked it up and examined it. It was hot to the touch. There were really two disks, not one, with a hairline joint between them. And the two blades had serrated edges with the hooks pointing in opposite directions. He winced and dropped the disk. This was for the forensics guys.

Footsteps rang out as a group of commandos clattered down the secret stairway and grouped before him as they took in the scene. One of the commandos spoke into his throat microphone. 'Mission accomplished. Round them up.'

'Thanks, guys,' Imran was grateful. If they hadn't arrived when they did, it would have been his corpse on the floor.

A thought struck him. He glanced at his watch. 6.30 p.m. He had two phone calls to make. Vijay Singh and his friend, the woman, were in danger.

Threat To Kill

Colin, Shukla and White looked at each other. They had been waiting in the lobby for half an hour, but there was no sign of Vijay.

'Maybe he's gone up to his room to freshen up first,' White had suggested.

'It isn't like Vijay to disappear like that, not when he told us he'd join us in the lobby,' Colin had said earlier, but agreed to wait for a while.

Now, after 30 minutes had passed, Colin was getting restless. 'Let me check out his room,' he said and sprang to his feet before the others could respond.

After 15 minutes he was back, a worried look on his face.

'What happened?' Shukla read the concern in Colin's eyes.

'He's not in his room. I checked out the parking lot and the car is there. But there's no sign of Vijay.' He hesitated. 'And I went to check if Radha knew where he was, but she's not in her room either. I don't think they would have left the hotel together without letting us know. Something's wrong.'

Shukla looked worried. He knew his daughter would not have gone anywhere, even if accompanied by Vijay, without letting him know first.

As if on cue, White's mobile phone rang. He put the phone to his ear and his eyebrows went up. 'Yes,' he said into the phone, 'it's me, Greg White. And yes, I have the others here as well. Okay.' He disconnected the call and glanced at the screen as he put the phone away.

'Farooq,' he said, in response to the unasked question that hung on the lips of the other men.

He didn't have to say more.

'He's here?' Colin was shocked. 'How...?'

White shrugged. 'I don't know. He was calling from Vijay's mobile phone.'

Colin understood that if Farooq had Vijay's phone that meant that his friend was either captured or dead. 'What did he want?'

'He's got Vijay. And Radha. He wants to talk to all of us. Let's go up to your room. I can then call him back and put him on the speaker phone.'

'Farooq has my daughter?' Shukla's eyes widened with horror. He sat down on one of the sofas next to them and buried his face in his hands.

'Dr. Shukla,' Colin sat down next to the older man. 'We need to talk to Farooq and find out what he wants. They are alive and we have to ensure he keeps them that way.'

In Colin's room, White dialled Vijay's number and put his phone on speaker mode.

Colin and Shukla gathered around him.

'Gentlemen,' Farooq's smooth voice greeted them. 'You've all been quite a nuisance so far, especially Vijay Singh. One step ahead of me all the time! But that's all history, isn't it? I'm a step ahead of you now.'

They listened silently, not interrupting.

'Where are Vijay and Radha?' Colin asked, when Farooq had finished gloating.

'With me. And they're going to stay with me until you give me what I want.'

'What is it that you want?' White asked, though Colin already knew the answer.

'My demand is simple. I know you went to the Barabar caves. And I know what you found there. A riddle—the final step to finding the location of the secret.' He paused. 'I want to know what it means. It points to the location that I'm looking for. Tell me, and I'll let them go.'

Colin despaired. 'I don't know the meaning of the verse. None of us does.' He glanced at Shukla and White, who nodded supportively.

'I believe you,' Farooq said, after a pause. 'You just stumbled upon the riddle today. You haven't had time to decipher it. But you've been pretty good at unravelling the clues so far. I'm sure you'll get this one, too. Here's the deal. I'm giving you two days. Forty-eight hours. Spend that time wisely. When I call back, I want the location of the secret.'

'And what if we can't get the answer to the riddle?'

'Well, then, that's tough luck,' Farooq's unctuous voice was calm. 'You'll never see your friends again. And there's a lot we can do with the woman. Before we kill her.'

The phone went dead.

'We have to spend every minute of the next 48 hours trying to find out what that verse means,' Colin said sombrely. He knew he would do his best, and so would the others. But would their best be enough?

Mission Patna

Imran stood in Vaid's office. For the last hour he had tried calling Vijay's phone to warn him about the threat from Farooq, but Vijay's phone had just kept ringing. It was too much to hope that Vijay wasn't carrying his cellphone or was not responding for some other reason. It was more likely that he was too late.

And now it looked like his plan would also come to naught. 'I don't get it,' he stared at Vaid in disbelief. 'What justification are they asking for? Don't they have all they need? Do they want Farooq to present himself before them? Bloody bureaucrats!'

He had been summoned by Vaid minutes ago and informed that the mandarins in the Home Ministry had asked for justification to deploy the 50 commandos Imran had asked for to be despatched to Patna. It was this news that had provoked his outburst.

Vaid regarded Imran calmly. While he knew that Imran's question was rhetorical, he could understand his subordinate's frustration.

'You know better than anyone that we can't follow up every lead we get,' he tried to reason with Imran. 'The Home Ministry believes that with the death of Bheem Singh, the plot has been foiled. There was no mention of Farooq in your conversation with him. They don't want to fly a planeload of commandos all the way to Patna for nothing..'

'I know that's procedure. But, surely they know that Bheem Singh spoke about his partners? That would have been in the recording of our conversation.'

'It was there. I don't know if they've gone through the recording in detail. But even if they have, they probably think that after Bheem Singh's death, the partners are leaderless, rudderless and directionless.'

'Vijay Singh and his friend, Radha Shukla, have been kidnapped,' Imran said quietly.

Vaid raised his eyebrows.

'Yesterday, I authorised a tap on Vijay's mobile phone. Just in case. Sure enough, just about an hour ago, Farooq called the others using Vijay's phone. And told them to decipher some verse in exchange for their lives.'

Vaid leaned forward, his curiousity piqued. 'Did Farooq refer to himself by name?'

Imran knew what Vaid was looking for. But he also knew that this hope was futile. 'He didn't.'

'There's nothing else we can do, then. We need evidence that Farooq is at large and in Patna. Find me something and, I promise you, I'll have the commandos flown there with an hour's notice.'

Imran sighed. He knew Vaid was right. Eyebrows had already been raised at his surreptitious mission at Bheem Singh's farmhouse. Never mind that he had unearthed the terrorist plot of the century. He had broken the rules. If he had the commandos flown to Patna and they didn't find Farooq, there would be trouble. And he had no way of knowing if Farooq would actually make good his threat. After all, he wouldn't yet have heard of Bheem Singh's death. What would he do when he knew? Suppose he decided to call off the search?

'I've also put a trace on Vijay and Radha Shukla's mobile phones,' he informed Vaid. 'If Farooq uses either phone again, we'll locate him. I'll find him and call you.'

'You're going to Patna?'

Imran smiled grimly. 'I want to make sure we nail that bastard.'

33

Day 8

Patna

Farooq beamed with satisfaction at his two prisoners. 'Finally, I have you where I want you. Your friends are going to work out the last clue you found at Barabar. And once we have that clue, the secret of the Nine will belong to us.'

Vijay and Radha sat on the floor before him. Radha's hands had been unbound but Vijay's hands were still tied behind his back.

After a short, bumpy ride in the SUV, through narrow lanes and dark alleys, they had arrived at a three-storey house in a nondescript section of Patna. Both prisoners had been dragged into the house, where they had been dumped in this room. There was no one in the room apart from the three of them; Farooq's armed goons stood guard outside the door.

Vijay didn't like the fact that their captors had made no effort to blindfold them or confuse them in any way about the location of the building where they were being held captive. It was as if Farooq didn't really care if they were able to identify the place later or not. He guessed that Farooq didn't mean to let them leave. That was a sobering thought!

But he still put up a brave front and he could see that Radha was doing the same. She was a strong woman; he had always known that, but to see her hold up in the face of the kind of adversity they were now confronted with was a different thing. His respect and admiration for her had increased by several notches. As had his sense of despondency.

Vijay stared back angrily at Farooq. 'You're never going to get away with this.'

'Really? And who is going to find you? Not your friends.'

'The Maharaja,' Radha said suddenly. 'Bheem Singh. Greg White will inform him and he'll organise a rescue party for us.' Her eyes flashed at Farooq . 'You and your gang of thugs will go to jail.'

Farooq smirked. 'Gang of thugs, eh? You really don't know who you're dealing with here, do you?'

A sudden fear took hold of Vijay. 'Who are you?' he demanded. 'And what are you after?'

There was a genuine look of surprise on Farooq's face. 'You mean to say you don't know what the secret of the Nine is?' His voice rang with disbelief.

Vijay shook his head. 'No. We know that the brotherhood of the Nine was created by Asoka to conceal a great but dangerous discovery. But we don't know any more than that.'

Farooq laughed heartily. 'You've gone to such great lengths to decipher the clues left by the Nine and travelled across India following the trail of their secret but you have no idea what you seek? This is rich.'

Vijay flushed. He didn't like the way Farooq put it, but he was right. All he had been focused on was following the clues in his uncle's message and finding the secret. He and his friends had been so caught up in this that they never really gave a thought to the actual nature of the secret. He felt a bit foolish, recognising the truth in Farooq's words.

'Do *you* know what the secret is?' he countered aggressively.

'Of course,' came the immediate reply. 'We've known all along. We found out 10 years ago.'

'We?' Radha didn't understand.

Farooq seemed to mull over something.

'No one is going to come to your rescue,' he said finally. 'And there's no way you can escape us now. So I guess there's no harm if I tell you now. After all you've gone through, perhaps you deserve to know.'

He barked out an order and one of his men scurried into the room with a chair. He settled down comfortably, after dismissing the guard. 'Let's begin with ancient history. You are right about Asoka the Great and the discovery of the secret which led to the birth of the Nine in the third century BC. Fast forward to 500 AD, when the first Maharaja of Rajvirgarh stumbled upon the Nine and an ancient lost book of the Mahabharata.'

'Wait a minute,' Radha interrupted. 'Rajvirgarh? Isn't that Bheem Singh's ancestral kingdom?'

Farooq grinned wickedly. 'Yes, I'm speaking of Bheem Singh's ancestor, the man who founded the kingdom of Rajvirgarh when the Gupta Empire crumbled. The stone book was the *Vimana Parva*, that was deliberately not recorded and available for the masses, unlike the other books of the Mahabharata, when the oral tradition gave way to the written one. The book described a secret weapon from the gods that the Kauravas were about to employ on the battlefield with the help of the King of Magadha. But with the abrupt end of the war that weapon was never deployed.'

'That's what the inscription said,' Radha looked at Vijay. 'The one on the wall of the secret chamber at Bairat. You remember Papa translated it for us.'

Vijay nodded as it was Farooq's turn to flush. 'I never saw that inscription,' he admitted reluctantly. 'But it doesn't matter now. We don't need it.'

He resumed his story. 'The Maharaja discovered that his court astronomer was, in reality, a member of the Nine and tried to get the secret out of him. But the astronomer disappeared and was never seen again.'

He chuckled. 'Until 2001. When the Taliban destroyed the Bamiyan Buddhas.'

Vijay's hopes began to sink. Farooq's words were ominous. Was he connected in some way to the Taliban?

'There were caves hidden behind the statues,' Farooq continued, 'caves that were hidden away for 1,500 years. In one of those caves, the Taliban found the skeleton of a man and a treasure trove of ancient documents. Texts that had somehow survived the ravages of time. They also came across a metal disk with inscriptions. Our long-lost astronomer from Rajvirgarh had finally been found.'

Radha and Vijay exchanged glances. So this was where the second metal disk had turned up.

'Unfortunately,' Farooq continued, ignoring them, 'the Taliban couldn't read the texts. They were written in Kharosthi. So the ignorant louts sat on them for a while without knowing their significance.'

'So how did you get hold of them?' Vijay demanded. He was trembling despite himself, in anticipation of Farooq's revelation of his links to the notorious former rulers of Afghanistan.

'Patience,' Farooq admonished him. 'I'll come to that in a bit. But first, here's something you didn't know.' He grinned again, clearly enjoying himself.

'Around the same time as the discovery of the texts, in early 2001, I was approached by the Nine with an invitation to join them. One of their members had died and they were searching for a replacement.'

'You mean the Nine are still around?' Vijay wondered aloud. 'I thought they had died out centuries ago?'

Farooq looked directly at Vijay. 'It was your uncle who extended the invitation. He was a member of the Nine...and their contemporary leader as well.'

He was greeted by expressions of disbelief.

Vijay found his tongue. 'Is this another of your tricks? Uncle, a member of the Nine, and their leader as well?'

Farooq stared back at him, his gaze unwavering. 'I know it's hard to believe. But it's true.'

'It does make sense,' Radha said slowly, addressing Vijay. 'It would explain the clues he left in his emails to you. It also explains how he was so well-informed about the locations of the clues we've followed so far. That's probably also how he came to possess the metal disk we found in his locker.'

'Oh, that wasn't with him to start with,' Farooq clarified. 'The disk and the key to the disk were never kept with the same person; always two different people. It came to him when I killed the member of the Nine who possessed it. Two years ago.' His eyes flashed angrily. 'He never told me he had it. They had a secret code by which, if something happened to one member, anything they possessed was passed on to another member whose identity they knew, until the member who died was replaced.'

There was silence once more. They could both imagine what had happened to the rest of the Nine. Vijay's mind flashed back to the softboard at his uncle's desk; the eight news clippings that reported the mysterious deaths of eminent people all over the world. Had they been the other eight?

Farooq was speaking again. 'I was delighted to accept his invitation and I joined the Nine. It was an honour. It didn't matter that India and Pakistan harboured political animosities. As a nuclear scientist, I felt the Nine had no political or geographical boundaries. But that was short-lived. After 9/11, when the US invaded Afghanistan and killed thousands of innocent civilians after overthrowing the Taliban, I joined Al Qaeda. The West had no right to attack and kill innocent Muslims without provocation.

'The US had long helped Pakistan with its covert nuclear programme and I had come to regard America as a friend. But 9/11 showed me that it was a marriage of convenience for the Americans. I began to hate America and when Al Qaeda approached me, I joined them. I had planned to pass on critical components of the Pakistani nuclear programme to Al Qaeda so they could assemble a nuclear bomb.'

Vijay's hopes sank even lower. Farooq was a member of Al Qaeda! What moment of madness had led him to entangle with a man who was proudly confessing to being a terrorist? He clung on weakly to the only hope that seemed to be left for them: Bheem Singh. Surely the Maharaja would be able to command resources that would lead to their rescue?

And another question had begun to trouble him. What was there about the secret of the Nine that was of such interest to Al Qaeda?

Farooq was speaking again and his next words shattered Vijay's hopes. 'I met with one of Al Qaeda's partners, a powerful consortium led by an Austrian businessman, Van

Klueck and Bheem Singh. They had been unsuccessfully searching for the secret of the Nine since 1990, when Bheem Singh had discovered ancient documents in a secret chamber in Rajvirgarh fort; documents that spoke of the *Vimana Parva* and the missing astronomer.'

'What?' Radha couldn't believe her ears. 'Bheem Singh is a partner of Al Qaeda?'

Farooq was grinning from ear to ear, enjoying their shock and visible discomfort. He had known that they were pinning their hopes on the Maharaja.

Vijay's expression grew gloomy and forlorn as he digested this revelation. There was no hope of escape left for him and Radha. He looked at Radha and saw the same conclusion in her eyes.

'So Bheem Singh knew you were a member of the Nine?' Radha demanded.

'Of course not. I wasn't going to tell them everything. I'm pretty sure they held back a lot of secrets from me.'

Farooq waited for a while before taking up the narrative again. 'Bheem Singh and Van Klueck had searched high and low for clues to the secret of the Nine. They even sent a squad of assassins to the Temple of the Tooth near Lhasa. The assassins massacred the monks and made off with the ancient texts that were hidden in a vault in the temple. But they couldn't find the metal disk and the key which were so vital to the search.' He shrugged. 'Naturally. One disk was with the Nine. The other was with the astronomer, buried behind the Buddhas at Bamiyan.'

He leaned forward and looked at Vijay.'Now, I'll answer your question about how I got the metal disk and the texts. Luckily for us, before the Taliban was overthrown, the disk and the texts were passed on to Mohammed Bin Jabal, an Al Qaeda leader. But it wasn't until 2003 that I got to see them. I immediately realised they were important, though I had never imagined what they would lead to. I took them to Vikram Singh, who didn't yet know about my links to Al Qaeda. He translated them for me and I learned the truth about the secret of the Nine.'

He looked at Vijay. 'Unfortunately, your uncle began wondering where I had found the disk and the texts. And when I asked him which member of the Nine had the key, he became suspicious. He secretly placed me under surveillance and discovered that I was working for Al Qaeda. He confronted me and threatened to expose me.' A shadow crossed his face. 'I gave him a chance. I told him if he let me know who had the key, I'd leave him alone and that would be the end of it.'

'But he didn't.' There was pride in Vijay's voice.

'I had to go underground. While I lay low, I got involved with Lashkar-e-Taiba, who had ambitions of becoming the foremost Islamic defender of the faith. I also informed Bheem Singh and Van Klueck about the discovery. One of the texts mentioned a hidden location and gave instructions on how to find it. But that wasn't where the secret was hidden. Instead, we found a small hoard of weapons, fairly sophisticated considering their antiquity, which we reverse engineered to build our own armoury.'

Radha and Vijay recalled the examples Shukla had given them, in an earlier conversation, of the so-called celestial weapons that had been used in the Mahabharata; terrifying weapons that could kill thousands at one stroke and lay entire regions to waste. It was a sobering thought.

'That contraption you used to blow up the vault door,' Vijay recalled the events at the vault in Delhi, 'was that part of this hoard?'

'One of the original weapons,' Farooq beamed. 'Not one of the replicas we built. Imagine it. A weapon thousands of years old, still in pristine working condition. And amazingly lightweight as well. That metal—we couldn't figure out its composition—was lighter than aluminium or even carbon fibre.'

Vijay remembered seeing how the device had been folded up to less than half its size and the manner in which it had been carried away. Having witnessed the power of that device, the fact that a terrorist organisation like LeT had access to weapons like this was frightening.

'Does that mean there is some truth to the legends of the Mahabharata?' Radha wondered. 'That the war actually did happen in ancient times?'

'Doesn't matter.' Farooq was dismissive. 'The weapons were powerful, but that isn't what we were looking for. Though we did find an incomplete manual that described how to build the ultimate weapon of the Kauravas, the one described in the *Vimana Parva*. Using the manual, we built a prototype. But it didn't work the way it was supposed to. We realised we needed to find the location where the weapon was hidden. Which meant we needed the key to the disk. So, we began looking for the key.'

'And murdered the members of the Nine, one by one,' Vijay said, bitterly.

Farooq sounded enthralled by his memories. 'We used the weapons we had built using the secret hoard we had discovered.

I was fond of your uncle. I didn't want to kill him. Which is why I left him for the last, hoping that one of the others would have the key.

'No wonder your uncle had such an advanced security system installed at the fort,' Radha remarked. 'He knew his life was in danger.'

'And you murdered him.' Vijay's voice was low, but the pain of his uncle's death had returned. He was also angry with himself for having unwittingly aided a terrorist organisation in getting their hands on a secret that the Nine had strived for centuries to keep concealed.

'So what is this secret?' Radha returned to the question that had led to these revelations.

'An amazing weapon delivery system,' Farooq hissed, his eyes brightening. 'One that we will use to carry out our threat.' He smiled superciliously. ' We are going to attack the G20 summit in Washington. Al Qaeda has become obsolete and redundant, a toothless paper tiger. It is time for them to be replaced by an organisation that is more innovative and persistent. The time has come when the world will sit up and take note of Lashkar-e-Taiba!'

34

Day 9

The Hotel Ashoka Palace, Patna

Colin, White and Shukla were gathered in Colin's room. He hadn't slept much the previous night and, from the linguist's face, it was evident that he hadn't either. Colin placed a sheaf of papers before the others and this included some of the printouts they'd referred to in their earlier meetings.

'I've been thinking about the verse all night,' Colin began. 'About who the Mother could be and how we can locate the forests where the verse says she lives. But it didn't get me anywhere. Then, I realised that I was probably thinking too much about the Mother and not enough about the meaning of the verse. Perhaps if we start with the first line and try and understand each line, as we did with the inscriptions on the metal disk, we may get somewhere.'

'The first line seems easy,' White offered. 'The chambers that echo would be the Barabar caves, I think.'

Colin nodded. 'That's what I thought as well. So, if we stand at the Barabar caves and look south, what do we see?'

He picked up the map of India from among the papers. It was the same map that they had referred to in the study at Jaungarh a few days ago, with the locations of all the edicts of Asoka marked out on it.

'I'm guessing we are still looking for locations of Asoka's edicts. There are only two places south of Barabar where the edicts are located,' Colin pointed out the two locations along the eastern coast of India. 'At least the ones that are nearby. All the others are way down south, near the southern borders of his empire.'

'Dhauli and Jaugada,' White read off the map.

'I think one of these two should be the one referred to in the verse,' Shukla concurred.

'The verse says that we should look southwards to *the harbinger of the Lord's birth*. Any ideas what that means? Who is the *Lord*?'

'*The harbinger of the Lord's birth*,' Shukla mused. 'These verses were written by members of Asoka's court. In which case, the *Lord* is most likely Lord Buddha.'

'And was there a portent that heralded his birth?' Colin inquired.

Shukla's thoughts were distracted by his concern about his daughter. Was she safe? Were they treating her badly? He shook away the thoughts with an effort and replied slowly, thinking hard.

'I haven't heard of any legends about a sign or omen heralding Buddha's birth. But, in art, Buddha's conception is normally depicted by a dream of his mother, Maya, in which a white elephant enters her womb. I don't know if this depiction comes down all the way from Asoka's time, but that is the only "harbinger" I can think of.'

'It must be the one, then.' Colin looked convinced. 'The next line says: *In a dream*. Do you think it is one sentence deliberately split into two lines to confuse the reader: *To the harbinger of the Lord's birth in a dream.* That could mean the elephant in the dream.'

He reached out for some of the printouts and began scanning them.

'If we look southwards from Barabar, where do we find a white elephant? Could it be a painting of a white elephant? As you say, this is the depiction of Buddha's conception in art.' Colin frowned.

'Listen to this.' White began reading aloud from the sheet of paper in his hand. 'At Dhauli, near the ancient town of Tosali, is an Asokan inscription carved into a rock. Immediately above the inscription is a terrace, on the right side of which is carved the forepart of an elephant, four feet tall. The elephant is a symbol of Lord Buddha and has now become an object of popular worship.' He looked around. 'What do you think?'

'Could be.' Colin was perceptibly excited. There was a ray of hope, after all. 'Okay, if we assume that the elephant at Dhauli is the one that can be seen when we look southwards from Barabar, what next?'

'We come back to the Mother.' White was matter-of-fact. 'Which is where we got stuck in the first place.'

'I don't get it,' Colin admitted. *Passing over the Mother.* What could that mean? Who is the *Mother*? And how does one pass over her? They didn't have planes in those days.'

'Could this be a reference to some ancient statue?' White wondered aloud.

'If it was a statue it must have been someone famous at the time,' Shukla suggested. 'But I can't think of any woman from that period whose fame has persisted through the centuries.'

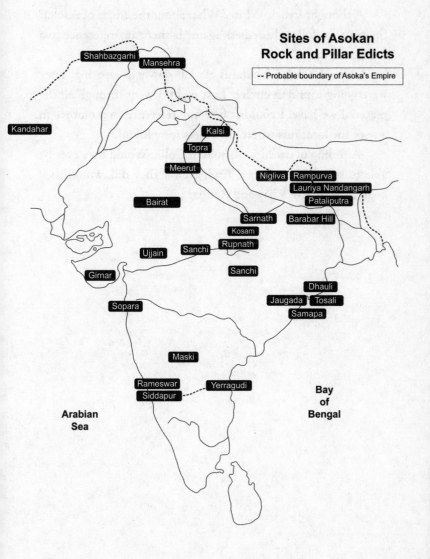

Sites of Asokan Rock and Pillar Edicts

-- Probable boundary of Asoka's Empire

Shahbazgarhi
Mansehra
Kandahar
Kalsi
Topra
Meerut
Nigliva
Rampurva
Lauriya Nandangarh
Pataliputra
Bairat
Sarnath
Barabar Hill
Kosam
Rupnath
Ujjain
Sanchi
Girnar
Sanchi
Dhauli
Jaugada
Tosali
Sopara
Samapa
Maski
Rameswar
Yerragudi
Siddapur
Arabian Sea
Bay of Bengal

A thought struck White. 'What about the edicts of Asoka? Suppose we follow his edicts again? Is there any reference to a mother in them?'

Colin shook his head, his elation slowly dissipating. They were going round in circles. 'Last night, I went through all the material we have. I couldn't find any reference to a mother in any of the locations where the edicts were found.'

A feeling of dread took hold of Colin. Would they ever be able to solve this mystery? And, even if they did, would they be in time to save Vijay and Radha?

35

Day 10

Patna

White and Colin strolled down the road where their hotel was situated. The previous day had passed without any further breakthrough in their attempts to decipher the riddle. Even today, they were no closer to solving the puzzle. They had just three hours left to find the right answer for Farooq. A shop they were passing caught Colin's eye. He stopped and pointed to a row of colourful brochures on the shop counter.

'Travel brochures.' Colin began thumbing through them. The shop was a little travel agency. 'These are local tours. Looks like there's lots to be seen around here.' He was desperately looking for a way to take his mind off the problem of the clues. Perhaps if he was able to stop thinking about the problem he might get some new ideas that would lead to a breakthrough.

He picked up some more pamphlets and flipped through them, now genuinely interested. 'Seems like Barabar isn't really on the tourist circuit,' he observed. 'There's no reference to the caves in any of these brochures.'

White looked like he didn't understand but he, too, picked up a brochure and looked at it.

'Tours of Bihar and Jharkhand,' he read out the title of one. The owner of the travel agency, observing what seemed to be two American tourists browsing through his itineraries, hurried to the main counter.

'Very good sights to see, sir,' he began, addressing Colin. 'Not very far from here, sir.' He glanced at the brochure Colin was perusing. 'Interested in ancient history, sir? You come to right place.' His sharp eyes had observed Colin scrutinising the brochures, searching for a mention of the Barabar caves.

'Lots of ancient sites, sir,' the travel agent continued, thinking he was homing in on the kill. 'Hazaribagh plateau. Not far from here. Many old sites; Banadag megaliths, ancient burial stones of the Kolarian tribes, Bawanbai Hills. Ancient manmade hill, according to the legends.'

He paused to see if his words were having any effect. Not satisfied with what he saw in their faces, he persisted. 'North Karanpura valley. Stone tool culture. Rock paintings. Very old. Karanpura valley. More rock paintings.' Pausing, he looked at his two prospective customers again.

'There's more, much more,' he continued, obviously feeling that he hadn't impressed the American tourists sufficiently with his sales pitch. 'Sitagarha Hill.' He passed a brochure to White from the back of the acrylic brochure rack. 'Important Buddhist site. 300 BC. Sacred hill. Forms the figure of a Mother Goddess. Worshipped by the Birhor tribals.'

White smiled and took the brochure from him.

Colin froze. He reached out and grabbed the brochure the agent had handed to White.

'What...?' White began but stopped as he saw the expression on Colin's face. 'You got something?'

Colin didn't hear him. He was engrossed in reading the contents of the brochure. When he had finished, he looked at

White, a big smile on his face. 'Thank you.' He passed a ₹500 note to the travel agent. 'Thank you very much! You don't know how helpful you've been.'

'No mention,' the puzzled travel agent replied, wondering what he had done to earn the money. However, he accepted it with grace even though he was disappointed that the two prospects wouldn't convert to paying customers.

'Time to get back to work.' Colin turned around and, for the first time since Vijay and Radha had been kidnapped, the shadows and worry lines had disappeared from his face.

36

Day 10

The Ashoka Palace Hotel, Patna

Shukla, White and Colin were gathered in Colin's room. Vijay's laptop occupied the desk in the room and papers were strewn all over the bed.

On returning to the hotel, Colin had disappeared into his room, and they hadn't heard from him until a few minutes ago, when he called the other two men to join him in his room.

'We have a hope,' Colin beamed, 'to save Vijay and Radha.'

A look of anticipation flitted across Shukla's face and White nodded.

Colin held up the pamphlet they had earlier picked up from the travel agent. 'The travel agent talked to us about Sitagarha Hill.' Colin opened up the brochure and began reading from it. 'According to this, Sitagarha Hill is the site of an ancient Buddhist settlement. Located in the Hazaribagh plateau, a stone-carved stupa and iron relics have been excavated along with stone pillars and heavily engraved stone blocks. Artefacts from the site have been dated to 300 BC.'

He paused. 'I did some research on stupas. They are hemispherical shrines, usually built over a relic of the Buddha. And listen to this.' His face shone with excitement. 'The sacred hill of *Marang Buru*, also called *Juljul*, forms the recumbent landscape figure of a reclining Mother Goddess. On the south face is a 65-foot-long stone face, called Mahadeva by the Birhor tribals. Mahadeva is a term alternately used for Lord Shiva and Buddha. The Birhor tribals still worship this hill as their Mother Goddess.'

Shukla's face radiated hope as he guessed the direction in which Colin was heading.

'So you think this hill, in the shape of a reclining Mother Goddess, is the "Mother" that the verse refers to?' White had also understood the connection Colin was trying to make.

Colin nodded. 'What else?' He pulled out the map of India with the locations of Asoka's edicts. 'Look at this.' He drew a straight line from the Barabar caves to Dhauli, where the carving of the elephant stood.

They gazed at the red line on the map. The line passed through the states of Bihar, Jharkhand and Orissa.

'Don't you see it?' Colin drew a rough circle on the map, which the line passed through. 'I've checked around twenty different maps of eastern India just to be sure. The line passes over the Hazaribagh plateau. Remember what the riddle said.'

They recalled the last cryptic verse on the ball of rock they had found at Barabar.

From the chambers that echo,
As we lift our eyes to the south
To the harbinger of the Lord's birth
In a dream
Passing over the Mother
Who lies amidst the forests green, reposing,

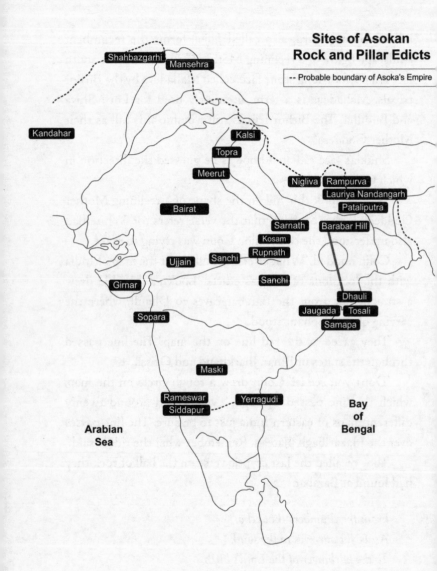

Sites of Asokan Rock and Pillar Edicts

-- Probable boundary of Asoka's Empire

Shahbazgarhi
Mansehra
Kandahar
Kalsi
Topra
Meerut
Nigliva
Rampurva
Lauriya Nandangarh
Pataliputra
Bairat
Sarnath
Barabar Hill
Kosam
Rupnath
Ujjain
Sanchi
Sanchi
Girnar
Dhauli
Jaugada
Tosali
Sopara
Samapa
Maski
Rameswar
Siddapur
Yerragudi
Arabian Sea
Bay of Bengal

Holding within her bosom,
Hidden for Millennia,
The Secret of the Nine.

'According to the brochure and the Internet,' Colin continued, 'the Hazaribagh plateau is home to dense tropical forests. I think these are the *forests green*. And the hill of the reclining Mother Goddess is the Mother, reposing within the forests. I believe that is where we will find the location where the secret of the Nine is hidden.'

They looked at each other. It had to be more than mere coincidence.

'You could be right.' Shukla's eyes shone with the prospect of saving his daughter and discovering a secret hidden for thousands of years. 'The text in Beger's diary, the one written by Surasen describing his discovery, also talked about the secret being hidden within a hill for centuries.'

'All this time we've been thinking that the secret, whatever it is, had been removed from its original location and hidden away somewhere else by the Nine.' White shook his head, smiling. 'It's been in the same place all along. Exactly where it was found. In a cavern within this hill.'

The air tingled with electric anticipation. Suddenly, the secret of the Nine seemed to be more than a myth; more than a fantasy. Finally, it appeared to be within their reach.

Colin's face grew sober as he realised that this discovery would now belong to Farooq. They had to pass on this information to him if they wanted their friends back safe.

He looked at his watch. 6.00 p.m. Half an hour to go before Farooq called. They had just about made it.

There was a knock on the door. All three men turned to look at it.

'Intelligence Bureau. Please open up.' The voice was authoritative.

Colin looked puzzled. 'Who's that?'

'The Indian equivalent of Homeland Security in the US,' Shukla explained. 'You better open up fast. It's probably a case of mistaken identity.'

Colin looked at White, who looked uneasy. 'You alright?'

'Yeah,' White muttered. 'Just nervous about Indian cops. Heard a lot of stories about them. None of them good.'

'Don't worry, it's probably nothing.' Colin opened the door.

Three men stood there. Colin instantly recognised the man who led the group. It was the same policeman who had come to Jaungarh Fort to get a sketch made of Farooq and Imtiaz.

'Can I come in, please?' Imran nodded to Colin, as he produced an identity card from the Intelligence Bureau.

'Sure,' Colin looked confused as he stepped aside to allow Imran to enter. 'Didn't you say you were with the Gurgaon police when you visited us at Jaungarh?'

Imran allowed the shadow of a smile to play on his lips. 'Actually, I didn't say who I was with. I was working undercover. If your definition of undercover includes an IB officer playing a local policeman!'

Colin introduced Shukla and White. 'Is this regarding the case?' he asked. 'We really don't have much more to tell you.'

'Oh, yes you do.' Imran's face was grim. 'I know about Vijay and Radha. Trouble is, you don't know about Farooq Siddiqui. He is a very dangerous man. He is linked to Al Qaeda and Lashkar-e-Taiba. We have been on his trail for a while, but we didn't want to move in on him until we knew exactly what he was after. Now we know.' He told them about the threat issued by LeT to bomb the G20 summit.

Greg White's face was ashen and Shukla too was white with terror. His daughter was being held captive by one of the most dreaded terrorist groups in the world.

'And I know that you were engaged by Bheem Singh to come to India,' Imran addressed White, 'So I'm sorry to inform you that he, too, was mixed up with Farooq in this web of intrigue. What's worse, Bheem Singh was one of the ringleaders. But we don't have to worry about him now.'

'You've arrested him?' White's face had turned a darker shade of grey. He wasn't taking the news very well.

Imran shook his head. 'Unfortunately, no. There is much he could have told us. But he's dead.'

He decided to come to the point. 'I know that Farooq has been in touch with you and wants you to decipher some sort of verse for him,' Imran continued. 'We tapped Vijay's phone and we've been listening in on the conversations he's been having with you. Now, here's what I want you to do.'

He looked around at the group. 'Have you deciphered the verse?'

Colin nodded.

'Good.' Imran smiled grimly. 'Now, when Farooq calls in around 30 minutes from now, I want you to tell him the answer to the verse but only after a very long negotiation.'

'How will that help?' Colin enquired.

'We've located his hideout,' Imran explained. 'It will take us 45 minutes to reach. I need you to keep him engaged in conversation. So negotiate for Vijay and Radha's release. Put forward terms and conditions. Give him a detailed explanation of how you solved the mystery. Anything. Just keep him talking. Please. It will give us time to reach there.' He held Colin's gaze. 'This is our only chance of getting Vijay and Radha out of there alive. Believe me, Farooq has no plans to free them. Once he gets the information he needs, your friends will die.'

Colin pondered this for a few moments, exchanging glances with Shukla and White. Both men nodded. This seemed to be the only way out.

'Fine.' Colin exhaled sharply. 'We'll do as you've asked. Please get them back.'

Imran nodded grimly. 'I'll do my best.' Inwardly, he wasn't so confident. He had a plan, but it depended on so many other factors, there was no way to be sure what would happen.

As Imran left the room, White said, 'I'm sorry but I need to go lie down for a while. I hope you don't mind.'

'Sure, no problem,' Colin said, half distracted, as White left the room. Shukla stayed, still looking pale and petrified.

A thought briefly crossed Colin's mind but he pushed it away. There was no doubt the news about Bheem Singh had come as a shock to the archaeologist. But it seemed to him that White looked more *angry* than unwell! But that didn't make sense. Colin shook his head. He was imagining things. He had more important things to worry about right now.

A Moment of Happiness

Vijay sat on the floor of the room in which he was being held captive. For some reason, his captivity didn't bother him. But his mind was still in turmoil. He struggled to come to terms with his hopelessness. He questioned the use of trying to understand his emotions when they were confronted with death. Farooq intended killing Radha and him. There was no hope for them.

Something went off in his brain. He realised what had happened. He had fallen in love with Radha. For a few moments, he allowed the thought to wash over him and luxuriated in the warm, ecstatic feeling that accompanied it. Then he pushed the thought away. What a time to discover love! When they were doomed to be killed. But then, if they lived, would she reciprocate his feelings? She had shown no signs of any special feelings for him.

He sighed. Life was a bitch.

As if to reinforce his conclusion, two of the LeT fighters entered the room. An AK 47 was pointed at him and one of the men gestured for him to rise and follow them.

A Daring Attempt to Escape

The room where Radha had been dumped had no furniture apart from a hard, lumpy cotton mattress that had served as her bed in one corner of the room. The floor was dirty but thankfully there didn't seem to be cockroaches or rats around; at least, she hadn't seen any.

The power situation in Patna wasn't very good. The lights would go off every few hours or so and the blackout could last for anywhere between half an hour and several hours. It seemed that the building didn't have a backup generator or inverter, at least not one connected to this room. During these blackouts the room would be in complete darkness with each sound amplified a thousand times. She had heard lizards scraping along the wall as they scurried from one shelter to another but no other sounds had disturbed those hours of solitude, silence and darkness.

She really hadn't any cause to complain about the way she was being treated. She was given three meals a day; simple food, but she never went hungry.

Farooq hadn't made an appearance since the first day when he had spoken to both of them. Neither had she seen Vijay since then. She, too, had been left alone though Farooq had kept her mobile phone with him. She wondered how Vijay was faring, and hoped he was safe.

Her solitude over the last two days had been difficult for her, though she fought to keep her hopes alive. Often, when the lights went off, the darkness and silence weighed down on her mind, enveloping it, numbing it and distorting her emotions and thoughts. It was in those moments that she felt most disheartened.

She longed to be able to get away and tell the others. The Indian government needed to know. Other governments needed to be informed. If what Farooq had shared with her was true, the world was running out of time.

There was a sound at the door and she looked up. One of Farooq's men entered. He looked at her and wordlessly indicated that she was to follow him.

Wearily, she got to her feet. The gunman strode away, not bothering to look back at her, confident that she had nowhere to run.

The guard led her down the corridor, until they came to a large room with rattan furniture strewn around in a haphazard fashion. Farooq occupied a large sofa , directly facing the door. A bottle of whisky and bottles of soda stood on a table in front of him. He held a half-empty glass of whisky and soda. Some of the other men held glasses of whisky as well.

Vijay stood before Farooq, his hands bound behind his back. She realised that Farooq wasn't taking any chances after Vijay had escaped from his clutches on an earlier occasion. She also realised that the men believed that she was easy prey, which was why she was allowed more freedom than Vijay. After the initial feeling of resentment at being considered weak just because she was a woman, it dawned on her that this gave her the slimmest of chances of getting away. She decided to stay alert and look out for the slightest opportunity for their escape. No matter what the odds, she wasn't going down without a fight. And she knew that neither would Vijay.

Despite her strong resolve, she shuddered at the lascivious grins that appeared on the faces of the men as she entered the room.

Vijay looked relieved to see her. He didn't look very well, though there was no evidence that he had been physically mistreated in any way.

What was that emotion behind the concern in his eyes? It shouted out to her that he reciprocated her feelings for him. Her heart quickened. The man she loved was standing next to her, but she couldn't tell him that she loved him, too.

'Forty minutes to go,' Farooq said by way of a greeting. 'Your friends better have been successful in figuring out the location of the secret.' He ignored Vijay who was staring angrily at him and focused on Radha. He grinned, an evil, leering grin. 'And after I get what I want, we'll take care of you.' He looked at his men. 'Won't we?' He laughed and the other guards in the room laughed as well. She didn't like the look in their eyes.

Vijay was standing like he was carved out of stone. Radha could see the fury in his eyes. He was making a conscious effort to restrain himself. His face, stony and black, betrayed his anger, his urge to fight and break free. Farooq was mocking her, mocking him, knowing fully well that they were like birds with clipped wings, able to flutter around but incapable of taking flight.

A shiver ran down her spine. The true extent of their predicament struck her like a blow in the face. These men had no intention of letting them go. Any hope that he would eventually set them free was now gone. And now, it was also clear that they didn't intend killing her immediately. And she knew what that meant!

Tears welled up in her eyes as she realised the hopelessness of her situation. But she was determined not to show her fear; she knew it would only embolden the men.

Smiling with grim satisfaction, Farooq lifted his glass. 'To the weapon of Lashkar-e-Taiba!' He exclaimed in Urdu.

'The weapon of Lashkar-e-Taiba!' The other men echoed the refrain, some of them thumping their boots on the floor.

Radha tried to hide her trembling hands behind her back.

Then, it happened.

The power went off and the room was plunged into darkness.

'Radha, go!' Vijay's shout was immediately followed by a thud, the sound of the sofa overturning, a crash and the sound of glass shattering. She heard Farooq yell out in pain and curse. The room exploded in commotion.

For a moment, she froze. Then she realised what had happened.

Vijay, seeing the opportunity, had jumped Farooq, knocking down the table and the rattan sofa. By the sound of it, he had probably rolled over after that, unable to stop himself with his hands bound, and crashed full tilt into some of the other terrorists.

She realised that her opportunity was at hand.

It would mean leaving Vijay behind, but she knew what he was thinking. One of them had to escape and get word to the government about the threat. Vijay had created this opportunity knowing the risk he faced by being the one left behind.

The fact that the lights had gone out meant that the house didn't have an inverter. Even if there was a generator that fed power to this room, she had a few precious seconds before someone started it.

Someone shouted in Urdu. 'Secure the woman!'

Radha racked her brains, desperately trying to recall the direction of the door through which she had entered the room and realised that it should be directly behind her. She turned around and sprinted out of the room. Shouts rang out as men closed in on where she had been standing and realised that she was no longer there.

Farooq's voice rose over the clamour, speaking in Urdu 'Fools! She must not get out of the room!'

A light came on behind her, dimly lighting the room she had left. Someone had lit a candle. Its weak light did little to pierce the gloom in the corridor that stretched before her, though it did help ensure she didn't bump into anything in the dark.

She ran down the corridor.

The passage forked before her. Darting down the passage on the right, she ran blindly, hoping she was going the right way.

If she was caught...

She shuddered, not wanting to think about the possibility. She noticed rooms on either side, with their doors shut, on either side of the passage.

A beam of light pierced the darkness. Someone had switched on a torch.

There was a shout as the torch silhouetted her in the passage. The men following her had reached the fork in the corridor and had seen her.

The light from the torch also outlined a door at the end of the corridor. *Where did it lead to?*

Radha increased her pace, her breath coming in short bursts. How long would she be able to keep this up?

Reaching the door, she jerked it open.

A landing led to a staircase that descended to a lower level. She just caught herself from tumbling headlong down the stairs.

For a split second, she hesitated. Was she going the right way? Or was she getting herself into a dead end?

The sound of the men pursuing her grew louder as they approached.

Quickly making up her mind, she sped down the staircase, moving as fast as she could in the darkness.

While the darkness had helped her escape, it was also slowing her progress. The men pursuing her had no such handicap. They could move faster than her and would catch up soon.

There was a window at the next landing. She paused to steal a glance outside. There was a moon in the sky which dimly lit up the surroundings. Though the streetlights were off she could make out one thing that mattered.

The street was one level below.

Her gamble had paid off.

Her hopes rising, she darted down the rest of the staircase using the balustrade to maintain her pace.

The stairway ended in a large room. Through the curtainless windows, she could see the street outside.

The lights came back on again.

Behind her the men raced down the staircase.

The stairway led down one more level, into the basement, which was enveloped in darkness. She noticed a door each, to her left and right. Both doors were latched shut.

Radha hesitated. She had to make a choice of which door to try and she didn't have time for mistakes.

The door on her left. It was directly below the window from which she had seen the street. That had to be the front door.

She raced to the door and struggled with the latch which seemed to be jammed.

She rushed back across the room and tried the latch on the other door. It slid back smoothly and noiselessly. She turned to see where her pursuers were and saw them enter the room.

They saw her immediately and advanced towards her, evil grins on their faces.

Desperate, Radha backed up against the door she had just opened. It gave way behind her and she lost her balance, falling back into the room it led into.

Suddenly, shouts erupted from upstairs.

The group of men stopped, looking at each other as if trying to make sense of what they had heard.

The shouts came again, spurring the men to action. All of them, except one, raced back up the stairs. The lone remaining man walked up to the door and stared at Radha, anger in his eyes. Wordlessly, he slammed the door in her face and Radha heard the bolts being shot home. She heard him shout something back to the men upstairs. He was probably letting them know that he'd locked her up.

She was a prisoner once more.

Day 10

Somewhere in Patna

As the lights blinked on again, Vijay found himself being hauled up roughly and hurled across the room. He crashed into a wall and lay there, dazed, breathing heavily. He tried to sit up but before he could, Farooq was at his side, pulling him up by a handful of his hair.

Vijay shouted out in pain but it only seemed to encourage his tormentor.

'Think you are smart, are you?' Farooq hissed in his ear. 'If I didn't have to keep you alive until I got my answers, you'd be dead by now.'

He flung Vijay away from him, then kicked him hard in the ribs, following it up with another kick for good measure. Vijay buckled with pain but clenched his teeth and forced his screams back. He was not going to give Farooq the pleasure of knowing that he was hurting him. But he knew he couldn't hold out for much longer if the man persisted. Just then, Vijay's mobile phone, which was with Farooq, rang and the LeT leader looked at it with astonishment. As Vijay looked on, he disconnected the call and put the phone back in his pocket.

It promptly rang again.

This time, Farooq answered. 'What the hell do you think you are doing calling me on this number?' he demanded angrily. 'You know the plan. I...'

He stopped midsentence, as if abruptly cut off by the caller and his jaw dropped. Vijay surmised that he was getting some news that he hadn't anticipated. He wondered what it was.

'Are you sure about all this?' Farooq asked finally after hearing the caller out.

He fell silent again, listening to the reply.

'Fine. Change of plans. We'll leave immediately.' He disconnected the call and looked at Vijay. 'Your friends have deciphered the verse,' he smirked. 'And now they'll be joining you. All of you will die together.'

Vijay wondered how Farooq knew, because he certainly hadn't been speaking to any of his friends. But he didn't have time to think further. 'We leave immediately!' Farooq barked to his men and immediately they galvanised into action. Two of them dragged Vijay to his feet and supported him out of the room.

'What about the woman?' Vijay heard one of the men asking Farooq in Urdu.

'Forget her. We have more important things to worry about,' Farooq shot back. 'Call the others back. The Intelligence Bureau knows our location. We have to leave before they find us.'

Vijay's heart leaped. This meant that he and his friends weren't the only ones who knew about Farooq.

'She has been locked in the room downstairs,' one of the men informed Farooq.

'Doesn't matter. Let's go,' Farooq responded.

Vijay smiled to himself. If the IB was hunting the LeT leader, then they would come to this safehouse sooner or later. Even if Farooq and his men escaped with him as captive, Radha would be found.

Farooq's next words, however, dashed his hopes to the ground.

'Burn the building to the ground.'

A Little Too Late

Imran's phone rang. He was in a police jeep, being driven to Farooq's safehouse. He looked at the number. It was from one of his men in the surveillance team, who had been despatched to the safehouse as soon as its location was tracked down. Their job was to keep a watch on Farooq and his men and report in if they noticed any developments.

'Have the commandos reached?' Imran looked at his watch impatiently. He knew that as soon as Farooq learned about the location of the secret, he would waste no time in leaving Patna. So, he had detoured to speak to Vijay's friends in the hope that they would be able to delay Farooq's departure from the safehouse just long enough for the commandos to reach.

'No,' came the reply from his agent outside the safehouse. 'And I think Farooq's slipped out. The building is on fire.'

Imran cursed as he disconnected the phone. He had lost Farooq.

And he didn't know where to start looking for him.

Marching Orders

Colin knocked on White's door and the archaeologist opened it. He was looking normal now. The short rest must have done him good.

'Your phone,' Colin explained. 'Farooq calls us on your phone.'

'Oh, I'm so sorry,' White apologised, looking sheepish. 'I should have left my phone with you. I wasn't thinking straight.' He fetched the phone from his desk.

The two men walked down the corridor to Colin's room.

As if on cue, the phone rang. Vijay's mobile number flashed on the screen.

Farooq's smug voice floated over the phone. 'You have the information I want.'

It was a statement, not a question, but Colin answered him anyway. 'Yes.'

'Well?'

'We've solved the riddle.'

'And what is the answer?' There was an edge to Farooq's voice that Colin hadn't heard before. He remembered Imran's instructions.

Delay them as long as you can.

He just hoped he wasn't putting Vijay and Radha in any more danger than they already were.

'The secret location is in the Hazaribagh plateau.'

'And what makes you believe that?'

'Before I tell you that or the exact location, I want to know how and when you will hand over Vijay and Radha to us.'

'Do you take me for a fool?' Farooq's voice strained with fury and something else percolated through. Was it an undercurrent of desperation? Colin couldn't be sure.

'Do you know what your friends just did?' he continued, his voice shaking with anger. 'They tried to escape.'

Colin's heart sank.

Farooq's next words made his blood run cold.

'My patience is running out. I don't have either the inclination or the time to negotiate. If you don't give me what I want then that's fine. You'll never see your friends again.'

Colin hesitated. He considered his options. There was no guarantee that Farooq would return Vijay and Radha to them after learning where the secret was hidden. On the other hand, if he didn't get the information, both of them were doomed.

There was only one thing to do. Colin could only hope that Imran reached the safehouse in time.

'Sitagarha Hill,' he told Farooq. 'The Hazaribagh plateau.' He explained to Farooq how they had arrived at this conclusion.

Farooq seemed to doubt his explanation. 'And how do I know you are being completely honest with me?'

Colin didn't have an answer.

'There's only one way to be sure,' Farooq interrupted his thoughts. 'You'll show me the way to this hill to prove that this is indeed the place.'

'And you'll let them go then?' Colin persisted.

'I want you to leave Patna immediately. All three of you.' Farooq ignored Colin's question. 'Leave for Hazaribagh now. I will meet you there and together we will go to this hill. If what you are saying isn't true...' He left his threat hanging but Colin understood perfectly.

'One more thing. Switch your phone off. Now. I don't want you to switch it back on until you are near Hazaribagh. I'll be checking to see that you've followed this instruction.

Don't let me find your phone on. Call me when you're approaching Hazaribagh.'

The phone went dead.

Colin hung his head.

'Did he come around?' White inquired, looking anxious.

Colin shook his head. He quickly explained to the others about Vijay and Radha's aborted attempt to escape and Farooq's demand.

'We must be going.' He rose. 'Farooq asked us to leave Patna immediately. I'll get the X Trail out and meet you in five minutes at the main porch.'

Trapped in an inferno

Radha had switched on the light in the room.

There were no windows and it was pitch dark inside. She had found the light switch by going around the room, by sticking to the walls, and feeling her way.

The room seemed to be a storehouse. There were empty boxes and cartons lying around. In one corner, cotton mattresses were stacked into piles.

Bedding for the terrorists, she assumed.

Outside, silence had descended. She wondered what was happening. With a feeling of dread she hoped that Vijay was okay—though she had a nasty suspicion that Farooq would be vindictive and punish him for her attempt.

What would happen to her now?

She suddenly realised that the air had become somewhat hazy. Radha looked at the door and saw, to her horror, tendrils of smoke seeping into the room from under the door.

Horror gripped her. Was there a fire in the building?

She flung herself against the door and beat at it with her fists, screaming at the top of her voice.

Had no one in the building realised there was a fire?

The smoke grew thicker and she heard the fire crackle and spit outside in the hall. She backed away from the door, trying to find a place where the smoke was thin so she could breathe. Her eyes were stinging and she began to cough. She had read somewhere that most victims of fire died not from burns but from suffocation.

But it was no consolation to her that she wouldn't be burned alive. No one seemed to be coming to her rescue.

She was going to die anyway.

Outside the safehouse, Imran leaped out of the jeep as it screeched to a halt. The commandos had reached, and he saw that they had taken up defensive positions around the house.

Three fire tenders stood by as firemen battled the flames. An ambulance had accompanied the fire tenders on Imran's instructions.

But they were too late.

The birds had flown the coop. Farooq and his men were gone.

Imran walked over to the commander of the commandos, a young officer who introduced himself as Major Kishore Verma.

'Is there anyone in the house?' Imran was concerned that Vijay and Radha may have been left behind to perish in the fire. Farooq had no use for them now that he knew his destination.

Verma shook his head. 'We've been trying to figure that out, but the fire was raging when we got here. The heat sensors are going haywire with the fire itself. It's difficult to detect a human presence inside. And the firemen think it isn't safe to go inside just yet. It looks like they used some kind of chemicals to start and feed the fire, to keep it going for a while.'

Imran looked Verma in the eye. 'There were two hostages. If they were alive when Farooq left, I don't want to lose them to the fire.'

One of the commandos in the command vehicle gave a shout. He had been sitting with his eyes glued to the heat sensor, one of a range of equipment that the government had invested in after 26/11.

'There's someone inside!' he exclaimed. The flames had diminished sufficiently to allow the sensor to detect a human presence in one of the rooms.

'Only one?' Imran asked.

The commando nodded.

'Did you get a lock on its position?' Verma enquired.

The commando nodded. 'The room directly opposite the front entrance.'

Verma quickly explained the situation to the firemen and two of them agreed to break into the house.

'I'm coming with you,' Imran declared. 'There's no time to argue. Let's go.' He felt a sense of responsibility for what had happened,

A hat, gloves and a jacket along with a gas mask were quickly procured for Imran and he followed the two firemen. 'There,' Imran pointed to the door opposite them as they entered.

The firemen raced across the hall and broke open the door. At the far end of the room, Radha lay on the floor. Without breaking stride, the three men lifted her and sprinted out of the building with her.

Within moments, the paramedics with the ambulance had taken charge and begun trying to revive Radha.

Imran stood outside the ambulance, his face grim.

Would Radha make it?

38

Present Day

Day 10
Patna

'I can't tell you how grateful I am to you,' Radha smiled at Imran. They were both in the police jeep, Radha having spent the better part of an hour in the ambulance and then in a local hospital.

Imran smiled back. 'I'm just glad we made it in time.'

A serious expression replaced Radha's smile. 'So, Farooq fled because he got wind that you were onto him?' Imran nodded. 'Yes. We had tapped Vijay's phone and minutes before the fire started, Farooq got a call updating him about Bheem Singh's death and also informing him that the Intelligence Bureau knew what he was upto.'

The first thing Radha had done on recovering was to tell Imran about Bheem Singh, only to discover that Imran was from the IB and already knew.

'So, you have a leak at the IB'?

Imran shook his head. 'Not the IB. There's only one person who has known all this and yet gone unnoticed and unsuspected all this while.'

'Who'? Radha racked her brains but couldn't figure it out.

Imran told her.

Radha's eyes widened in horror. 'Are you sure?'

'I'm positive. We ran a match of a sketch with his photograph. A perfect match.'

'And Farooq asked Colin to get the others and join him near Hazaribagh,' Imran informed her.

Radha was really worried now. 'We have to do something.'

'We are. We are meeting the commandos in 15 minutes. We go with them to Sitagarha Hill.' Imran had tried calling White's mobile phone but it was switched off. There was no way of contacting them.

Radha had been dumbstruck when she heard, from Imran, about Sitagarha Hill and Colin's explanation about why this hill had seemed to be the obvious location of the secret.

It all fitted together so well.

'How will we find the hill?' she wondered.

'I know the place,' Imran replied. 'The Border Security Force uses the site as a heavy artillery range.'

His mobile phone rang. 'Hi, Vishnu,' he greeted the caller and lapsed into silence, listening intently. 'Good,' he said finally, 'I'm glad that's been worked out. If the state Home Secretary is working with you and the BSF have agreed to help, that's great. Hell, we don't even know what's going to happen.'

The caller responded and Imran seemed satisfied. 'Okay. Thanks, Vishnu. We'll see you in Hazaribagh.'

Radha looked enquiringly at him as he hung up. 'Vishnu Prasad,' Imran explained. 'The District Collector of Hazaribagh district. We don't know what lies in that cavern within Sitagarha Hill but I just can't believe that the secret that LeT is after is the only thing that's in there. I asked the

DC to get the town of Hazaribagh evacuated. Just in case. The town is barely 20 kilometres from the hill. I don't want any civilian casualties if something goes wrong. We are dealing with a small army of LeT men armed with sophisticated weapons. We can do without them running amok in a town full of innocent civilians. Before LeT gets to Hazaribagh, there won't be a soul there.'

Radha was curious. 'You seem to know everything,' she remarked. 'The brotherhood of the Nine, the clues, the search, even the secret.'

'Not everything,' Imran smiled at her. 'A bit. Courtesy Bheem Singh. And I want you to fill me in on the rest. Ah, here we are.'

They had reached the rendezvous point. Three five-ton camouflage trucks stood there, filled with men garbed in black body armour—the elite commandos of the Indian army, armed to the teeth with INSAS 5.56mm light machine guns, AGS 17 Plamya 30mm automatic grenade launchers, Carl Gustav 84mm recoilless rifles and Glock 17.9mm pistols.

Imran and Radha hopped into the leading truck. Imran looked at Radha. 'You're sure you want to do this?' She had insisted on coming along as she thought she might be able to help with clues at the site.

'Absolutely,' she replied. Imran nodded to the driver of the truck and the convoy trundled onto the highway that led to Ranchi.

39

Day 10

The Patna-Ranchi highway

Colin rubbed his eyes wearily. He had driven without a break for four hours, since leaving Patna. Darkness enveloped them like a shroud.

They were alone on the highway.

They had passed the town of Nawada two hours ago and several villages after that, as the highway snaked through open fields, which had now given way to dense forests.

'Where are we supposed to meet Farooq?' White suddenly spoke up. He and Shukla were sitting quietly in the backseat of the X Trail.

'He didn't say.' Colin responded before slowing down and stopping at the side of the road. He turned to White and held out his hand.

'It's about time you switched your phone on.'

White did as directed.

As if on cue, his phone rang.

'I'm glad to see that you followed my instructions.' Farooq's smooth voice came over the phone's speaker. 'Where have you reached?'

'I don't know where we are.' Colin fought back his anger and frustration, trying to keep calm.

'Have you passed an ancient ruin in the forests along the highway?'

'No. We are in a heavily forested area, though.'

'Then you must be very near Hazaribagh. Look out for the ruin to the left of the highway. You can't miss it. Stop there and wait for us.'

The phone went dead.

Colin drove on slowly, clinging to the left side of the highway. They all peered out, trying to catch a glimpse of the ruin that Farooq had described. It was dark in the forest and they had to strain to make out even the outline of the trees.

'There. In that copse of trees.' White saw it.

Colin jerked the car to a halt as White indicated a section of the forest they had just passed. He reversed slowly to the spot and switched off the headlights.

Darkness immediately descended upon them, welcoming them into its folds. Colin alighted and the others joined him, staring at the forest until they could discern the faint outline of a structure, barely visible among the trees.

They stood there in silence, waiting. The moments seemed to pass at a snail's pace. Where was Farooq? Colin thought.

Suddenly they noticed two points of light that pierced the veil of darkness that hung over them. The lights moved slowly towards them, growing larger and brighter as they drew near. More lights appeared behind the first set. A convoy approached them.

'Farooq' Colin breathed. Did the man have Vijay and Radha with him?

As the convoy drew near, they discerned six black Ford Endeavours which drew to a halt in front of the X Trail. Men jumped off the SUVs and ran towards them, carrying UZIs.

Behind them, carrying a revolver, was Farooq.

Colin perked up suddenly as he saw that Vijay was with them. His hands were bound, his face was bruised and he looked weary, but he was alive.

The moment of elation was short-lived. Nothing had prepared him for what happened next.

Farooq tossed an UZI to White while Vijay and his friends stared, open-mouthed.

'You sure took your time in coming,' the archaeologist said heatedly.

Farooq shrugged, his demeanour clearly showing that he did not like being questioned.

Vijay stared at the two men, his head spinning. What was happening?

'Okay, let's get this show on the road,' White said dismissively. 'We've lost enough time.'

Farooq turned to his men. 'Get these three into their car and let's get moving.'

40

Day 11

The Patna-Ranchi highway

'Where are we?' Radha had fallen asleep almost immediately after leaving Patna, tired and stressed after the events of the last few hours. The revelation that Bheem Singh was one of the bad guys and that a trained assassin was impersonating Greg White had come as a rude shock to her. It didn't help that her father and her friends were in the hands of men for whom killing was just another day's work.

'We're close to Hazaribagh,' Imran offered helpfully.

'They must have reached Sitagarha by now,' Radha mumbled.

'We're going as fast as possible. These trucks weren't built for speed.' Imran looked at her. 'Tell me, did Farooq reveal any of his plans while you were in his captivity?'

Radha told him everything that Farooq had shared with Vijay and her. 'It's a great plan,' Imran conceded. 'The consortium uses LeT as a front. No one will ever know. LeT gets to fulfil their ambition of becoming a great terrorist organisation, bigger and more effective than Al Qaeda. And the consortium can build an arsenal with the kinds of weapons they've already developed. As producers, they control the inventory. They issue a few to LeT, who target the G20 summit and allows the consortium to install their own men as state heads. Everyone is happy. LeT gets its 15 minutes of fame. The politicians realise their political dreams. And the consortium controls the world. Power and profit is theirs for the taking. The perfect plan.'

Radha mulled over his words. 'And there's nothing anyone can do to stop LeT from carrying out their threat,' she said finally. 'They've hit upon the one weapon that no armed force in the world possesses a defence against.'

Imran agreed with her. 'I saw it with my own eyes. The prototype they've developed. I wouldn't have believed it if I hadn't seen it. Van Klueck is still alive, even if Bheem Singh is dead. And their political backers will ensure that LeT is able to develop and deploy their weapon. There's only one thing that can stop them now.'

They both knew what that was. The commandos had to reach Sitagarha hill in time.

41

Day 11

Somewhere beyond Hazaribagh town

As they drove along the highway, Vijay mulled over what had just transpired. Greg White was in league with Farooq. And Bheem Singh. And it explained a lot. How Farooq had known about their movements, for one. He chided himself for not suspecting White. Then, again, his uncle had asked him to speak to White. But what was the archaeologist's interest in allying with Farooq?

'What does an archaeologist have to do with LeT?' He asked White as they clambered into the X Trail.

'I'm not an archaeologist. My name is Murphy. I took out White the day he arrived from the States.' With that terse response and a lopsided grin, Murphy had steered the car towards their destination.

Vijay realised that he should have seen it earlier. Time and again when Murphy, as White, had been asked to contribute with his knowledge as an archaeologist and historian, he had failed to tell them anything meaningful. That, alone, should have rung alarm bells. But he had been so intent on following the trail of clues that nothing else had seemed to register for him. And now, they were in a fine soup.

As soon as they had been bundled into the SUV, Shukla asked the question that Vijay had been dreading.

'Where's Radha?'

Vijay averted his eyes. How was he to tell Shukla that Farooq had left his daughter to be burned alive in the safehouse? 'I don't know,' he mumbled finally, settling on the truth, however tenuous it was. Even though he knew that Radha had virtually no chance of escaping from the fire, he hoped with all his heart that she had somehow made it out alive. But the odds had been heavily stacked against her. But there was no time to think about this. Right now, two other lives depended on him—on his ability to lead Farooq to the secret of the Nine. He had to find a way out of their predicament.

Shukla lapsed into silence, brooding over Radha. He, too, nurtured the hope that she was alive, somewhere in Patna.

They drove past Hazaribagh town. After a while, they turned off the highway and onto a narrow road that was almost as bad as the road from Bela to Barabar.

Vijay brought Colin and Shukla up to date on his kidnapping, his captivity, the attempt to get Radha to escape, Bheem Singh's relationship with LeT, the terror threat to the G20 and the great secret that Farooq had revealed to them on the first day of their kidnapping.

'The secret of the Nine is the blueprint for a sophisticated technology,' Farooq had told them. 'A technology the world has dreamed of for long. Perhaps these dreams were influenced by the fact that the technology did exist thousands of years ago. It's the stuff of fantasy and only now have scientists begun taking the first steps to make it possible again. And this technology lies in the cavern within that hill.'

As he spoke, Vijay recalled the conversation he and Radha had had with Farooq on the first day of their captivity.

'What are you talking about?' Vijay demanded.

Farooq grinned at their incomprehension. 'The *Vimana Parva* gave a detailed description of the nature and impact of the weapon. According to this text, the *vimanas* being built by the King of Magadha would swoop down on the battlefield from the air, unseen. They would launch arrows that would decimate the Pandava armies and win the war for the Kauravas.' He paused for effect.

'They had discovered how to make their *vimanas* invisible.'

Vijay struggled to put his thoughts into words. The man was either crazy or was stringing them along.

'You're joking,' he said. 'Invisibility! It's found only in fantasy stories. Harry Potter, Lord of the Rings, that's where you'll find your technology.'

For a moment, Farooq seemed to be on the brink of exploding. Then, he drew a deep breath and composed himself. 'This is no joke. The concept of total invisibility has moved from the realm of the fantastic to the realm of the possible. You probably aren't aware of this, but science has begun taking its first steps towards making things invisible. And I am not talking about camouflage technology. This is real invisibility— the ability to bend light so that it goes right around an object, instead of reflecting off it, resulting in the object becoming invisible to the human eye.'

Vijay shook his head. 'I don't believe this is possible. I've studied physics, too.'

'I'll explain.' The scientist in Farooq came to the fore, and he settled himself comfortably in his chair as if preparing to deliver a lecture.

'You know how visibility works. Light reflects off something and renders it visible to the eye.'

Both Vijay and Radha nodded. This was basic science.

'All naturally occurring matter displays properties that are determined by its atomic make-up,' Farooq continued. 'The amount of light that is reflected or refracted depends on the interaction of the electromagnetic waves of light with the atomic particles of matter.

'There is a group of matter called anisotropic metamaterials. This group comprises materials that are not naturally occurring, but are artificially synthesised. Being artificial composites, their properties are not dependent on their atomic particles, but on the properties of the materials that make them up and the shape or pattern in which these materials are put together to make the metamaterial. There is a lot of research going on into this nowadays.

'Theoretically, anisotropic metamaterials have a variable refractive index and can actually bend light, so that if an object is sheathed in metamaterials, light isn't reflected or refracted but is simply guided around it. All natural materials bend electromagnetic radiation in one direction; away from a line perpendicular to their surface, or away from normal. Metamaterials, on the other hand, can be arranged so that their index of refraction forces waves to travel a path that bends towards normal. By diverting the waves upwards, around the object and then down again, the object, from a visual point of view, doesn't even exist. Moreover, if the light waves can be guided around the object in such a way that it returns to its original course, not only is the object rendered invisible, but it doesn't cast a shadow either. So an aircraft, for example, sheathed in metamaterials will be invisible to the naked eye.'

'And that is your plan? To steal this technology and use it for terror?' Vijay's scepticism seeped into his voice.

'Correct. We will use this technology to attack the G20 summit in Washington three months from now. In one stroke, 20 governments will be wiped out.'

'You'll be discovered before you can try anything.' Vijay attempted bravely, trying to strike at Farooq's confidence. 'Discovered?' Farooq smirked. 'We've already told them. And they're in a flap, trying to figure out why we've announced our plan three months before executing it. But the world can't defend itself from what it can't see! An invisible plane, carrying a deadly payload—how can any security agency in the world detect and stop it?'

'Radar.' Even as he spoke, Vijay realised the futility of his argument. 'You'll never get close enough to do any damage.'

'You aren't thinking straight,' Farooq replied scornfully. 'As you know, microwaves are the electromagnetic waves used in radar and their wavelengths are measured in anything from millimetres to metres. The wavelengths of visible light are measured in nanometres. If the technology is able to manipulate waves of visible light, manipulating microwaves is hardly a challenge. Perhaps you haven't heard of contemporary experiments being conducted using metamaterials that can manipulate microwaves. Using a sheath of metamaterials, an aircraft can be invisible to radar. And, though DARPA is only now working on trying to create metamaterials minute enough to manipulate light waves, this technology existed thousands of years ago. So our aircraft will have two sheaths. The first one will make them invisible to radar. And once we are close to our target, we will activate the nanoshield, which will render them invisible to the naked eye. Mission accomplished.'

'There's a flaw,' Vijay persisted, unwilling to give up. The thought that LeT could spring a shock on the world and they had unwittingly aided them was hard for him to accept.

'And that is?'

'Granted, a sheath of metamaterials will bend light around the aircraft, as you have explained. But, since the light that would normally enter the aircraft is now diverted around it anyone sitting inside will have a problem seeing out of the aircraft.'

'You haven't been reading the latest developments in this field,' Farooq shook his head. 'Recently, Chinese researchers have claimed to have developed an anticloak that, theoretically at least, takes care of this problem. The technology can be made assymetrical. The anticloaking material is an anisotropic metamaterial that is impedance-matched to the refractive index of the invisibility cloak. By pressing the anticloak against the invisibility cloak, some light could be guided inside to allow a person inside to peep out. That will enable the occupant of the aircraft to see outside while remaining invisible to an external observer. Research is ongoing into this aspect of the technology. It would seem, though, that the ancients had solved this problem.'

'What about the visible spectrum?' Vijay demanded, as another potential problem presented itself to him. 'The different colours of the spectrum exist on different wavelengths. How is it possible to simultaneously divert the different wavelengths in the visible spectrum?'

'I don't know how the ancient scientists who developed the invisibility shield overcame this problem,' Farooq admitted. 'And that's where the location of the secret comes in. Our prototype is not completely invisible. We've missed something vital in putting it together; which is why we need the original shield or the blueprints of the technology to put it together again.'

'If it wasn't you telling us all this, I would never have believed it,' Colin remarked when Vijay had finished. 'No wonder the IB guy was all worked up about Farooq.'

Abruptly, the X Trail lurched to a halt. They looked around at the thick forest that surrounded them. The six Endeavours stood a short distance ahead, their headlights illuminating the trees around.

As they alighted, they saw something being tossed out of one of the Fords. It landed on the forest floor with a heavy, dull thud.

'Our guide,' Farooq explained, 'who brought us this far. But it seems he didn't want to go further, so Maroosh took care of him. We don't need him from here.'

Vijay, Colin and Shukla stood frozen, shocked by the brutal murder of the guide. Murphy beckoned to the Pakistani scientist and both men walked off to one side, conversing in low tones. Farooq issued instructions to a couple of men who nodded and took up positions around the vehicles.

'The hill lies straight ahead,' Farooq informed them as he returned. 'If we follow this path, we should be fine.' He looked at the three captives. 'Any funny tricks and you'll follow the guide, not us.' He chuckled at his own pun.

Five men broke away from the group and brought up the rear, ensuring that the prisoners were surrounded.

Farooq stalked away to join Murphy and the two men led the group as they pushed through the forest, their powerful flashlights lighting up the path through the trees.

The path ran more or less in a straight line and the gradient slowly increased as they progressed deeper into the forest. Shukla's breathing became heavier and Vijay supported him. They had followed the path for half an hour when Murphy called a halt. As they clustered together, he pointed ahead.

'There.'

Before them, barely discernible, was the silhouette of a rocky wall.

Vijay's heart raced with anticipation, despite their predicament. Was this it?

On reaching the rock wall, they discovered that it fronted the hill, winding around the base for a considerable distance. The hill loomed above them as they halted in its shadow, the darkness deeper here than in the rest of the forest.

'Now what?' Murphy looked at Vijay.

Vijay thought fast, his mind flashing back to Surasen's account of his discovery which Shukla had read out to them from Beger's diary. If this was the hill Surasen had come upon, there should be an opening hidden by the rock face.

'Shine your flashlights on the rock,' he directed and, with one accord, multiple beams of light converged on the rock wall.

They made their way along the wall, moving slowly, searching for an opening or any sign of a blocked entrance. Vijay was sure that the original Nine had closed the opening and hoped that they would find some sign that indicated where the cavern entrance once stood.

But there was nothing. The wall stretched for almost 60 feet around the hill but they came across neither opening nor any sign. As they came to the end of the wall, Vijay asked them to light up the gap between the wall and the hill. He stepped forward to enter the fissure but Farooq summoned him back and motioned to one of his own men to check the narrow gap.

The man walked slowly, cautiously, feeling his way around the narrow passage between the wall and the hill. And disappeared.

After a moment, a shout came to their ears, followed by a string of unintelligible words.

'What's he saying?' Murphy asked.

'There's nothing there.' Farooq shouted out something to the scout and turned on Vijay, his anger carving deep lines on his face in the light of the torches.

Vijay didn't understand. He made his way into the gap. The terrain, the wall, the fissure, all matched the description in Surasen's narration.

With one difference.

There was no entrance into the hillside.

He emerged from behind the wall, looking perplexed. A sinking feeling took hold of him. Had the Nine brought them so far only to lead them into a dead end?

Or had they been mistaken in their conclusion about Sitagarha hill being the location of the cavern?

42

Day 11

The outskirts of Hazaribagh town

The convoy of trucks drew to a halt and Imran hopped out. Radha jumped out as well and they walked together to where a white Ambassador car, with a beacon, stood. As they approached, the man standing outside the car came forward to meet them.

'Good to see you, Vishnu,' Imran greeted the District Collector of Hazaribagh warmly.

'Good to see you, too, Imran.' The DC was in his mid 30s, with jet black hair cut short and a pencil-thin moustache.

Radha was introduced to him.

Vishnu smiled at Radha and, addressing Imran, said, 'I know you're not going to tell me who she is and why she is here.'

'No. Long story. We don't have too much time. We have to be on our way.'

'That's why I said I'd meet you here rather than you taking a detour through the town. You'd lose an extra half-hour that way.' Vishnu glanced at the commandos in the trucks. 'And you'd fall behind whoever you are chasing.' He grinned at Imran. 'I don't suppose you can tell me what you're up to? Evacuating Hazaribagh town in the middle of the night, accompanying three truckloads of Black Cat commandos into the forests of Hazaribagh. Whatever it is you're after, it must be big.'

Imran grinned back. The two men seemed to know each other well. 'National security. Can't tell you. But you're right. It is big. How's the evacuation going?'

'The BSF have been a great help. We'll be through in a couple of hours.'

''What did you tell the people?'

'Section 144. Earthquake prediction.' Vishnu looked at Imran. 'It wasn't easy, though.'

Imran understood. Disaster management policies and contingency plans sounded good on paper. Putting them into action, however, was a different thing. 'We must be going.' Imran said, finally, to Vishnu. 'You'd better get away as well. Just in case.'

Vishnu's face was serious. 'Take care of yourself, Imran.' He nodded to Radha. 'You too, Radha. And I hope you catch whoever you are after.'

He got into his car and drove off as Radha and Imran made their way back to the truck and clambered in. They were close to their goal.

But would they reach in time?

The Final Task

The tension was palpable and Vijay was sweating profusely.

Then, Colin had a flash of inspiration. 'Hang on. Wasn't there something about a stupa being discovered around here?'

Vijay stared at Colin, wondering what he was jabbering about. His mind was numb with the pressure of their fate hanging by a thread, accentuated by a lack of sleep and the tension of the last few days.

Colin realised that Vijay hadn't seen the brochure from the travel agency, and he quickly explained.

Vijay, too, made the connection. 'The original entrance was definitely here,' he explained. 'Behind the rock wall. The Nine must have blocked it up and camouflaged it so it looked like the rest of the hillside. With the passage of 2,000 years all trace of their handiwork would have disappeared. But they must have built an alternate entrance. The stupa will mark that entrance.'

Farooq's eyes bored into Vijay for a moment, then he turned around and barked instructions to his men who fanned out, searching for a stupa.

Tense moments passed. Murphy stood by impassively, his face inscrutable. Farooq, however, paced up and down wordlessly like a lion in a cage.

A shout came out of the darkness.

Farooq strode swiftly in that direction, followed by the rest of the group.

Two men had their flashlights trained on a small stupa blackened with age. If there had been a protective wall around it, the centuries had devoured it. What stood before them was a hemispherical stone mound, 10 feet high, bereft of carvings or stonework.

Vijay held his breath as he and his friends approached the stupa.

'Let's split up and examine the face of the structure. You know what we are looking for,' he directed them.

Colin and Shukla nodded and broke away. The stupa seemed to be consistent with the pattern the Nine had followed.

It had been carved out of stone, not bricks and plaster like many other stupas; it had been built to last.

Shukla made the discovery. 'Here,' he called out.

They quickly hurried to the far side of the stupa and found him standing before the only ornamentation on the structure.

It was a stone column that extruded around six inches from the stupa, parallel to the ground. The base of the pillar, where it met the stupa, was ornately carved with miniature lions. But it was the face of the pillar that was visible to them that bore the unmistakable sign of the Nine, within a circle of lions.

The nine-spoked wheel.

They looked at each other excitedly, almost forgetting that they were surrounded by terrorists.

Farooq and Murphy came up to them and stared at the pillar. Murphy looked at Vijay. 'Well?'

The pillar was profusely carved and to anyone not familiar with the sign of the Nine it was difficult to comprehend the nature of their discovery.

'It's here.' Vijay looked around. What did the sign mark? If it indicated an entrance, then where was it?

'How can you be sure?' Farooq eyed him with suspicion.

Vijay ignored him. 'Keep looking,' he instructed his companions. 'It has to be here somewhere.'

They wandered among the broken columns and pillars scattered around the stupa, probably remnants of some other ancient structure that had stood here. But there was no sign of anything that would indicate an entrance to the cavern within the hill.

Shukla stopped at a short stone cylindrical pillar and stared curiously at it. It was three feet in height and resting on a stone base that rose up from the ground to a height of three inches. Near the tip of the pillar were small, hollow stone loops.

Vijay and Colin saw his interest in the pillar and joined him in examining it.

Did it offer any clues?

Colin looked back at the horizontal column on the stupa which had the wheel engraved on it.

The same thought struck all three of them together.

It was pointing straight at the circular pillar Shukla had stopped by. The horizontal column was fixed at exactly the same height as the height of the circular pillar. This had to be more than a coincidence.

'Lights!' Vijay called out and the LeT men trained their flashlights on the stone pillar.

'It's built to slide.' Colin pointed at the thin stone slab that formed the base. The pillar seemed to be mounted on grooves and if they could slide the pillar along the grooves, they were certain that beneath the base of the pillar, they would find another entrance to the cavern of the Nine.

'We need ropes.' Vijay looked at Farooq, who barked orders once more.

The LeT men ran thick ropes through the stone loops on the pillar. They then tugged hard at the ropes.

The pillar didn't move.

More men joined the effort, straining every muscle.

But the pillar refused to budge.

Vijay frowned and squatted, examining the grooves on which the pillar was mounted. 'The pillar can't be slid in this direction,' he announced after a few moments. 'There's an edge of rock wedged in between the grooves, locking it in place. Try pulling in the opposite direction.'

The LeT men now moved to the opposite side and heaved on the ropes.

This time, the pillar moved with a jerking motion, shuddered and then toppled over to the ground with a soft thud.

Carved into the stone base was a hollow, forming a sturdy stone handle. It had been concealed beneath the pillar.

Ropes were looped through the handle and pulled. Slowly, the base stone began to rise as centuries of dirt and mud fell away from its edges. It finally fell over, exposing a dark hole in the ground.

Flashlights were immediately trained on the opening, revealing a stone staircase that descended into the depths of the ground and disappeared into darkness.

Farooq motioned to two men who obediently disappeared down the stairway. A few moments later, a muffled shout reached their ears. They were quickly herded forward, led by Farooq and Murphy.

In the light from the flashlights they noticed that on either side of the staircase were bare stone walls polished smooth, though not as finely as the walls of the caves they had seen at Barabar.

The stairway took them deep under the forest floor. As they stepped off the final stair, they stood in a square chamber and looked around, in awe. It was large enough to accommodate at least a 100 people. Whoever had built the chamber had taken pains to burnish its appearance, polishing the walls to a high degree of smoothness. The roof was about 30 feet above their heads.

The LeT men spread out.

Shukla gazed around, wondering why the chamber had been built. He knew this question would remain unresolved, the answer hidden in the mists of time.

There was a shout from one of the LeT men who had gone ahead to explore.

Farooq and Murphy stalked over to him, followed by the others. The light of the torches revealed openings in the rock wall opposite the rocky stairway entrance.

'Not another riddle.' Colin groaned.

They stared at the sight before them.

Nine archways had been cut into the rock wall. Each arch rose to a height of 10 feet and bore an inscription above it. But this time the telltale wheel was of no help.

Each arch bore an engraved wheel above the inscription.

'What does this mean?' Farooq demanded angrily. His tension was palpable. He hadn't been expecting the final stage of the journey to be this challenging.

But it was clear that the Nine hadn't meant their secret to be discovered so easily. Even if someone solved the clues and made it this far, they had to go through further tests before they achieved their goal.

Shukla had been studying the arches. 'I've read about tricks like these,' he said softly, his eyes still gleaming. The excitement of treading a path that hadn't been trodden for over 2,000 years, of finding the only existing structures built in the time of Asoka the Great, and of being so close to finding the secret of the Nine, had momentarily overcome his fear and apprehension of being held hostage by LeT. 'Entrances like these were built to ensure that only a select few could access them. Enter the wrong doorway and you could find yourself in a trap, a maze, or worse.'

'So, which one is the correct doorway?' Murphy's gaze bored into Shukla.

Vijay looked at the old scholar, hoping he could make sense of the inscriptions above each archway. They were unintelligible to him.

'The inscriptions are in Magadhi.' Shukla gazed fervently at the engravings, straining to read them. Farooq noticed this and ordered the flashlights be trained on the inscriptions.

'Can you read them?' Vijay urged Shukla. 'I mean, are they still legible?'

To his relief, Shukla nodded. 'They've been sheltered here for a long time, protected against the elements, so they're in good condition.' He pointed to each inscription, as he read them out from left to right.

'*Isvara, Jeevas, Prakriti, Samay, Karma, Dukkha, Samudaya, Nirhodha, Marga.*'

Colin frowned. 'I recognise the first five. I remember you telling me about the five basic truths of the Bhagavad Gita. But what are the others?'

Shukla looked at him. 'The four basic truths of Buddhism; *Dukkha* (the truth of suffering), *Samudaya* (the truth of the cause of suffering), *Nirhodha* (the truth of the end of suffering), *Marga* (the truth of the path that frees human beings from suffering). Together, these nine words represent the foundation of Hinduism and the basis of Buddhism, the two major religions that originated in India. If there was any doubt that Asoka was responsible for this or connected with this structure in any way, this removes that doubt.'

'Good.' Murphy walked up to Shukla, 'Then you can also figure out which one is the correct doorway.'

Shukla shook his head. 'I have no way of knowing which one to choose. There are no clues here.'

Farooq strode up to Shukla, a hard look on his face. 'We have not come this far to fail. We must find the path to enter.'

Then, without warning, he suddenly lashed out and struck Shukla in the face with his gun. The elderly man crumpled to the rocky floor of the cavern, blood streaming down his face.

Vijay opened his mouth but before he could speak, help came from an unlikely source.

'No.' Murphy stepped forward swiftly and placed a hand on Farooq's arm as he had taken a step forward, as if to kick Shukla who was lying prone on the ground. The Pakistani was venting his frustration on the weaker man, but Murphy knew that Shukla was a valuable resource.

'We may need him.' Murphy warned. 'There may be more inscriptions that only he can read.'

Farooq's face was a mask of fury as he turned on Murphy. For a few moments, the men seemed to be engaged in a battle of wills. Then, with a visible effort, Farooq composed himself.

'Fine. But I want this puzzle solved. Now.'

Colin stepped up. 'I think I know the answer.'

Farooq looked at him, his scepticism showing in his face. If a scholar like Shukla couldn't solve this riddle, what chance did an American have? 'You do?' He didn't trust him. 'Then tell me what it is. And just to be sure that you won't try anything funny, your friend here can go through the arch first. You and the old man will remain with us. If you're wrong or lying, then you'll have sealed your friend's fate. But if you're right, he'll be back to guide us through.'

Colin stared at the brutal mask that leered at him. He had no doubt that Farooq meant every word of his threat.

He swallowed and looked at Vijay, less confident now. What if he was wrong? Vijay nodded back imperceptibly, reassuringly, and Colin faced Farooq once more.

'I don't know much about the *Gita* or Buddhism, but I remember the emails Vijay's uncle sent to him.' He turned to Vijay. 'What if your uncle had hidden a clue to this in his emails? We now know that he was a member of the Nine. What if he had left a clue to help you make it through this stage?'

Vijay frowned. 'You could be right. There was a lot in the emails that we initially thought was redundant and had been put there just to confuse anyone reading them. But I can't think of anything that could relate to these inscriptions.'

'The second email,' Colin urged.

Vijay thought hard. What had the second email said? *Everything isn't always the way it looks. Sometimes you need to look deeper within. Study, the Bhagavad Gita, it is the source of much knowledge. The subject of the Gita, though mixed up, is a mark upon us for our future lives, and will lead you through the door to knowledge, which you must unlock. In an ocean of maya, there is always an island of satya.*

He shook his head.

'The same clue that led us to the key.' Colin pointed to the central arch and at the inscription above it. He silently prayed that Vijay would arrive at the same conclusion as he did and corroborate his line of reasoning.

Vijay gazed at the arch, still uncomprehending. It was flanked by four arches on either side. Fatigue lurked on the fringes of his mind, threatening to overpower it. He fought it, concentrating on Colin's words. What had Shukla said the fifth inscription was?

Isvara, Jeevas, Prakriti...Samay...Karma...

It struck him like a brilliant flash of light; like the flashbulb of a camera going off in the dark. It had to be the central doorway. Colin was right.

He felt a new surge of energy course through his body, washing away all his exhaustion.

'Karma,' he said aloud and Colin beamed at him, jubilant.

Vijay stepped forward and extended his hand for a flashlight. One of the men handed him one.

Colin walked up to join him. 'You're not going in there alone.'

Vijay smiled at him gratefully.

Farooq watched as the two friends made their way towards the central archway. They paused at the threshold, then, with a backward glance and a deep breath, they plunged into the darkness.

43

Day 11

The forests near Sitagarha Hill

Radha watched admiringly as the commandos methodically organised themselves in dead silence. No words were spoken, not even in whispers. The entire formation was complete in seconds, using just sign language.

Weapons were checked and the men split up into groups. A thrill coursed through her as excitement mixed with apprehension; a potent cocktail that made her heart race.

But the men around her seemed devoid of emotion, oblivious to danger—another day, another mission!

They had reached a part of the forest that was reasonably near their goal but still distant enough for them to remain undetected. The trucks would remain here while they proceeded on foot. In the centre of the formation, created by the teams of commandos, were Radha and Imran. The men were invisible in the darkness and barely audible except for the occasional rustle of undergrowth. There were no flashlights. Each commando was equipped with night-vision goggles.

Silently, slowly, like a gargantuan many-headed monster, the commando force made its way towards the goal.

It is All an Illusion

Vijay and Colin walked down the passage, shining their flashlight ahead. The bare stone walls that stretched before them were unpolished and unadorned. The rock floor however was level and flat.

As Vijay walked, he wondered if Shukla was safe with the terrorists back in the chamber. He didn't trust Farooq, and the flashes of anger the LeT leader had recently displayed suggested that he was losing his grip on himself. Vijay also knew that each of them was safe only as long as they were useful to Farooq.

They stopped as two archways appeared. Engravings in the rock above each arch jumped out at them as the two trained their flashlights on them.

Vijay frowned. The archway on the right appeared to be carved into the rock and meant only as decor. 'This doesn't make sense,' he said.

Colin agreed. 'After all we've seen of the Nine, why would they create two archways when one of them can't be used? Now, if they'd given us a choice between the two and we had to decipher a clue to make that choice, I'd have been happier.'

Slowly, cautiously, they entered the archway on the left. It was a straight passage that sloped downwards after a while.

Vijay frowned. 'This seems to be going deeper underground. Wonder why.'

They continued along the corridor, careful to keep their elbows and hands from brushing against the jagged walls. The passage had narrowed considerably since they had entered it, and despite their cautiousness they had picked up a few bruises and scrapes from the rough walls.

They followed the turns of the passage until they reached a lone doorway.

Vijay stared at the arch suspiciously. What lay beyond?

Colin shot him a glance. 'What do you think? I smell something.'

Vijay grinned. 'Probably dead rats. There must be scores of them here. But I have to agree with you. I've got a bad feeling about this.'

'We can't go back. Farooq will kill us. And that's not a joke.'

'On the other hand, it's just a feeling we have. There must be something beyond that archway.'

'I'm not sure I want to find out what. In Hollywood movies there's normally a mummy or dragon or some frightening beast that lurks beyond archways like this one. And, in case you haven't realised by now, that's not an encounter I'd relish.'

Vijay smiled. Even at a time like this, Colin managed to be humorous. 'Ancient Indians never mummified their dead. So there won't be any mummies here. And dragons are found in Chinese lore, not Indian mythology.'

'What about demons?' Colin countered. 'I recall Dr. Shukla saying something about demons in the Mahabharata.'

'Yes,' Vijay agreed gravely. 'There are loads of demons in Indian mythology. All kinds. *Asuras, Rakshasas...*'

'Save the names and descriptions,' Colin interrupted him hurriedly. 'I think I'm better off not knowing.'

He poked his head beyond the archway and stood looking for a few moments. Then, he withdrew and grinned at Vijay. 'This you've got to see.'

Vijay flashed his torch through the archway and walked through it, into an enormous cavern. The darkness of the cavern was impenetrable as far as his eyes could see.

He raised his eyes to the roof of the cavern, and his jaw dropped.

While the roof was cloaked in darkness, the blackness itself seemed to be alive with a million dots of twinkling light. Had they not known that they were deep underground and now stood in a chamber carved from the bedrock, they would have easily believed that they had emerged from the confines of the rock and into the open, under the starlight.

They switched off their flashlights for a few moments and savoured the beauty of the sight. It was like gazing at the night sky from the top of a mountain, with no clouds or smog to obscure their view, no city lights to dim the brilliance of the stars.

'It's a replica of the night sky,' Colin murmured, outlining with his hand the constellations he knew. 'Look, there's the Great Bear—the Big Dipper is clearly visible. And that's Orion—there's his belt.'

They stood gazing for a while, identifying a few more constellations, wondering at the skill and ingenuity of the builders of this cavern. Who had they been? How had they created such an amazingly life-like representation of the night sky? And why?

Finally, they tore their eyes away from the spectacle overhead and turned their attention to their surroundings. All around them stretched an opaque canopy of darkness. The beams of their torches only scratched the skin of the darkness but failed to cut through its flesh.

'D'you think this is it?' Colin whispered, overawed. 'The cavern of the Nine?'

They looked at each other and then moved forward together, slowly, cautiously. Who knew what the Nine had planted in this cavern to safeguard their secret?

Suddenly, they stopped. Something was visible in the torchlight. They crept closer until they could see it clearly, though it was still some distance from them.

It was a pillar, four or five feet tall and black in colour, which was why it was not easily discernible. It had blended in with the darkness of the cavern until they were close enough to it to see it in the light of their torches.

But it wasn't the appearance of the pillar that astonished them. It was the fact that it seemed to be floating in the air, around four feet above the floor of the cavern. They flashed their torches along its length and above the pillar, to see if it was somehow suspended from the ceiling. But they could see nothing—the pillar was apparently not anchored to either the floor or hanging from the roof of the cavern.

They flashed their torches around the cavern. More pillars came into view; scattered around the cavern, frozen in the air at different heights above the floor.

Vijay looked troubled. 'Something's wrong.'

'Agreed. A cavern with the night sky for a ceiling and now levitating columns. Not my idea of normal,' his friend responded.

They approached the pillar closest to them, hoping to discover its secret once they examined it closely.

Abruptly, Colin grabbed Vijay's hand and jerked him back. His torchlight played along the floor, below the pillar, and Vijay realised why, even though the pillar was around three or four feet away from them.

Barely a foot from where they stood, the floor of the cavern plunged sharply and disappeared. One step more and Vijay would have dropped off the edge. Colin had spotted the break in the floor in the nick of time.

Beyond the edge of the floor, the light from their torches glinted off something black and wet.

'A subterranean lake?' Vijay was mystified. He flashed his torch before him and Colin did the same.

The pillars were all suspended in mid-air above the water which seemed to stretch away as far as they could see. The water was black and still, not a ripple disturbed its surface.

'What is this place?' Colin wondered. 'This looks like an artificial water body to me.'

'It does,' Vijay agreed. 'But there must be a source of water to keep it filled over the centuries. Perhaps there's an underground spring that empties into the lake.'

'Now what?' Colin looked at Vijay. 'We can't go forward. And we can't go back. This is a fine mess. And I feel like any moment Gollum's going to pop out of the lake, hissing "my precious."'

'Why would the Nine create an alternate entrance to the cavern, make those nine archways which only someone familiar with their thinking could get past, only to lead to a dead end?' Vijay frowned as he tried to search for an answer. 'We're missing something here.'

'I think the answer is connected to the suspended pillars. There must be a logical explanation for this illusion.'

Vijay grabbed Colin by the shoulders. 'That's it,' his eyes were shining with excitement. 'Thank you, buddy. I never thought I'd ever hear myself say this, but you're a genius.'

'Huh?' Colin looked bewildered.

'I think you may have just helped us find the answer to this puzzle.'

Eerie Stillness

The commandos had come to a sudden halt. They had apparently detected movement ahead. Or a presence.

Radha kept close to Imran, following his lead, though she wondered how much experience he had in operations like this.

She looked around. The teams that had flanked them on the journey, all but invisible in the darkness of the forest, had disappeared. Something was afoot. She shivered and Imran smiled at her reassuringly.

A man suddenly screamed from somewhere up ahead, shattering the stillness, making her jump. There was a flurry of sharp claps followed by silence.

The team of commandos escorting them signalled that they should move forward.

As they advanced, Radha understood the reason. Her heart leaped as she discerned the X Trail standing behind six Ford Endeavours. Bodies lay scattered on the ground around the cars, LeT men who had been taken out by the commandos.

Radha averted her eyes from the sight of death and concentrated instead on praying that her father, Vijay and Colin were safe.

The commando to her right signalled again, asking them to move forward and they continued their trek through the forest.

Day 11

Sitagarha Hill

'What d'you mean?' Colin stared at Vijay as they squatted on the rough floor of the cavern.

'Illusions. Remember Uncle's emails? He mentions illusions twice. We had tried to interpret those lines without luck and given them up as junk that had been added to confuse the reader of the emails, in case they fell into the wrong hands.'

Colin thought hard, trying to remember. 'I remember only one reference to illusions. The fourth email.

If something happens to me, you must seek out the Nine. If you look for a deeper meaning, you will find it. Two thousand years of history, which I have safely guarded for the last 25 years, is yours to unlock. Follow the path of truth and you will find your way through any illusion.

'There was another reference. In the second email.' Vijay repeated the line from the second email for Colin. '"*In an ocean of maya there is always an island of satya*". One meaning of *Maya* is illusion. So, for example, the world is an illusion, everything material is *maya*. And *satya* means truth.'

'Right.' Colin got it now. 'So this cavern is *maya*, right? The stars, these suspended pillars; a magnificently created illusion.

So where's the island of truth? And the path of truth that we're supposed to follow to find our way through these illusions?'

'There,' Vijay pointed across the water into the darkness. 'I'm betting there's an island in the centre of this lake.'

Colin grinned at Vijay, despite their circumstances. 'You're kidding. What d'you think, the island is invisible?'

Almost as soon as the words left his mouth it struck him as well.

'Holy crap!' He looked at Vijay. 'You could be right. After all, these are the guys who have the secret of invisibility hidden away somewhere in this hill.' He looked around in awe. 'It certainly explains the illusion of the pillars. They aren't suspended—their lower portions must be shielded with an invisibility cloak. And it is possible that there is an island out there that is also shielded so we can't see it.'

Vijay grinned. 'You got it, kid. An island of truth hidden behind an illusion of invisibility. See, my brilliance is beginning to rub off onto you.'

Colin scowled at him. 'Okay Brainy One, how do we get to the island then? Figure that one out.' He held out his hand. 'No wait, I think I've got it. There should be an invisible bridge over the water if our theory is correct.'

'Our theory?' Vijay put on a mock indignant expression.

Colin grinned happily at him. If they were right, this cavern wasn't so much of a mystery after all. 'We find this invisible bridge by following the pillars. Some of them must be supporting a path across the water, right?'

'Let's go,' Vijay started towards the nearest pillar. It hung above the water two feet out from the shore. He extended his leg and felt around for a bridge over the water.

Nothing.

Vijay looked at Colin. 'Guess it isn't going to be all that easy, huh?'

They went to the next pillar that was nearer to the shore but fared no differently. The next four pillars all yielded the same result.

Just as they were beginning to feel that they may have been wrong about the invisible bridge, Colin found it and stepped onto it. He looked down at his feet. It seemed uncanny, standing on what seemed like thin air, with the dark waters of the lake clearly visible directly below his feet. 'This invisibility shield really works, doesn't it? Farooq wasn't kidding. No wonder he wants it so badly.'

Slowly, painstakingly, they made their way over the water, testing the space around them before taking each step until they suddenly came to what seemed to be an invisible wall across the bridge.

'It feels like plastic,' Colin remarked as he felt along the wall. 'Wait a minute, what's this?' He felt around what seemed to be a receptacle in the wall. 'I think there's a slot here for the key.'

Vijay cursed. The key would most probably open this door as well. But it was lying in his room in the hotel in Patna.

'Don't fret, dear boy,' Colin grinned at him as he took the key out of his pocket. 'You forget that you are in the company of a genius. Knowing that we were coming to the den of the Nine, I was pretty sure we'd need it somewhere.'

Concentrating hard, he tried to fit the key into the invisible doorway, until the key slid home with an audible click. He turned the key clockwise and, suddenly, a doorway appeared before them, as if materialising out of nowhere.

'Open Sesame.' Colin grinned at Vijay, thrilled that they had been right. He stepped through the doorway onto a rectangular metal platform enclosed on all sides by a metal wall that towered at least 30 feet above them. The floor and walls were all black like the pillars, no doubt forged from the same metal that had been used to craft the metal disk.

Vijay followed Colin inside and they flashed their torches around the room. Eight pillars, each two feet tall, stood in a tight circle in the centre of the room. The metallic walls were bare.

'Now what?' Vijay asked.

As if in response to his question, there was a loud groaning sound followed by a grating sound of metal scraping against metal. The sound seemed to come from above them and they trained their torches on the ceiling.

To their horror, the ceiling, studded with long black iron spikes, was descending towards them.

Almost simultaneously, the metal platform that formed the floor of the room jerked sharply. Through the doorway they had used to enter the room, they saw the suspended pillars outside, above the lake, begin to move upwards.

'Another illusion?' Vijay frowned and then the realisation hit him. 'Shit! This is no illusion!'

Colin threw him a panic-stricken glance. 'The island is sinking into the lake!'

They looked at each other in horror. The room was descending into the lake and the ceiling, with its spikes, was collapsing on them. If they weren't impaled alive, they would surely drown.

'There has to be a way out ,' Vijay muttered, looking around. 'The Nine wouldn't allow someone with the key to enter here only to die.'

'The pillars,' Colin strode swiftly towards the eight columns in the centre of the room.

They split up and began examining the pillars, running the light from their torches along the length of each column, looking for inscriptions, a slot for the key; anything that might indicate how they could extricate themselves from this predicament.

The platform continued to sink into the lake and the ceiling continued its inexorable descent towards them.

They completed their examination of the columns.

Nothing.

Both men fought to keep panic at bay. They had to stay calm if they were to find a means of escaping a sure death in this cavern.

'Think. Think,' Vijay said. 'There's got to be something that works.'

He looked up. The sharp ends of the spikes, gleaming in the torchlight, were now barely two feet above their heads now.

Colin flashed his torch on the floor. 'Water's coming in,' he reported on the thin film of water on the floor of the room, which had drawn level with the surface of the lake.

In a few minutes the spikes would descend all the way.

Or the chamber would fill up with water from the lake.

Either way, they were rapidly running out of time.

'Wait a minute,' Vijay said, his mind grasping at straws. 'Why are there eight columns and not nine?'

'This is no time to be thinking about the number of columns, man,' Colin's voice was strained.

'Think,' Vijay urged. 'Everything we've seen so far has revolved around the number Nine. Because that was the number of people in the brotherhood. Why change the pattern now? And why eight? What's so unique about the number eight?'

Colin was thinking fast now. He realised that Vijay was possibly onto something. In any case, they were out of options. 'Didn't Radha say something about the wheel of law having eight spokes?' He suddenly recalled the conversation they had had when they discovered the key embedded in the painting in Vikram Singh's study.

Vijay beamed at him. 'Brilliant. I swear I'm going to give up joking about your intelligence. You've got it. The wheel of law.'

Colin hadn't figured it out yet. 'Okay, so I agree I'm a genius. And I like the oath you've just sworn. But how is it going to help us?'

Vijay glanced upwards.

The spikes were now inches away from their heads.

They would have to get on their knees to do this. He knelt and asked Colin to do the same.

'Here's what I think. If the Nine have replaced their favourite number with the number eight for no other reason than to depict the wheel of law, then there's only one thing that this circle is here for. It's a wheel, and a wheel should move.'

'That sounds logical.' Colin perked up.

Both men grasped a column each and put their shoulders against it, straining to move the columns in a clockwise direction.

Nothing happened.

The water in the room was now a foot deep and the spikes were almost touching their heads.

If this didn't work, they would be impaled on the spikes before the water claimed them.

'Try counterclockwise,' Colin panted.

They tried applying force in the opposite direction.

This time, with a loud grinding noise, the columns moved. As soon as the wheel, formed by the columns, began moving, the grating noise of the descending ceiling ceased and the platform, the room was built on, stopped jerking.

The two men looked at each other and heaved again. The wheel of columns moved again, reluctantly, complaining at being disturbed after 2,000 years.

It was hard work; moving the columns while on their knees, their clothes soaked with the water flooding the room, but Vijay and Colin kept at it. This was their only hope.

As they pushed, they realised that the platform had begun jerking and shuddering again, but water wasn't flooding into the room any more. They glanced upwards and saw that the ceiling, too, had begun retreating upwards.

'Keep pushing!' Colin shouted above the din made by the columns and the ceiling. 'We have to get it back to the original position. Only then will the invisible bridge be at the same level as the floor of this room.'

Vijay nodded. Their hands and shoulders were sore from pushing against the columns, but they kept going.

After what seemed like eternity, the circle of columns shuddered and stopped moving.

Both men sat back, leaning against the columns, gasping.

'I'll say one thing,' Colin grinned at Vijay, having recovered his composure and good humour, now that their ordeal was over. 'This beats bungee jumping in New Zealand.'

'Agreed,' Vijay grinned back. 'Let's get out of here before something else happens.'

'But what do we do now? Go back to Farooq?'

Vijay shrugged. 'Frankly, I don't know if there's anything else we can do.'

They rose and made their way out of the open doorway. They didn't stop to celebrate their freedom but raced up the tunnel, overjoyed at being free after what seemed like a lifetime.

As they emerged from the tunnel, their breaths coming in gasps, Colin grabbed Vijay's arm and pointed at the second archway, the one they had earlier rejected as useless. Something had happened while they were in the cavern of illusions. The second archway was no longer carved into the rock. The arch now framed a yawning gap. There was an entrance here to another tunnel; an entrance that, somehow, had been concealed earlier and was open now.

'D'you think that the turning of the wheel had something to do with the opening up of this archway?' Colin wondered aloud.

Vijay nodded, excited now. 'I don't know what happened, or how, but clearly the only way to get this archway opened was by going through that cavern. This was another test by the Nine to ensure that their secret was protected.'

They entered the second archway. The tunnel they were now in was broad but unfinished. It turned at sharp angles and soon they had no sense which direction they were heading towards. After a while, the passage began sloping upwards then abruptly ended in a small rocky chamber which had a stairway carved into the rock.

Cautiously, they moved forward, wary of any surprises, flashing their torches around the chamber, which was bereft of any adornment or carvings.

Was this the last stage of their journey to find the secret?

With mounting excitement, they made their way up the staircase, uncertain of what they would find at the top.

Disappointingly, they emerged into yet another tunnel that was blocked at one end by a sheer wall of rock.

'I'm sick of being underground,' Colin grumbled.

Vijay grimaced. The awareness of being deep below the surface of the earth wasn't a pleasant sensation. But they had no choice. They had to move on.

To their immense surprise, they had barely taken a few steps when the passage came to life with a dim light.

They looked at each other, barely able to contain their excitement. Both spoke at the same time.

'This is the passageway Surasen described in his text.'

'This is the passageway that leads from the opening in the hill to the cavern of the Nine.'

Both men laughed as they realised how close they were to discovering the secret of the Nine.

'Race you there. Bet I can beat you.' A rush of adrenalin had revived Vijay's energy, buoyed by the thought that they were finally within reach of their goal.

Both men were well matched in physical prowess and together burst through an archway that lay at the end of the tunnel.

Skidding to a halt, they gazed around, awestruck. They were in an enormous cavern that was lit up by the same soft light that had illuminated the passage. The roof of the cavern soared high above their heads, probably three or four hundred feet above them. The depth of the cavern was immense. It stretched away from them on all sides, in all likelihood running the length of the hill. Whether it was manmade or natural they couldn't tell, but it took their breath away.

But it wasn't just the dimensions of the cavern that shook them. The secret of the Nine lay before them, revealed in its full glory.

They had known about the legend from the *Vimana Parva*. They also knew about the invisibility shield. But nothing could have prepared them for the sight that now greeted their eyes. It was the same sight that had overawed Surasen when he had stepped into this very cavern 2,300 years ago.

Frustration!

In the chamber below the stupa, Farooq, Murphy and the LeT men waited. An hour had passed since Vijay and Colin had left them.

The time had passed with great difficulty for Farooq, who paced the length of the chamber like a caged tiger, his face dark with anger and tension, unable to come to terms with the fact that he had little control over events. He hated the fact that he had to rely on Vijay and his friends to decode clues, decipher verses and inscriptions and make sense of what had to be done. The presence of Murphy only added to his frustration; it was because Murphy was employed by the people he was partnering with, that he had made peace with him.

And now, Vijay and Colin had disappeared. He wasn't concerned about what might have befallen them. He was worried about how their disappearance would affect the success of his mission.

'Where are they?' he growled at Shukla.

'They'll be back,' he replied warily. He was worried about Vijay and Colin. But he also feared Farooq's visibly growing irritation. 'If we have patience—'

'Patience is one thing I can't have now. You and your friends have been nothing but trouble for me.''

'They may have run up against some difficulty,' Shukla countered, keeping his voice low lest he inflame the Pakistani. 'Perhaps we should have all gone together.'

Farooq didn't take kindly to what seemed to be a challenge to his decision to send Vijay ahead.

'You think I made a mistake?' he snarled. 'So now I'm responsible because they've disappeared?'

'No, I wasn't suggesting that,' Shukla began, sensing Farooq's rage peaking, backing up a few steps.

But it was too late. Farooq had been suppressing his tension, frustration and anger and now, finding an outlet for release, it exploded like a volcano. He rushed at Shukla and repeatedly struck him viciously with the gun, attacking his face and body until the elderly man collapsed under the ferocity of the onslaught. He then aimed the gun at him.

For a few moments, silence hung like death over the group as the scientist glowered and stared down the barrel of the gun at the prone scholar. To the rest of the group, it seemed like a miracle when Farooq finally lowered the gun and flung it aside.

His rage dissipated, Murphy's words rang in the Pakistani's head. If Vijay had fallen prey to a trap laid by the Nine, then he may need Shukla to point him in the right direction. He couldn't kill him. Not now. Not until he could be absolutely sure that Shukla was dispensable.

'Let's move,' Farooq growled. 'If those two have killed themselves in there, that's their bad luck. And if they haven't, then we'll find them and kill them for disobeying my orders.'

Two LeT men helped Shukla to his feet and he grimaced with pain. Blood dripped from the cuts on his face and head and stained his clothes.

Farooq gestured to his men to follow him and strode through the central archway.

Sitagarha Hill

Farooq stood before the two archways and squinted at the inscriptions carved above them.

More riddles.

He had begun to tire of the repeated occurrence of riddles and puzzles. He was longing to get the secret in his grasp, but was being befuddled at every step of the way by the intricate puzzles that the Nine had laid out.

Farooq gritted his teeth as he fought to control his frustration. He was a scientist and yet, here he was, playing the games of a 10-year-old child on a treasure hunt.

He pursed his lips, drawing comfort from the thought that this would soon end. He turned to Shukla, who had also been studying the inscriptions.

'Well?' Farooq stood before the scholar, hands on his hips, and waited.

'It says that we've come to the final test. If we pass this, we prove ourselves worthy. If we fail, we are doomed.' Shukla spoke haltingly, resting his head against the wall.

Farooq frowned. 'That isn't much of a clue.'

Shukla shook his head weakly, wincing in pain with the movement. 'There's more. Each archway has a separate inscription above it. The one on the left is *Maya*. The other one is *Satya*.

'And?'

Shukla sighed, his breath ragged as he spoke. 'Roughly translated, *Maya* means illusion. And *Satya* means truth. According to Vikram's emails, we should follow the path of truth and not that of illusion.'

As he spoke, a look of horror spread over Shukla's face as a thought struck him, momentarily overcoming his pain.

'Oh my God,' he whispered. 'I hope Vijay and Colin chose the right archway.'

'Well, if they didn't, that's just too bad for them.' For Farooq, it meant two less people to manage on this journey. And, going by the inscriptions, it seemed that he didn't need anyone any longer. Not even Shukla, if this was the final inscription. And definitely not Vijay and Colin.

'Leave him here,' he instructed, gesturing to two men. 'You two will stay with him while we go ahead and secure the prize.'

Without another word, he turned towards the archway on the right and led the group through it.

They didn't know it but Vijay and Colin had passed this way just a few minutes ago.

In Close Pursuit

Imran and the commandos gazed at the open hole in the ground.

Verma motioned and the commandos instantly regrouped and silently descended the stairway. Presently, they reached the outer chamber where the LeT fighters had stood not so long ago. Imran stood with Radha and Verma before the nine arches and contemplated the inscriptions.

'Which way?' Verma whispered.

Imran shrugged. 'I have no idea,' he whispered back.

'I wish Papa was with us,' Radha whispered. 'He would know.'

Imran nodded. 'No doubt LeT has made good use of his expertise.'

'What do we do?' Verma urged. 'We are losing time.'

First Victory

Shukla sat propped up against the wall and tried to shut his mind to the agonising pain that racked his body. The two LeT men stood by, sullen and silent, upset at having been left behind. They couldn't understand why Farooq hadn't disposed of this man. But they didn't dare argue or challenge him. Suddenly one of them raised his head.

'Did you hear something?' he asked the other in Arabic.

'No. What?'

I thought I heard voices. Do you think someone was in the jungle and found the entrance?'

The other man laughed. 'Who would be wandering in the jungle at this time?'

'I think I should go and see.'

His companion sighed. 'Go. Suit yourself, Nasir. But I'm keeping the torch. We don't want this one getting away in the dark. Farooq will have our skins if we lose him.'

They had just one torch between them.

Nasir moved back up the tunnel that led to the nine arches and the chamber beyond. Perhaps it was his mind playing tricks on him. But he had to be sure. If he was right, and there was someone around, Farooq would ensure that he suffered for his oversight.

He came to the archway and paused, waiting for a while. His comrade had the torch and its light barely reached this far into the tunnel. The cavern was dark and silent, like a monster lying in wait for its prey.

He wasn't afraid of death. But something about the darkness in the chamber unnerved him.

He moved forward again and emerged into the main chamber. The surrounding darkness welcomed him and enveloped him like a shroud.

The commandos watched in surprise through their night vision glasses as the LeT fighter emerged from the central archway. While they could see him, he was blinded by the darkness and was moving slowly, feeling his way along the wall.

They were swift to react.

A gesture from Verma and a commando sidled up silently to the unfortunate LeT man, plunging a knife into him, covering his mouth to muffle any sound. It was over in seconds.

They now knew which archway to enter.

The commandos swiftly passed through the tunnel, moving towards the dim light of the torch that was with Shukla and his guard. They crept forward and saw the second set of archways. Clearly visible in the torchlight was the prone form of Shukla and the second LeT fighter.

Radha couldn't restrain herself and gasped in shock as she saw her father's condition.

The LeT fighter looked up in surprise at the sound.

His first reaction was shock as he realised what was happening. Then, he lifted his weapon to fire.

But Verma was faster. The blade of the knife glinted in the light of the torch as it flashed through the air and buried itself in the LeT fighter's chest. He fell back, his gun chattering as his finger, which had been on the trigger, involuntarily spasmed.

Then, there was silence. The commandos looked at each other. They were thinking the same thing. Had the noise of the gun reached the other terrorists? Radha rushed to her father. 'What happened?' Her voice trembled with shock as she examined her father.

Shukla perked up on seeing her and the commandos. He realised that there was now a chance, however slim, of stopping Farooq before he reached his goal. He seemed to draw strength from these thoughts, and explained how Farooq had assaulted him.

'You don't know how glad I am to see you, but we need to hurry. Farooq and his men went that way.' He pointed to the right-hand fork. 'And Greg White is an imposter. His real name is Murphy.'

'We realised that, only a bit too late,' Imran admitted.

'What about Vijay and Colin?' Radha asked anxiously.

Shukla averted his eyes. 'They went into this tunnel leaving us in the chamber outside. We haven't seen them since. There was an anxious edge to his voice, although he looked visibly relieved on seeing that his daughter was safe.

Verma looked around. 'Okay boys,' he addressed his men. 'Let's move. Now, we'll have to deal with the main group. They won't go down without a fight.'

'We'll help Dr. Shukla back into the main chamber and up the stairway,' Imran said.

'I'm not going back to the forest,' Shukla protested. 'I'm coming, too.'

Verma looked at him. 'I don't mean to be rude, Dr. Shukla, but from now on this is a strictly military operation and we can't have civilians involved. My men have a job to do and they can't do it effectively if they have to watch out for you.'

Shukla stood still for a moment, consumed by a yearning to go on. He was so close to seeing the secret of the Nine with his own eyes; a secret that had been hidden away for thousands of years. But he realised the truth of Verma's words and nodded.

Verma pointed to two of his men. 'You will go with them. Wait for us in the forest.'

The men supported Shukla between them and went back up the tunnel, accompanied by Imran and Radha. The rest of the commandos followed Verma through the archway that had *Satya* inscribed on the rock above it.

Sitagarha Hill

Vijay and Colin gaped. Having learned what the secret of the Nine was, they had expected a library housing documents, blueprints; texts that described how to build the invisibility cloak Farooq had described.

Anything but the sight they gazed upon now.

Stretched out, to their left, running the length of one half of the cavern, as far as they could see, was a row of horizontally inclined metal cylinders; all seemed to be made of the same metal that the disk with the verse had been forged from.

On the opposite side, to their right, the cavern was mostly empty with a few stone blocks scattered around. A portion of the wall adjoining the entrance contained hollow chambers in which plaques made from the same black metal were neatly stacked.

The metal cylinders were cigar-shaped with one end blunt and the other end tapering to a conical nose. Attached to the belly of each cylinder was a set of six wheels, arranged in pairs along the length of the cylinder with a set of wings curving away from the body mid-length and two horizontal, stubby wing-like protrusions at the blunt end.

There must have been at least a 100 of these machines. The two men stumbled into the cavern, unable to believe their eyes.

'Oh sweet Lord!' Colin gasped. 'Don't tell me.'

Vijay nodded, awestruck. They had both guessed what they were gazing at.

'The *Vimana Parva*,' he said, softly. 'This is the fleet of aircraft that the King of Magadha had built to defeat the Pandavas.'

Colin gazed at the *vimana*s. Something about them seemed to be a bit strange, yet amazingly familiar, but he couldn't put his finger on it.

The two men walked along the row of the machines. They seemed sturdy enough considering their age, and there wasn't a trace of rust on them.

'Can you imagine,' Vijay said excitedly. 'Aircraft that are thousands of years old. I wonder what fuel they used for them.'

It suddenly stuck Colin. 'There's no cockpit,' he said, staring hard at the machines. 'And no vertical stabiliser. Just those two little thingummies at the rear.'

Vijay looked curiously at Colin.

'Don't you get it? They look more like pilotless drones than regular aircraft. I'll bet they are equipped with explosive warheads.'

'You're right,' Vijay said, examining the *vimana* nearest to him. 'So that's how they got around the problem of the invisibility cloak blinding the pilot. If you don't have a pilot, you don't have to worry about that problem.' He looked at Colin. 'Remote-controlled drones, like stealth bombers, flying over battlefields thousands of years ago? How does one explain the existence of this kind of technology in prehistoric times?

'Well, the King of Magadha certainly didn't equip his *vimana*s with the secret weapon, like the book said,' Colin grinned. 'After all, we can see them, can't we? If they had the invisibility cloak, we wouldn't know they were here.'

'That's not relevant' said a voice interrupting them and they turned around to see Farooq at the entrance of the cavern. 'Whether they have the sheath or not isn't important. Who knows if these tin cans will even fly after all these centuries have passed.' His voice rose. 'What matters is the blueprint, the design for manufacturing the sheath. This weapon will now belong to LeT.'

He swaggered into the cavern, beaming. If he was surprised to see Vijay and Colin safe and alive, he didn't show it. His whole attention was taken up by the discovery in the cavern. His plan had worked, the mission was a success and the secret weapon of the Nine was finally his.

Vijay thought fast. It was now or never. Addressing Farooq, he said, 'You can now let us go. You've got what you wanted.' A knot formed in his stomach as he uttered the words. The LeT *had* got what they wanted. And he, Vijay, had helped them secure their prize. But he had no choice! He suddenly frowned. 'Where's Dr. Shukla?' All the LeT men and Murphy were now in the cavern but he couldn't spot Shukla.

'In safe hands,' Farooq grinned. He then turned to his men and shouted. 'I want a complete list of all the plaques before we begin loading. And move quickly if you want to get out of here fast.'

Some of the LeT men looked upwards nervously. The fact that a hill rested above their heads was an unnerving thought. It was apparent that some of them felt an unfamiliar oppressiveness, almost as if the weight of the hill was slowly, but surely, bearing down upon them and crushing them to the ground.

One man hefted the black duffel bags he had been carrying and disappeared up the tunnel that formed the sole entrance and exit for the cavern.

Vijay found his tongue again. 'Well,' he said. 'You don't need us any longer. Now, let us go.'

Farooq's face twisted in a cruel smile.

A loud explosion came from the direction of the tunnel at the entrance, accompanied by the rumble of falling rock.

'We've blasted open the original entrance, the one that was sealed by the Nine,' Farooq explained, beaming. He was delighted with the way things were going now. 'A controlled explosion; just enough to create the opening we need without bringing the hill down on us. We can't take all this stuff back the way we came.'

A man shouted across the cavern and Farooq crossed over to see what he had found. A look of delight crossed his face.

'We've found them!' he shouted out to his men. 'The designs for the future armoury of LeT.'

The LeT men whooped, in unison, expressing their delight. Vijay walked over to Farooq. 'Let us go. Now that you've got the secret, we're not going to be in your way.'

'Oh, yes, that,' Farooq smirked, enjoying the sight of Vijay pleading for their freedom. 'You're not going anywhere. What made you think that I'd let you go?'

All this time, Vijay had nursed a hope, however remote, that Farooq might let them go once he found the secret. He realised now that Farooq had always intended to dispose them off when they had outlived their utility.

'You see,' Farooq explained. 'I meant it when I said you would die. The woman is already dead. And now that I have your friends here, they will die with you.'

Vijay felt a burning rage well up within. All this time he'd been consoling himself with the thought that he had helped

LeT solely because it was the only way he could save his friends. Now, he found himself confronted with the bitter truth that they were doomed. He had hoped that Radha had somehow survived. But he had been wrong. Radha was dead. The woman he had fallen in love with was dead! There was no way out of this situation now. And what was the point, even if there was?

Fuelled by desperation at their plight, something snapped within him. Like a condemned man, with nothing to lose, his rationality dissolved and he allowed his anger to consume him. With a roar, he lunged at Farooq, and rained blows on the surprised Pakistani scientist. The LeT men and Murphy were taken unawares and even Colin looked on shocked. Farooq collapsed to the floor under the force of Vijay's assault.

The LeT men quickly overcame their initial shock at Vijay's onslaught and rushed to Farooq's aid. They swarmed around Vijay and Farooq and hauled Vijay off their leader. Vijay disappeared under a group of men, as they used the butts of their rifles to bludgeon him.

Colin tensed but before he could even think of a possible course of action, he heard Murphy's voice in his ear. 'Don't even think about it.'

Farooq stood up, helped by two of his men, his nose and mouth bleeding, his shirt torn. He spat a mouthful of blood and wiped his face with a sleeve.

'Wait!' he shouted to the men who were attacking Vijay. 'I don't want him dead. Not yet.'

Colin rushed forward to help his friend, who had blood streaming down his head and face. His shirt had patches of blood from cuts on his body and he winced in pain as Colin helped him up.

Farooq hobbled over to Vijay and jabbed a finger at him. 'You will pay for this,' he rasped. 'Before I kill you, I will put your friends through a slow, painful death. And you will watch them die. You will hear them scream for mercy and beg for a quick death. I will show you what it means to mess with me.'

He turned to a group of his men. 'Take them into the entry tunnel,' he instructed, 'and keep them there. The rest of you, get back to work!'

The LeT fighters prodded Vijay and Colin before them into the passage they had travelled through not so long ago. A soft light still suffused the tunnel but instead of the rock wall at the far end, they could see the newly blasted opening in the hillside, through which a soft breeze now blew into the passage.

Inside the cavern, Farooq suppressed his anger over Vijay's audacious attack and focused instead on his success. LeT would finally rule the world.

Day 11

The entrance to the heart of Sitagarha Hill

The commandos stood at the foot of the rocky staircase, which
would take them to their final destination.

While making their way up the passage they had
suddenly heard a muffled explosion accompanied by a sound
they couldn't explain. The ground underfoot trembled and
a portion of the rock wall behind them collapsed with the
vibrations. They stopped and waited, wondering what it was.
What were the terrorists doing? Surely they weren't blowing
up the hill?

When the rocks stopped falling, Verma signalled to one
of the commandos who ran up the stairway, noiselessly. He
returned in a few moments and gave an all-clear signal, following
which the other commandos made their way up the staircase.

In the tunnel outside the main cavern Colin shifted
uncomfortably. They were sitting on the rock floor of the
passage. Vijay was feeling stupid for having let himself be driven
by his anger and frustration. He had just made things worse for
them. Instead of a quick death, they were all now doomed to a
painful, long-drawn-out one. He knew that Farooq would be
as good as his word.

'I'm sorry,' he had mumbled to Colin as the LeT men had shoved them along the tunnel. 'I don't know what came over me back there. I'm really sorry.'

Colin knew Vijay well enough to understand that it was only human of him to break down in the face of the deaths of two people close to him and the hopelessness of their own circumstances. He, too, was afraid.

Colin stood up. He was tired of sitting cross-legged on the floor and began to walk towards the entrance of the passage that led to the forest outside.

One of the LeT men turned sharply to look at him and raised his weapon slightly. Colin held up his hands. 'Hey, I'm just stretching my legs.'

Satisfied that the American wasn't attempting to escape, the fighter turned back to his mates, their conversation punctuated by low laughter.

Colin walked slowly to the opening in the ground through which he and Vijay had entered the passage. And stopped short.

A face smeared with black colour was looking into the passage. The man was dressed all in black.

Colin staggered back in shock.

Before he knew it, the man had silently bounded out of the opening and was by his side, clamping a hand over his mouth and holding his arms in a vice-like grip. Swiftly, silently, more men poured into the passage.

'Indian commandos,' the man holding Colin hissed in his ear.

Colin relaxed but was confused. He couldn't help wondering how Indian commandos had reached Sitagarha.

But his hopes lifted. Perhaps all wasn't lost yet.

He turned around and saw that Vijay had been similarly silenced while a few commandos set about taking out the LeT men. It was all over in seconds; the terrorists guarding the duo, caught unawares, were quickly and silently overpowered.

Colin's captor released his grip and the commandos herded him and Vijay towards the entrance to the passage. Colin caught a glimpse of the men; black clad figures armed with automatic weapons, and, good heavens, was that a grenade launcher?

A thrill ran down his spine as the reality of the commando operation sank in and they hurried out of the tunnel and breathed in the fresh night air of the forest. It was refreshing after their long sojourn underground.

Vijay too welcomed the arrival of the commandos. He had given up all hope in the cavern. 'What about Dr. Shukla?' He suddenly remembered.

Wait and Watch

Verma lay on his stomach and watched the scene before him. The LeT men milled around the cavern, busy as ants, gathering metal plates and stacking them in piles, as if hoarding food for the winter. They were not expecting company.

But he was worried. This was very different from the brief he had been given at HQ. His mission was to take out the terrorists. No one had said anything about the fleet of *vimanas*. He studied the machines through a pair of binoculars and came to a decision.

He crawled back to join the rest of his men, who were a short way down the tunnel.

He signalled to the men to explain the strategic points where the LeT fighters were; they would need to take out these points first. His men nodded and, dividing into three groups, took up their positions. The two smaller groups flanked the opening and one large group stood ready in the centre.

Each group would open fire at one of the strategic points indicated by Verma, while the larger group would take advantage of the element of surprise and the cover provided by the other two groups. With the disarray they hoped to cause in the process, they would charge into the cavern to immobilise the rest of the terrorists.

There was one thing they had to avoid. Firing at the metal cylinders!

Verma had his sights set on Murphy. But first, he had a final task to complete.

A Happy Reunion

'Dr. Shukla is safe with two of my men,' Verma joined Colin and Vijay after briefing his men. 'We need to hurry. All of you have to get out of here. Fast.'

Colin supported Vijay as they hurried after Verma, trying to keep up with him.

They saw a group of people standing near the stupa, but in the near darkness they could only make out the silhouettes. Verma had reached the group and was addressing one person in particular.

'...we can't risk it. We could be sitting on a gunpowder keg here.' He turned to his men, waiting alongside the group, 'Come with me. I'm going to need you.'

The three commandos raced back towards the hill.

Colin and Vijay came up to the group and stood there, gaping. Before them stood Imran and Radha. Colin ran towards them with a cry of delight. Vijay stood rooted to the spot, looking like he had seen an apparition.

'I can't believe it,' Colin kept repeating as he hugged Imran and Radha in turn. He looked back at Vijay.

Like someone waking from a trance, Vijay, now beaming, finally began walking slowly towards them. The tension and the anxiety weighing upon his mind, had suddenly disappeared. The sight of Radha, safe and sound, was like a sunbeam that had dissipated the fog of worries that had clouded his mind.

Vijay recognised Imran as the police officer who had visited the fort just a few days ago. He didn't know what Imran was doing here and how or why Radha was with him, but it was clear that Radha's escape and Imran's presence were somehow linked.

He turned to face Radha, looking at her intently. She returned his gaze, uneasy, unable to interpret his expression.

He stood for a few moments then hesitatingly raised his hand to stroke her hair gently. There were tears in his eyes. To Radha's great surprise he put his arms around her and folded her in a warm embrace.

Radha blinked back her own tears. She now knew for certain he loved her. She returned his embrace.

'I'm sorry to break up the reunion, but we have to get out of here now,' Imran broke in. 'You two see what's in the cavern?'

Vijay and Colin nodded.

'Come on, then. You can tell us what you saw once we're in the car.' He looked at Vijay. 'I'll help Dr. Shukla. Can you make it with Colin?'

Vijay nodded.

'Let's go then. We don't have too much time if what Verma said is true.'

Ambush!

Inside the cavern, the LeT men were hard at work, stacking the plaques and creating a list. The plaques were surprisingly light, considering they were made of metal, and the men were able to work swiftly.

Farooq had come across a four-foot-long strip of metal which, seemed to disappear when he turned it over. Even though he could feel it, hard and cold in his hand, he couldn't see it. He excitedly realised that this was what they had been looking for all along. A sample of the sheath engineered centuries ago by ancient scientists.

This meant that they now possessed the design as well as a physical sample of the invisibility shield. Finally, they would be able to replicate and manufacture the sheath on a large scale. His mind raced as he thought of the possibilities that would open up for LeT.

His thoughts were rudely interrupted as a volley of shots rang out through the cavern. He looked up angrily, ready to curse. This was no time for his men to indulge in irresponsible firing. They had a job to do.

He was stunned to see some of his fighters drop to the ground. And then, another round of shots raked the cavern.

Verma and the commandos had opened fire, felling several LeT men. The effect was immediate and as they had expected. The terrorists scattered, unable to comprehend that an armed force had come upon them. Men ran helter skelter, looking for shelter from the attack, as they fumbled with their weapons.

Murphy immediately took cover behind one of the cigar-shaped *vimana*s.

At a signal from Verma, a group of commandos rushed into the cavern, their guns blazing.

48

Day 11

The forests near Sitagarha Hill

Imran, Vijay and the others, in the meanwhile, were driving away from Sitagarha Hill. No one had spoken a word since they had left the stupa and begun the trek towards the SUV. Imran broke the silence now, as the X Trail charged through the forest, bumping and jerking its way through the trees.

He introduced himself and explained quickly how he had found Radha after Bheem Singh's accidental death. 'So what did you guys see in there?'

Colin told him.

Imran nodded, 'Verma said that the cavern contained what looked like missiles and they may be loaded with explosives. If that's true, then there's no knowing how unstable the chemicals may be if those things really are thousands of years old. Anything could set them off. That's why Verma asked us to leave immediately.'

There was silence as the implication of this announcement sank in. What would happen to the commandos if there were explosive warheads in the *vimana*s and if they did, somehow, go off?

'Couldn't they nail the terrorists without going into the cavern?' Colin asked. 'I mean, if those doodahs have explosives in them, all they have to do is fire at them and bring the roof down on the LeT.'

'Exactly what I asked him,' Imran shook his head regretfully at the choice the commandos had had to make. 'They can't be sure that the *vimana*s are loaded with explosives. They're up against men who are willing to die. The commandos have just one shot at getting it right. The only way they can do their job is to go in there and kill every single terrorist. And hope that nothing else happens.'

Imran looked at Radha and passed her his mobile phone. 'Check if there's a signal yet. I didn't get one in the forest.'

They had reached the side road that led from the forest to the highway.

Radha nodded. 'There's a signal.'

'Good. Dial the last number called—Vishnu Prasad.'

'The DC?' Radha dialled Prasad's number.

Imran nodded. 'There are two dams around Hazaribagh; Tilaiya and Konar. Both are roughly the same distance from Hazaribagh, around 50 kilometres away. Tilaiya is to the north, so that puts it at around 70 or 75 kilometres from Sitagarha hill. Konar is to the east, beyond Sitagarha. That makes it around 30 kilometres from the hill. If something happens in that cavern, we need to make sure that villages around these dams, and along the rivers they are built on, are evacuated.'

Radha, in the meantime, had got through to Vishnu Prasad and put him on the speaker phone.

Imran quickly explained the situation to the District Collector, who was shocked to hear the news.

'There are several villages around there,' Prasad said. 'But, they are small villages so it won't take long to evacuate them.

But we can't get to them in time. We'll try calling the village headmen and they'll have to mobilise the evacuation. Thanks for the warning.'

Firefight!

Verma glanced quickly around the cavern and became aware that the LeT men had recovered from their initial paralysis and were now putting up a fierce resistance.

They had quickly found secure positions for themselves behind the stone blocks that were lined up near the wall, towards the vacant part of the cavern. This gave them an advantage over the commandos who were now without any protective cover, except for the covering gunfire from their comrades within the tunnel.

As Verma looked on, he saw his men put the second phase of their plan into operation. A lone commando, hefting a rocket-propelled grenade launcher, appeared in the opening of the cave.

He aimed for a particularly troublesome corner of the cavern where a bunch of LeT militants was holed up behind massive stone blocks. The RPG found its mark, blowing up several of the terrorists.

The LeT guns fell silent, and Farooq cursed. Right now, his men were at a disadvantage and he shouted out for them to dig in and defend, rather than go on the offensive.

Emboldened by the success of their plan, which appeared to have momentarily given them the upper hand, the commandos advanced, taking up positions behind some of the stone columns. The commando with the RPG launcher also advanced into the cavern and took up a position that gave him a clear line of sight to another group of LeT fighters, who were ensconced behind a stone block deeper in the vacant section of the cavern.

Suddenly, two LeT men darted out from the cover of a block that was adjacent to the tunnel opening, right behind the commando with the RPG launcher. The commandos had been oblivious to their position.

Now, as the commando readied to fire the RPG launcher a second time, these LeT men dived at him. He was taken by surprise and fell to the ground, the launcher flying out of his hands with the momentum of the assault.

The two LeT fighters were quickly despatched by the other commandos but the damage was done. The grenade had been launched at the moment of impact, but it was no longer bound for the target it had been meant for.

Instead, it sailed over the heads of the LeT fighters and into a far corner of the cavern which was unoccupied.

Time seemed to slow down as the grenade arched downwards, missing the LeT men. This was the opening they needed. Exulting at their luck, they roared with one voice and rushed forward for a counter-attack, shooting wildly as they advanced. With the RPG launcher down, the momentum of the attack had turned.

The grenade exploded as Murphy and Verma looked on. Nothing could have prepared them for what happened next.

This futile explosion was succeeded almost immediately by a huge blast, as if a stockpile of ammunition had gone up in flames.

49

Day 11

The Ranchi-Hazaribagh highway

Imran and the others were speeding towards Hazaribagh. They hoped that they had put enough distance between them and Sitagarha Hill. Imran was hoping that the whole operation would go as planned and nothing untoward would happen.

But he knew that was wishful thinking.

The sky had begun to lighten as the first fingers of dawn began to creep across the sky.

Abruptly, the SUV bucked as if the road had taken on a life of its own, and shivered violently. Imran had to wrestle with the steering wheel to stop the car from skidding off the highway.

'What...?' Radha began, then broke off as the road before them, illuminated by the SUV's headlights and the growing light of dawn, began to disintegrate before her eyes. Large cracks opened up and Imran grappled with the steering wheel wildly to avoid them.

Vijay and Colin peered through the rear windscreen to see what was happening. The road behind them had been torn apart, as if a pair of giant hands had taken each end of the highway and pulled them in opposite directions.

'What was that? An earthquake?' Colin's voice trembled.

Imran shook his head. 'Seismic shockwave. Something has happened at Sitagarha; something big enough for a seismic shock of this intensity to be generated.'

He now knew that Verma had been right about the *vimana*s. The encounter between the terrorists and the commandos must have set off the unstable explosives in the *vimana*s.

He pressed the accelerator to the floor and the SUV leaped forward with a roar. 'It isn't over yet. The airblast shockwave is yet to come. If the seismic shock was any indication, that isn't going to be a breeze. Pun not intended.'

As if his words were some kind of spell, there was a loud thunderclap, the car windows and windscreens shattered and the vehicle was buffeted by a strong gale.

Imran reached out and knocked out the shattered windshield so he could see ahead of him. The SUV swung wildly and he fought to keep it on the road. He felt as though invisible hands were taking turns to pull or push the car violently in different directions; the steering wheel seemed almost useless in his hands.

Almost simultaneously, the ground under them shook violently again and something big thumped hard against the side of the car. The door bulged inwards with the impact. There was another loud thump on the roof which immediately caved in and they saw a large branch blow away after having struck the car. More branches slammed against the shattered rear windscreen and windows, spraying the occupants of the cabin with shards of smashed glass and letting in smaller branches, twigs and leaves, along with the gale that was now rocking the SUV.

Radha screamed and they looked at the road ahead in shock. A crack on the left side of the road was widening and advancing directly across the road ahead of them. In a few seconds, it would stretch right across the highway, leaving them with no space to escape it.

Imran pressed the accelerator to the floor. The engine roared as the SUV charged ahead, racing alongside the swiftly advancing crack. He said a silent prayer as he tried to focus on the road through the leaves and branches that swept past them and into the car, because of the absence of the windshield.

Just as the fracture began to devour the narrow path Imran had been driving on, the SUV zipped forward, its two left wheels bumping over the narrow wedge of the fast-growing crack.

Imran now exhaled audibly and allowed the car to slow down just a bit. For a moment there, he thought that they were going to plunge into the abyss that had opened up across the highway!

Then, it was over. Silence descended on them, apart from the roar of the SUV. Through the open windows they saw the devastation around them. Trees had been blown over and those that were still standing had had branches and leaves ripped off them.

Imran stopped the SUV, leaving the engine idling and they all clambered out, shaken and bruised.

'Oh, my God!' Colin whispered. He was facing the direction from which they had come, the direction in which the hill was located.

They turned to look at what had disturbed Colin. The ruined forest stretched out on either side of the highway. Apart from the devastation, they saw a column of flames that had shot up to the heavens, brightening the dawn sky behind them.

Before they could comprehend the sight before them, there was a loud blast from the direction of Sitagarha hill.

Almost immediately, there was a second, bigger and louder explosion that seemed to tear through the forests around them.

'What...what's happening?' Radha's face was white as she stared at the column of flames.

'The seismic and airblast shockwaves travel faster than sound,' Imran explained. 'The hill's blown up.'

Fury of Fire

As Imran and the others left the forest for the highway, a huge orange jet of fire shot out towards the roof of the cavern and shrapnel flew at the LeT men, who fell like ninepins.

Verma stared in horror at the space that had seemed vacant until now, and where now indistinct shapes suddenly materialised out of nowhere, engulfed by flames that had begun to devour that part of the cavern.

The King of Magadha had apparently succeeded in equipping part of his fleet with the sheath of invisibility. The grenade had strayed from its path and exploded right in the middle of the fleet of invisible aircraft.

As the cavern and the foundations of the hill shook, a second explosion followed, bigger than the first one. The cavern erupted in a fury of fire as the row of *vimana*s, visible and invisible, exploded, blasting the upper half of the hill to smithereens. Boulders and rocks, along with blasted pieces of *vimana*, were ejected high above the forest.

All that was finally left of the cavern and the hill was a smoking crater in which rocks pelted down from the sky.

The Aftermath

Imran steered the SUV through the deserted streets of Hazaribagh. The roads were torn and shredded like the highway, testifying to the intensity of the explosions at Sitagarha.

They gazed at the buildings they passed. Some now had great cracks running along their sides, others had partially or fully collapsed walls or roofs and a slum they passed had been razed to the ground. There was not one window that had a glass pane intact and the roads were littered with shards of glass. Electric cables had snapped and lay like lifeless snakes curled on or along the sides of the roads.

It was a sorry sight and Radha was glad that Imran had had the presence of mind to have the town evacuated. Who knows what loss of life and injuries may have resulted had the inhabitants of Hazaribagh been here? Imran pulled over and dialled Vishnu Prasad. 'The dams,' he said and listened for a while. 'Thanks,' he said finally as he hung up.

The others looked at him curiously.

'All safe,' Imran reported, but he was unable to bring a smile to his face as he said, 'The villages were evacuated. Fortunately, the dams are still standing. They were apparently built to withstand an earthquake much stronger than the seismic activity generated by the explosions.'

But the fate of the commandos was seared into his mind.

50

Day 12

Jaungarh Fort

Vijay sat on a balcony of Jaungarh fort and surveyed the countryside, gloomily. The sun was sinking below the hills on the horizon, reflecting his mood. The view of the countryside was breathtaking. The dying sun wrapped its cloak around the landscape, throwing long shadows upon the ground. At the base of the hill on which the fort stood, lights twinkled in the houses huddled together in the village that had, in centuries past, been defended by the fort.

From Sitagarha they had returned to Patna, from where they were flown in a military aircraft to Delhi, after Vijay and Shukla had received medical attention. The media had been full of reports about the mysterious explosion at Sitagarha hill that had levelled half the forests of Hazaribagh and caused devastation on an epic scale. Tremors from the explosion had been felt as far away as Patna.

Speculation was rife as news reporters linked the midnight evacuation of Hazaribagh town with the devastation at Sitagarha Hill. The government had refused to issue a statement, with the Home Minister saying that he would only comment after a probe led by a scientific team. There was no mention of the IB's involvement in the mission. Or of the commandos. It was as if they had never existed.

Vijay reflected on the events of the last few days. He had set out to solve the clues in his uncle's email. And look what had happened. They had found the secret of the Nine and almost lost it to Farooq and the LeT. If it had not been for the selfless act of the commandos, the world would have been a different place once the LeT carried out its threat.

But surely this wasn't what his uncle had intended? His uncle knew about Farooq's motives. Why, then, had he sent Vijay on a mission that would deliver him and the secret into the hands of LeT?

And then, there was the other emotional storm that was playing out in his head. In the turmoil of the last few days he had discovered love. And yet, was there a future for Radha and him? They both had their individual ambitions to live for...

Day 12

The Brotherhood lives on

Vijay sat up in bed and switched on the bedside lamp. Sleep wouldn't come to him. Earlier that evening, he had dropped Colin off at the airport.

He was alone in the fort now and had stayed up reading before deciding to try and sleep. But there was too much on his mind.

He got out of bed and switched on his laptop. There was something that nagged at him. He didn't know what it was, but it had also contributed to his difficulty in falling asleep.

What he did know was that he still hadn't resolved his uncle's intentions in sending him the emails.

Without quite knowing why, he pulled up the emails his uncle had sent him and gazed at them. There they were, straightforward enough, now that they had been fully deciphered and their directions followed.

Something tugged at his mind. Despite all that had happened, including the destruction of Sitagarha hill, he had a subliminal feeling this saga wasn't over yet, that there was more to come.

But what more could there be?

He glanced over the emails again and contemplated deleting them.

He took a deep breath and opened the first email. Quickly glancing at it, he deleted it and opened up the second email. The nagging feeling returned. As if something was trying to steer his thoughts in a certain direction.

What was it? He studied the email, reading it slowly and carefully. But they had exhausted the meanings buried in this email.

Or had they?

Everything isn't always the way it looks. Sometimes you need to look deeper within. Study, the Bhagavad Gita, it is the source of much knowledge. The subject of the Gita, though mixed up, is a mark upon us for our future lives, and will lead you through the door to knowledge, which you must unlock. In an ocean of maya, there is always an island of satya.

Vijay sat back and mused.

Why was this particular email troubling him? Was there an even deeper meaning in this email?

Sometimes you need to look deeper within.

Or was he being over-analytical? He had grown so accustomed to discovering multiple hidden messages in the emails that it was difficult not to look for more meanings behind every word.

A thought suddenly swam through his head. He sat up, considering it.

Was it possible?

For a moment, he sat still, trying to dismiss the thought. It seemed incredible. But the harder he tried to banish it, the stronger it seemed to get.

He walked out of his bedroom, and through the corridors of the fort, switching on the lights as he progressed deeper into the fort, until he came to a room that had been constructed around the hillside. This was a room with a huge mural depicting the discourse by Lord Krishna to Arjun the Pandava, on the battlefield of Kurukshetra. The discourse known as the Bhagavad Gita.

He switched on all the lights in the room and stood gazing at the mural, musing over the second line of the email.

Study, the Bhagavad Gita, it is the source of much knowledge.

His mind raced. This line had first helped them isolate the study as the location of the key. But this line also contained the second reference to knowledge, within this email. Was there a connection between this line and the last line of the email which also mentioned the *Gita*, and spoke of the door to knowledge? Was there another meaning to the *Subject of the Gita* other than the obvious reference to Karma which they had already interpreted?

He trembled with excitement as he considered the possibility that the email might be pointing to this mural.

The subject of the *Gita* could also mean the discourse itself, which was represented in this painting.

But what was the *door to knowledge?*

Vijay walked closer to the painting and studied it closely. It was a painting that was common in India and he could find nothing exceptional or different about it.

Unless...

He moved closer to the wall and examined the chariot. Only one wheel was visible in the painting.

He held his breath as he studied the wheel and then exhaled sharply.

The wheel of the chariot had nine spokes.

There *had* been another hidden message in the email. What did it lead to?

Vijay sat on the floor, now wide awake, and tried to reason it out. If the clue in the email was taken into consideration, it would mean that his uncle had hidden away something in the fort; something that was connected to the secret of the Nine, something that could be classified as knowledge...and something that fitted the description of being '2,000 years of history'.

What could it be? And where could his uncle have hidden it?

He examined the painting again. Perhaps he had missed something. There must be more in the painting to guide him.

Was it the horses? There was nothing special about them.

He studied the figures of Arjuna and Krishna but there was nothing unusual in them either..

It was difficult to search for something when he had absolutely no idea what he was looking for. He sighed and examined the chariot but there was nothing out of the ordinary there either.

What about the wheel? Apart from the nine spokes, did it have anything that stood out? He took in the rim, the spokes and the axle, a portion of which was visible.

Nothing there.

He turned his attention to the centre of the wheel and started.

In his earlier scrutiny of the painting, the hub of the wheel had appeared to be a dark black solid circle. Now, he realised that where the hub should have been, there was a concave cavity. Armed with this knowledge, he now discerned a thin hairline crack in the painting that he hadn't noticed before. It was barely visible and extended from the missing hub towards the floor and the ceiling, perpendicular to them.

Vijay felt his excitement growing. The last time they were guided by this email they had found the key to the disk, in a painting in his uncle's study. Was there a link between the key and this painting?

Only one way to find out.

He darted out of the room and sped up the stairs to the study. It took him seconds to find the key and fly down the stairs, back to the room with the mural.

Would it fit?

He slowly slid the circular key into the concave cavity in the mural, his hands trembling with anticipation.

It fitted perfectly.

Vijay could barely contain his excitement.

He turned the key to the left. It locked in with a click. Holding his breath, he turned it in a clockwise direction.

There was a series of clicks and whirrs, then the wall split at the crack he had seen, the two halves of the painting sliding aside with a soft rumble.

Vijay stood transfixed at the archway carved into the rock of the hillside.

The door to knowledge, which you must unlock.

It now made sense.

He stepped into the darkness beyond the arch. As he crossed the threshold, a soft light played around him and he realised that he was in a tunnel carved out of the rock. It led into a chamber within the hillside.

Entering the chamber, he looked around with awe. Row upon row of stainless steel shelves lined the rocky walls; each bore stainless steel containers.

Against one wall stood a stainless steel table upon which were placed a thermograph and a hygrometer. The thermograph indicated a temperature of 65 degrees Fahrenheit and the hygrometer showed humidity at 35%.

He felt the caress of cool air against his skin and heard the faint hum of an air conditioner.

What was this place? And what was in the steel containers?

Vijay realised that his uncle had gone to great lengths to build this chamber. But what was its purpose?

He strode up to a row of shelves and examined the containers. Each one had a label on it and they were all in a strange, unknown script. He opened one container. Inside was a roll of microfilm.

That explained the air conditioning and the thermograph and hygrometer; they were to ensure that the microfilm was preserved.

What was on the microfilm?

Next, he noticed a screen set up at the far end of the chamber, with a machine before it. It was a microfilm reader. The desk also had a sheaf of papers with notes on it.

Vijay browsed through the papers. The notes were in his uncle's handwriting. He was reading a paragraph that described the engine of an aircraft that used anti-gravitation as a means of propulsion.

He switched on the microfilm reader. Images appeared on the screen; lines of script, unreadable and undecipherable. He had never seen this script before. But he knew what he was looking at.

Whether it was as the leader of the Nine or simply as a member of the Nine, who was well-versed in ancient Indian languages, Vikram Singh had been tasked with the responsibility of deciphering the ancient library of the Nine. They had seen the abandoned shell of the library in the cavern at Bairat. But here were the contents, safely preserved, and his uncle had been engaged in translating these into English.

Vijay looked around. The shelves nearest him bore containers with labels in English. He understood. His uncle had also preserved the English translations on microfilm.

He now noticed that there was a drawer in the steel desk. He slid it open. It was empty, except for an envelope. To his great surprise, it was addressed to him.

Vijay pulled out a single sheet of paper. It was a letter. He recognised the handwriting as his uncle's.

It was dated six months ago.

My dearest nephew, Vijay,

If you are reading this letter then it means that you have lived up to my expectations and decoded my messages. It also means that you now know about the Nine and the secret that the brotherhood have guarded for over 2,000 years. What you don't know yet is that I am the last of the Nine—their leader in the 21st century.

I am sorry I had to keep this from you but I was bound by the code of the Nine.

Your presence within my microfilm chamber implies that I am dead, probably killed by someone who was once a trusted friend and colleague but who turned against the values and principles of the Nine. But that isn't important. What you must know, however, is that your life may also be in danger, now that I have shared this knowledge with you.

It is my sincere hope that my decision to share my secret with you will not put your life in peril. And I hope you will understand that I have no other choice.

Now, to speak of a matter close to my heart. I am the last surviving member of the Nine. I must pass on my responsibility to someone I trust. And I trust no one more than you, Vijay. So, I am asking you to shoulder the burden I bore for 25 years and become the custodian of the secret of the Nine.

A word about this secret. When the brotherhood of the Nine was founded by Asoka the Great, 2,300 years ago, the nature of the secret was known to the founding members of the Nine. However, the oath of secrecy and the confidentiality surrounding the identity of the Nine, even as members were replaced through the centuries, meant that the nature of the secret and its location were forgotten over the years. Only the puzzle remained to identify the location of the secret. Even I did not know what the secret was until a few years ago.

The reason why no member of the Nine was able to locate the secret until now is because no one person had all the clues necessary to solve the puzzle. It was only six months ago that I came into possession of all the parts of the puzzle that had earlier been with different members of the Nine. I managed to solve some of the clues, but have done so half-heartedly. For it was six months ago that I realised that, having killed the other eight, the traitor whom I had expelled from the brotherhood, would come for me. And this realisation was sealed by an email he sent to me. Since then, finding the secret has not been a priority for me. My concern then was more about handing over the baton to you.

The secret has remained hidden for over 2,000 years. I have no interest in learning where it is concealed. You are the only person, other than I, who now has access to all the parts of the puzzle that can help locate the secret. The choice is yours. But I implore you to resist the temptation to search for the secret of the Nine and let it remain buried wherever it is, for eternity, because this was the purpose for which the Nine was created.

There is, however, another part of the secret that you need to know. What you see about you is a library containing scientific knowledge accumulated over centuries from all parts of the world. Succeeding generations of members added to the original collection of knowledge discovered by the founding members of the Nine to create the greatest treasure trove of knowledge the world has ever known. This must remain concealed just as the Nine have protected it for centuries.

I have faith in your ability to discharge this responsibility.

I am truly sorry, Vijay, for burdening you with this charge without your consent. But there is no other whom I deem fit to exercise this duty.

May God bless you,
Your loving uncle.

Vijay put the letter down on the table, his feelings mixed. At first, a surge of resentment rushed through him; displeasure at his uncle for believing that he could task him with this responsibility.

But there was another feeling that rose up within him almost immediately, quelling the resentment.

A feeling of pride.

His uncle had chosen him to succeed him as a member of the Nine, a brotherhood that was legendary for its selection of members. The enormity of the responsibility was something he would only appreciate with time.

The feeling that had been bothering him suddenly deserted him. He realised now that his uncle had had no intention of sending him on a search for the location of the secret. Rather, in this letter, he had urged him against it. The emails hadn't been intended to be a trigger for the search he had embarked on.

All his uncle had wanted was for Vijay to find this chamber and take on the responsibility of guarding this library.

Sometimes you need to look deeper within.

If you look for a deeper meaning, you will find it.

Vijay shook his head wistfully. His friends and he had looked too deep within. Overlooking the clues that would have led him to this chamber, he had followed the clues that led him to Sitagarha instead. What a fool he had been!

But then, perhaps it was best it worked out this way, Vijay mused. The secret was now destroyed and beyond the reach of anyone. His mind was surprisingly clear and calm and there was an amazing clarity to his thoughts. Even if the secret cavern was no more, the secrets lived on in this chamber, in this library.

He didn't *want* to deny the responsibility his uncle had passed onto him.

He was now a member of the Nine.

He *was* The Nine.